Raves for the novels of Marshall Ryan Maresca:

"Superb characters living in a phenomenal fantasy world, with a detective story that just sucks you right into the storyline. Marshall Ryan Maresca impressed me with *The Thorn of Dentonhill*, but *A Murder of Mages* has secured me as a fan." —*Fresh Fiction*

"Veranix is Batman, if Batman were a teenager and magically talented. . . . Action, adventure, and magic in a school setting will appeal to those who love Harry Potter and Patrick Rothfuss' *The Name of the Wind*."
—*Library Journal* (starred)

"Books like this are just fun to read."
—The Tenacious Reader

"The perfect combination of urban fantasy, magic, and mystery." —Kings River Life Magazine

"Marshall Ryan Maresca is some kind of mad genius. . . . Not since Terry Pratchett's Ankh Morpork have we enjoyed exploring every angle of an invented locale quite this much." —B&N Sci-fi & Fantasy Blog

"Maresca's debut is smart, fast, and engaging fantasy crime in the mold of Brent Weeks and Harry Harrison. Just perfect."
—Kat Richardson, national bestselling author of *Revenant*

"Maresca offers something beyond the usual high fantasy fare, with a wealth of unique and well-rounded characters, a vivid setting, and complicatedly intertwined social issues that feel especially timely."
—*Publishers Weekly*

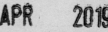

A
PARLIAMENT
OF BODIES

A novel of
The Maradaine Constabulary

MARSHALL RYAN
MARESCA

DAW BOOKS, INC.
DONALD   A.   WOLLHEIM,   FOUNDER
1745 Broadway, New York, NY 10019
ELIZABETH R. WOLLHEIM
SHEILA E. GILBERT
PUBLISHERS
www.dawbooks.com

Acknowledgments

A Parliament of Bodies was a challenging book to write, and I'm grateful to all the little ways people made it easier.

It's a cliché, but where would I be without my wife, Deidre Kateri Aragon? Probably not writing the acknowledgments to my ninth novel, that's for certain. She's a friend and partner and a source of unending support. As is the rest of my family—my son Nicholas, my parents Nancy and Lou, and my mother-in-law Kateri.

I have been blessed to have Sheila Gilbert as my editor. She's been an absolute joy to work with as we've shaped the *Maradaine* stories into what they are. The entire team at DAW (Betsy, Josh, Katie, Leah, and Lindsay) have made this book and this series (and series of serieses) everything they can be.

Daniel J. Fawcett deserves a world of credit for everything that is in these books, the foundation for the world behind them. He's been the proverbial "guy in the chair" for me all these years, and I am ever so grateful.

Finally let me talk about the beta-readers: Miriam Robinson Gould and Kevin Jewell. They're the ones who've been there for the run of Maradaine and offered priceless advice on how things work in the story. Miriam, especially, has proven to be an effective emotional barometer for the things that happen in the story. I do some mean things to my characters, and Miriam always lets me know when I break her heart.

Reader, this book broke her heart a lot. Fair warning.

A
PARLIAMENT
OF BODIES

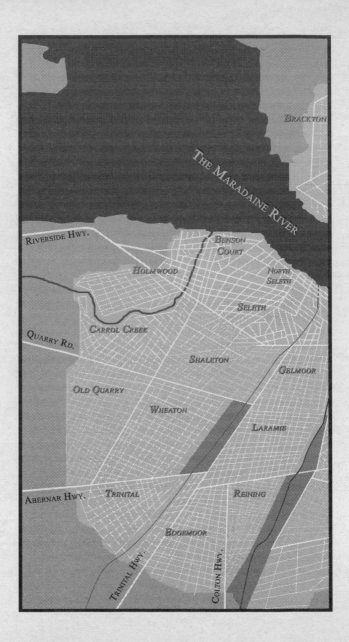

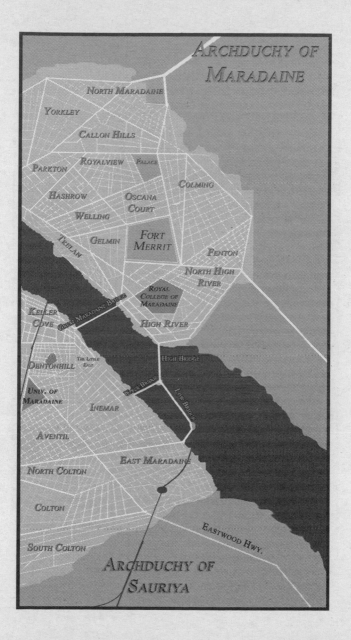

ARCHDUCHY OF MARADAINE

NORTH MARADAINE

YORKLEY

CALLON HILLS

ROYALVIEW

PALACE

PARKTON

COLMING

HASHROW

OSCANA COURT

WELLING

GELMIN

FORT MERRIT

FENTON

TREBAN

NORTH HIGH RIVER

KELLER COVE

GREAT MARADAINE BRIDGE

ROYAL COLLEGE OF MARADAINE

HIGH RIVER

DENTONHILL

THE LITTLE EAST

HIGH BRIDGE

UNIV. OF MARADAINE

MELT BRIDGE

LOW BRIDGE

INEMAR

AVENTIL

NORTH COLTON

EAST MARADAINE

COLTON

EASTWOOD HWY.

SOUTH COLTON

ARCHDUCHY OF SAURIYA

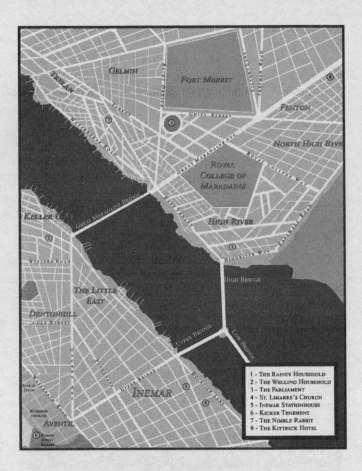

1 - THE RAINEY HOUSEHOLD
2 - THE WELLING HOUSEHOLD
3 - THE PARLIAMENT
4 - ST. LIMARRE'S CHURCH
5 - INEMAR STATIONHOUSE
6 - KICKER TENEMENT
7 - THE NIMBLE RABBIT
8 - THE KITTRICK HOTEL

Prologue

DAYNE HELDRIN DID not care for his apartments in the lower floors of the Parliament building. They were well appointed and comfortable, certainly, but it didn't change the fact he was living there in exile.

"Exile" was an extreme term. But his "residency" at the Parliament, acting as a liaison between the government, the King's Marshals, and his own Tarian Order, was clearly an intentional isolation from the rest of the Order at the chapterhouse. He spent half his time running around the city. Even yesterday, a Saint Day, he was occupied by minutia and kept out and about on pointless errands, hand-delivering messages that any page could carry. He was being used as a footman in a political game and he didn't know who the players were, what the game was, or even what the board looked like.

But he would perform the duties assigned to him. As long as he was a Tarian—even as just a third-year Candidate—he would strive to be an exemplar of the ideals of the Order. He would serve the needs of the Parliament, serve king and nation, be the shield between all and harm.

The apartment had a shield hanging on the wall. His shield, in theory, but not a true Tarian shield. It was something the Parliamentary staff only put here as a display, some form of placation. To make him feel like a proper Tarian, when he was almost certain to be cashiered once the third year of his Candidacy ended in nine months.

And all for one mistake, not saving the right person from the wrong man.

Now that wrong man might be here, in Maradaine.

After his morning exercises, Dayne made a simple breakfast of tea and oats, and sat down with the newssheets. A seventh murder, by the person the newssheets were calling the "Gearbox Killer," was splashed over several of the papers. Sensationalist pabulum, using human life as the currency to sell paper and ink. Each story focused on the most lurid and gory of details. Dayne read through them all as he ate, even though it made his stomach curdle. He had to push through, learn more. He wasn't certain, because the name hadn't appeared yet, and with that name the gloating need to claim responsibility for these deaths. Not yet.

But everything else looked just like the stories in Lacanja from last year. He was certain that these murders were the work of the same man. He made a note of the inspectors on the case. They needed to know what he knew.

His reverie was disturbed by a knock on his door. Dayne answered it, one of the newssheets still in his hand.

"Morning, Dayne." Jerinne Fendall, the capable young woman who was now a third-year Initiate in the Tarian Order, strode into his apartment with confidence. She had earned that confidence as far as he was concerned. Over the past few months, he had developed a certain kinship with her. He had never had any siblings, but Jerinne was much like a little sister. And to him, she was little, even though she was taller than almost any other seventeen-year-old girl. But most people only came up to Dayne's chest.

She had been there at his right arm through several

challenges—eager to learn, eager to help. She was, in many ways, his hope for the future of the Order. Presuming that she wasn't kicked out before finishing her Initiacy.

"Shouldn't you be at the chapterhouse?" he asked her as she came in.

"Morning drills are done, and the rest of the third-years are working with their mentors for the rest of the day."

"So you came to me," Dayne said. Her Initiacy was in trouble, despite her martial skill and placement in the rankings. For some reason, Grandmaster Orren had prevented her from establishing a formal mentorship with one of the Masters or Adepts in the Order, instead insisting that she be informally assigned to Dayne. There was a nominal excuse that involved her recovering from injuries, but from everything Dayne had seen, Jerinne was fully healed and back on her feet.

Maybe she was being punished for her fellowship with him. Maybe they were both too politically inconvenient, and they were being cordoned off from the rest of the Order. Like a quarantine.

"Still following that?" she asked, looking at the newssheet.

"Unfortunately," he said. "I was hoping to talk with Hemmit and Maresh today about it."

"But before you do that . . ." she said, an energetic gleam in her eye.

"We can't continue this much longer. Once the Parliament session begins—"

"I know, I know," Jerinne said. "But I need further sparring practice if I'm going to keep my ranking. Can we run through the Shield and Staff Drills?"

He nodded. "Let me just—"

He was interrupted by the clanging of alarm bells, the likes of which he had never heard before. He didn't even know there were bells like that in the Parliament building. Something must be catastrophically wrong.

He grabbed a sword off the wall and tossed it to Jerinne, and then grabbed the shield for himself. The weight of it was all wrong, but it was the best he had right now.

He charged up the stairs to the entrance floor of the Parliament. He could already hear the commotion there. The alarm bells continued, but people were also shouting and crying. At the top of the stairs, one of the King's Marshals was doubled over, retching.

"Is it an attack?" Dayne asked him.

"It's horrible—" the marshal, a very young one, said. "I've never . . ."

Another marshal was in a panic. "Get the chief! Call the Yellowshields! Call the Fire Brigade! Call everyone!"

Dayne followed the focus of their attention—through the main doors leading to the Parliament floor, the very seat of the Government of Druthal. He went to see, but didn't get past the doorway.

It was a horror beyond his worst nightmare.

And yet so familiar. This was certain, now. It couldn't be a coincidence that this atrocity of engineering and gearwork and bodies and pain, on such an unimaginable scope, had been delivered literally to Dayne's doorstep.

Sholiar was here.

"Jerinne," he said quietly, forcing his voice to be as calm as possible. "Can you run?"

"Yes, but—"

"Run across the river, to Inemar. As fast as you can."

"Why?"

"Because we need Inspectors Minox Welling and Satrine Rainey. Immediately."

Chapter 1

SATRINE RAINEY WOULD never have guessed that she would make a habit of waking up before sunrise to go to Absolution at Saint Limarre's Church. In her nearly forty years, she hadn't ever bothered with the ritual. Her soul was probably beyond salvation; she had accepted that. But she needed to talk, and she was filled with secrets too terrible to hold in, but too dangerous to entrust to anyone.

Anyone but Sister Alana, under the silence guaranteed by the rite of Absolution. Sister Alana would never tell her secrets. The ritual was taken very seriously by both the government and the church, so nothing said under Absolution could ever be used in persecution or prosecution.

Even the secrets of a not-so-former spy turned Constabulary Inspector.

Of course, Sister Alana was more than just a Cloistress of the Blue in the Church of Druthal. She was an old friend—the only person left from Satrine's childhood on the streets of Inemar who could be called that. Most others from those days were dead, jailed, or wasted. Hardly any of them were someone she would have considered a friend even back then. Her own mother—that waste of flesh named Berana Carthas—had abandoned her when she was twelve. Just left to live with some man who didn't want to deal with a daughter.

Sister Alana was the only person who knew everything about who she was, who she had to become, and who she was now.

She knew Satrine well enough to be sitting on the back steps of Saint Limarre's, looking out at the small burial field behind the church, waiting with pastries and two cups of tea.

"I didn't tell you I was coming today," Satrine said as she walked up.

"Didn't need to," Sister Alana said, standing up and embracing Satrine. "I saw last night's newssheets. Tea?"

"It seems too hot for tea." It was now autumn, but the sweltering summer heat still hadn't broken. Even now, before the sun had properly showed itself over the towers of East Maradaine, the heat was oppressive. For the past few months Satrine had forsaken the traditional coat of a Constabulary officer, usually wearing just her shirtsleeves and inspector's vest.

"You'll drink it anyway," Sister Alana said, sitting back down on the steps. She was right. Satrine may have made a habit of seeing Sister Alana early in the morning, but she wasn't accustomed to it. Most nights she barely managed to sleep at all. She took the tea and sat next to the cloistress. "How was your Saint Helsen's Day?"

The fact that yesterday had technically been a holiday—both the equinox and a Saint Day—had barely registered on Satrine. She worked the whole day, and there was no particular observance she would make to Saint Helsen. She didn't even know Saint Helsen's story.

And in thinking that, it came to her, courtesy of her telepathically induced education. Saint Helsen, Savior of Harvests. The Sickle-Bearing Pilgrim.

"It was work. And you know that."

"Bless those whose work keeps us safe."

At least last night she went home at a reasonable

hour. She was able to eat dinner with Rian and Caribet, spend time taking care of Loren. She hadn't realized how much Rian had sprouted over the summer. Her eldest daughter was now almost as tall as she was, and looked far older than her nearly fifteen years. Her summer working the glove counter at Henson's Majestic store had done wonders for the girl's maturity. And the money helped. For the first time since Loren's accident, it didn't feel like they were just scraping by each day.

"The girls go back to school today," Satrine said idly.

"You aren't here to chat about the girls."

"No," Satrine said.

Sister Alana closed her eyes for a moment. "May our voices only be heard by God and the saints, for our words are for no one else."

"Thank you," Satrine said. "So what did you read in the newssheets?"

"Many things, most of which probably had nothing to do with you and yours."

"Aventil had another street war last night. Nine dead, including two constables."

"Aventil isn't supposed to be your problem."

"I'm in the Grand Inspection Unit now," Satrine said. "The whole city is technically my problem." In truth, in the months since they had launched the GIU, it had been a steep learning curve of what the new unit meant. They were supposed to handle the big cases, the ones that had a wider scope than any one precinct. What it really meant was fighting with stationhouse captains, officers, and patrolmen over jurisdiction and resources.

"You've been sweating over Aventil for the past few weeks."

"Why shouldn't I? Welling and I work one case, and right after that, gang wars explode. Two of the gangs are determined to destroy each other, another splinters into two factions, and I just wonder . . ."

"If you could have stopped it then?" Sister Alana sighed. "Please, Satrine. Aventil has been a nightmare since we were girls. You couldn't have saved it. You definitely didn't start it."

"And then there's the new case. Cases."

"The children?"

"No, that one is on Mirrell and Kellman."

"I thought you and Minox were working it."

Satrine sighed. Minox had pushed the idea that a series of missing children—mostly street rat kids like she and Sister Alana had been when they were Tricky Trini and Lannie Coar—were part of a larger case that warranted deeper investigation. Evidence had connected those missing children to a handful of other cases involving children from working-class families, and even a few from minor nobility. Minox had put the pieces together—notably the similar witness reports from all over the city—to show that there was some sort of larger conspiracy to kidnap children. Though for what, he still had no idea. Satrine suspected another fighting ring, or something even more disturbing.

Once Minox had presented his evidence to Captain Cinellan, the case got a lot more notice. That meant it wasn't going to be handled by the inspectors who handled "the strange ones." Not by Satrine Rainey, who was still loathed throughout the city Constabulary for faking her way to an Inspector's rank with forged orders, or by Minox Welling, the Uncircled mage who still had the threat of Inquiry hovering over his head. So the pile of files for the missing children went to Mirrell and Kellman. Satrine didn't understand why—they weren't very inquisitive or investigative. A delicate case that involved a lot of moving parts, that was not their forte.

"No, we're working the Gearbox Murders. That's what the gaudier newssheets are calling it."

"Yes," Sister Alana said. "I rather like the gaudy newssheets. There's something honest about the level of viscera they commit to."

"You're talking about the ones with the drawings." Satrine picked up a pastry. She was going to need something in her system for this.

"I really have to ask," Alana said, picking up one of the newssheets she had stacked next to the steps. "These contraptions you find the victims in. They aren't actually this elaborate, are they?"

Satrine took the paper from her. The sketch showed a monstrosity of machinery, with gears and blades and some poor woman caught in the thing while bits of her were being sliced off. As gruesome as it was, there was also an almost comical aspect to it, as the machinery also had strings, candles, mice in wheels, and a whole assortment of elements that were purely the artist's imagination.

"Nothing like that," Satrine said. "Most of the time we never even saw the machine. . . . I'll spare you the gore. There were five deaths—that we know of—before we realized they were connected. Now seven."

"Who are they?"

"Victims from every part of the city, each found in a different part of the city. No rhyme or reason behind it. Men, women, old, young, rich, poor."

"Noble?"

"Not yet. But . . ." She hesitated to voice her thoughts.

"Go ahead."

"Whoever is doing this, they've got resources. They've got time. And they want attention. If it isn't nobility, or at least someone with money and influence, I'll eat my vest."

"And this theory of yours has met with resistance?"

Sister Alana hit on the point. "Minox doesn't think so. He thinks this is someone with a message. There's a grand scheme to it."

"A grand scheme for what?"

"He's not sure. He can't figure out the message."

"And so his theory holds more credence than yours why? After all, the theories don't exclude each other."

"It doesn't, just . . ." Satrine sighed, taking a bite of the pastry. "When he gets his hunches, he just digs into them like a crab on the beach."

"Did he spend the night in the stationhouse?"

"Probably," Satrine said. "If I were to predict—"

Before Satrine could finish that thought, the back doors of the church burst open, and a young blond woman in nightclothes stormed out, swinging a great candlestick like a sword. "Betrayal! Beware the betrayal and escape the darkness!"

Satrine was on her feet, instinctively grabbing her handstick, but Sister Alana had already reacted. In swift motion, she ducked the swinging candlestick, popped back up, and knocked the blond woman in the face with a perfect punch.

The blond woman dropped to the ground, and then looked around rather confused.

"Sister Alana," she said curtly. "Why am I in the back garden in my sleeping attire?"

"You were having one of your spells again, Sister Myriem," Sister Alana said. "Go inside and clean yourself off. I'll come to check on you shortly."

Sister Myriem stood up and dusted herself off, giving Satrine a polite nod before returning inside the church.

"She's still a problem?"

"Not for long," Alana said with a heavy sigh. "Or at least, not mine. She's going to be transferred to Saint Bridget's. Not my doing. The other cloistresses here are terrified of her."

"Really?"

"This fit was a sedate one for her," Alana said. "In a few weeks, she'll be gone. May the saints forgive me, but I will sleep easier."

"I wish I could." Sleep hadn't been easy . . . all summer, frankly. Between the rigors of the job and the strain of caring for her husband, it had already been hard enough. The words a Lyranan spy had whispered in her ear had set her thoughts spinning every night. "You're working with a traitor."

Sister Myriem screaming "Betrayal" in her fit didn't help. Something about that young woman was just unnerving. She didn't blame Alana for wanting to be rid of her.

Alana guessed her thoughts. "Do you honestly suspect Minox is a traitor of some sort? In collusion with corruption?"

"Not at all," Satrine said. "But I can't shake the feeling. Pra Yikenj spoke with . . . conviction. And she had proven insightful before." Satrine's first encounter with Pra Yikenj had been a little over fifteen years before, when the spy had noticed Satrine was pregnant before Satrine had.

"She wanted to rattle you." Alana glanced about furtively. "And your other masters? What do they think?"

"Druth Intelligence isn't telling me anything new, other than to remind me that there's some sort of corruption in the Constabulary that they worry about. Which . . . isn't useful to tell me."

"So what will you do today?"

Satrine was about to answer, when she heard the pounding of feet and a wheezing breath that was oddly familiar. "I think I'm about to get summoned to the stationhouse."

And then Phillen Hace, newly minted Senior Page in the Constabulary, raced into the churchyard. "Inspector Rainey."

"Phillen," Satrine said calmly, picking up her tea and sipping it. "Did Inspector Welling send you in search of me?"

"Yes," Phillen said.

"And did he presume to tell you to find me here?"

Phillen looked guilty for a moment. "Yes."

"Has he been there all night?"

"Near as I can tell, ma'am. I mean, I slept."

"Fine. Be with you in a moment."

"Yes, ma'am," he said with a bit of a salute. He gave a nod to Alana. "Begging your pardon for interruption, your glory."

"Always, son." As Phillen went to the street, Alana sighed and looked at Satrine. "Never the time we need."

"Come to the house sometime," Satrine said. "I would love you to meet the girls."

"I'll try. I don't get much chance to cross the river."

Satrine let Sister Alana embrace her one more time and went off to where Phillen was waiting patiently for her.

A thought crossed her mind. "You do go home sometimes, yes?" She had never thought to ask the boy that. He always seemed available when Welling sent him, at any hour.

"No point, ma'am. Ain't had a home for a year, save the stationhouse. And that's the best year I've had."

"What about your mother?" Satrine asked. "You've mentioned her before."

"I have, indeed," he said. "That year I brought up? It's been the year she's been in the Quarry for theft and grift."

"Oh, I'm sorry," she said. She knew he had no fondness for his mother—she understood that all too well—but she also understood it wasn't easy to feel nothing for one's mother.

"Don't be," he said. "I'm the one who got her nabbed and ironed."

"How long does she have left to serve?"

"Five days," Phillen said as they approached the stationhouse. "It should be interesting."

"Let me know if there's anything you need," Satrine said. Phillen nodded and dashed off. She steeled herself and went into the stationhouse. There was surely about to be some form of aggression or difficulty facing her, from the patrolmen or the desk sergeants, or most likely Miss Nyla Pyle, the floor clerk for the GIU who hated Satrine with cold fire. All that she was used to.

That was part of her every day.

———————◆■◆———————

Sleep had not been a priority for Minox Welling for the past few days, catching only a few hours in the station-house bunk to refresh his mind before returning to his analysis of the "Gearbox Killer" murders.

He had to confess, it was possibly the most singularly troubling case he had ever encountered in his time as an Inspector Third Class in the Maradaine Constabulary. He had never before seen a case where the murderer had no apparent motive beyond the thrill of killing. That, and the message Minox theorized was hidden within the murders.

"There is no thrill to killing," Joshea Brondar said. "I spent three years in the army trying to avoid it if I could."

"That's you," Minox said quietly. "Men like you and me are fundamentally decent. But to the deranged mind—which is clearly what we're dealing with—there is."

Joshea picked up one of the charcoal sketches of the crime scene. "Is it all right if I look closer at this?"

Joshea was not a member of the Constabulary, but when the Grand Inspection Unit had been formed, Captain Cinellan called for an adjacent force of specially trained patrolmen to use in extreme situations. That had involved Joshea—a military veteran—being brought in as a trainer and consultant. Minox had wondered who had suggested Joshea, as he hadn't. Not that he minded having Joshea in proximity, especially in moments like this when he needed to talk through his ideas and get a different perspective.

Ideally Minox would consult with Inspector Rainey, but he respected that her time away from the station-house was not his to monopolize. Her family situation was one that required her attention, which was radically different from his own. The Welling household operated just fine in his absence, save his mother's worry that he was not taking care of himself.

Joshea was an excellent substitute in these moments, especially since he was one of the few people in this city—beyond family or fellow Constabulary—who Minox enjoyed talking to. And Joshea seemed to enjoy it as well, making a point of coming to the stationhouse in the early hours of the morning. Perhaps because it gave him a legitimate excuse to visit with Minox. Joshea's family were no fans of the Constabulary, and surely did not approve of his current employment.

They definitely would not approve of the true connection between Joshea and Minox: they were both Uncircled mages.

"It should be fine," Minox said. "You've been cleared for a certain level of access to active cases. There's nothing here that isn't also in the newssheets."

"Saint Hesprin preserve me," Joshea whispered, kissing his knuckle and touching it to his chest. "This is really what the body was like when you found it?"

"The latest," Minox said. "The tragedy is this one was definitively preventable. And for whoever our killer is, I think that was part of his design."

"How was it preventable?"

"The crate arrived in Talon Circle sometime between six bells and seven bells in the morning. It sat there, ignored, for at least four hours until it became active, in the full sight of a sizable crowd. The victim—"

"Nantel Emmarik?" Joshea raised an eyebrow. "That's an Eastern Druth name. Oblune or Monim."

"You think that's relevant?"

"It stands out. Do you know anything about the victim?"

"Very little at this point. But he was alive in the crate for those four hours. Alive! If anyone had gone up to that crate and examined it, called a constable to investigate it . . . Mister Emmarik could have been saved."

"Possibly," Joshea said, looking at the sketches. "The device activated, the crate opened, and this happened?"

He handed the sketch back to Minox. This was an official sketch from Leppin's charcoal artist—a young boy who didn't balk at the gore, but lacked the artistic craft Minox would have preferred the sketches to have. Despite that, it accurately depicted the state the body was in when the GIU arrived on the scene. Arms and legs twisted at impossible angles, rib cage ripped open, and the poor man's head—which had a metal cage screwed onto it—had been forced to spin two full circles.

The witnesses had described it all happening in front of them. They had described Emmarik's screams.

Those people would never be the same again.

Joshea didn't flinch from the depictions, though. "It's just—you see those hooks in his wrists and ankles? The way the cage is bolted to his skull? I imagine that if he had been discovered before the box went off, it would have been impossible to extract him without killing him."

Minox sighed and looked at the charcoal sketch again. It was likely Joshea was right about that, and Leppin—the stationhouse's examinarian and expert on causes of death—had made the same assessment. Mister Emmarik was probably doomed from the start. "I would argue that there would still have been a chance for him. If I had been there—"

"No," Joshea said. "You can't go thinking you can solve anything with magic, especially something like that."

"I'm not saying—"

"In fact, I don't know why you stopped taking the *rijetzh* to help keep it under control. I thought we were figuring out the ideal dosage."

Minox nodded. "I'm afraid for me it isn't as simple as merely dampening my ability." He held up his left hand, currently gloved despite the sweltering heat of the stationhouse. "While using the *rijetzh*, I have no control over my altered hand."

"I understand how that might be frustrating—"

"My condition with my hand is more than frustrating."

Minox had spent the last few months adapting to how his hand had changed. It was no longer flesh, that was certain, though to the touch it still had the same texture and pliability. But it was now black, with an almost metallic shine, and he had almost no direct sensation through it. He could still use his hand indirectly—controlling it by focusing magic through it. The *rijetzh*—the Poasian spice Joshea introduced him to—hampered his magical ability, and with that the functionality of his hand. Joshea liked dosing himself with *rijetzh*, keeping his magical ability under tight control, but for Minox it was no longer an option.

Adding to the frustration was that he truly was at a loss regarding his hand. With no access to Circled mages or their knowledge, he didn't know what his hand even was now, or why it had changed.

There were several possible factors to craft theories with. That arm was the one that had been broken by the strange, magic-draining spike that Nerrish Plum had used in his ritual mage killings when he had attempted to make Minox his fourth victim. It was impossible to determine what effect the exposure to that may have caused, especially since the spikes had gone missing from the evidence lockup, including all record of them. Minox found that deeply troubling, on many levels. Leppin told him he was taking further precautions now to protect evidence and records. Right now the only ones who knew the spikes were missing, and with that the breach in security at the stationhouse, were the two of them, Inspector Rainey, and Captain Cinellan.

Minox had also been exposed to the Tsouljan flower pollen that became volatile when magically activated. That, in all likelihood, was what had put him into a sickened state, and thrown his magical abilities out of alignment at the time his hand changed. Minox was certain that the change in his hand was already underway, and the sickness merely accelerated it. He also wondered if the *rijetzh* was a contributing factor.

There were too many potential factors.

"If you can't control it—" Joshea started.

"Then someone else can," Minox said. He had already had that troubling experience a few weeks ago, in his encounter with the Aventil street vigilante the Thorn. The Thorn, who was also a mage, was capable of exerting control over his altered hand. "That is unacceptable."

Strangely enough, Minox learned that he could, through the hand, exert control over the Thorn's mystical tools. He and the Thorn eventually reached an understanding, even a tenuous kinship—but Minox couldn't overlook the fact that if the Thorn could control his hand, some other mage might as well. Especially a highly trained Circle mage.

And Circled mages did not like Uncircled mages. Nor did they care for Constabulary. So Minox was one of their least liked people in Maradaine.

"You're just nervous about what's hanging over your head. Today is the eightieth day, yes?"

"That doesn't give me comfort," Minox said.

His position as an inspector in the Maradaine Constabulary was at risk, due to being an Uncircled mage. He would not have been allowed to serve in the Constabulary as a Circled mage, even if he had had the opportunity to train and become Circled. But now he faced an official question of his fitness to serve. His magic—raw and untrained and out of control in his sickness—had caused damage and chaos. Questioning his fitness was completely just.

Today was the critical day. Constabulary regulations dictated that once a request for an Inquiry of Fitness had been put in, the hearings had to begin within eighty days, which meant that the first interview had to be done today, or the formal inquiry would have to be dismissed. Minox would be relieved—his position would no longer be in danger, for now.

Today, at the eighty-day mark, he had not even been informed of anyone being appointed to his Inquiry board. As far as he knew, there was no one to conduct an interview today. So at the end of shift today, the Inquiry would be dismissed. But it also meant that the cause behind the Inquiry—valid cause, Minox agreed—would never be properly answered, and could be raised again.

He'd rather face the Inquiry now and have it resolved.

"Just get through today," Joshea said. "Corrie told me your captain doesn't even think the Inquiry is necessary. I bet he didn't take it seriously, and said so when he put in the formal request."

"It's not his to take seriously—nor is it my sister's place to gauge his feelings. But he isn't part of the Inquiry, other than to observe and abide by the board's recommendations."

Inspector Rainey came up to the inspectors' floor, approaching their desks at a strident pace.

"I should go," Joshea said. "But good luck today."

He left before Minox could say a proper good-bye, going out toward the back stairway. When Minox turned back, Inspector Rainey was at their desks.

"Did I interrupt something?" she asked.

"We were just discussing the case," Minox said.

"Was that—" She paused, and her face showed that same hint of reserved distrust she'd been displaying for the past three months. Ever since the Tsouljan compound, and Minox's hand changed. "I'm sure it's fine. They brought him in here, after all."

"I've been going over the evidence for these murders—"

"All night?" she asked. "I keep telling you to stop that."

"My mother is in agreement with you, but that is not of the moment."

"You should listen to your mother," Rainey said. "Did you sleep at all?"

"A few hours. I should have had tea ready for you—"

"It's fine, I've had a cup already today. So what did you determine?"

Minox put together the various sketches and notes he had compiled and handed them to her. He had learned over their months of partnership that she preferred to be presented information with a bit of neatness and organization. "I've theorized that each of the victims we've found has been chosen to send a coded message."

She raised an eyebrow—she was intrigued. "What sort of code?"

"Bear with me, because this is possibly a coincidence that I have ascribed meaning to . . ."

"What sort of code?" she asked again.

He went to the slateboard by their desks and started writing. "The first body that was found: Edgin Follickar. Then Nalia Askent, Barrin Imber, Reb Latty, Astin Unger, Ialana Restin, and now Nantel Emmarik."

"Right. And we're certain there's no connection between any of them. Is there?"

"As individuals, no. Nothing I've found suggests a common element among these people."

"So what's the code?"

Minox underlined the first letter in each of the victims' family names. "If you take the first letter of their family names, in the order they were killed, it spells 'failure.'"

Rainey looked at the slateboard. "I suppose it does. Interesting, but it could be a coincidence."

"I acknowledge that," Minox said. "But there's another part to this." He underlined the first letter in the victims' given names. "What does that spell?"

"Enbrain." Inspector Rainey looked shocked, and there was a degree of acknowledgment on her face that indicated she was finding his theory credulous. "'Enbrain failure,' that's the message?"

"Imagine that," Minox said, taking the sketches from her hands and laying them out on the desk, "someone went through the pains of these elaborate, torturous murders of seven random people . . . entirely because their names would spell out a message."

"Wait, wait," Rainey said, sitting down. "You think this entire thing is just to make some sort of threat on Commissioner Enbrain?"

"I think this is the . . ." Minox considered his next words carefully. "This is the overture of a greater plan targeted at the commissioner."

Whatever Inspector Rainey was going to say next was interrupted by shrill whistles through the stationhouse. A senior page—one Minox was not personally familiar with—came running onto the floor. "Where's Jinx and Tricky?"

Minox grit his teeth. He hated the "Jinx" nickname he had acquired, though he knew Inspector Rainey took more ownership over the "Tricky." "It's Inspectors Welling and Rainey to you, page. What's on?"

The page didn't seem remotely rebuked. "There's an emergency call. Needs the GIU and the Special Response Squad. Told it needed to be you."

"By?" Minox asked as he grabbed his coat off the desk. He had noted that Captain Cinellan had not yet reported to the floor, nor were there any other inspectors. At this hour, that was odd.

The page shrugged. "I was told. Come on." He darted back to the stairs.

Inspector Rainey was on her feet, checking her crossbow. "Let's see what's on. How else are we going to earn our keep?"

Minox wished he had a valid argument against that, but he didn't. Putting on his coat, he followed Inspector Rainey after the page.

Chapter 2

SATRINE AND WELLING raced after the page to the street, where Sergeant Iorrett was already waiting with twelve of his men and Corrie Welling—the Special Response Squad that Joshea Brondar was training. They were all dressed in riot armor—heavy coats and helmets and wide shields supplementing their crossbows and handsticks.

"What's going on?" Satrine asked. "You told the page to call us?"

"We've got a situation," Iorrett said.

"That's a time-wasting statement," Welling said.

Corrie spoke up, rushing her words. "There was a heist on a rutting silverwagon as it was heading over The Lower blasted Bridge."

"That seems ill-advised," Welling said.

"Damn right it was," Corrie said.

"Here's the scene," Iorrett said, scowling at Corrie. He whistled to his people to start moving. "Inspector Mirrell was on hand when it was going on—"

"Why was that?" Welling asked, following the squad. Satrine was thinking the same thing. Mirrell lived in Gelmin, west of the stationhouse, regularly taking the tickwagon in. For Mirrell to be on The Lower Bridge—north and east of here—was odd.

"I couldn't say, specs," Iorrett said. "This is what I

know, from the brief from the patrolman on the scene—we should move faster, by the way." He broke into a jog, as did the rest of the squad.

Satrine took that as a cue to match his pace if she wanted to hear the brief.

"Like I said, Mirrell was on the scene, and he tried to intervene, but the silverwagon, along with Mirrell, the original guards, and the robbers, all crashed into a teashop in Lower Bridge Square at the end of the bridge."

Satrine nodded. She was familiar with the teashop. "It's a small place, right across the street."

"What requires our intervention?" Welling asked.

"Because the rutting robbers took Mirrell and the folks in the teashop hostage!" Corrie almost shouted.

"Ah," Welling said. "So we're supposed to intervene somehow? This isn't our usual sort of case."

"Yeah, well . . ." Iorrett said with a shrug as he ran. "That's what I know."

The street corner was pure chaos. The armored carriage was smashed into the front of the teashop, blocking the doorway in. The entire shop face was a wreck, and there wasn't a good way to see inside. The driver must have managed to trigger the yoke release before the carriage crashed, as the horses were off to one side, the only calm element on the scene.

People in the streets were crowding around, and the few patrolmen on the scene were struggling to keep them back. Two Yellowshield teams were also on the scene, holding back and waiting for directions from the Constabulary.

Satrine took point on that. "Corrie, take half the squad and secure this area. Who's in command right now?"

"Ma'am?" one of the patrolmen came over. "Hently, ma'am. I was the one who was here when it happened, put in the whistle calls."

"Tell us what you know, Hently," Satrine said. Welling still seemed to be taking in the scene, with a distinct lack of urgency. Perhaps because he usually arrived on a scene after the bodies were found, not during an active incident.

"Wagon came down the bridge, and the driver lost control and released the horses before it hit the teashop. Now the robbers, I couldn't properly tell you what they were doing or how, but they were all on the top of the carriage, one grappling with the driver from what I saw."

"While it was driving?" Welling asked idly, still glancing around the scene. "And Inspector Mirrell?"

"He was hanging on it as well. I think. It went by in a blur, sir."

"I'm sure it did." He approached at an almost languid pace. "I presume once you had men here, you secured that back alley, where the teashop surely has its kitchen door."

"Yes, sir," Hently said. "I've got one of mine back there."

"Iorrett," Welling said. "You still have six more men at your disposal?"

"That's right, Inspector."

"Put two on the alley, stage three back here with crossbows, and you and your last man move in as close as you can to those windows."

Satrine thought that was all well and good, but didn't properly address the situation. "Has there been any communication with them inside the shop?"

Welling added, "And do we have any intelligence on the robbers?"

"Yes, sir, ma'am," Hently said, looking at them both. "Shortly after the incident, when I tried to get close, I heard Inspector Mirrell call out that I shouldn't come closer. That the robbers had him under aim, and the driver, the teashop keeper, and three patrons also at arms."

"So they have crossbows," Satrine said.

"They may have *a* crossbow," Welling said. "It's entirely possible that they took Mirrell's. And we cannot see inside?"

"No, sir. The shop already had very few windows, and the ones that weren't blocked or wrecked by the carriage they managed to cover up."

"Back door locked, yes?"

"Of course," Hently said. "I was going to try and crack it down, but I think Mirrell realized that and told me not to."

"Very good, Hently," Welling said. "A word, Inspector Rainey?"

He stepped away from Hently and the rest of the patrol officers, as much as could be done in this situation. The crowd was growing, including a few newsprint folks. Satrine recognized Rencir, from the *South Maradaine Gazette*. That man was sometimes friendly with Welling, but he was a pain in the side to most of the Constabulary. More often than not, he strove to paint them in a negative light.

Welling still glanced about, as if he were observing an interesting social event. "Are you not taking this seriously?" she asked him.

"Of course I am," Welling said. "Serious, but not urgent. We must deprive the robbers of their perception of power. We cannot act too quickly or rashly. We cannot appear to be desperate to rescue Mirrell or the civilian hostages."

Satrine let out a sigh of relief. There was a logic to his casual behavior here. She should have trusted Minox a bit more. "What do you think?"

"The only intelligence we have is from Hently's report, including what he heard from Mirrell. We cannot proceed without more information. Thus we must talk to them."

"You have a plan for that?" she asked.

"Of course," he said. "You're going to do it."

She raised an eyebrow. "You know I've never done anything like this."

"Not precisely, but that's fine."

"You, however, actually have done this before."

When Imach radicals had taken hostages in Ironheart Ward, Welling had tried to negotiate with them. Of course, that ended somewhat disastrously.

"That was a different situation, and frankly, my mental capacity at the time was suspect. This is—" He paused for a moment. "This is not the sort of thing inspectors typically do."

"Yet here we are."

"Indeed." Something was swirling in his brain. "We were explicitly summoned." He started to glance around the area. If he was on the track of something, it was best to let him continue down that path.

"All right, I'll try to engage. And you?"

"I'll try to determine how many robbers we have, where they are, and the risks to the civilians inside. You just keep them talking."

Satrine nodded, and moved over to the broken entrance. Now that she was closer, she saw there was a bit of a gap between the carriage and the doorframe. Someone could slip through there, possibly, but slowly. Not too useful.

"Hey, is everyone all right in there?" she called out. "This is Inspector Satrine Rainey. I just want to make sure everyone is all right."

"They sent a rutting skirt?" a man yelled out.

"Inspector skirt," Satrine said. "Are you one of the hostiles?"

"Quite a word, Inspector. You presume I'm hostile?"

That was interesting. The man's tone was light, like he didn't consider the situation serious. "You've crashed a silver bus and have taken people hostage. That's fairly hostile."

"That's one way of seeing it," the man said. "Don't reckon I agree."

This wasn't a fruitful path to take. "Are the hostages safe and uninjured?"

"I suppose they are."

"I need to talk to the inspector in there with you."

"Oh, I don't know about that, skirt," he said. "I can't very well let him just flap his lips about what's the score in here."

This guy was very odd. She waved Hently over to her.

"Ma'am?" Hently asked.

"Did you speak directly to Inspector Mirrell?"

"When?"

"When he told you to bring Welling and me over here."

"No, no, I didn't," Hently said, looking a bit confused. "Well, I called out, and the man in there said that Mirrell said—"

This was beyond strange.

"Sir?" she called out to the man in the shop. "What do I call you?"

"Hebbler," he said. "That's name enough for you."

Something about that hit a memory for Satrine—something familiar she couldn't quite place. Not just the name, but the whole phrase. In not placing it immediately, she recognized that it must be an actual memory of her own, rather than one of the inserted ones from her psychic education. Those were usually perfect.

"All right, Hebbler," she said, moving a bit closer to the shambles of the door, "then tell me what you want."

"Oh, well, there's still the matter of me and my boys getting this silver and getting out of here."

"That's not likely."

"That's what the hostages are for, skirt. To change the odds."

"Tell me about the hostages."

"Well, there's the nice teashop man and the driver. And there's the cranky lady, the pair of old gentlemen, and of course, the two Constabulary inspectors."

"Two?" Satrine asked. "Who do you have besides Mirrell?"

"A skirt named Rainey."

The door opened up, and three sets of hands pulled her inside.

———◆—◆—◆———

"They grabbed her!"

One of the other footpatrolmen came running into the alley while Minox was still examining the back entrance. He hadn't determined any further insights from the alley, save that much about this whole situation seemed wrong.

"Be clear," he said. "Who grabbed who?"

"The robbers inside! They grabbed Inspector Rainey and pulled her inside!"

Minox came out of the alley. He didn't say it, but what they were describing sounded patently impossible. Inspector Rainey would not be "pulled inside," certainly not without giving significant resistance.

"Who saw it?" he called out as he emerged onto the street. He focused on his sister, working to keep the crowd back. "Corrie? Did you see what happened?"

"Hmm?" she said, her attention on the crowd, the shop, the ground—anywhere but eye contact. "No, I rutting didn't see anything."

That was atypical behavior.

"Specs?" Iorrett said. "What's the word?"

Minox glanced around. Eyes were all on him. "I am the ranking on scene? Very well." This was very curious. There should have been a patrol lieutenant, if nothing else. This was not a role for an inspector. Of course, it was his duty to assist in any way within his power, and he would do so willingly. But that didn't change the fact that the entire scenario was incongruous.

Given the apparent severity, it was shocking that Captain Cinellan hadn't come onto the scene himself, especially with one of his lead inspectors being held hostage.

Where had Captain Cinellan been this morning? He hadn't been in his office, or even come onto the GIU floor. His position as captain of the GIU often put the politics of the office on his desk, forcing him to go to meetings with city officials, but he still checked with the inspectors each morning.

This morning had been different. No captain, Mirrell on the bridge.

Minox considered all this for a moment, and then approached the door with the crashed silverwagon in it. "This is Inspector Minox Welling of the Grand Inspection Unit. Who is claiming authority for the malefactors here?"

"I'm the leader, champ," a voice said from the other side of the door. "What can I do for you, Mister Welling?"

"An expeditious surrender would be ideal, sir," Minox said. "I insist on knowing the status of your hostages."

"They're all fine, including your Inspector Rainey," the man said. "So what are you going to do, champ?"

Minox checked his crossbow—loaded with blunt tips. Painful and incapacitating in most cases, but usually not fatal. "Corrie," he called to his sister. "You and Iorrett, come here."

She came over with Sergeant Iorrett. Strictly speaking, they were the same rank, but she wasn't even twenty years old. Iorrett was over thirty, and she deferred to him entirely in her body language. At least she did right now. Typically, Corrie yielded to no one, especially Iorrett.

"You got a plan, specs?" Iorrett asked.

Also atypical. Iorrett was normally aggressive, even insubordinate to Minox. He would be putting forth a plan of action. Demanding it, even.

And they were geared for full action, the special response their squad was being trained for. Except their crossbows also had blunt tips loaded.

"I do," Minox said plainly, though it wasn't entirely true. He had a deduction, and was going to act as if his supposition was true. "I need you to place some of your people at either end of that alley to watch that back door. The rest will be with me for a frontal assault."

"A what?" Corrie asked, looking at him for the first time.

"If it comes to that," Minox said, though he had already played out in his head the most likely way this situation would go. "But put the plain footpatrolmen on crowd control. This will be best handled by your people."

"What's the plan?" Iorrett asked.

"The plan is to follow my lead," Minox said. "I assume this situation is the sort of thing you've been training for over the past two months, yes?"

"Yes, sir—" Iorrett started.

"Then get your people in position. On my signal, you will need to move in fast to neutralize any threats to civilians expediently. Can I trust you to do that, Sergeant, or do I need other officers here?"

"Yes, sir, we can do that," Iorrett said sharply. He barked out a few orders to his people, and they positioned themselves at the alley and around the wagon.

Minox went back over to the door of the teashop. "Sir, can you hear me?"

"Ayuh, specs. You got something to say?"

"I do. You have to the count of ten to release your hostages and come out peacefully."

"Or?"

"There is no or. In a few moments you will be ironed and arrested. Right now you have the opportunity to minimize your own discomfort."

"I think you ought to negotiate a bit better than that," the leader said.

"Ten," Minox said. He kept counting as the man sputtered on.

"Now, look, specs. We're prepared to offer you one of these folks, but you have to—"

"Three," Minox said, having counted to that.

"But we should—"

"Two—"

"I don't think—"

Minox pulled in as much magic energy as he could easily muster, channeling it through his altered hand.

"One."

"Wait—"

Minox didn't wait. He nodded at Iorrett, and with a massive push of the energy—so strong it caused his hand to burst into blue flame—he yanked the silver-wagon out of the doorway, exposing the teashop within. Three men with knives and crossbows were standing in the teashop, with Inspectors Mirrell and Rainey kneeling on the floor in front of them. Four other civilians were off to one side.

"Go," he said to Corrie and Iorrett, which was about all he could manage. He hadn't realized how much moving that wagon would take out of him.

Iorrett and Corrie, in unison with the rest of their squad, leaped forward with their shields up and crossbows trained.

"Drop your weapons and raise your hands up," Iorrett said. "This is your only warning."

All three robbers moved in an instant, but not to drop their weapons. The two with knives went at Mirrell and Rainey, and the third—the one with the crossbow—snapped up his aim and shot at one of the civilians.

Minox didn't think—the magic surged out of him toward the bolt flying at the woman's chest. In an instant, the bolt had turned to ash. He had done that out of instinct, and as a result, he felt as weak as a kitten. Foolish on his part, since it was unnecessary.

He didn't even glance over at Mirrell and Rainey. "I trust you two are all right."

"We wouldn't have been," Mirrell said. He was still kneeling on the ground, the "robber" behind him holding the knife against his throat. But the two of them were now completely relaxed. Mirrell looked rather annoyed.

"In a real crisis situation, possibly no," Minox said. "But this clearly was not one."

"You didn't know—" Mirrell started.

"I did," Minox said. "I had deduced rather quickly that this scenario was some sort of exercise or test, rather than an actual hostage situation." He glanced around at the robbers, the civilians, and the members of Iorrett's squad. "And clearly the focus of this test was me."

"No," Mirrell said quickly as he got to his feet. "It was a training exercise for the squad to . . ."

"Sewage, Inspector," Minox said. He rarely employed vulgarity, but it fit in the moment. "The squad, I noticed, had crossbows loaded with cloth-wrapped blunt tip quarrels. Minimal injury in case they had to fire. The path the silverwagon supposedly took from the bridge to crash into this teashop was unlikely, and certainly the driver would not have had the chance to trigger the horse release. Third, you had no reason to be in this area, and Inspector Rainey and I had no reason to be specifically called, unless this test was for me."

"It could be—"

Minox shook his head. "You couldn't let Inspector Rainey know until we were already engaged, but you made a point of removing her from the scenario as quickly as possible, to force me into a command position."

"And this was sewage," Rainey said, now brushing off her slacks. "I almost took Mirrell's eye out when they grabbed me. Sorry."

"It's fine," Mirrell said.

"Wasn't apologizing to you," Rainey said. "I had no idea about this, Welling."

"No apology needed." He looked over at Corrie. "Nor from you. You were clearly aware, but was ordered not to say anything. Everything about your nature this morning told me you were harboring a secret."

"Captain's orders," she mumbled.

"Captain?" Minox called out. "I suppose you can come out from wherever you're watching."

Mirrell pointed over to an office building on the

opposite corner. "He's up there with Kellman. They'll be down in a bit."

The lead robber came over to the three of them, now all smiles. He was a young man with an almost impossibly pretty face. "This was fun," he said. "If you need to do this sort of thing again, the Birch Street Players are at your disposal."

"Birch Street?" Rainey asked. "Where is that?"

"Out in Seleth," Mirrell said.

"That was my idea." Inspector Kellman came over from the office building. "I figured we needed folk that you two wouldn't recognize from your own stages."

"Westtown," the actor said, now using a West Maradaine accent very similar to Inspector Kellman's. "I imagine you don't get out there much."

"No," Rainey said. "But next time don't pick a character and dialogue from plays. Even obscure ones."

"No one's seen *Hebbler's Heartaches*."

"All the Gestin plays have had a resurgence on the north side," Rainey said, nodding her head toward the bridge.

Minox shook his head, still looking for the captain to emerge. "This all seems to be an unwieldy and expensive endeavor simply to test my . . . what were you even testing?"

"Your fitness, Mister Welling."

This came from the woman Minox had saved from the crossbow shot—though surely that whole thing was some form of stagecraft to make him think she was in danger. She was a primly dressed woman, in a high-collared dress and her dark hair up in a tied bun, under a small hat. She approached and offered a gloved hand to him.

"Kendra Morad. Special advocate and advisor from the offices of the Archduke of Sauriya."

"Miss Morad," Minox said, taking the hand. "I presume you are here for a purpose connected to the Inquiry I am under."

"You presume correctly, Mister Welling. I'm in charge of the Inquiry board."

"And how are your findings?"

"Incomplete, Mister Welling. Intriguing, but incomplete."

"Sloppy, that is what they are!" This came from a flamboyantly dressed man—a yellow-and-green suit and several rings on each finger. Minox had met this man once before, that he was certain, but he couldn't recall the circumstances. He chose, therefore, to address the captain, who was walking a few paces behind him. Captain Brace Cinellan had his head down, as if his years of service to the Constabulary were weighing particularly heavily on him today. He looked harried, exhausted.

"Captain," Minox said. "I trust I performed adequately, given that I saw through the ruse and acted accordingly. I would not have risked Inspectors Mirrell and Rainey in any situation I believed was legitimate. And I presumed correctly."

"I understand, Welling," the captain said. If Minox had to guess, the captain was embarrassed by this whole test. He had likely been forced to impose it on Minox. "This is—"

"Quentin Olivant," the flamboyantly dressed man said with some disdain. "Lawyer and member of the Lord Preston's Circle."

"That's the educationally focused one," Minox said. He had been reading up on the larger circles of late.

"Yes, you met one of our prominent members a few weeks ago. Professor Gollic Alimen?"

The magic professor on campus, who had worked himself into a frenzy just from looking at Minox.

"And he contacted you?" Minox asked.

"I became aware that your service in the Constabulary, as an Uncircled mage, was growing increasingly troubling. And that you were under Inquiry. It would be remiss to not step in and assist in the proceedings."

"Which are still mine, Mister Olivant," Miss Morad said. "And we will proceed as I see fit."

"As you wish, Miss Morad," Olivant said. "I can tell you what I observed. Messy, uncontrolled magic. The equivalent of using a bonfire to heat your tea."

"Your opinion means very little to me, Mister Olivant," Minox said.

"But not to me, Inspector," Miss Morad said.

"Of course, Miss Morad," Minox said. He glanced about at the assembled group around him. "Surely the middle of a public square is not the place to discuss this."

"No," Captain Cinellan said. "This whole exercise was absurd." He glared at both Olivant and Morad. "I should never have consented to it."

"I thought it important to observe the choices and tactics Inspector Welling makes under pressure."

That made sense. "Mirroring the events in the hospital ward, yes." Looking at his sister, he added, "I'm surprised they didn't make you one of the hostages."

"I told them this was rutting sewage and I didn't want any part of it."

"It was a good training exercise for our squad," Iorrett said.

"Shut your rut hole before I sew it," Corrie said, gripping her handstick.

Captain Cinellan stepped up, putting his hand on top of Corrie's. "As Minox said, let's take it off the street."

"Indeed," Rainey added. "We have work to do."

Whistle calls of all sorts pierced the air, coming from the other side of the bridge. Calls came for crowd control, Yellowshields, bodywagons—all blended together. Even with the river between them, it was such a cacophony, it was impossible to ignore.

"Should we be responding?" Kellman asked.

"It's north side," Cinellan said. "That ain't our problem."

"I thought the whole city was our problem," Rainey said.

"Only when we're asked."

Minox wondered how much of that was Cinellan's own tribalism, his desire to focus on his own neighborhood, and how much was weariness from the politics he now faced as captain of the GIU.

Amid the crowd and confusion of The Lower Bridge and the surrounding square—a situation only made more congested by their continued presence—Minox noticed a young woman racing down the bridge. She stood out for several reasons—one was her obvious skill. She was dodging her way around people, bounding up on the railing to get past them, anything she could do to cross the bridge at best speed.

The other was the uniform she was wearing, one Minox had rarely seen anyone wear in Maradaine: that of the Tarian Order.

The Tarians were an ancient order, an entrenched part of Druth history from a time before there was Constabulary, established army, or anything resembling standards for protecting the common civilianry from evil and lawlessness. He remembered that when he was a child he'd listen to his Uncle Terrent tell stories of Old Druthal or the Shattered Centuries, where the heroes were from one of the Twelve Elite Orders of old. These people were the predecessors of law enforcement in Druthal, and for many people, the only source of justice.

Minox had always held them in high regard, from the shield-bearing Tarians to the Vanidian woodsmen to the Braighian pikemasters.

Most of those Orders had disbanded or evolved into something new. The Yellowshields—like his cousin Ferah—came from the Ascepian Order, and still bore the same emblem on their coats. The Hanalian Order became the King's Marshals. Others just faded away.

The Tarians persisted, mostly as a nostalgic relic. Minox knew they were still around, but had never met a member. It was actually surprising that a young woman like this—or any person her age—would be a part of the Order.

"Constables!" she shouted as she leaped down the steps from the bridge to the square. "I need inspectors! Right away at the Parliament!"

"The Parliament?" Kellman asked. "What the blazes happened up there?"

"Not our jurisdiction," Captain Cinellan said. "Young woman, there was no need for you to run here. Anything at the Parliament is handled by the King's Marshals."

"No, I—" She now paused to catch her breath. "I need specific inspectors from here, from Inemar."

"It's not—"

"Captain," Miss Morad said sharply. "This is wasting time."

"Who do you need?" Rainey asked. She gave an odd glance to Minox.

"Two inspectors," the Tarian girl said. "Wenning and . . . Casey?"

"Welling and Rainey?" Mirrell asked.

The Tarian girl snapped her fingers. "That was it. Yes. Where can I find them?"

"We're here," Minox said, stepping forward with Rainey now at his shoulder. "But like the captain said, an incident at the Parliament isn't our jurisdiction. We can't take a case from there."

"You don't understand," the girl said. "This is your case. The Gearbox Killer."

That changed things, but Rainey put it to voice before Minox could. "He placed a body in the Parliament?"

"No, ma'am," she said. "He placed a monstrous machine on the Parliament floor, and there are over a dozen people in it."

Chapter 3

"**C**APTAIN, WITH YOUR permission," Minox said, pointing toward the Tarian and the bridge. He fully expected the captain to grant it, there was no meaningful reason not to. If this was another strike from the Gearbox Killer, they should go directly there to investigate.

"Absolutely not."

This did not come from the captain, but from Miss Kendra Morad.

"Who is this?" the young Tarian woman asked.

"Kendra Morad. Special advocate and advisor from the offices of the Archduke of Sauriya."

"Good for you," the Tarian said. "But I need constables. These two."

"Captain," Rainey urged.

"I agree with you," Captain Cinellan said to Rainey. "If this young woman is right, you two need to investigate."

"I am raising an objection, Captain," Miss Morad said.

"And I've made a note of it."

"Captain," Miss Morad said sharply. "The regulations are clear that I need to start the proceedings with Inspector Welling today—"

"Then you shouldn't have waited so long," Rainey said. "We have a job to do, Miss Morad."

"I need—"

"It is somewhat urgent," the Tarian girl pressed. "I don't know how stable the scene is there."

"Please silence yourself, Miss Fendall," Miss Morad said to the Tarian girl. Upon her shocked expression, she added, "Yes, I know exactly who you are."

That silenced the girl.

Miss Morad turned to the captain. "I have the authority—"

"Your authority does not extend to interfering with my people's investigations," Captain Cinellan said. "You wasted your own time with this charade you insisted on. Now—"

"Cap, we could go," Inspector Kellman said. "I mean, that way—"

"Not possible," Minox said. "Miss Morad, you waited eighty days to have our interview. You can wait a few hours more."

"It must be today—"

"If I consent to granting you an extra day, can we continue?" Minox asked. He looked to the captain. "Surely, I have the right to extend that limitation."

"Minox, you shouldn't—" the captain started.

"Fine," Miss Morad said quickly. "But I will join you and observe what happens."

Miss Fendall took this as cue enough, and returned to the bridge. Inspector Rainey and Miss Morad went behind her.

Corrie grabbed Minox by the arm before he had a chance to follow. "Be careful with that one, Mine. She's a rat."

"I have to abide—"

"Watch your blasted self, you idiot," Corrie said. "But I'm at your arm in all this, get?"

"Favor me this," Minox said, taking some dried meat from the pouch on his belt. He always carried extra food on his person for moments like this when he used more magic than he had expected to. "Send a page out east, get Jillian to come to the Parliament."

"You want Jilly?" Corrie raised an eyebrow at that. "You think she—"

"She's better than Leppin's boy, especially with anything . . . gruesome. Please."

"I'll get her myself," Corrie said. "Eyes up, really."

"You as well."

"I thought you expressed urgency, Inspector," Miss Morad called from the foot of the bridge.

Minox saluted to his sister and went off.

"Fendall, is it?" Inspector Rainey was asking the Tarian girl.

"Jerinne Fendall," she said, "though how this woman knew that—"

"Please, Miss Fendall," Miss Morad said. She was doing an excellent job keeping pace with the rest of them, despite her apparent mature years. Minox wanted to break into a run, or even commandeer a pedalcart, but he felt like he needed to exhibit decorum around Miss Morad. She exuded an air of respectability, a brassbound temper that made Minox feel like he was found wanting. Even at the brisk pace, she was an avatar of poise and posture. "Your exploits with your companion, Mister Heldrin, made you something of a minor celebrity in higher circles."

"Exploits?" Minox asked.

"I'm surprised you didn't know, Inspector," Miss Morad said. "I thought researching newsprints from the whole city over was part of your process."

Minox wracked his memory. Had there been stories of note that involved Tarians? There had been something involving the assassination of a handful of members of Parliament some months back, and then something else with the election. He hadn't paid it much mind, because it didn't reflect on the cases he had been working on.

But he did remember that cousin Evoy had paid

attention to those stories. Fixated, even. That was noteworthy.

"I'm aware of those events. The names hadn't stayed with me. I note what matters, not minor celebrity."

"You should note who is doing what. Some would say these Tarians did the job when the Constabulary failed."

Minox wasn't going to rise to that bait. "We all work on the side of justice. Credit isn't important."

"And yet you've also made a name in the news-sheets."

"Infamy, perhaps," Rainey said.

"Notoriety, either way," Miss Morad said.

"Ma'am," Miss Fendall said sharply. "We're about to head into something pretty gruesome. You sure you want to see this?"

"I've kept up on the story, in researching Inspector Welling. I'm fully prepared."

While Miss Morad was engaged with Miss Fendall, Rainey stepped into pace with Minox.

"You all right?" she asked in a low voice.

"I was expecting something to occur today. I wasn't thinking it would involve these dramatics, but I'm fine."

"I meant, you just did some heavy magic. Hungry?"

She offered a bit of dried fruit from the pouch on her belt. Their months together had put them in a rhythm, and they both carried an emergency supply of food for him. Since the changes that altered his hand, his appetite had become even more voracious, but he had also learned how to manage it.

"I'm fine for now," he said.

"All right," she said. "But we're near my house. So I actually know the good food carts here."

"I'll keep that in mind."

Miss Fendall was now half a block ahead of them, so Minox and Rainey picked up their pace to catch her.

When they reached Parliament Square, the scene was already chaotic. A dozen Yellowshield carts choked the streets, while Constabulary formed a barricade around the grand building, keeping the crowd far away from it.

Despite living in Maradaine his entire life, Minox had rarely crossed the bridges to the north side, and never had cause to visit the seat of the government. He had never been particularly interested in it, as the decisions of a hundred pampered men rarely had any real impact on his own life. The "august body" was far removed from the day-to-day of life in Maradaine, especially for the hardworking people of the city services.

He remembered something from his schoolboy lessons though, which always struck him as ironic. Some two hundred years ago, when the Parliament was founded, Maradaine was also rebuilding from the Incursion that had taken place at the beginning of the eleventh century. Much of the rebuilding work was done by common folk, under the promise that their loyalty to Maradaine and Druthal would be rewarded, that they would have a voice in the new nation. But when the Rights of Man were written and the Parliament was finally convoked, those folk were blocked out. Instead, their reward was to be named the "loyal families." The families who put the city back together would form the foundation of the Constabulary, the Fire Brigade, the brick and pipe men, and the other city services.

One of those was the Welling family. Marius Welling—Minox's many-times-great-grandfather—had been a key man who helped form the Constabulary and organized a large part of the rebuild efforts. He had been so vital to the work that one of these north side neighborhoods bore his name.

"Welling?" Inspector Rainey said. "Sure you don't need to eat something?"

"No," he said. He must have been in a bit of a reverie. "We'll need to push through to those barricades."

"Make a hole!" Miss Fendall shouted. People in this part of town, at least, gave respect to a uniform. The crowd parted and let her lead the three of them up to the barricade.

"You can't come through here," the patrolman said almost instinctively as they approached.

"I'm afraid we must," Minox said. "Inspectors Welling and Rainey with the Grand Inspection Unit."

"Really?" the patrolman asked. "Are you two supposed to be here?"

"We were called for."

"I'm going to have to check on that."

"We're in a rush," Miss Fendall said.

"Let them through," someone else called. The patrolman reacted immediately to that, and as he moved the wooden barricade over to let them pass, Minox could see why. The man who gave the order was Commissioner Wendt Enbrain. He approached them in an almost feverish state.

"Satrine," he said, sweeping Inspector Rainey in a panicked embrace. "I just . . . I never . . ."

He then looked at Minox as well as Fendall and Morad, and regained a bit of composure. "Inspector Welling." He took Minox's hand and shook it warmly. Minox had only met the man in passing a handful of times, but he clearly had a long history with Inspector Rainey. Of course, her infirm husband had worked closely with the commissioner as an Inspector First Class out of Capital Plaza. "I'm very grateful you two are here, but . . . why . . . how . . ."

"We were summoned by Miss Fendall," Minox said.

Commissioner Enbrain gave her another look. "Tarian? But why—it doesn't matter. Doesn't matter. I'm very glad to see you, Satrine. It's horrible. Horrible."

She gave a glance to Minox, a single look that communicated a great deal. He understood her meaning, and he had deduced the same thing. Whatever was happening on the Parliament floor, whatever horrors they were about to see, it had some sort of direct and personal impact on Commissioner Enbrain.

Enbrain failure.

<hr />

Corrie Welling still hadn't grown used to the sergeant's braid on her shoulders. She knew damn well nineteen was a young age to earn it, and she also knew plenty of the old hands in the stationhouse felt the same way.

Especially guys like Rezzo in the stables. That steve had been on horsepatrol for years, and when he hurt his back he was taken off the streets to mind the horses. Never rose above the rank of patrolman, old enough to be Corrie's father. And now she outranked him.

"What's a sergeant doing down here?" he asked as she came down to the stables. "Thought this girl was too fancy to walk through the dung piles."

"You shouldn't call yourself a rutting dung pile, Rez," she said.

"Funny girl," he said. "What you doing down here?"

"Need a damn horse, why else?" Corrie said.

"Most of the horses are out on patrol. Don't know if I have one that's worthy of a sergeant."

"Stop pouring sewage down my throat. I just need to ride out east."

"Do you now?" This wasn't Rezzo, but rutting Iorrett, leaning against the stable door. "What's the story?"

"I got a job to do, Iorrett," she said.

"Not by me you don't."

"I don't blazing well answer to you, tosser."

"Yeah, but we've got training to do. Go over what we did on that exercise."

"Exercise?" Corrie spat on the ground. "You have the rutting nerve to call that heap of sewage an exercise?"

"What happened?" Rezzo asked.

"Oh, shut your rutting breadhole," Corrie said, and

then turned back onto Iorrett. "You actually are saying that helped us?"

"Hey, I know you're chuffed because the whole thing was made to tag your brother—"

"What to her brother?" Joshea Brondar came into the stables. He was looking crisp, despite just being in shirtsleeves. He somehow managed to make dressed-down working-man clothes look like style. He didn't make Corrie's heart patter like he did her cousins—both Ferah and Nyla couldn't get enough of him—but she understood why they felt that way. Of course, as much as he charmed them, the only Welling he had much interest in was Minox. Probably because they were both untrained mages, as blazing crazy as that was. But Joshea's magic had saved her, saved Tricky, saved Minox. So she wasn't going to say a split of anything about it to anyone. Joshea's secret, his rutting business.

"We're talking about that training exercise," Iorrett said.

"Rutting sewage. Get me that horse, Rez. Now."

Rezzo ran off.

"Yeah, how did that go?" Joshea asked.

"You knew?"

"Yeah, I—" Corrie didn't let him finish, grabbing him by his suspenders.

"You blazing well knew they were doing that to Minox?"

"Do what to Minox?" He looked at Iorrett. "I thought it was an exercise for your squad. The captain told me to sit it out, which is fine, but—"

"It wasn't for us, you rutting stone," she said.

"It was useful to us," Iorrett said under his breath.

"No, it was a rutting setup to test Minox, rigged by the folks who are doing his blasted Inquiry."

Joshea's eyes went wide, then narrowed with cold anger. "I had no idea. I—another officer taken hostage, civilians at risk. I should have seen the connection." He slammed a fist against the wall.

"So what did you blazing know?"

"Only the scenario. I swear, I thought it was a training setup for your squad."

"Corrie," Iorrett spat at her. "It don't matter. This ain't his fault or my fault. We all did what we were told. Jinx—"

"Don't you rutting—"

"Inspector Welling," he quickly corrected. "He knew a reckoning was coming for him, that he was being investigated. So it didn't look like he expected, but we did our job. Like we were supposed to."

"I'm sorry, Cor," Joshea said.

"So am I," she said. "You all had me betray my own blood."

"I really had no idea that's what it was."

"Yeah, well, now you rutting know," she said. Rezzo came over with a saddled horse. Not one she was familiar with, but it looked like a solid, strong one. She took its reins from him.

"Corrie," Iorrett said sharply. "We still got to debrief on this, talk about how it went."

"Talk amongst your rutting selves, bastard," she said. "I got an assignment from one of our inspectors. That's our rutting job."

She pulled herself up on the horse and kicked it into a jog before she could hear whatever sewage Iorrett was going to throw at her. She didn't give a damn.

She had to head out east, and find another cousin, one she hadn't talked to in over a year. She'd never go out east to talk to Jilly on her own, but Minox asked her to. And right now, she'd walk through the blazes just to bring him a drink. It was the least she could do.

◆—◆◆—◆

Satrine had known Commissioner Wendt Enbrain for years, and she had never seen him in such a state as this. His face was decidedly green, with a sheen of sweat over it that was too much even for this autumn heat wave. He raced his large frame as he led them up the Parliament steps to the main entrance. These grand doors, under the flag of Druthal, were the ones that were to be used by the press and the common people who had business in the Parliament building. There were ten other entrances surrounding the building, one for each archduchy, which led to their specific portion of the Parliament floor. Eleven formal entrances, and surely several more for functionaries, services people, and deliveries.

Satrine knew all that about the Parliament, despite never setting foot in the place. Her telepathic education was now filling her thoughts with details and history and familiarity, as if she had been coming here for years.

The top of the steps outside the doors was another area of barely controlled chaos. Yellowshields were encamped here, as well as King's Marshals, a smattering of Army and Navy officers, even an Intelligence colonel in uniform. On top of that, people who Satrine presumed were members of the press were trying to get to the doors, shouting questions.

"What's happening?" Satrine asked Enbrain.

"A violation, the likes of which—" He trailed off, the silence lasting too long. His face showed her enough—he had seen something which had struck him to his soul.

"Sir," Welling said. "What can you tell us?"

"It's—" He choked up. "I'm sorry. Let's get you inside."

"Are we even allowed inside?" Welling asked.

"We'll manage." That was the Tarian girl. Jerinne. Couldn't be more than a couple years older than Rian. Satrine was amazed this young lady could be so sure of herself, so poised. Of course at that age, Satrine was in Waisholm, pretending to be a dead noblewoman and actively guiding events to put her lover on the Waish throne.

Her own youth was not a typical point of comparison.

Jerinne went straight for the first door, only to have a King's Marshal get in front of her.

"What are you doing, girl?" he asked.

"We have business inside," she said.

"Ain't no one going inside who isn't cleared."

"I was in there when it was found," Jerinne said.

"Then you should have stayed inside."

"Son," Enbrain said, coming up to the marshal. "We're going in."

The marshal glanced at Enbrain, Satrine, and Welling. "Constabulary is supposed to be keeping the crowd back at street level. We don't need you up here."

"We're inspectors," Satrine said. "Apparently you have a murder in here that needs our attention."

"I've not heard of bringing in street constables," he said. "This is the province of the marshals."

"Special circumstances," Enbrain said. "Step aside."

"Pardon me," the young marshal said, putting a hand lightly on Enbrain's chest to block him. "I don't yield to you, sir. I know who you are, but I don't answer to your authority."

"Do you answer to mine?" An older man in a simple but fine suit had come over, giving the marshal a hard glare.

"Your Honor," the marshal said. "You, of course, can go inside." Clearly this old man was a member of Parliament.

"The commissioner and his people will be joining me," the Parliamentarian said.

"And the Tarian girl?"

"Absolutely." He turned to Jerinne and gave her a familiar wink

The young marshal led them all in. "I'm going to tell my first that they're here under your authority, though, your Honor."

"Do that," the Parliamentarian said. Once they were

inside, beyond the marshal's hearing, he took Enbrain into an embrace. "Wendt," he said. "I'm so sorry. Rest assured—"

"Everything that can be done, I know. Which is why I want these two as part of the investigation."

The Parliamentarian offered his hand to Satrine. "Alphonse Montrose."

Montrose. One of the leading men in the Parliament, head of the small but earnest Populist party. One of the chairs from the Archduchy of Maradaine. Logan had voted for him a couple of times.

"Inspector Satrine Rainey," she said, taking his hand. "My partner, Minox Welling."

"Your Honor," Welling said, shaking the man's hand.

"What do we know?" Enbrain said.

"I don't know much of anything yet," Montrose said. "But I'm determined to find out."

"Shall we not dally further, then?" Welling asked.

"We've heard there's a monstrous machine," Satrine said. "With several victims."

"Several victims, yes," Enbrain said. "Hopefully there's something that can be done for them."

"Done for them?" Welling asked. "Do you mean to say—"

"Yes," Enbrain said. "Many of them are still alive. But—"

Enbrain didn't get any further before Welling bolted to the doors.

"Wait!"

A large man—possibly one of the tallest men Satrine had ever seen—put himself between Minox and the door. He was also wearing a Tarian uniform, a shield strapped to his arm. "I can't let you go through that door."

"Sir," Welling said, his hand firmly on the handle of the door. "It is imperative that we take action and save as many of the victims as we can."

"I agree," the Tarian said. "That's exactly why you can't open the door."

"I don't—"

"Inside there is a machine of death and butchery, devised by a brilliant madman. There are over a dozen people trapped within the machine, and more already dead. We cannot safely . . ."

"That doesn't explain—"

"And the machine has many elements and moving parts. Some of which are connected to these doors."

Welling let go of the door handle.

The large Tarian hadn't raised his voice a bit—the whole time he spoke with calm, quiet assurance.

"Dayne," Jerinne said. "These are the ones you asked for."

"You're Inspector Welling," the large man said, offering his hand. "Dayne Heldrin."

"Of the Tarian Order," Welling said, taking the offered hand.

Dayne approached the rest. "You must be Inspector Satrine Rainey."

"I know about you," Satrine said, taking his hand as he came over. "My daughter brought home that pamphlet."

"I didn't ask for the press," Dayne said. "I just do what I can to save lives."

"Our paramount concern . . ." Welling started.

"Of course, this way," Dayne said, leading them to a stairwell. "The press gallery is safe to enter from."

The gallery door at the top of the stairs was watched by another King's Marshal. "We're in the process of a rescue, Mister Heldrin," he said. "It's very delicate." A small squad of Yellowshields were encamped outside the door. Clearly they had been instructed to stay out of the Parliament for the moment, but Satrine couldn't imagine why. Surely their skills were needed inside.

"These two inspectors are experts in this machinery

and the methods of the killer," Dayne said. "You shouldn't try anything until they've gotten to see it."

The marshal fretted for a moment, glancing at Dayne, and then Parliamentarian Montrose. "All right, but it's on you. If Chief Quoyell asks, I wash my hands of it."

"Such nobility," Dayne said as he went in. He turned back to Satrine and Welling. "You will want to steel your stomachs. This is not something to look upon lightly."

"I've had more than my share of that," Satrine said, pressing through. She had heard so much of what a horror was awaiting them, she was certain that nothing could live up to the myth.

Five steps into the Parliament hall, that was belied. If anything, the atrocity machine had been minimized.

"Sweet saints and sinners preserve me," she whispered.

From the press gallery, they had a perfect view of the whole Parliament floor. Down below, there was an atrocity of machinery and people. Ropes, chains, gears, and pipes. Weights and counterweights. Blades, hammers, spikes, and clubs. And blood. An untold amount of blood.

The chains and gears and pipes formed a sort of spiderweb, connecting to devices on the floor that clicked and whirred, pulling chains and pushing pipes, changing the tension on the ropes. All of those spread out to the doors around the circular hall.

And then there were the people, shackled into chairs in a rough circle around the machines. All the chairs moved.

Everything moved. The people trapped in the device were being pulled and dragged around the Parliament floor in their chairs, and the deadly instruments around them spun and slammed and cracked. The people were gagged with leather straps, so none of them could cry out. They all could struggle just enough to make it clear that they were still alive. Most of them were strapped to the chair in such a way that their faces were covered by horrific masks, masks that were also contraptions of gears and blades and springs.

By Satrine's immediate count, there had been eighteen people total—mostly men but three were women, all relatively youthful. Twelve were still alive—including all three women. The other six had been sliced, shredded, and ground by the horrific machine.

And yet, as everything moved, the hall echoed with clicks and clangs and pounding that almost became music. It had a rhythm, a sonorous beauty that in any other circumstances might bring a tear to one's eye.

Satrine's eyes were full of tears.

Welling's hand was on her shoulder. She looked at him and saw his eyes were just as full. She had never seen any such emotion from him before.

"We can save these people," he said.

"And then let's find this bastard."

A half-dozen King's Marshals grabbed them both and pulled them back to the door.

Chapter 4

◄━━━━●◄ ►●━━━━►

SATRINE ELBOWED ONE of the marshals in the gut, forcing him to let go. With one arm free, she drew out her handstick and cracked it across another's wrist. In a moment they all let her go.

"I've been manhandled enough today," she snarled. "How dare you grope us like that?"

"You shouldn't be up here," one of the marshals said, rubbing his arm. "You might have triggered—" He then looked and saw Dayne, Commissioner Enbrain, Montrose, and the rest. "Oh. I didn't realize."

"Of course you didn't," Montrose said. "Did you think they would have just wandered up here on their own?"

"Well, no," the marshal said. "Just Chief Quoyell said no one was supposed to be up here."

"And where is Chief Quoyell?" Dayne asked, stepping forward. "He was actually supposed to be up here. Even the Yellowshields needed to be staged outside."

The marshal pointed to the other side of the gallery, where three other marshals—including one with stars on his shoulders—were assembling a rope and pulley device that extended over the gallery floor.

"What's their intention?" Welling asked.

"Lower themselves down to disassemble the device, getting the people out of there."

Commissioner Enbrain pushed forward to the gallery railing to look down to the floor. "Is it possible? Can they do it?"

"Get down there? Sure," the marshal said. "Once they get that thing ready, it should be no problem."

Dayne came over to Welling and Satrine. "The marshals who first opened the main door downstairs—when they did that, it started these machines in motion. That's when the first three people died."

"You saw it?" Welling asked.

"I saw right afterward."

"And that door is, I presume, inaccessible?"

"Once the machine was started, spinning and whirling blades blocked the door, as well as the other entrances on that level. I sent Jerinne to fetch you two, and I tried to get through. But my attempts were futile."

Satrine noticed that his uniform coat was sliced and cut on the arms.

"He means his interference triggered another part of the device," the marshal said, glowering at Dayne. "That's part of the problem. We try to do much of anything—like open a door down there—we trigger something else. And the deaths speed up."

"Speed up?" Welling asked.

"The thing is like a clock," the marshal said, pointing at the moving gears. "Every minute they're all pushed or prodded or knocked. And on the hour . . ."

"Someone dies," Welling said.

"And we already figured out opening any door anywhere but the gallery makes the clock go faster," Dayne said. He scowled and shook his head. "He wanted an audience."

"We have to stop it," Satrine said. It was clear Dayne had a specific "he" in mind, but this wasn't the moment to address it.

The marshal sneered at her. "I don't know what makes you think you are part of the 'we,' Inspector."

"I called them in," Dayne said.

"And I want them here," Commissioner Enbrain added. Satrine came back over to him, looking down at the people on the floor.

"Which one is it?" she asked him softly.

He looked over at her, his face stricken, and then pointed to one of the victims. "That one. My nephew Niall."

His nephew. Of course. Enbrain was a widower, no children of his own. He was close to several of his nieces and nephews.

Welling looked over. "And the rest of these people? Do we know who they are? What is their connection to each other or the rest of these murders?"

"We've identified some, and those are Parliamentary functionaries. I presume they all are," Mister Montrose said. "Niall there is my head clerk. The ones I recognize have similar positions with key members of Parliament."

Welling nodded, moving closer to the edge of the railing to look down. He was absorbing it all, his eyes darting all over the machinery. "Windup. Spring tension. Releases started when doors were opened. We presume that if we had left everything alone, it would run its course over eighteen hours and everyone in there would be dead."

"How does that help?" Dayne asked.

"Information always helps. Our immediate priority, of course, is rescuing the people alive down there. But we must learn all we can about what is happening, so we can use that information to find the killer."

"About that—" Dayne said.

"Yes," Welling said, holding up a finger in the big man's face. "I'm certain you have critical knowledge, and I'll want to interview you fully. But that will have to be after the immediate crisis is resolved."

"After it is resolved I need to interview you, Inspector."

Satrine had forgotten that Miss Morad was still with them. She had to admit, she was impressed by the woman's moxie. Most people wouldn't be able to stomach being in this room, let alone doing so with such a stern, disinterested expression.

"In due time, Miss Morad," Welling said, giving Satrine a look. He then turned to the marshals who manhandled them when they first arrived. "Of those marshals with Chief Quoyell, which of them is the engineer?"

"The what?" the first marshal asked.

"Engineer. Machinist. Tinkerer, clockmaker? Anything of the sort?"

"I don't—"

Welling shook his head, "They're going to get everyone killed. Miss Fendall!"

"Yes?" Jerinne asked.

"My sister—the officer with the colorful tongue—do you recall her?"

"Oh, saints, yes," Jerinne said, with almost too much enthusiasm.

"She'll be coming this way with a charcoal sketcher from the Constabulary. Please make sure they are able to get in here."

"All right," she said, looking to Dayne for a moment for approval, and then ran off.

"Inspector Rainey," he said, looking to her, "I'm going to attempt to engage the rest of the marshals—you will intercede on my behalf, Mister Heldrin?"

"Of course."

"But we need someone with some experience with machinery like this on hand, and quickly."

Satrine looked back down at the monstrosity. "I don't know who would—"

"So I presume you do not at the moment?"

He knew her telepathically induced education sometimes needed a trigger for her to actively access it. But in this instance, it didn't help. "Nothing like this was needed to be a princess." There had been an Intelligence officer outside. Perhaps there was someone out there she could reach out to. There had to be people in Intelligence who had experience with this kind of machinery. Gadgeteers or security consultants. "I have an idea, though."

Welling nodded. "I always have trusted in your ideas. Mister Heldrin, with me."

He stormed off to walk around the gallery to where the marshals were working with the pulleys. They had already started to lower someone to the floor.

"Satrine," Enbrain said. "We have to save everyone, but Niall—"

"We'll do anything we can for him," she said. "I'll be back."

As she left the gallery, she noticed Kendra Morad calmly writing in a notebook as she followed Welling to the other side. With everything else happening right now, the last thing anyone should be worried about was an inquiry into Minox Welling. If Kendra Morad couldn't see him for the dedicated and tireless city servant that he was, she had no business judging anyone.

◆——◆◆——◆

The East Maradaine Stationhouse was so damn quiet, it was rutting unnerving. Corrie had expected what she usually saw in the front office of their own stationhouse— scabs and other rats ironed up and waiting on benches for the desk sergeants to process their paperwork; shouting and threats and the sense that a fight would break out any minute.

Instead this house had a handful of sergeants and clerks silently writing and filing, no one waiting to be brought into lockup, and a distinct lack of shouting.

Not a proper stick house in the slightest.

A clerk who must have been old enough to have hired Granny Jillian back in the day was at the front desk. "Can I help you, miss?"

"Yeah," Corrie said, coming closer. The lenses on her spectacles were thick enough to stop a crossbow bolt. "I'm looking for—"

"Oh, my!" the old lady said. "You've got your sergeant's stripes. So few young ladies have those on their collar."

"Right, well—"

"And look how young and pretty you are. How old are you, now?"

"I turn twenty in a month," Corrie said. "I'm looking for—"

"Sergeant before you turned twenty, and for a lady constable as well. That's incredible. That sort of thing would never have happened when I was your age."

"I need—"

"But girls today are so very remarkable, I'm just amazed at all you are accomplishing. We've quite a few accomplished girls in this stationhouse, I can tell you—"

"Yes, and I need to—"

"But none of them have made sergeant before they turned twenty, that is for certain. Where are you coming from?"

"The Inemar house," Corrie said, biting her tongue before she added additional invectives to that.

"Oh, Inemar, yes, that's some rough and tumble." She peered with her giant glasses. "Probably how you have that scar by your eye. Probably how you earned those stripes."

"Yes." Screaming all sorts of profanities would feel wonderful but help rutting nothing.

"Are we holding someone who's supposed to go to you? We don't see as much trouble in this house."

"No," Corrie said. She had to get this out before the old bat interrupted her again. "I just need to find Jilly Welling."

"Oh, Jilly. Lovely girl, lovely. Yes, she's right there." She pointed to a desk in the corner, where a honey-brown-haired woman was working, her back to the floor.

"Thank you."

"Oh, you're a Welling!" the old woman said, tapping Corrie's badge. "I didn't know she had another sister."

"Cousin," Corrie said. "Excuse me."

She pushed her way through the office floor to the desk. "Jilly, I need you—"

She realized the mistake before she even finished the sentence. But it was too late.

"Jillian is down in the examinarium, as she always is," the young woman said without even looking up. "Even if you didn't use your eyes, you could use common sense."

It wasn't Jilly, but her twin sister Sherien.

"Sorry, Sheri."

Sheri looked up, hard eyes. "Corrianna. What ever are you doing so far from your milieu?"

Corrie never understood how these cousins talked like they were so properly rutting educated. It wasn't as if they hadn't all gone to the same public prepatory in Keller Cove.

"I came looking for Jilly, but the lady at the front desk pointed me in the wrong rutting place—"

Sheri winced like she had been physically slapped.

"But now I know to go to the examinarium, so I'll be out of your hair." She bit back a "blasted" and "damned" that she had wanted to throw in there.

"You've never been here, and you'll get lost," Sheri said, getting to her feet. She brushed off her long skirt as if it had gotten rutting dusty just sitting at her desk. "Come along, and I'll show you."

"You don't—" Corrie started, but it wasn't worth it. She was rutting glad that things were already this civil. No need to poke the dog anymore. "Thanks."

Sheri led her down a hallway to a dark stairway. "So, Corrianna, you've been promoted to sergeant. When did that happen?"

"Couple months ago. You didn't hear?"

"Well, Father didn't mention it, but he might not have taken note of it."

Uncle Terrent had been a sergeant for twenty years, never getting promoted to officer or inspector. But he was walking the streets here in tony East Maradaine. Not that Corrie had seen him or the twins much in the past couple years.

"And you?" Corrie asked, though she didn't know why she was bothering with pleasantries. "Anything new for you?"

"Work in the day, cause in the evening, it keeps me busy."

"Cause?" Corrie regretted asking as soon as it came out of her lips.

"The only cause, Corrianna: suffragism."

"Right. Aunt Emma is working in that, too. Her and Nyla."

"Hmm," Sheri said coldly. "We're a different chapter of the movement." She opened up the door that was clearly marked "Examinarium" and led Corrie in. "Jillian? Are you down here?"

Jilly was there, sitting at her desk right next to a slab with a dead body on it. She and Sheri were exact doubles, except Jilly had changed her hair to a short boyish cut instead of Sheri's prim bun. She also had painted her face in a way that made her look almost like the corpse she was sitting next to.

"Corrianna," she said in a way that was almost musical. "Don't tell me that all the girls downtown are short-cropping."

Corrie realized Jilly was talking about her own hair. She touched it reflexively. "This? Nah, some machie bint chopped it off me in a riot."

"Savage," Jilly said, almost excited at the prospect.

"Language, Corrianna," Sheri said.

"So why have you come to haunt us?" Jilly asked. "Please don't tell me your mother sent you here to convince us to get Father to come up to the house."

"No, no," Corrie said. "Nothing like that. This is business."

"Well, I have work to do," Sheri said. "Corrianna, it's been a pleasure to see you." She didn't sound like it had been anything of the sort. "Jillian, I'll see you at sign out." She left.

"What business do you have with me?" Jilly said, getting to her feet. "I didn't realize you were interested in me or my sister."

"Don't rutting say that, Jilly," Corrie said. "I've never given you any damn grief for anything."

"No, I suppose not. Still, it's not like you've ever come to see us."

"You don't exactly head into Inemar or come all the way out to the house."

"We don't care about the stupid house," Jilly fired back. "Why do you all insist—"

"Hey, hey," Corrie said, putting up her hands. "I don't give a pig's whistle about the house or whatever grief your pop and the rest have. Live how you want."

"So what do you want?"

"Minox asked me to come get you," Corrie said.

"Minox? Asked for me?" Jilly's voice softened a little. "Whatever for?"

"He's been working this case, the springbox murders?"

"The Gearbox Murders," Jilly said. With a tone that seemed far too energized for Corrie's taste, she added, "Those have been gruesome."

Jilly was always fascinated with the gruesome.

"Yeah, well, there's another one, and it's apparently big. Minox asked for you to come out to join him."

Jilly's hand went to her sketchbook and charcoals. "Don't you have sketchers in your Grand Inspection Unit?"

"Minox told me he needed you. And right away."

"Hmmm," Jilly said, drawing out the word like she was sipping a fine wine or something. "Well, I'm glad that Minox, at least, recognizes talent."

Corrie didn't want to say a rutting thing to that.

"Let's just get moving, before it's too late. We got to get across the river."

"Really? What, is this murder in the Parliament or something?"

"Exactly."

Jilly snatched up her gear. "Then what are we waiting for?"

———— ◆ ◆ ————

Minox rushed through the gallery seats to navigate his way to the other side, fully aware of the looming presence of Dayne Heldrin right behind him.

"Forgive my brusqueness, Mister Heldrin, but I assume you have a formal position of authority here in the Parliament?"

"Formal, yes," Heldrin said. "But the exact nature of my authority is nebulous."

"I appreciate your honesty here," Minox said. "And I must act quickly. Are you at least versed in Parliamentary rules and procedure? It is a significant gap in my knowledge. I am counting on you, especially since the marshals surely have standing."

"I can help with that, Inspector."

"Good," Minox said. They were now a quarter of the way around the Parliament hall. The change in angle did nothing to mitigate the horror below. Out of the corner of his eye, Minox also noticed Kendra Morad following behind him. He wanted to behave as if it didn't bother him, that her observation was welcome. But she unnerved him, and that drew his concentration away from the task at hand.

And this task would require all his focus.

Minox came up on the two marshals who were lowering the third. Speaking directly to the one with chief's stars, he said, "I'm going to have to insist you cease this operation immediately and cede authority in this matter to the city Constabulary's Grand Inspection Unit."

"And who the blazes are you?" Chief Quoyell

asked, his brass name badge so polished it shone. He was an older man, most of his hair, which appeared to have been at one time the same red as Inspector Rainey's, was either white or gone.

"Inspector Minox Welling of the aforementioned Grand Inspection Unit. If you direct your attention over there, you can see Commissioner Enbrain speaking with Mister Montrose. I'm afraid it is imperative that this situation fall under our authority."

"You have no authority or jurisdiction here." He turned to Heldrin. "Was this your doing, Tarian?"

"I called in Inspector Welling, yes."

"Always meddling," Quoyell said. "But you have no cause or reason for claiming authority over the King's Marshals."

"Save one," Minox said. "You, Chief Quoyell, and everyone under your command, are suspect in this matter, and therefore cannot be allowed to supervise or interfere in the investigation."

"How are they suspect?" This came from Kendra Morad.

"This is outrageous!" Chief Quoyell said.

"But utterly sensible. As you said, Chief, this is your jurisdiction. And, specifically, maintaining the security and integrity of the Parliament is the responsibility of you and your men. This," Minox said, gesturing to the mechanical horror below, "is a monstrous failure of your security. Which means your people—and by reflection you—are either corrupt, culpable, or incompetent. Regardless, you cannot be allowed to continue this investigation."

The whole time, their man kept lowering himself to the Parliament floor. It didn't escape Minox's attention that he was almost all the way down.

Chief Quoyell did seem slightly fazed by this argument. Or at least shamed. "Exactly why this is our responsibility. No one else's."

"And who are you accountable to?" Minox asked.

"King Maradaine XVIII."

"And the people," Heldrin said. "I can easily let the press know that your pride and incompetence are impeding a proper, independent investigation."

"Which is what you need, Chief." This came from Kendra Morad.

They all looked at her.

Miss Morad continued. "Your obstinacy is hurtful to yourself and your fellow marshals, to the process of neutrality, the process of justice, and the king himself. None of these things have been particularly popular in the press of late."

Chief Quoyell was almost red-faced and sputtering. "Who is this woman?"

"She's a special inquisitor with the Archduke of Sauriya," Minox said.

That seemed to have some effect on Chief Quoyell. Perhaps, despite his claims of only being accountable to the king, the threat of archducal authority had some sway over him. "Yes, of course, ma'am. But there is a matter of protocol. City Constabulary has no jurisdiction or authority here. Even if I ceded ours—"

"Which you should," Morad said.

"I can't give run of this situation to a Constabulary Inspector. He doesn't have the clearance to—"

"But I do," Heldrin said. "My role is to liaise with the Parliament, the marshals, and with that mandate—from the king himself—I am empowered to take independent action in service of the security and safety of the Parliament. I'm claiming that authority now, Chief."

"Hey, Chief," the man on the floor called out. "I'm able to get at the first victim here. Looks like just a few leather straps holding her in. I should be able to—"

Minox almost leaped over the railing. Heldrin grabbed him by the belt to keep him on the gallery.

"Doesn't he know—" Minox started to say, but he could see the man was already starting to unbuckle the leather strap on the woman's wrist. "Stop!"

It was too late. As soon as he undid the buckle, a grinding sound emerged from the machinery below.

The marshal below looked around, as if he couldn't identify exactly where the new noise was coming from. Then he scrambled to undo the strap on the woman's other wrist. She was still otherwise immobile, and her mouth was gagged, but even from this distance Minox could see the terror in her eyes. She desperately tried to thrash out of the chair while the marshal struggled to set her free.

"Haskin!" Chief Quoyell yelled.

The grinding then transformed into a series of pops.

The chair the woman was sitting in suddenly split apart, the two halves of the chair pulling in opposite directions. The woman in the chair was torn open, blood and viscera dropping to the floor in a sickening splash.

In place of the chair, a great pike sprung up, and the blade buried itself in the marshal's skull.

"Oh, sweet saints," Heldrin said.

Minox turned on Chief Quoyell, pointing an accusing finger at him. "Two more deaths. That was on you, sir."

"That was my man!"

"And an innocent woman whom we might have been able to save!"

"Inspector!" Miss Morad called forcefully.

Minox quickly realized why. He was pointing at Chief Quoyell with his left hand, and it was glowing in a blue nimbus through his glove. He pulled the energy down while putting his hand into his pocket. He hadn't even realized that he had been pouring his anger into his hand.

Looking Chief Quoyell in the eye, he said, "We need to handle this situation with deliberate care. This is possibly the most dangerous, volatile thing any of us have ever encountered."

"Possibly," Quoyell said, glaring at Minox.

"We cannot underestimate the genius behind it."

"I can tell you about—" Heldrin started.

"Oh, damn it, Dayne, I don't need to hear this

madness again!" Quoyell said. "Fine, I'll acknowledge that we don't know what the blazes we're doing with this. Are you happy? Does that help those poor bastards down there?"

"It's a start," Heldrin said.

"Very well," Quoyell said. He yelled over to Commissioner Enbrain and Mister Montrose, who both were stricken pale by the further carnage below. "This mess is yours now, Enbrain! You and yours can take the fall for it!"

He stormed off to the nearest exit.

"Well, Inspector," Miss Morad said quietly. "What's your next step?"

Chapter 5

SATRINE TOOK THREE steps out of the Parliament gallery before she stopped to lean against the wall, let the horror of it wash over her. She took deep breaths, hoping her stomach would settle itself from the horrible churning. That she had kept her breakfast inside her this long was incredible. She hadn't even consciously realized the extent she had been saturated by the slaughterhouse scent of the room until she was outside it. She could still smell it on her clothes.

After a moment, she realized the Yellowshields outside the door were staring at her.

"Have you even seen what's in there?" she asked them.

"No ma'am," one—the squad leader—said. "A lot of people have emptied their stomachs over it, though. Or worse. Water closet is over there if you need it."

"I'm fine," she half lied.

He nodded, coming a bit closer to her. "It's probably almost as bad in there, based on the sounds I've heard."

She waved him off, heading down the stairs to the lobby.

She spotted the Intelligence officer she had seen earlier—or, at least, someone in a formal Intelligence uniform. Those were not something often worn in public, but this sort of situation was unusual. The officer—a woman with a sallow face and short-cropped hair that made her almost look Lyranan—was talking to man in a fine bespoke suit and another in an Army uniform. Satrine swallowed down the bile in her throat and approached.

"Ma'am?" she asked. "Might I interrupt for a moment?"

"And you are?" The stripes on her collar marked her as a colonel in Druth Intelligence, making her one of the highest ranked people in the organization.

"Inspector Satrine Rainey of the Grand Inspector's Unit." No look of recognition crossed the woman's face, and her companions looked distinctly annoyed by the interruption. Satrine added, "And formerly of Innetic Project?" Bringing up the official name of the project that encompassed her mission to infiltrate the Waish nobility and place the man Druth Intelligence wanted on the Waish throne should get the attention of anyone with a colonel's stripes.

"Innetic Project?" the man in the suit asked.

The colonel's eyes widened for a moment, and she grabbed Satrine by the arm. "Of course, Inspector. Forgive me for not remembering you. Gentlemen, a moment, please?" She squeezed hard and pulled Satrine aside.

"I apologize—"

"You had no idea who those men were and you mention something like Innetic?" She glared hard at Satrine. "Who the blazes are you?"

"I told you, Inspector Satrine Rainey. Though I understand I'm still on the Register as Satrine Carthas."

"Someone on the Register wouldn't—"

"You can blame Grieson."

The colonel almost shuddered with revulsion. "You're one of his pets."

"That isn't the term I would use."

"It doesn't matter. You have my attention, Inspector. What is it?"

"Thank you, Colonel. There are, last I knew, twelve

men and women trapped in that atrocity machine in need of rescue."

"I've heard. And you're coming to me, why?"

"I'm actively investigating this case. We—"

"Who is we? I thought the marshals were in charge of the situation."

"Commissioner Enbrain wanted me and my partner to be on hand."

"Surely not to interfere with the marshals. You don't see me bringing in a team."

"In fairness, ma'am, would I even see that?" Satrine raised her eyebrow just a bit.

"Valid point," the colonel said. "But this isn't our dance."

"But given that the music is playing," Satrine said, lowering her voice a bit more, "I imagine you've got people who know the steps."

"Intelligence doesn't—"

Satrine knew the rest of the sentence. "Doesn't 'operate within Druth's borders.' I know the line. I know it's far from true."

"We're not allowed to take official action." The colonel gave a little wink. "And with something this big, and public, unofficial action isn't an option."

"But you might have something to pass on to someone who can take official action."

"And you think it should be you instead of the marshals?"

"We all want the same thing."

The colonel scoffed. "I think that's far from the truth. But I actually pay attention to the goings-on in Parliament and national politics."

"I just work the city, ma'am."

"I'll see what I can do," the colonel said. She gave Satrine an odd regard. "But that isn't even what you came to me for."

"No," Satrine said, realizing she had let the colonel walk her around. She had asked for a favor—not the one she came here for—without intending to, and the colonel knew damn well that put Satrine at a disadvantage now. Satrine reviewed the exchange they just had, and didn't even realize that she had been manipulated. It had felt so natural.

Blazes.

"The machine those people are trapped in, it's beyond our ken, and I'm certain the marshals are equally lost. From what I have seen about this killer's methods, a rescue attempt could result in more deaths—"

A snapping sound echoed through the entire lobby, emanating from the direction of the Parliament floor.

"So it would seem," the colonel said.

"Is there anyone on the Register, or in uniform, who has experience with machinery like this?"

The colonel nodded. This time, no guile—at least, none that was obvious to Satrine. "I don't know exactly, but I'll send word." She walked off.

Commissioner Enbrain came down from the gallery with Mister Montrose, both of them pale and clammy.

"What happened?" Satrine asked as she approached.

"The marshals' rescue was a fiasco," Enbrain said. "Chief Quoyell yielded command of the situation to the Constabulary."

"That easily?" Satrine asked.

Mister Montrose shook his head. "Quoyell already knows his head is on the block with this whole mess. Something like this defiles the Parliament floor. The sheer scope of the undertaking, the manpower required . . . I can't even comprehend how it was accomplished."

"But it's a colossal failure on his part, right," Satrine said.

Enbrain nodded. "Welling is . . . examining the situation. I'm not entirely sure. But he's alone up there."

"What about the Tarian?"

"He's organizing something on Minox's instructions. And I'm going to get our people to take charge of the building, secure all entrances and locations."

"Sweep the whole building," Satrine said. "It's entirely possible there are more victims secreted away somewhere, or the killer with whatever infrastructure he used to set this up."

Enbrain nodded grimly. "I can't imagine someone perverse enough to concoct all this wouldn't want to watch his performance."

A point so simple Satrine wanted to kick herself for not thinking about it. "Get our patrol people on identification. We need to know everyone who is here, and everyone who should be here but isn't."

Enbrain gave her a slight smirk.

"Sir," she added.

"Giving orders suits you, Satrine," he said, putting a hand on her shoulder. "I'll put people on it. Go to your partner."

Satrine went back up to the gallery, the slaughterhouse. This time the scent hit her even harder.

Now the gallery was empty, save Welling and Miss Morad. He was perched on the gallery ledge, watching everything below with the intent he usually reserved for studying his slateboards. Miss Morad had taken a seat in the back of the gallery, scribbling in a journal and keeping one eye on him.

"What do we know?" she asked, joining him on the ledge.

"Failed rescue attempts will be fatal," Welling said. "Our killer had planned for that."

"Whoever he is, he either has connections in the marshals or the Parliament to achieve this level of infiltration," Satrine said. "This is—"

"A massive security failure, yes," Welling said. "Which—"

"Suggestions collusion or collaboration." If he could finish her sentences, she could do the same with his. "Now that this is under our jurisdiction—"

"That is probably a temporary thing. I imagine Chief Quoyell is planning something to embarrass us and reclaim control."

"He can try," Satrine said. "But I've asked the commissioner to have footpatrol sweep the whole building. There may be other victims, other devices—"

"Or our killer watching all this somehow. I presumed."

"And we're working on getting identification on every person in this building. I suppose that includes our Tarian friends. Do we know what Heldrin's exact job or authority is?"

Welling shrugged. "It seems to be nebulous. I haven't fully questioned him—that will have to wait until after we've finished rescuing these people and examining the machinery. But I like him."

Minox Welling flat out declaring he liked someone was rare. And his judgment of character was something Satrine tended to trust. He liked her, after all, when no one else did.

"So how are we rescuing these people?" she asked. Eleven trapped people were still down there, bound and gagged and swirling about like toy tops. They must be devastated with fear right now. And the killer left them their eyes. They could see everything, but never scream. And all eleven could see two constables looking down, and were probably wondering why they weren't doing anything to save them.

"Right now?" Welling's focus never left the whirling machinery on the floor. "Learning."

━━━◆━■▶━━━

Dayne had spent the last half hour gaining authority over the situation in the Parliament—giving instructions to the constables as Commissioner Enbrain authorized them to secure the building. Normally, Dayne had found the Constabulary to be as obstructionist as the King's Marshals when it came to giving respect to a member of the Tarian Order. Maybe it was the gravity of the situation, maybe it was Enbrain's own shock at having his nephew be one of the victims, but the commissioner had been nothing but courteous.

Dayne found Jerinne outside one of the doorways, at watchful attention.

"What's the word?" he asked her.

"Still looking for the folks Inspector Welling asked for. What's the mood in there?"

"Tense. Horrified."

"About right," Jerinne said. "What's the plan?"

"Now the marshals have yielded the investigation—and the rescue—to the Constabulary."

"The rescue? How's that going?"

"The first attempt by the marshals was disastrous. But we need to do something."

"I could send word to the chapterhouse . . ."

"We don't have anyone there who is an expert. We need—" He glanced over to the clock on Saint Fenson's church across Parliament Square. It was almost the top of the hour. If the machine kept to form, someone else would die shortly. "I need to get back inside, quickly."

"But—" Jerinne said.

"Later," Dayne promised, going back inside.

Dayne raced up the stairs to the gallery, to find Inspector Rainey watching her partner, who was sitting on the balcony ledge, looking down on the machine below. Kendra Morad, the strange woman who seemed to only be here to observe Welling, stayed a respectful distance away.

"What's he doing?" Dayne asked Inspector Rainey.

"He's studying the machine. He feels it's all he can do right now."

"And you?"

"Waiting for local Fire Brigade to come with rescue armor, Yellowshields at the ready. Commissioner Enbrain is discussing the plan with them."

"There is a plan?"

"No one is too keen to drop down there after the marshal was killed." She glanced around. "I saw Quoyell skulking about a few minutes ago with a few of his men, but he's gone for the moment. I think he's got his own plan. How well do you know him?"

"Quoyell? Not very. He's pretty new in the position of Parliament Security."

"New people under him, too? Or old guard who may resent him?"

Dayne shrugged. "A bit of both. Why?"

"This is a massive failure at his feet, and I've got a sense in my gut about it. He's the type to do something to reclaim control."

"You might be right."

She mused, looking off in the distance, sounding out the man's name. "Coy-yell," she said, slowly. "That's how he pronounces it?"

"Yes," Dayne said, slightly confused. "Why?"

"Just an unusual name is all," she said.

"Inspector Rainey," Welling said from his perch.

She approached, and Dayne stayed with them. "What's going on?"

Welling didn't take his eyes off the machine below, still clicking and whirring as the victims were spun around the floor.

"I've worked out some of the obvious patterns of the movements, the victims, and the dangerous elements. It is all in clockwork precision."

"How does that help us?" she asked.

"I think—and I stress think—I know who will die next, and how. We may be able to use that knowledge to save him, if nothing else, until we can properly disarm and rescue all parties. Do we have a timeline on that, yet?"

"Enbrain is putting people together. I could go check."

A particularly loud click on the floor took Minox's attention. "I'm afraid we're at a critical juncture. The question is, how can we interfere without triggering a punitive cascade like the one that killed the marshal and the woman?"

Dayne felt his blood raise. "We need to save whoever is next, no matter what. Who is it, and when?"

"Seconds now," Inspector Welling said. He pointed to a young blond-haired man. "The axe on that arm—the one that's winding back!"

Dayne saw it. "It'll crash down, cracking open his skull." He instinctively jumped up on the ledge.

"Stand firm, Mister Heldrin," Welling said. "On my mark, throw your shield at his head."

"So I kill him first?" Dayne asked.

"Trust me," Welling said. The axe kept creaking back, as the arm it was housed on moved into position and locked in front of the blond man bound to his chair. Welling tapped his fingers in a count.

"Inspector—" Dayne said, holding up his shield, ready to throw.

"Just—now!"

The axe released, and Dayne hurled the shield. Right before either made contact with the young man's head, the shield spun off course, rocketing past the man's face by inches. The axe crashed into the shield, imbedding itself into the metal. The crunching sound it made was sickening, but then the axe started to wind back again, now with the shield attached to it.

The young man's head was unmolested.

"How?" Dayne asked.

Inspector Welling was holding out his gloved hand, which was glowing bright green. The glow subsided, and Welling dropped back, his breath heaving.

"Not quite as clean as I wanted," Welling said. "I wanted to get the shield back up here, but I didn't realize how much force that axe struck with. Amazing."

"You all right?" Rainey asked. She handed him something from her belt pouch, which he took and ate without question. The exchange was automatic between them, an instinct they shared.

"Nothing a few minutes' rest and something to eat wouldn't cure," Welling said.

Dayne raised an eyebrow. "A mage in the Constabulary?"

"Uncircled," Welling said. "That's part of why she's here." He indicated Miss Morad, who silently observed the goings-on.

"I understand," Dayne said. He knew something about being second-guessed by petty bureaucrats. A reason why he was likely not to be promoted beyond his Candidacy. He looked down to the machine. "Still eleven alive down there."

"If my estimates are correct," Welling said, moving to one of gallery seats, "we've bought ourselves about an hour before the next death. But I haven't figured out the entirety of the patterns. And there's more going on that can be accounted for by spring tension or clockwork winding. It's genius. Mad, ugly genius, but genius nonetheless."

Dayne nodded. That's exactly what Sholiar was. "I know about the man behind this. I've faced him before, in Lacanja."

Welling looked to Rainey, and she nodded. "We will want to interview you properly on the matter," she said. "But first—"

"Eleven souls to be saved," Dayne said. Absolutely, that was the first priority. Dayne would not—could not—let another person die when he could prevent it. And certainly he wouldn't let Sholiar further desecrate this august hall with his atrocity.

Dayne would give his own life before that would happen.

<hr />

Corrie wasn't prepared for the madhouse around the Parliament. Marshals and sheriffs had blockaded off the street in a three-block perimeter, seizing up traffic for half a mile in every direction. Judicious use of her whistle moved people out of her way, and more than once she guided her horse up onto the walkways. Jilly, clutching her waist, seemed bemused by Corrie's methods and choice of words when people didn't move away.

They let her through the initial blockade easily enough—just saying that an inspector had called for a charcoal sketcher seemed to be enough credibility to get through the first blockade.

As they got to the Parliament building itself, that changed.

"Oy, you can't bring your horse up through here," some marshal or sheriff said to her. "You got to leave this road clear for the Yellowshields."

"Fine," Corrie said, sliding off the horse. As Jilly dropped down, Corrie handed the reins to the guy. "I've got to escort her inside, so you can tie her off over there."

"Listen, girl—"

"That's 'Listen, Sergeant,'" she said. "I don't have rutting time for your sewage. The inspectors in there asked me to bring this charcoal artist inside, and they want her rutting now, so why are you holding up the matter? Tie off the blazing horse."

She marched off before he could say anything else.

"Is that all true?" Jilly asked as they went up the steps.

"True enough," Corrie said. "I mean, for all I know, Minox and Tricky got shut out once they got here. I mean, who rutting has authority here?"

"Tricky?"

"His partner—you don't know. She's—don't tell her I said this, but she's all right. But most folks at the stationhouse hate her. Including Nyla."

"Nyla hates someone? I didn't think she had it in her."

"She's got a rutting streak of anger like you've never seen. She had a gentleman caller the other day—"

The story was going to have to wait, as that chippy in the Tarian uniform came up to them.

"Hey, you—you're the sister, right? And you're the one she's bringing?"

"Good eyes, kid," Corrie said. "They have you running all over, huh?"

"It's what I do. This way." She led them through the main doors, passing by the marshals and other folks who were in the lobby.

"Saints, this really is the Parliament, ain't it?" Jilly said.

"Someone was killed in here?" Corrie asked, but she already could tell it was worse than that. It wasn't just the size of the crowd, but the caliber. Even Commissioner Enbrain was here, as well as a whole mess of swells in fine suits with silk ascots.

"Brace yourself," the Tarian girl said.

They were led up to a gallery overlooking the Parliament floor, where Corrie saw the most horrible thing she'd ever seen in her life.

A clock-click later, she was emptying out her stomach all over the Tarian's boots.

Jilly, on the other hand, wasn't very affected.

"Well, this is quite a thing," she said, going over to Minox.

"Jillian," he said calmly. "You're wearing a lot of eyelining."

"Learned it from your mother."

He nodded. "Can you capture sketches of all this?"

While Corrie sat down on the floor, Jilly looked over the horror. "It's a lot. It'll take some time."

"Then I appreciate you getting to work."

Jilly pulled out her sketch paper and charcoal pencils and got to work on it.

Tricky came over to Corrie. "You can sit out or go back if you need to. Don't torture yourself with this horror."

"I can handle it," Corrie said. "I just—"

"No one should have to handle this," Tricky said.

"You all are," Corrie said, getting to her feet. Her

rutting stomach still wanted to rebel, though. "Sorry about your boots, kid."

"Not the worst thing I've been hit with," the Tarian said.

Corrie looked up at Tricky. "Why ain't, like, all the rutting sticks, sparks, and Yellowshields, and everyone else in here, getting these folks the blazes out of here? Why are folks just standing around out there?"

"Partly a pissing match over who should do what," Tricky said. "Right now, though, this is on our lap, and Minox doesn't think too many people should be in here until we figure out what's what with this atrocity. Too many people could set something off—."

"What do you rutting mean, figure it out?" Corrie pointed down to the floor, resisting her stomach's urge to rebel again. "You confused about saving those tossers down there? That's what we do!"

"I'd love to," Minox said, not looking away. "But this is filled with tricks within tricks, including spider-wires to the doors. I think too many bodies in here could trigger another consequence."

"We already lost one marshal," the big Tarian said. Corrie hadn't even realized this guy was here, though she didn't know how she could have missed him. If she stood on her toes, she might come up to his chest. And, saints, did he have a chest. And arms that looked like most men's legs.

"We've got all sorts of backup out there," Tricky said. "Once we're ready for them, we call them in."

A young patrolman walked in, and in a moment he swore and threw up as well. He, at least, didn't hit anyone.

"I'm sorry," he said.

"It's all right," Tricky said. "Do you have a report or news or something?"

"Which one of you is Satrine Rainey?" he asked.

"That's me," Tricky said.

"You're needed in the lower levels."

That sounded blazing suspicious, and Tricky clearly thought so as well. "By whom?"

The patrolman looked troubled. "By a guy who said to tell you 'Don't cry louder than your six sisters.'"

That sounded like rutting nonsense, but it perked Tricky up. "Take me to him."

Chapter 6

THE PATROLMAN LED Satrine down several rounds of spiral staircase, going so far down they must be underground. She didn't know this officer, and instinct drove her to hold on to her handstick as they went down. There was no real reason to believe she was being led into a trap, or not to trust this patrolman, but being led to strange underground passages did nothing to calm her already frayed nerves.

But no random patrolman would have known proper code phrase to pull her away.

"What is all this?" she asked.

"I think part of it are offices for the marshals, but supposedly it's tied to old catacombs and such. I've heard stories—"

"Right," she said. Everyone had heard stories of the lost and forgotten tunnels beneath the city, and she was sure half of them were true. But this did mean there was a whole new set of security weak points that she hadn't even considered.

The patrolman led her to an alcove where two men were waiting. One was dressed in a fancy suit, but had a burlap sack over his head and shackles on his wrists.

The other was Major Grieson.

"You can go, young man," Grieson told the patrolman, who scurried off.

"Is this where you keep yourself, Major?" Satrine asked. "I'm a little busy."

"I know you are, that's why I'm here. The Gearbox Killer has moved to the next level, right?"

"That's underselling it."

"I've heard. You're looking for an expert to help disarm it, aren't you?"

"Yes, but so far we haven't found anyone."

"You talked to a woman, a colonel in Intelligence, yes?"

"Right." Satrine wasn't sure where he was going with that.

"Yeah, she—she's apparently sabotaging that search. Blocking people from coming in for security reasons, that sort of thing."

That was absurd. "Why is she—"

"Politics and absurdity. I can't go into it. Instead, I've snuck an expert in here."

"But—"

"I can't go into it, and you don't want to know." He gave a signal that he didn't want to talk details in front of the bound man.

"Fine. He's an expert?"

"The kind that definitely would not get through a security screening."

"Do you have to talk about me like that?" the man said from under the hood. "I'm a perfectly legitimate businessman."

"Now," Grieson said. He pulled the hood off to show a handsome young man, with thick curly hair. He looked like he was of Kieran descent.

"And you are?"

"Dressed fantastically," he said, looking down at his outfit. "Really, Major, I understand the urge to undress me, and I appreciate these fine clothes, but . . ."

"Shut it," Grieson said. "If anyone asks you, he's a Parliamentary functionary who's helping you. Don't ask him about himself, and don't you talk, either." He handed a satchel to Satrine.

The Kieran shrugged. "Whatever you say, but you could have asked nicer. My brother—"

"—Will put up with it," Grieson said sharply. "Take him up, use his knowledge, and then bring him back to me."

"He's shackled. That's going to stand out."

"Oh, this," the Kieran said. With a twist of his wrists, the shackles fell off. "Seriously, Major. Strip me down and shackle me. My wife will wonder about your intentions."

Satrine took the man by the arm. "You're not going to give me any trouble, are you?"

"Saint Senea forbid," he said. "I've got a family and bakery to get back to, after all."

Satrine led him back up the stairways to the upper gallery, where Welling was now pacing back and forth, counting numbers quietly, while his odd cousin continued to sketch. Heldrin came over to her.

"Who is this man?"

The Kieran extended his hand to Heldrin. "I'm the expert you all need, apparently. Wow. The Parliament floor. Never thought I'd see this."

"You've found someone?" Welling asked. He glanced over at them. "Who is he, besides someone who doesn't actually own the suit he's wearing?"

"I really don't," the Kieran said, coming over to the ledge. "But I think I should get to—great Saint Jontlen!"

"I'm sorry, mister . . ." Welling fished for a name.

"Nothing to apologize for," the Kieran said in an awed voice. "This . . . never seen anything quite like this."

"I doubt many people have," Welling said. "But what can you do to help us?"

"Well, let's see. You've got my tools there, lady?"

Satrine sighed. She handed him the satchel.

"What sort of experience do you have with this sort of thing?" Welling pressed.

"The sort you don't tell to Constabulary inspectors," the Kieran said. "But watching people die horribly isn't my style, so let's not quibble. I'm guessing this moves like a clock, and kills someone on a regular interval? And time is short?"

"About five minutes to the next one," Welling said.

"Right." The Kieran limped over to the rope pulley the marshals had left behind. "Big guy, come over here."

"It's Dayne."

"Glad to hear it. Who knows about this building?"

"I do," Heldrin said, approaching the pulleys.

"Right, so here's my first question—is there a furnace or something below us?"

"I think so," Heldrin said. "Why?"

"Well, there's definitely a heat source doing something with this contraption," the Kieran said, grabbing the rope. "Because something is slowly cooking that dead man's face."

"What does that mean?" Satrine asked. The Kieran scurried down the rope to the floor.

"Careful!" Heldrin called to him.

"Of course," the Kieran said. "I don't intend to end up like that fellow. But I've got to get a better look at this stuff."

"The heat?" Satrine prodded.

"Oh, right. Most of this, on first glance, is running on prewound clockwork. Spring torsion. Plus there's some—oh, that's very clever." He squatted down to look under one of the chairs.

"What?"

"All right," he called out. "Wow, it's like I'm a member of Parliament."

"Focus," Welling said. "Three minutes."

The Kieran nodded, looking at the parts of the machine with feverish intent. He started walking, which Satrine thought seemed like a terrible idea, but then she realized he was moving in time with the machine, keeping himself from getting knocked by any of the moving parts. "Right. So there's got to be a source of power to keep all these gears and bobs going, right? The main things are torsion springs— a series of them—that're unwinding in this box right here." He pointed to the large dome that was in the center of the room. "But I bet those springs are being rewound by a counterweight force, like in a hallway clock."

"What's the counterweight?" This question came from Minox's charcoal-sketching cousin.

"That's the—oh, hello, didn't see you before—the genius. All these chairs our victims are strapped to, they're slightly off the ground. They're the counterweight."

"Blade!" Welling shouted.

The Kieran ducked as one of the spinning blades whirred over his head. "Didn't see that one, thanks."

"So how do we—"

"Here's what I think I'm seeing, though that's the real problem. The heat."

"From the furnace beneath this room."

"Yeah," the Kieran said. He crouched down and gingerly touched the floor, and then one of the pipes, pulling his hand away quickly. "My guess is, that's a failsafe if we try to stop the rest."

"Failsafe?"

"Yeah, right," the Kieran said. He looked back up, and for the first time his expression was dead serious. "Someone who's fast, run. We need that furnace shut down."

Satrine didn't wait another moment.

◆━━◆▪▷━━◆

Satrine was halfway down the stairs before she realized Jerinne was keeping pace with her.

"You don't know your way around here," Jerinne said, taking the lead. "I'll show you the furnace."

"Lead the way," Satrine said. As they pounded through the lobby, Satrine called out, "I need Fire Brigade with me, and Yellowshields up top. Now!"

She kept after Jerinne, not bothering to see if the Brigade boys really were following her.

Down two flights of stairs, and then through several darkened corridors—but not quite as deep as the catacombs where she met with Grieson—until they reached a heavy metal door, with some kind of wheel on the front instead of a handle.

Jerinne strained to turn the wheel, but it didn't start moving until Satrine helped her.

"I'm guessing," Satrine grunted out, "that when we had people search the building, they didn't look in here."

"Probably . . . not . . ."

The wheel finally gave way, and the door opened.

The heat coming out of the room was intense. Satrine felt the hair on her neck singe just from the gush of air that came out.

Jerinne held up her shield in front of Satrine. "Let's go."

The shield kept the worst of the heat off them, but Jerinne had to hold the shield low enough to see over, and the crackling heat dried out Satrine's eyes. She kept blinking and could barely see.

"Is someone there?" a voice called out. "Help!"

Satrine used the voice as a lighthouse, leading her way deeper into the heat.

Three men were shackled at the ankle, throwing wood into the furnace in front of them with frantic madness. They were drenched in sweat, stripped down to their skivvies. "Help us!" one of them shouted. "Get us out of here!"

There were so many questions racing through Satrine's head that none of them could find voice.

"Why the blazes are you feeding the furnace?" Jerinne shouted. "We need to shut it down!"

"Because of that!" one of the men shouted. He pointed to a device mounted to the top of the furnace. In the center of the device was a glass tube with some liquid sloshing back and forth. "We have to keep that hot!"

"Get us out of here!"

Satrine took the shield from the Tarian girl and moved closer to the men. The shackles around their ankles were thick iron, no keyholes. These were never meant to come off.

"Where are those brigadiers?" Satrine snapped. "We need tools to get them free."

"We need to stop the fire burning!" Jerinne shouted back. "They said—"

"No!" one of the men said. He seemed the only one remotely in his senses. The second was still madly throwing logs at the fire, while the third was half collapsed with exhaustion.

Jerinne got closer to the mouth of the furnace, peering at the device. "What's the story with this?"

"He told us—" the maddened man said. "He showed us! If that stuff cools, this whole room explodes in a fireball!"

"Is that possible?" Jerinne asked, seeming to aim her question at Satrine.

"Wouldn't put it past this madman," Satrine said, though she had no idea. She slammed the shield against the chain holding one of the men in place. All she accomplished was denting the shield.

Two fire brigadiers ran in. "The blazes is going on in here?" one asked.

"We've got to get these men free!" Satrine shouted. "And douse that furnace!"

"No!" one chained man yelled, throwing another log on.

The brigadiers pulled at the chains. After their fruitless attempt, one of them looked up. "Maybe with a doorcracker?"

"Worth a shot," the other said, and he ran off.

Satrine knocked the wood out of the reach of the three men. "We've got to stop the fire."

"You don't understand!" one shouted. "If it doesn't keep burning—"

"I got it, thanks," she said. "I don't care."

Jerinne had found a barrel of sand, and was throwing handfuls into the furnace. "Do you have a plan, Inspector?"

"Not really," Satrine said. She used the shield as a scoop and hurled more sand into the furnace. The sand started smothering the flames.

"You're going to get us killed!" the chained men shouted.

"Help get them free," Satrine said. "I've got this."

"What about if they're right about that thing?" Jerinne asked, nodding at the glass tube mounted over the furnace door. The liquid in the glass vial was already more like honey than water.

"Then we need a plan," Satrine said.

She hoped one would come to her before too long.

❖ ❖ ❖

Minox was out of time. Inspector Rainey had responded to the urgent call to douse the furnace, but there was no way she could get it cooled before the next scheduled murder.

"Sir!" he called down to the trapmaster—there was no other word to describe him, and he was obviously the sort who had found himself on the wrong side of the law more than once. "We need to act quickly, or that woman with the dark hair will be killed."

The trapmaster gingerly glanced at the woman, and the aspects of the device immediately around her. "Are you sure?"

"Reasonably," Minox said.

"What do you need?" Heldrin called down.

"It's just . . . I think something more is happening in a few moments."

"More as in—"

The trapmaster crouched next to the larger box of

the machine. "I mean, if I'm guessing right, we're gonna get something of a grand finale now."

"Is that possible?" Jillian asked.

"Anything is possible," Heldrin said.

"Can you cease the operations?" Minox called down.

"I'll be honest, this is the trickiest bit of blazes I've ever seen," the trapmaster said. "I may be able to disarm the triggers on the chairs and the strap, but not while this is still moving." To accentuate his point, he dodged out of the way of a swinging pike. "And as far as it still moving is concerned, there seems to be a lot of redundant gearwork."

"Meaning?" Minox asked. Talk was getting more and more pointless.

"Meaning—here, look, big gear right here." He pointed to it. "I could jam something in there and gum it up. But there's another gear over here that seems to be doing the same thing. So jamming one might not make a difference, as long as the other gear is working. Or one of these is a dummy that's doing nothing."

"How can you figure it out?"

"Another hour or two."

Heldrin went over to the rope. "We need to take more direct action before it's too late. Dark hair is in danger?"

"I believe so, but our expert—"

"No, she definitely is," the trapmaster said, slinking over to that woman. "Just she's not the only one. This whole thing is like a clock—"

"I had ascertained that."

"And it's time for the big bells."

And in that moment, the motion of everything accelerated. Bells started to ring in the machine. Blades and axe heads all rose up for powerful, fatal swoops down.

"That can't be rutting good," Corrie said.

"Heldrin!" Minox called. The Tarian was already on the rope, dropping down to the floor.

"Wait, there's—" The trapmaster dove under a blade to reach the woman. "Maybe if I jam that gear, I can stop hers, but I can't jam all the gears."

Bells grew more frantic, and the grinding gears added to the cacophony. Heldrin was on the floor, going for his shield.

The bells suddenly stopped, and everything swung down with deadly intent.

Minox reached out with every bit of will and might he had to grab hold of the machine.

Everything stopped.

The gears ground, then blades inched and pipes and chairs strained and pushed, but Minox held it all still, surrounding everything in a green, sickly glow of magic. It took every ounce of concentration he had, and it fought against him.

If he released the magic, it would all crash down.

"What happened?" the trapmaster asked. An axe head was inches away from the woman with the dark hair, and he was enough in its path he would have been sliced as well.

"Welling?" Heldrin called up. He had his shield in front of one of the other victims, though it looked like it wouldn't do any good with death coming from three different directions. "Are you—"

Minox found himself unable to speak. His jaw was clenched, teeth grinding. He couldn't spare an ounce of concentration away from holding the machine in place.

Fortunately, Corrie was there. "Start to get them rutting out!" she shouted. Then she ran to the doors, first blaring her whistle, and then shouting. "Yellowshields, sticks, all hands! Get your worthless asses up here!"

◆━━━◆◆◆◆━━━◆

The blades and gears were frozen in place, but straining to move. Dayne hadn't expected Inspector Welling to have this kind of power as a mage, but in this moment he wasn't complaining.

"Friend!" he shouted to the mousy fellow. "We need to get all these people out now!"

"I'm with you," the mousy man said. He was on the chair with the woman who had the dark hair. "Help me with this, big guy."

Dayne came to him, ducking underneath the staves and spikes to reach him. "We must—"

"Yes, in haste," the mousy man said. He had pried open a panel under the chair. "Oh, but isn't this a beauty. Grab her shoulders."

Dayne did as instructed. "What am I—"

"On my mark, pull her toward you. Ready?"

"Yes—"

"Now!"

The man released something, and Dayne pulled her forward. Her wrists were still strapped to the arms of the chair, but when he pulled her up, a spear shot up out of the seat of the chair. Had she still been in it, she would have been skewered. She flailed in panic, attempting a scream that the gag over her face wouldn't let her make.

"That's one," the mousy man said, undoing the straps on her ankles. When he released her wrists, she desperately clung onto Dayne.

"I need to—" Dayne tried to say, but the woman was half-clawing him.

"Get her out. I'm on the next one."

The gears and blades jarred for a moment, surging an inch before holding again. Inspector Welling cried out.

Dayne rushed over to the rope. A team of Yellowshields were now up on the gallery, with Fire Brigade hurling down ropes.

"Should we come down?" one of the Yellowshields asked. Dayne glanced over at Inspector Welling. He seemed to be barely holding on to whatever he was doing to keep things together.

"Only two," Dayne said. "We shouldn't risk too many bodies down here."

With the help of the Fire Brigade, two Yellowshields quickly shimmied down the ropes to the floor. Dayne passed the woman to them—they nearly had to pry her off—and they quickly got her to the top.

"Friend?" Dayne asked.

"Got this one free," the mousy man said, undoing one of the young men. "Each chair is different. But—"

Dayne helped the young man to his feet. "Explain later."

"Right." He moved to the next chair, gingerly touching pipes and the floor on his way. "I think that furnace is shutting down. Hope that does what I think it will."

"Which is?"

"Stop the main force of the machine."

Dayne had passed the second victim to the Yellowshields, and watched as the mousy man—truly a marvel with his hands—undid the next one. "You've got a knack for this."

"Fear is a fine motivator," the mousy man said. "How much longer can his magic hold?"

Dayne looked up again. Inspector Welling was pale and sweating. He looked like he was barely holding on. The sketch artist had stopped her work to hold him upright.

"Work faster."

A great cracking sound came from inside the main hub of the machine.

"What was that?" Dayne asked as he pulled the third victim away.

"That depends on if we're lucky or unlucky." The mousy man sprang over the fourth chair—which held a dead man—to the fifth. A tool in each hand, moving like lightning, he snipped and clipped and opened, freeing the next victim. Not losing a step of his rhythm, he said, "If we're lucky, the strain of fighting against the magic snapped something in the machine, causing significant internal damage. But—"

"But?"

The green glow around the machinery flickered away, and the weapons all surged another inch. Then the glow resurged fiercely.

"But we might be profoundly unlucky." The man was nearly shouting, and he savagely undid the bindings on the woman. "Saint Senea, stay with me today."

"Shouldn't you—"

"Hush." With a snap and a crack, the woman was released. "How many left?"

"Five."

The next one was Niall Enbrain—Mister Montrose's assistant, the Constabulary commissioner's nephew. There were a series of five circular blades that were in position to slice into his face and neck—each of them now only a breath away. While he was bound and gagged, Niall was trembling with fear, his eyes in a mad panic. He was bound by multiple iron rings around his head, chest, and legs.

"Oh, this one is a nightmare," the mousy man said.

"Can you—"

"Too much, too much. Get behind him."

"What are you—"

"Can't get him out." He took his tool to the arms holding the circular blades. "Better remove these instead." With quick motion, he spun the tiny nut holding the first blade in place, letting it clatter to the floor.

"What do I—"

"This is just on a cursory glance, but this chair doesn't look like it has a separate trap." The second blade was removed. "This one looks like he was never supposed to have a chance to get out of it."

The inspector had said something about the commissioner before. Was it possible that in all this chaos, Niall Enbrain was the true target of it all? Did Sholiar's madness have that much method?

The third blade dropped.

"And so?"

"So I'm guessing those arms of yours aren't just for show," the mousy man said. Fourth blade removed.

"Soon as I get this last one, yank the whole blasted chair out of place."

"What'll that do?"

Inspector Welling let out a primal, horrible scream as the mousy man was removing the fifth blade. All the arms of the device surged. Instinctively, Dayne grabbed the chair and pulled it away with all his might. It came off its housing and he fell backward.

"Son of a—" the mousy man cried. His hand had been sliced, bleeding profusely. The machine burst to life, every arm and blade spinning madly. Of the four people still trapped in chairs, two were killed instantly. Dayne looked to Niall, who was seizing and gurgling through his gag.

His neck had been sliced open.

<hr />

"Get us out of here, you crazy skirt!"

Satrine had half a mind to leave these three behind, especially if the glass vial was about to explode in a ball of fire. The liquid inside it was thickening and turning orange.

The fire brigadiers had returned with a doorcracker, taking it to the chain holding the three men.

"Hurry up! He showed us! That thing is about to burst!"

"We're trying! These chains ain't breaking!"

Satrine could tell that the doorcracker wasn't going to do the job. "Get the blazes out of here," she told them. Jerinne was still throwing sand in the furnace, but it was nothing but ash and embers inside now. Satrine grabbed Jerinne's shield, saying, "You too."

"Ma'am, I shouldn't let you—"

"That's not how it works, girl," Satrine said. "Everyone run."

"We can't run!" the crazed man of the trio said.

Satrine didn't listen, instead she knocked the glass vial off its mount with the shield, catching it before it shattered on the ground.

"Are you rutting crazy?"

"Probably," Satrine said, tossing the vial into the furnace. She then slammed the furnace door shut and turned back to the trio.

Jerinne and the brigadiers hadn't gone anywhere, still struggling with the chains.

"You think that'll hold it?" Jerinne asked.

"Let's see," Satrine said, putting herself between the furnace and the men.

"I should take the shield, be the one holding the line," Jerinne said.

"Worry about them," Satrine said.

Something snapped, and one of the men was free: the one who was already exhausted. He barely had the strength to crawl. Jerinne pulled him to his feet and hauled him to the door.

The crazed man lost what little bit of sanity he must have had left and attacked the brigadier closest to him. The other brigadier tried to help his partner.

Satrine didn't have time for this foolery. She drew out her handstick and cracked it against the madman's back. He dropped, and she put her irons on him.

"We should rutting leave him," one brigadier said, working on the sane man's shackles.

"Not our job," Satrine said. "Get that last one clear."

Pops and cracks came from the furnace.

"That's not a good sound," she said.

The stable member of the trio shook his head. "I'm telling you, skirt, it's going to be bad. You got to run!"

Satrine held up the shield in front of him and her. "I'm the last one out of here."

Cracks and hisses came from the furnace.

The chain snapped. The stable man stumbled and ran, and the brigadiers struggled to get the crazed man up.

"Let's go, stick," one of them said, dragging the man toward the door. Satrine was right behind them, but the sane man had slipped and fallen.

Satrine pulled him up on his feet, and Jerinne was there with her.

"Now, ma'am!"

Jerinne pulled the man away, and in that moment, the sounds from the furnace became a hollow, horrible rattle.

Satrine looked back and saw the whole room had become fire.

She raised the shield in front of her face before she was blown back against the wall.

Chapter 7

MINOX WAS IN a daze of gray and fog when he realized wine was being poured into his mouth.

"Stop," he tried to say, pushing the wine pourer away. His vision cleared a bit and he saw it was Jillian. She pulled back as he spat out the wine in his mouth.

"You all right?" she asked.

"I am decidedly not," he said. "But wine is hardly the solution." He reached for his belt pouch, but it was empty. Foolish.

"Sorry, I didn't know what else—"

"It's fine," he said. "Thank you for the intent." He felt as weak as a newborn; he couldn't even get up from the chair he found himself sitting in. The upper gallery of the Parliament. He struggled to remember exactly what had happened on the floor, but the strain of trying to hold the machine in place had taken all his focus. Most of the time, he couldn't even see.

"What happened?" he asked.

"Eight people were rescued," she said. "The last three . . . they didn't. And there's one who could go either way."

Minox took this in. "What about young Mister Enbrain?"

"I don't know who that is."

Minox tried to stand up, but his legs might as well

have been boneless. "He's—he's the nephew of the commissioner. Where is the commissioner now? Or Mister Heldrin?"

"Heldrin is the big Tarian? He's still down there with the thief."

"That's hardly a suitable term for the expert."

"It's what he clearly is, though."

Minox always appreciated Jillian's bluntness, as well as her sharp eye for details, regardless of the unsavory nature of what she was looking at. It was what made her such a gifted charcoal sketcher. She had no fear of the dead, nor any revulsion to gore. Even with something as horrific as this, she had set to work sketching the details as quickly as she could.

"Are they both well?"

Jillian glanced over to the balcony railing. "I think they both took a couple of knocks and scrapes, but most of their blood is still inside their skin."

"And the machine?"

"It's . . . not moving anymore."

"Did you get your work done?"

She smirked and showed him the sketchbook. She had done an excellent job capturing the essence of the machine.

"Where is Inspector Rainey?" Minox tried to pull himself up. It was no good—his arms were as weak as his legs.

"She's your partner? Ran off to the furnace, I guess."

"Find—find her. Or Corrie. . . ."

"Corrie got swept up carrying victims out with the Yellowshields."

"Right. Can you look for her? Now that the immediate danger has passed, we can begin our proper investigation."

"You'll be all right here?"

"I can call for Mister Heldrin if I am in a dire state."

Jillian chuckled. "Minox, if this right here isn't what you call a dire state, I'm curious what would qualify. Be back in a shank."

She left his view, and a moment later Miss Morad was right in front of Minox.

"Very interesting, Inspector," she said quietly.

He had honestly forgotten she had been here all this while, observing.

"I hope this was informative to you," he said.

"Rather. Far more interesting than the false emergency we used to test you."

"And your verdict?"

She shook her head. "That isn't procedure, Inspector Welling. Now, I recognize that you have spent yourself quite thoroughly in this venture. While my intention was to hold our hearing this morning, it would be neither fair nor just to force you back to the stationhouse for such a thing in your current state."

Minox wasn't sure what that meant her intentions were. "What are you proposing?"

"Based on my understanding, you are probably ravenous. In dire need of nourishment, no?"

"Rather."

"All right. Unless my reckoning is off, it's a bit past eleven bells in the morning. Take care of yourself, finalize whatever details you need to here for your investigation, and then report to your stationhouse at two bells. We will begin the Inquiry then. If you are not there, there will be consequences to your career."

Minox nodded. "That is fair, Miss Morad."

"I refuse to be anything but." She sighed. "You're going to need assistance." She went over to the railing and called down. "Mister Heldrin, are you doing something useful, or mostly sulking?"

Heldrin replied. Minox couldn't quite hear what he said, but it did not sound like a very civil response.

"Yes, well, that can't be helped now, sir. If you could come back up here? There's a more pressing situation."

Another displeased reply came, but shortly after that, Heldrin came up over the balcony ledge. "What's going on—Inspector!"

"No need for alarm, Mister Heldrin," Minox said.

"I've never seen anyone that pale who wasn't dead or Poasian," Heldrin said.

"Neither yet," Minox said.

Miss Morad spoke with commanding authority. "He needs to eat, and quickly. He can't even walk on his own, so you'll have to bring him."

"But all this—" Heldrin said lamely.

"Can hold. There are scores of officers and officials outside. What needs to be done can be handled without Inspector Welling, at least for a short order."

"Who are you, again?" Heldrin asked.

"As far as you're concerned, I'm the right hand of the Archduke of Sauriya. But simply put, I have urgent business with Inspector Welling that must be conducted today, and I have other arrangements I must make in the meantime. You are a Tarian. Your charge is to protect and care—"

"That was the Ascepians—"

"Help him, Mister Heldrin. I cannot have him at diminished capacity right now. It would not be just."

"Get me on my feet," Minox said. "And if you can assist me to anyplace with food right now."

Heldrin pulled him up. Minox still couldn't bear his own weight without leaning on the man. "What about the rest of this?"

Inspector Rainey came in the gallery, covered in soot and ash and with a Yellowshield chasing after her. She had a decent gash on her forehead, oozing blood.

"What's going on?" she asked. "We got the victims out?"

"Mostly," Minox said. "You got the furnace shut down?"

"I got the furnace blown up. Our killer had more victims and traps down there. And some chemical stuff I'd like Leppin or someone to look at."

Minox nodded. "We should let Leppin and his crew comb over the site and catalog everything, have it brought into evidence."

Commissioner Enbrain came in with Good Mister

Montrose. "They're taking Niall to Riverheart Ward. They aren't sure if he's going to make it."

"I'm very sorry, sir," Heldrin said. "I know his blood is on my hands."

"And mine, sir," Minox said. Glancing at Heldrin's bloodstained hands, he added, "If not as literally."

"Nonsense. If not for you, he wouldn't have had a chance. So thank you. What now?"

Rainey spoke up, still brushing off the Yellowshield's attempts to tend to her. "We need to let our examinarian and evidence men sweep through and collect everything." She looked over to Minox, still being held up by Heldrin. "I think we both need to look after our own well-being in the short term before we can do any significant further work."

"Right, hold still!" the Yellowshield said, grabbing Rainey by the head.

"Leave me be," Rainey snarled. Despite that, she stayed in place while the Yellowshield finished cleaning and bandaging the wound.

The commissioner nodded. "Go have yourselves looked at or . . . whatever you need to do. I'll have patrolmen keep this place locked down, pages run for your examinarian, and so forth."

"Appreciated, Commissioner," Rainey said.

"You shouldn't be unattended," the Yellowshield said.

"I'll keep an eye on her." Jerinne Fendall was at the doorway. "Chief Quoyell and his boys are fuming out there."

"Let them," Heldrin said. "This lands on his shoulders, surely."

"Let's not be too hasty," Mister Montrose said.

"As you say, sir," Heldrin said.

Montrose sighed. "I just hope this can get sorted before the month is out. The Parliament is supposed to start convocation of the new assemblage, and we can't get to the work of governing with things like this."

"I think some members of Parliament would prefer

that," Jerinne said. Rainey gave her an odd look, and Jerinne continued. "If you've ever seen a session, it's basically an exercise in doing nothing."

Montrose chuckled. "You were the one with Seabrook at the end of the last convocation, right? Hopefully this new session won't be quite as absurd. Doubtful, but hopefully. I'll do what I can to placate Quoyell." He left with the commissioner.

The trapmaster popped up over the railing, his hand bandaged. "I think this is my cue to make myself scarce," he said, limping over.

"Did you hurt your leg?" Rainey asked.

"Not today, if that's what you're asking. Not to worry. If you don't mind, though, I'll see myself out and home."

"You know how to get out and not be noticed?"

"Inspector," he said with mock sincerity, "you wound me. I never walk into a room without figuring out how to slip away. Give my regards to the major, and tell him he owes me quite steeply for this one."

"Don't count on cashing that marker."

He shrugged. "It's been a thrill, gentlemen. Let's never have to do anything like this again."

Heldrin nodded. "You've saved many lives, sir."

"Next?" Rainey asked. "I suppose we send in the examinarium people, question survivors, as well as staff and the marshals."

"And Mister Heldrin here," Minox said.

"Absolutely," Heldrin said. "I'll tell you everything I know to help you catch Sholiar."

"You know the name of this Gearbox Killer?" Rainey asked.

"I have a lot to tell you both. Perhaps we should adjourn somewhere so Inspector Welling can eat."

Minox felt a chill run up through him—starting with his altered hand and moving through his body. "I'm afraid I must insist now."

"Right," Rainey said. "You know a place nearby, Mister Heldrin?"

"I definitely do," he said.

Minox needed to be almost carried by Heldrin, with Jerinne coming to help on the other side. As they left, Minox glanced back and saw that the Kieran gentleman was already gone.

———— ◆ ————

Dayne brought the inspectors down one of the service stairs and out the private doors to the street, avoiding all the bustle and madness in the Parliament halls and the square outside. It wasn't lost on him that the back hallways and functionary entrances were probably the exact method Sholiar had used to get his infernal machine of death onto the Parliament floor.

But even for Sholiar, this was an undertaking like none other. In some grand, horrific way, this was the man's masterwork.

Inspector Welling was nearly in shivers once they got him to The Nimble Rabbit. It was a selfish choice on Dayne's part, as it wasn't the closest place to get food for the inspector, but it was a place Dayne trusted, and they could speak about the situation away from the prying ears of the Parliament. That was crucial.

"Dayne!" Hemmit Eyairin jumped up from his usual table, where he sat with the other publishers of the *Veracity Press*, Lin Shartien and Maresh Niol. These three weren't mere journalists; they were seekers of truth, even if their more radical politics did not make their newssheet particularly popular on the north side of the city.

But they were also friends.

Hemmit came over and helped guide the nearly unconscious Welling to the table. Inspector Rainey and Jerinne joined them.

"Bread and water, quickly, and then some quick plates," Dayne called to the server.

Hemmit, a robust man of simple tastes and pleasures, looked at Inspector Welling's face. "What's wrong with the constable?"

"Not just a constable," Dayne said. "He's a mage, and he spent himself."

Lin—a mage herself of some small talent—scowled. "A mage in the Constabulary? I've never heard of that."

"It's true," Dayne said. "He—he saved most of the people caught in the infernal machine."

Inspector Rainey eyed Lin skeptically. "He's Uncircled. Is that going to be a problem?"

Lin scoffed at her, and then spoke with her natural Linjari accent even thicker and richer. "I'm told it's supposed to be. But I never really understood the fuss about it. Circle rules, circle politics are nothing but a bore."

"Really?"

Lin quickly flashed the tattoo above her heart to Rainey. "I would have avoided joining Red Wolf if I could have. I was told I didn't have a choice."

"Red Wolf?" Rainey raised an eyebrow, but said nothing more. She took a seat next to Welling, grabbing bread from the server and almost shoving it into his mouth. He swallowed it, and then reached for the water.

After a few gulps, he said, "There's no need to abandon decorum, Rainey."

"I've never seen you this bad off," she said.

"Then you've missed some of the worst moments of the past few months," he said darkly. "I think I can manage on my own now."

The servers brought out plates of charcuterie, cheese, picklings, and mustard. "Anything else?" he asked.

"Wine," Hemmit said. "Surely we'll need it."

"You always say that," Maresh said. "What happened over there, Dayne? We spent a bit of time among the madness outside, but once we realized that no one who knew anything was talking, we decided to leave."

"Probably wise," Dayne said.

"Can you talk about it?" Hemmit asked.

"Informally," Dayne said.

"It shouldn't show up in the print tomorrow, in other words."

"Newsprint?" Welling asked. "You're journalists?"

"The *Veracity Press*," Hemmit said.

Welling nodded. "I'm familiar with it. Prose is excellent. Point of view is unbalanced to the point of being nearly useless."

Maresh snorted. "He doesn't hold back."

Welling ignored him, piling meat and cheese onto bread and cramming it into his mouth.

Rainey took the bottle of wine from Hemmit and poured herself a glass. "You brought us out here to meet your newsprint friends?"

"Not specifically," Dayne said. "But I've found their counsel and perspective useful."

Rainey took a sip. "Fine. You've said you know something about the killer. Sholiar."

Hemmit raised an eyebrow. "Isn't that the—"

"Yes," Dayne said. He sat down, taking a deep breath. "Inspectors, I believe—and after the experience today, I am quite certain—that this killer is the same person I crossed with in Lacanja six months ago."

"In Lacanja?" Welling asked. "What happened there?"

"It began much like it did here. A series of deaths, at first seemingly unconnected, save their gruesome manner."

"This level of machinery? Of ingenious engineering?" Welling asked.

"I don't know if I want to say ingenious," Rainey said. "Doesn't it—"

"Give him too much praise?" Jerinne offered.

"Yes," Rainey said.

"This killer, whoever he is, is disturbingly sick," Maresh said. "There's nothing ingenious about wanting to cause suffering."

"Believe me, I would not want to praise him," Dayne said. "But we would be remiss to ignore his gift, not merely for sadism, but for all manner of engineering and craft. The man who pulled off the monstrosity we saw in the Parliament—"

"—Cannot be underestimated," Welling said. "We're all agreed on that."

"Then came the letters to the Constabulary. Written in code. And then he sent the key to crack the code."

"He's impatient," Rainey said. "Craving recognition."

Welling nodded. "I imagine he couldn't bear that constables couldn't read his letters."

"You may be right about his message, then," Rainey said.

"I'm certain of it now."

"Message?" Hemmit asked.

Welling took a moment. "We have reason to believe that his actions here were targeted at Constable Commissioner Enbrain. As his nephew was specifically victimized today—"

"Right," Dayne said. "Anyway, at the time this was happening, I was in my second year of Candidacy, serving with Master Denbar of the Tarian Order. Through other exploits, we had gained a small amount of celebrity in the city newsprints."

"As you have here," Maresh said.

"This got the attention of Sholiar, so he decided to make us his target. He kidnapped the son of a prominent family—the Benedicts."

"There's a Benedict in the Parliament, yes?" Rainey asked.

"There are four," Hemmit said. "The Benedicts hold a massive amount of wealth and power in Yinara—more than most of the nobility, save the archduke."

"Especially in Lacanja," Dayne said.

"How did this make you and Master Denbar targets?" Welling asked.

"The Benedict boy was the bait to force us to engage with him. Once Sholiar took him, he set the rules. He demanded a ransom, a method of delivery, location—all centered around Master Denbar and me being the ones to deliver it."

"So how did it go wrong?" Rainey asked.

She had put her finger on it.

"Sholiar's ingenuity. He separated Master Denbar and me, and I found myself facing Sholiar with an impossible choice: save the boy, or Master Denbar. And I thought Sholiar, in his hubris, had left me a third option: stop him and save them both. But it was my hubris he was exploiting."

Welling leaned in—and Dayne saw that Hemmit and the others did as well. Not that he was surprised—he had never truly relayed this to his friends, save Jerinne. She knew almost all his secrets and shames.

"What did you do?" Welling asked.

"I threw a barrel lid at Sholiar to take him down, and release his hold on his death machines. Then I rushed to save both Master Denbar and the boy. But . . . it was too late for Master Denbar . . . and the boy . . ."

"You failed them both?" This was Welling. His question, astoundingly, did not sound like he was judging Dayne. It was full of compassion.

"Worse. Somehow, who I thought was Sholiar was actually the boy, rigged up like some sort of marionette. When I threw the barrel lid at him—"

"You killed him?" Maresh asked it.

"No. But the boy would never walk again. Never be whole again. Thanks to me, falling for Sholiar's trick. As for Sholiar, he escaped. But not before letting me know. Mocking me."

"So it's personal to you," Rainey said.

"More than just that. I had lost my mentor, was run out of Lacanja, lost my—it doesn't matter. All of that, I could bear, if he had been brought to justice. But not only did he escape, half the Constabulary force didn't even believe he existed."

"How is that?"

"I am the only one who actually saw him. Saw his face, heard his voice. The Benedict boy never did."

"But surely the murders were documented—" Welling was now quite engaged, or had eaten enough to restore his vitality and pay attention. "Surely that there was a killer, this Sholiar, a name I assume he claimed for himself somewhere."

"In letters to newssheets."

Welling snapped his fingers. "Perhaps what was given more attention in Lacanja was ignored here. He may have written."

"Welling," Rainey said sharply. "We still don't know for certain it's the same person."

"The sadism, the mad genius, the engineering," Dayne insisted. "It's the same."

"And what did Lacanjan Constabulary think?"

Dayne looked down at the table, taking his glass of wine and finishing it. "A prevailing theory was that Master Denbar himself was the killer. That he engineered it all to raise the profile of the Tarian Order. And that I—"

Welling nodded. "That you stopped him, but maintained a story of Sholiar to protect his good name."

That had been it, and Welling had figured it out. He was the inspector Dayne needed on this.

"You can see how that's absurd. Master Denbar is dead, and the killings have started here, in Maradaine."

"Where you are, Mister Heldrin," Inspector Rainey said. "You have to see that you are the common element here."

"I recognize that. I . . . I know how all this sounds. But I'm telling you, these killings are Sholiar. He came and did this on the Parliament floor to taunt me. I am certain."

"Yes, but—" Rainey started.

"You could identify this Sholiar if you saw him?" Welling asked, talking over her.

"Yes, I believe—"

"Minox," Inspector Rainey said sharply. "Are you capable of standing now? We need to have a word."

◆━◆

Satrine was far too weary, given that it was barely midday, but she had already seen enough atrocity and pain to last for the rest of the month, if not her lifetime. And as much as she tried to play off the blow to her head as nothing to be concerned about, her thoughts were spinning and she was having a blazes of a time staying focused on the things around her.

But one thing she was focused on was Welling, and how quickly he was accepting Dayne Heldrin's story of this Sholiar character. That was troubling.

"We need a bit more healthy skepticism in this investigation," she said bluntly, once she had Welling pulled away from the table at The Nimble Rabbit.

"You doubt Mister Heldrin's account?" Welling asked.

"I think we can't accept it as scripture," she said.

"I understand that, on its face, it has elements of coincidence and circumstance that we would easily dismiss as fanciful in another situation."

"And why not this situation?"

Welling nodded—he was showing that he was taking her concerns seriously. A small thing he had made a point of doing of late. "Mister Heldrin's account shows little sign of dishonesty. He's telling us things that are painful to him, and his discomfort in revealing that reads as genuine."

"It may be genuine to him, but—" Satrine said. She stopped herself and took a breath. She was about to accuse him of lying, and she had no idea if he was right or not. "Look, I think—it's awfully convenient."

"What is?"

"That this killer is someone that only he can identify, and that the killer struck in the Parliament, where Heldrin is currently living. We need to look at him seriously as a suspect, or at least a collaborator, just as we need to be looking at the King's Marshals. No one should be above reproach."

Welling thought on this for a moment. "You are correct. Healthy skepticism, until we have further corroborating information."

"How are you feeling now?"

"Stable, if not to full strength," Welling said. "And you? You are, as usual, minimizing your injuries."

"I'll be fine," she said reflexively. "I think getting Heldrin's account is useful, but we need to look at every angle. We've got several victims to question, for one, as well as interrogating almost every King's Marshal."

"That is an element that troubles me the most," Welling said. "It's clear that the King's Marshals have a significant security problem, if not full-blown corruption in their ranks. We don't have the mechanism, or the authority, strictly, to investigate that."

"What mechanism do they have to investigate it internally? Do they have whispermen?"

"I don't know," Welling said. "If anything, such a problem would have to be handled externally. But the City Constabulary is not normally the body that could do such a thing."

Satrine mused. "It would require an organization that could be considered neutral and without bias, and has the approval of the Throne and the Parliament. And you know what group would qualify for that?"

Welling almost smirked—anything like a smile looked unnatural on his face. "The Tarian Order?"

"We might need Mister Heldrin," Satrine said. "But that doesn't mean we should blindly trust him."

"Agreed," Welling said. "But I do have to put trust in you."

"Like you don't already?" she asked.

"Of course I do," he said without hesitation. "But I mean that I need to head back to the stationhouse and face the Inquiry and Miss Morad. Which means—"

"Questioning the witnesses and the marshals now, while it's fresh, is on me." Satrine nodded. "I can handle that, but I'll keep Corrie on hand."

"Leppin and his people should be there by now."

"And that other girl—your cousin? The charcoal sketcher you called in."

"Have a runner deliver her sketches to my desk. Let's try to meet back at the stationhouse at five bells to review particulars."

She smiled. "I am not spending all night there, mind you."

He nodded. "Nor I, tonight, I think. For once, I think it crucial that I go home at the end of watch."

Satisfied with this, she led him back to the table. "All right, Heldrin—"

"Dayne," he urged.

"Dayne," she said. "You and Jerinne will be coming with me back to the Parliament. Hopefully Leppin will have some of his work done, and we'll have a bit of order with names and people. Because we have a lot of questions to ask."

"You think someone there knows where Sholiar is? Where he'll strike next?"

"I haven't a clue about that," Satrine said. "But the far more important thing is how he got his machine inside, and how he got his victims into place. And I'd bet you a week's salary there's someone in there—be it the victims or the marshals or even someone in the damned Parliament—who knows the answer to that one."

Chapter 8

◄━━━━◆━━►

"ALL RIGHT, EVERYONE take a rutting damned minute!" Corrie shouted over the din of people. There were a few shocked gasps and people clutched at their chests. Fakers, all of them. Corrie knew damn well there wasn't a person here whose language was just as salty as hers. Now, at least, the whole lot of city Constabulary, archduchy sheriffs, King's Marshals, military and Intelligence, Yellowshields, Fire Brigade, and everyone rutting else were staring at her.

How the blazes she got left with sifting through this mess of people in the Parliament, she had no idea. Leppin was on the Parliament floor, checking out the machine and the bodies. Commissioner Enbrain himself was here, but he was nowhere to be seen, having told Corrie and her people to "take care of it" until Minox and Tricky returned.

Wherever they went.

"Do I have your attention yet?" she asked. "Look, it's real rutting simple. I don't care who you are or who your daddy was, no one walks out of this building without checking in with my people at those doors there. Those are the only rutting doors out you blazing well use, hear? I want names, addresses, and papers if you got them. If you don't, unless you're the king himself, you will be waiting until we clear you."

A voice cut through the crowd. "And what if you are the prince?"

The crowd suddenly went down on one knee, and Corrie froze.

She was staring at Prince Escaraine—the rutting crown prince of Druthal, by all the saints—and her legs locked up. Saints, he wasn't just regal or handsome—and he was so blazing handsome Corrie felt a buzzing in her gut—but he was breathlessly elegant.

And if Corrie didn't get to her rutting knees now, she might lose her head.

Could a prince order a beheading? Was that even a rutting thing? Corrie had no idea.

"That, um, your Highness," she sputtered out, forcing herself onto one knee as she said it, "that is another exception we would make."

The crowd parted as he walked, and he approached calmly. Corrie was amazed at how casual and at ease he seemed, despite his bright silk blouse and ringed circlet on his head. A handful of King's Marshals—their uniforms marked differently than the ones Corrie had been neck-deep in here—kept a perimeter around him. These blokes looked like they would tear a person in half if they moved too close. "Forgive my intrusion in your investigation, all," he said, more to the crowd at large than to Corrie. "But something egregious and appalling has happened to our nation today, and my cousin felt the Royal House should take personal care at these events, this violation of the House of Free Men. If you could point me toward where any of our Good Men of the Parliament are congregating right now?" That last question was directed at Corrie.

Corrie's voice almost failed her for a moment. "I . . . that is, I believe one of them is up that way, Your Highness." She pointed toward the staircase where one swell had gone with the commissioner.

"Thank you." The prince turned to the crowd again. "I think it is so important, in the wake of this grief and tragedy, that we all do our best to cooperate with each other, so we can swiftly heal ourselves as a people, and bring justice forward."

He went to the stairs, and after he was out of sight, everyone else in the room let out a collective breath. Corrie wasn't the only person instinctively holding hers.

She got back on her feet. "All right, you all, you heard him," she said sharply, before anyone else could take advantage of the lull. "So let my people know who the blazes you are, why the blazes you're here, and what you rutting do, or saints help me."

The crowd started to work their way to the officers at the doors, now with a sense of calm and patience. That was something.

While Corrie watched folks line up, Tricky came over, flanked by two of those Tarians. Corrie still hadn't quite gotten their names.

"Anything interesting happen while I was gone?" Tricky asked.

"Just Prince Escaraine," Corrie said. She tried to make it sound like it was nothing, just to see how Tricky reacted.

"Really?" Tricky seemed more curious than surprised or nervous. That was rutting incredible. Corrie was still a puddle of nerves. "That must be why everyone is behaving themselves now."

"Probably. So what's next?"

"Are any of the victims in a state to be interviewed?" Tricky asked. "I'd love to know what happened to them, in their own words."

Corrie nodded. "We've got them—the ones who didn't need the Yellowshields or a proper doctor—all in a conference room to the side."

"And the marshals? Especially Chief Quoyell." Tricky nearly choked on his name, sounding out each rutting syllable.

"The marshals are sitting on their hands, and they ain't happy about it."

"I can imagine," the big Tarian said. "It's not like they're above reproach."

"They're down in their offices on the lower levels."

The big guy raised an eyebrow. "Those offices connect to corridors to other buildings."

Tricky nodded. "Yeah, I'm already aware of that sort of thing."

"I'm saying that no one is necessarily being securely kept on the premises. If someone—"

"I understand," Tricky snapped. Biting her lip, she added, "Look, Dayne, do you want to help?"

"Of course I do," Dayne said.

"Then find me building plans of this place. I need to know all the ways someone could get in and out. Especially with equipment."

Dayne scowled. "I don't know if there is a definitive plan. I mean, this building has existed in several forms over the past centuries, originally as—"

"Dayne," Tricky said sharply. "Just get me a map."

He nodded and walked off, and the young Tarian woman stayed at Tricky's side.

A woman approached them—Intelligence uniform. She made at Tricky like she had been shot from a crossbow.

"Inspector Rainey," she said sharply, giving Corrie and the others a bit of stink. "Do you intend to launch an investigation into corruption in the King's Marshals?"

Tricky didn't even blink. "I intend to investigate how a mechanical death machine—a thing that would probably take three teams of horses to bring here and twelve men to carry and assemble—ended up on the Parliament floor. Given that the marshals are in charge of security in this building, I'm going to question them. Whether or not that leads to a deeper investigation into the marshals themselves depends on the answers."

"I believe it is warranted, but I would insist that Druth Intelligence should take point on it."

"Druth Intelligence isn't supposed to investigate our own citizens, Colonel. I wouldn't even know what division should handle it."

"We can determine that on our own."

Tricky waved it off. "There is, right now, an established authority of jurisdiction for this case, and that lies on the city Constabulary and the GIU. But I hear Prince Escaraine is in the building, and he might personally override that. Until I hear otherwise, this building, this investigation, and anywhere it leads, falls in my lap."

"Inspector, you really should consider—"

Tricky turned away from the woman, looking to Corrie. "Where are my victims? The ones I can talk to?"

"I'll rutting show you," Corrie said. If Tricky wasn't going to give a trice about this Intelligence bint, neither would Corrie. She started walking, leading her to the conference room.

Something grabbed Corrie's arm—and it wasn't a hand. A band of yellow light was wrapped around her. Same thing happened to Tricky. The light pulled Corrie back, burning cold on her arm.

"I was speaking to you," the officer said, the yellow light coming out of her hand like a tendril. A rutting mage.

Dayne came thundering back, leaping between the mage and Corrie and Tricky. The yellow tendrils withered into nothing. "How dare you, Colonel?" he said.

"Do you even know me?" she snarled. "I could have your head, Tarian boy. And I mean that literally. Now, I will not be so rudely ignored."

"It's fine," Tricky said, rubbing her arm. "What is it you want, Colonel—"

"Colonel Altarn, Missus Rainey. Remember me and respect that."

"Altarn," Tricky repeated. She pushed past Dayne and got up in the colonel's face. "It's *Inspector* Rainey, ma'am. I have work to do. I'll send word to the High Office if I need you."

Tricky walked away, and Corrie ran to catch up with her. The two Tarians came up right behind them.

"Blazes, Tricky," Corrie said as they went up the stairs. "Remind me never to piss on your boots."

"You've got nothing to worry about," Tricky said. "Dayne, stop shadowing me."

"But in case—"

"I can handle it, son," she said. "Get me that map."

He scurried off—as much as a fellow that big could scurry. They reached the conference room.

"Who's in here?" Tricky asked, pulling her notebook out of her pocket.

"The four victims who weren't sent to Riverheart Ward. They're shook, but they're able to talk."

"Patrolmen with them?"

"Two regulars," Corrie said.

"All right. Get back to your people working the doors, get me all the names, every damn one of them. No one is off the hook."

"Not even Prince Escaraine?" Corrie asked.

Tricky laughed as she opened the door. "Yeah. Not even him."

———◆—◆◆—◆———

Minox took a tickwagon to make his way across the river back to Inemar. While he was no longer in a weakened state, his whole body was just weary. For once he wanted nothing more than to head home and sleep. But he had to go back to the stationhouse, had to face the Inquiry and Miss Morad.

Intellectually, he welcomed it—at least it would settle the matter of his status as an Uncircled mage in the Constabulary. But in his gut, he felt it was a colossal waste of time and energy. Time and energy he could be spending searching for this Sholiar, investigating the Parliament building and this machine. He knew he could trust Inspector Rainey to handle it all with intelligence and skill, but that was no substitute for being on it himself.

That was where he wanted to be right now. Shirtsleeves rolled up and working out the case. That was where he belonged.

He packed his pipe and lit it as he got off the tick-wagon. The new tobacco he was smoking now was decidedly inferior to his preferred brand, but Gasta ab Uhren wouldn't sell to him any more, so he had to find a new shop with a different proprietor. Minox was no longer buying his tobacco directly from the Fuergans, and it was clear that the Druth smoke shops were selling the dregs of the Fuergan crop.

He needed to make amends with Gasta ab Uhren. Or get someone to purchase it for him. Possibly Jace.

As he approached the stationhouse, he noted Joshea sitting at the fast-wrap stand. Despite the meal Minox had just had at The Nimble Rabbit, he would need a bit more sustenance to make it through the next few hours of Inquiry.

"Afternoon, specs," Missus Wolman said as he came over. "How many today?"

"Two," Minox said. "I didn't think you frequented this stand," he said to Joshea.

"But you do, and I wanted to get a word without anyone looking too suspicious." Joshea squinted at what Missus Wolman threw on her grill. "I have no idea what meat that is, and meat is my business."

"You and Inspector Rainey have some noted similarities," Minox said. "She's obsessed with figuring it out."

"You aren't?"

"I just eat what I can. This is here, it's easy, and it's decent." He took a wrap from Missus Wolman as she put the meat into a flatbread and passed it to him.

She turned to Joshea. "I'd be insulted but I know 'decent' is as high praise as he manages."

"I am very pleased to have you here, Missus Wolman," Minox said as he bit into the wrap. He looked at Joshea. "And why are you here?"

"I found out after it happened that the squad's actions today were some sort of test for you. I'm sorry. I never would have—"

"It's fine. I hadn't expected such an unorthodox

launch to the Inquiry, but I hold no ill will toward anyone who was compelled to participate."

"Iorrett and the others. They were downright gleeful. 'Good to see that freak taken down a notch.'"

Minox took that in. "They said that in front of you?"

"They know we're friends, but they don't know—" Joshea stopped for a moment. "They don't know what I can do. Things are happening in there, and I don't think it'll be good for you."

"I'm certain there are several people involved who would like nothing better than to see me forcibly removed from the Constabulary. Both among the constables and the mage circles. However, I have faith that, if nothing else, Captain Cinellan will not allow an unfair process to go forward."

"Can he stop it?" Joshea shook his head. "I heard about that woman . . ."

"Miss Morad," Minox said. "She is, without a doubt, someone who will gladly issue a negative ruling on me. But . . . I do not, in my assessment of her, think she would do so maliciously. She will likely be unkind to me, but not unfair."

"Nyla pointed her out to me," Joshea said. "Made my hair stand on end. And then that fop from the Circles . . ."

Minox nodded, finishing the last bite of the wrap. "Mister Olivant. He will be unfair."

"He looked at me strangely," Joshea said. "I kept my distance, but I'm sure he—"

"Do not trouble yourself with that right now. Or with my predicament."

"I feel responsible for your predicament. Maybe if that night, I had been more vigilant, made some other choice, then Inspector Mirrell wouldn't have—"

Minox risked putting a comforting hand on Joshea's shoulder. "This Inquiry was coming, one way or another, sooner or later. Do not place any blame on yourself. I certainly don't."

Joshea nodded. "You have to go in there now, I imagine."

"I do," Minox said as he turned toward the stationhouse. "Wish me luck, or prayers to the saint of your choice."

"Any and all," Joshea said, giving him a military salute.

Minox went into the stationhouse, making his way directly to the inspectors' floor. His cousin Nyla was organizing papers at her desk when he came up.

"Minox!" she said sharply. "What happened at the Parliament?"

"Too much," he said. "It's not something to talk about in polite company."

"I've read the preliminary reports," she said, holding up a file. "I meant you. Did . . . are you . . ."

In the past years, Minox had never heard Nyla directly address his status as a mage. She danced around the subject, as she was doing now.

"I'll be fine," he said. "Is the captain in? I'm given to understand the Inquiry hearing will begin in a few minutes."

"Right," she said, swallowing hard. "He's down in one of the interrogation rooms. That—that's where it'll be held."

Not quite what he had expected, though it was probably a tactic on Miss Morad's part to make him defensive. Treat him like a suspect.

"Fine, I'll—"

"I'll take you down," she said, leading him over to the back stairs. "I should tell you what to expect."

"I'm expecting there to be a hearing about my fitness to serve as an inspector."

"Yes," she said, her voice breaking just a bit. "But it's not that simple. You'll be in the main interrogation room, with Miss Morad, Mister Olivant, and any specific witnesses they call. Captain Cinellan will be in the listening room, with Mister Hilsom and two clerks to transcribe everything. And Inspector Mirrell."

"I was not expecting Mister Hilsom, but other than that, I am not surprised." Though there would be no need for Mister Hilsom to be present unless there was an intention for prosecution. Surely they didn't need him to sign off on Writs of Compulsion or Search. Miss Morad must have the authority to do that on her own. She ought to.

"Mirrell is supposed to give testimony about why you should be expelled! How could he do that?"

"Inspector Mirrell is the officer who made the initial complaint, and he was well within his rights to do so," Minox said. He shouldn't have to defend Inspector Mirrell, but he knew that Nyla was angry about this whole affair.

"I am going to be called in for questions," she said quietly. "I don't want to—"

"Be truthful in all things," Minox said. "Don't try to protect me."

"But—"

"Either I deserve to be here in this uniform or I don't. I won't have a lie be the reason I keep it."

She nodded. They had reached the door. "I'll see you when I'm called."

Minox went in. The room had been rearranged from its usual design, with Miss Morad and Mister Olivant sitting at the table, and a lone chair against the wall, presumably for Minox to sit in.

"Inspector," Miss Morad said lightly. "You're looking better than when I last saw you."

"I have recovered," Minox said. "Do I sit?"

"Please," she said. She looked over to the window, where supposedly Captain Cinellan and Mister Hilsom were watching. "Could we have some tea brought in here?"

"Are we making sure everyone is comfortable?" Mister Olivant asked. "Because I certainly am not comfortable being in here with . . . him."

"I did not ask you to be here," Minox said. "I'm

still not clear what stake you or your Circle have in this."

Before Olivant could answer, the door burst open and a young man stormed in, carrying a satchel of papers that was too stuffed to close properly. "You haven't begun yet, have you?"

"No," Miss Morad said. "Though I don't know who you are or why you think you can come in here."

The young man extended his hand to her, almost losing his control over his satchel in the process. "Cheed Cheever, with the Justice Advocate office."

"And what do you think you're doing here? This shouldn't concern Justice Advocate."

He put down the satchel. "I'm here to represent Inspector Welling in these matters."

"This Inquiry isn't a trial or a confession," Miss Morad said. "It's not appropriate for you to insert yourself in here."

"It's not?" Cheever asked, raising an eyebrow. "I'm sorry, but are you not deposing Inspector Welling with regard to the events leading up to this Inquiry? Are you not calling witnesses? Listening to testimony? Is Inspector Welling's career not at risk based on the results of this Inquiry?"

"That is all true, but—"

"And I know that Mister Hilsom is watching this right now—yes, hello, Zebram—so everything said in this room is evidence for potential future prosecution. And based on what? Being a mage."

"An Uncircled mage," Olivant said hotly.

"All the more reason I should step in," Cheever said, moving to stand next to Minox. "Justice Advocate's role is to protect the rights of people who have no other defenders."

Miss Morad shook her head. "This proceeding is not subject to—"

Cheever interrupted her. "The rights afforded to every free man in Druthal since 1015? And the

protections that mages explicitly should receive—
regardless of Circle membership, Mister Olivant—since
the decrees in 1023? Let alone that this hearing is implicitly unbalanced."

"Unbalanced how?" Minox asked. Cheever's performance here was interesting, and while he appreciated
the points the young man was making, he wondered if
Cheever was doing him more harm than good.

"You mean, besides the fact that Miss Morad is
both your prosecutor and judge? Where is the impar-
tiality?"

"Enough, Mister Cheever," Miss Morad said. "I am
authorized by the Archduke of Maradaine—"

"Who does not have the authority to undermine Inspector Welling's rights."

Miss Morad fumed at that. "I have no intention of
violating his rights!"

"Good," Cheever said. "Then you shouldn't mind
that I'm here to confirm that independently."

A young clerk came in with a tea cart. As she placed
the tea on the table, Cheever leaned against the wall.

"I think," Minox said carefully, "that for the purpose of making sure that the integrity of this proceeding cannot be questioned, it would be ideal for Mister
Cheever to stay."

"I suppose," Miss Morad said. "If for the sake of
appearances, if nothing else. Unless you object, Mister
Olivant?"

"Hardly," Olivant said. "But we've wasted enough
time. Can we begin?"

Chapter 9

ONE WOMAN AND three men sat in chairs around a conference table, huddled close to each other with blankets around their shoulders. Cups of tea sat in front of them, all untouched.

Satrine came in closer, giving a small nod to the two patrolmen to step outside.

"Hello," she said. "I'm Inspector Rainey. I know . . . I know you all have been through an ordeal, but it's critical that I ask you some questions while everything is still fresh in your minds. Is that all right?"

"It's fine," one of the men said. "I'm . . . I'm Harding Fain, and I think I'm the ranking person here."

"Stop making it about rank, Harding," the woman whispered. "No one cares."

"It's important that we—"

"Please," Satrine said, taking a seat across from them. Jerinne stepped up behind her. This girl seemed intent on shadowing her, staying at her side. Satrine didn't mind—having an armored knight with a shield and sword at her arm gave her a certain authority, on top of what her uniform and vest offered her. "That isn't something we need to focus on."

"Told you," the woman said.

"Let's start with what happened to you. When did you . . . when did it start?"

"Today is the third, yes? It's Ene?" Harding asked.

"I was home in my apartment on the evening of first of Oscan—it was Ren—having supper—"

"Alone?" Satrine asked.

"I live alone, yes. And I remember eating and then . . . then it's gray."

"Similar," one of the other men said. "Though I was with my wife. I don't—do you know if she's all right?"

"My husband isn't," the woman said, her voice choking. "He . . . he was . . . the demonstration."

Satrine instinctively reached out and took her hand. The woman gripped back hard.

"As best as you all can remember, you were home on Ren night, and then you don't remember what happened next?"

They all nodded.

"And then what?" Satrine asked.

"We woke up on the Parliament floor," Harding said. "All of us, stripped to our skivs and shackled to each other at the ankle. And we had contraptions strapped to our heads."

"Devices like the one you were in?"

"Not as elaborate," the man at the end said. He had been quiet all this time. He was young—they were all young—but he looked like he was barely out of university. "They were like bear traps, but with a child's springbox on it."

"Something like a springbox?"

"No, the actual toy," the woman said. "And all of them were slowly unwinding, playing their lilting music. The room echoed with that and the click-click-click of the springs."

"We all woke up down there, surrounded by crates," Harding said.

"Crates?" Jerinne asked.

"Wooden crates, stacked on the floor. The Parliament chairs and tables had all been pushed to the sides."

Satrine scowled a bit at Jerinne, then turned back to the group. "You all woke up down there together, all eighteen of you."

"Twenty-two," the woman said. "You couldn't see anyone's faces because of the contraptions—they were like masks—but there were twenty-two of us, each with a number written on the front of our masks."

"And you couldn't speak while it was on," the youngest said.

"So you couldn't identify each other?"

"I could identify my husband," the woman said. "He . . . he has—had—a scar on his chest that— It's distinct."

"The demonstration," the man with the missing wife said.

"Tell me, as best you can, what happened next," Satrine said.

Harding spoke up. "When we woke, we started moving, struggling. Several people were in a panicked state. No one could scream, but we all could hear that—that sound of the springboxes. It was . . . I never . . ." His voice faltered for a moment. "Then he appeared on the balcony."

Satrine stopped herself from saying "Sholiar"—she still had nothing but Dayne's word that that was the man's name, and she wasn't about to feed it to witnesses and poison that well. "He who?"

"He was—you couldn't quite see him, because he was wearing a mask—like a theatrical mask in the old plays? And a robe. So there was no sense of how big he was, what his shape was. He was just this figure up in the shadows in the gallery."

"But when he spoke . . ." the young man said hauntingly.

"Yes," Harding said. "He told us that we had to open the crates and start building. Build that machine. And if we didn't . . ."

"The demonstration," the young man said.

All three men looked to the woman, as if they expected her to tell this part.

"The man in the gallery," she said, her voice a rasp, like all possible screams and tears had long since been spent, "he said if we didn't do the work, didn't build to his orders, then the springbox would pop. And then a . . . he played a few notes on a flute, and suddenly one of the springboxes started unwinding much faster. My husband. The tune of the springbox raced. Duh-da-de-dah-de-dah-dah-dah. And then . . . and then . . . the springbox popped. And the contraption sprung open, tearing his head apart."

After a moment of horrified silence, Harding spoke again. "Needless to say, we worked. The man called out numbers and gave instructions of what everyone was supposed to do. The few times anyone balked or slowed, he'd play just a note or two on the flute. And everyone went back to it."

"For hours," the man with the wife said. "We must have worked on it the entire Saint's Day."

"It was genius, really," Harding said. "Every crate didn't just hold parts of the machine. The crates themselves became part of it. Everything folded up, connected, nothing wasted."

So that answered one key question—how the device was built on the floor. The victims were forced to build it themselves.

"Once it was done, then what?"

"When we were done, there were those eighteen chairs, those eighteen terrible chairs," Harding said.

"He told us the only way to get the devices off our heads and the shackles off our ankles was to fill the chairs. And that once all eighteen chairs were full, the last three could leave."

They all sat silently, looking at the floor.

"What happened?" Jerinne was the one who asked. No answer.

"What happened?" Jerinne was in a state, her face turning red. Satrine glared her down and waved her off. The last thing she needed right now was a half-cocked Tarian Initiate.

The young man spoke up. "We grabbed each other, forced each other into the chairs, strapped people in.

All of us." He looked down the line. "All of us. We fought."

"We fought to survive!" Harding said. "Every one of us." He looked at Jerinne, his eyes wet. "You would have done the same."

"I've taken an oath to the contrary," Jerinne said.

"All right," Satrine said. "I understand. And when you were fighting each other, what did the man do?"

"Laugh," the woman said. "And when all eighteen seats were full, the headpieces and shackles just . . . fell off. But not on the last three. He told them they had to wind the cranks and set the cords and chains that connected the machine to the doors. Once they did that, he guided them to the last door and . . . they left."

"Still with the devices and shackles?" Satrine asked.

Everyone nodded.

Likely the three in the boiler room. They hardly got a clean escape.

"All right," Satrine said, getting to her feet. "Have you all eaten? Other basic needs cared for?"

Heads shook at that one.

"All right," Satrine said. She went to the door and called over the patrolmen. "Make sure they all get fed and cared for, and then escorted home. They've been through enough." She looked back to them. "I'll want to interview you all again later, but for today . . ."

"Thank you, Inspector," the woman said. "I'm sorry we're not more help."

"Don't be sorry about anything," Satrine said. "You don't owe an apology to anyone after today."

She thanked the victims and left. Out in the hallway, Corrie was waiting with Leppin. The examinarian was looking as troubled as she'd ever seen him; a sheen of sweat bled through his leather skullcap. She would have thought that if anyone could handle this horror unscathed, it would have been him.

"What's the word, Leppin?"

"Ugly," he said. "I've got nine bodies on the ground, and . . . half of them, I got no way to identify them."

"We're not that rutting bad off with this," Corrie said. "The ones we know—Enbrain's nephew and the survivors, they're all clerks and attachés here, assigned to specific members of Parliament. The rest of the victims. . . . Those poor bastards are probably from here too."

"Makes sense," Leppin said. "Plus we got that one marshal."

"Him we can identify," Satrine said. Looking to Corrie, she said, "I need a list of all the victims, alive, dead, here, and in the boiler room."

"Boiler room?"

"There were three victims in there," Satrine said. "Not as bad off as these folks, but still survivors of something horrid."

Corrie looked a bit confused. "No one's mentioned them, but these rutting bastards are still all mixed up. They might have been sent to the hospital wards already. I'll sort it out."

"And the machine itself?" Satrine asked Leppin.

"Like the rest of the Gearbox deaths, it's now inert. A lot of it got wrecked in the boiler explosion and its own gears grinding itself up."

"That was Minox," Corrie said.

"What now?" Leppin asked.

"When the machine was poised to kill another," Satrine said. "Welling apparently held the machine in place—all the moving parts—with—"

"Ayuh, yeah. Blazes. That's quite a thing."

"Ain't it just, though?" Corrie said. "And now he's gonna get cat-dragged over it."

Satrine ground her teeth. She wished she had Minox here. He might have spotted something with these witnesses, some bit of their story that didn't fit, or some element that gave him one of his flashes of insight. Right now she just had one answer, but still so many questions. "Let's try and focus on our job here," she said. "It's what he would want us to do."

"Inspector!" Dayne came running up the stairs. "We've got trouble with the marshals!"

— ◆◆ —

While Miss Morad began an opening statement for the sake of the scribes on the other side of the curtain, Minox's thoughts were on the Parliament, the machine, and how this Sholiar character could have possibly achieved what was done there. It was impossible to achieve alone. Not merely the manpower—saints knew that there were plenty of people who would do the job for the right crowns—but the opportunity. Through intention or negligence, someone in the King's Marshals or one of the Parliament's administrative staff allowed this atrocity to happen.

Miss Morad wasn't saying anything of note or consequence, anyway.

"Now, I'd like to begin with direct questions to you, Inspector Welling."

"As you wish," Minox said.

"I'm reserving the right to object to lines of questioning," Cheever said.

"Object all you want, Mister Cheever," Miss Morad said. "Inspector, state your name and rank for the record."

"Minox Welling, Inspector Third Class."

"Date of birth?"

"Keenan twenty-fourth, 1189."

"Saint Helspin's day?"

"That is correct."

"And your mother is Amalia D'Fen Welling, daughter of Minox D'Fen?"

"Also correct."

"You were named after your maternal grandfather?"

"That is also correct," Minox said. It was getting tedious confirming things that Miss Morad already knew, and were part of the public record.

"But hardly relevant," Cheever said.

"Establishing all our particulars," Miss Morad said. "Your father was Rennick Welling, formerly a sergeant in the horsepatrol of Keller Cove."

"Correct, but in the last three weeks of his life, he was on temporary loan to Benson Court, riding the night shift."

"That . . . is not in the record," Miss Morad said, looking over the papers in front of her. "Do you know why that might be?"

"I cannot answer accurately, but I can speculate that it was due to an informal arrangement between the precinct captains."

"But it does explain why he was in Benson Court when he died, officially in the line of duty."

"I object to this," Mister Cheever said. "I can't see how it applies to the Inquiry at hand."

"I am establishing the inspector's history within the Constabulary."

"Inspector," Cheever said, "when did your father die?"

"In 1207."

"Eight years ago."

"Yes."

"And were you there?"

"No, of course not," Minox said. "At the time I was starting my first assignment as a patrolman, on horsepatrol in Inemar."

"Miss Morad, can you confine your 'establishing' to events that directly involve the inspector, and preferably of recent history?"

"Humor me, Mister Cheever, that I have a point. Inspector, you were just starting that assignment here in Inemar in 1207. Day shift in Inemar?"

"That's correct."

"Your first assignment after your cadet year was not, in fact, night shift horsepatrol in Benson Court?"

"No, absolutely not," Minox said.

"Can you explain this assignment letter in your file?"

She passed it over to him, which Cheever snatched, glanced over, then passed to Minox. It was a letter dated 1207, assigning him to the Benson Court Stationhouse, on the night shift.

"I've never seen this before," Minox said. "I can't attest to the authenticity of this letter, but I can say I never received it. I have no idea where it came from."

"There's no stamp on it," Cheever said. "This wasn't enacted."

"But it was written, until your father made a deal to get you assigned to Inemar on days, instead."

"That's entirely possible," Minox said. A Constabulary assignment to Benson Court on the night shift would have been incredibly dangerous, especially eight years ago when they were having the Warehouse Rows. That was exactly how Father had been killed, interrupting a heist of one of the old navy warehouses. And he had been an experienced constable, years in the saddle. He must have . . .

Minox found himself with tears in his eyes. He wiped them away.

Finding his voice, he said, "I was not aware of any such arrangement, but I cannot deny its plausibility. Rennick Welling was a dedicated officer of the Constabulary who believed in doing everything he could to protect the people of this city. Including me."

"So," Miss Morad said, "thanks to your father, you were assigned here. Made Sergeant in 1210, then Inspector Apprentice in 1212, and Inspector Third Class in 1214."

"You have all the information in my file," Minox said. He did his best to regain his composure. He wasn't sure what Miss Morad was doing, but he suspected that she was trying to emotionally manipulate him. Possibly as a test to see if he would lose control of his magic as a result.

He must not let her have that.

"My next question is, why take the inspector path instead of going for lieutenant, command of a squad?"

"Because inspector was always my goal, ma'am," Minox said. "Even as a page, I had a knack for examining crime scenes, finding evidence, piecing together the mysteries. I'm sure there's commendations in that file along those lines. I was not lacking for recommendation when I applied for Inspector Apprentice."

"No, certainly not. And when did your magical abilities manifest?"

"Also in 1212. A few months into my apprenticeship."

"At twenty-three?" Olivant finally spoke. Minox had thought the man had dozed off out of boredom.

"Yes, sir."

"That's—I've never heard of such a thing. Most manifest it between twelve and fourteen. I knew of one young woman who did at seventeen, but . . . twenty-three? No."

"It's true," Minox said. "I told it once to Major Dresser, of the Red Wolf Circle and former member of Druth Intelligence. He was surprised but not as incredulous."

"Do you have any specific questions, Mister Olivant?" Cheever asked. "Or are you just harassing the inspector?"

"I do," Olivant said. "Eventually."

"Hmm," Cheever said. "Seems like you just intend to interject at your leisure."

"Mister Olivant's role here is as my expert consultant," Miss Morad said. "His interjections are useful to me."

Olivant didn't look very pleased at that, but he had been looking displeased for some time now.

"I'm saying, can we proceed to something resembling the point?" Cheever asked.

"Yes," Miss Morad said. She reached under her table and pulled out a crate full of files. "These are all the cases you've worked on since the day your magic manifested. I would like to go over some of the particulars of each of them."

Chapter 10

$\mathcal{A}$S DAYNE LED Satrine along, he passed a note to Jerinne, and she ran off immediately. Likely some sort of Tarian business, and saints, could that girl run. She ran like the night couldn't catch her.

"What's happening?" Satrine asked.

"Quoyell is happening," Dayne said. "He's behind closed doors with your commissioner, Mister Montrose, and Prince Escaraine."

"And you think I should storm in there and stop him from doing whatever he's doing?"

"I think it's critical that this investigation be kept clear of, if not the marshals, at least from Chief Quoyell."

Quoyell. Something about that man sat wrong with Satrine, and it was deep in the back of her skull as to why.

No, not him—his name.

And she couldn't put her finger on why.

She shook it off. The man was just obnoxious, and that was probably what set the bad taste in her mouth about him.

She reached the door, Dayne waiting for her to take the lead.

"You want me to be the one to barge in on the prince and a member of Parliament?" she asked him.

"I didn't think of it like that," he said.

"I thought you were supposed to be protecting me, Tarian," she said, aiming for a playful tease, but feeling like she landed on a jaded barb. If nothing else, Dayne looked like a kicked puppy, as much as a man as towering as he was could manage.

"You're right," he said, taking the door handle.

"Wait," she said. "Let's not burn your capital just yet. I've got a sense you don't quite have much to spare."

"If you need—"

"Dayne," she said. "You've got the one constable who isn't going to be cowed by a prince. Trust me."

She opened the door and went in.

"—which is exactly why this is our problem," Quoyell was saying. He was standing at the desk, looming over Mister Montrose. Montrose had the look of a man who often had people attempt to intimidate him, and only found their attempts amusing. Enbrain was sitting on a couch, away from the desk, appearing to be lost in his own thoughts. Prince Escaraine—who Satrine assumed the handsome young man in the fur-lined jacket and silver circlet was—looked deeply concerned about Quoyell's point.

Just looking at Prince Escaraine triggered a whole history lesson in her head. Whoever had designed her telepathic education must have thought it was critical to know Escaraine's specific lineage. King Maradaine XV—the great-grandfather of both Prince Escaraine and the current king—was killed by a Poasian assassin in 1161, along with the queen and two of the king's three sons, Mardel and Calivar. The only royal survivor in the palace was Mardel's infant son, Ponoraine, who would grow up to be Escaraine's father. But the crown went to Prince Escarel, who was serving as a commander in the war in the Napolic Islands. His reign as Maradaine XVI was entirely on the war front, but he sent his wife—a Napolic woman—pregnant with his son Mastaine back to Druthal.

After Maradaine XVI died in battle, there was an outcry throughout the country that the throne should go to Ponoraine instead of a half-Napolic outsider. Ponoraine outright refused to challenge his cousin's rightful claim, and Mastaine ruled for twenty years as the charismatic and beloved King Maradaine XVII.

His son, Maradaine XVIII, was not charismatic or beloved. He was sullen and withdrawn, especially after the death of his queen and son two years ago. Prince Escaraine had the love of the people, and there were more than a few people who believed he was the "true line" of the Druth throne. Seeing him in person, Satrine could understand why he was so popular. He wasn't just handsome, he radiated an uncomplicated charm. She immediately bowed her head, not only showing proper respect and deference to his rank, but also giving herself a moment to absorb all the information that had just slammed into her skull.

"What are you doing here?" Quoyell asked her.

"I came to ask you the same thing," she shot back.

"This is a private meeting," he said.

"Shouldn't be," she said. Turning to the prince, she added with a touch of Druth highborn to her accent, "Begging your indulgence, your Highness. I would not presume to intrude upon you without your grace and permission, and will humbly withdraw should you command it."

The prince raised an eyebrow, and looked to Enbrain. "I was not aware we had women in the Inspector grade. And certainly not women of such impeccable grace."

"Rainey is a singular woman," Enbrain said, now focused on the conversation.

"Surely," the prince said. "I would not expect a member of the city loyalty to be so versed in etiquette."

Not every member of the "city loyalty"—a term both old and privileged, rarely used outside the nobility—had been a secret princess in Waisholm. But there was no need to tell Prince Escaraine that.

"I deeply apologize for my impertinence, your Highness. But I was made aware that Chief Quoyell was engaging in some sort of foolery that could impede my investigation."

"Your investigation?" Quoyell asked, almost raising his voice before looking to the prince. "Your Highness, as I said, we must maintain a certain order of things. A matter of this gravity must be handled by the marshals."

"Because the marshals have proven to be beyond reproach?" Dayne asked. "Need I remind you—"

"No, you needn't," Quoyell said.

Mister Montrose waved Dayne off a bit. "This circumstance is unique, on an order that none of our systems were designed to handle."

"What is that supposed to mean?" Quoyell asked.

"I mean," Montrose said, "that the breach in security and protocol—"

"Not to mention the sanctity of Parliament floor," Dayne interjected.

"Tarian," the prince snapped. "Do not talk out of turn."

Dayne bowed his head and stepped back.

"Mister Heldrin has a point," Montrose said. "We were lucky this didn't happen during Convocation, with more members of Parliament present in these offices."

Quoyell shook his head. "Begging your indulgence, sir, it's only because it was in the off session that this breach was possible. Just as members of the Parliament are away—mostly out of the city, save yourself and a handful of others—we are operating now on a crew of bone."

"I saw dozens of marshals today," Satrine said.

"Now, in response. And only because I wasn't even here when it started."

"No?" Satrine asked. "That is interesting."

"If I had been, all of this would have been handled in a quiet, dignified manner, rather than the carnival this fool started." He pointed at Dayne.

"I started? Your men had already sounded the alarm when I arrived."

"But you were here, Tarian. Your 'residency' is right in the building. Yet you saw nothing. Prevented nothing."

"I'm the one who brought in the inspectors in the first place!" Dayne shouted.

"Inspectors, Yellowshields, journalists. We could have kept this quiet!"

"Kept it secret, you mean!"

"And you want it all out in the open, right? So Dayne Heldrin, Tarian Candidate, can be the great hero in the newssheets again? And yet that still won't earn you your place as an Adept."

"Gentlemen, please," Satrine said.

"Did he tell you, Inspector, that he's going to be cashiered at the end of his Candidacy? That he will never be a full member of the Tarian Order?"

Dayne's head went down, his face and ears burning red. "That doesn't mean—"

"Because he screwed up and nearly killed a young man, grandson of one of the Parliament."

"I am still a Candidate—"

Quoyell drove further at Dayne, getting up in his face despite only coming up to the Tarian's chest. "And the only real connection between what happened to that boy and what's happening here, Dayne, is you. So maybe you're who she should investigate."

"I told you—"

"Cease this." The prince barely raised his voice, but the authority behind it sucked the steam out of both Quoyell and Dayne.

After a moment of silence, Satrine said. "Chief, if you weren't here when this was discovered, who was? Who was in charge of security yesterday?"

"As I said, we're on a rationed crew while the Convocation of the Parliament is disbanded. For the past month, we've had only ten men assigned here, and yesterday many were given the Saint Day off."

"And who was here?" Satrine asked.

"Inspector," the prince said. "Surely you don't suspect that the marshals themselves were culpable?"

"Specific suspicion is not the point, your Highness," Satrine said, lying to some degree.

"We had a breach," Chief Quoyell said. "We will determine what went wrong and correct it."

"Not good enough," Satrine said. Turning back to the prince, she said, "Your Highness, there was a catastrophic failure in their security, and that must be investigated, and independently of their office."

"Which we don't have a real mechanism for," Enbrain said. "The Grand Inspection Unit—which Rainey is a part of—is the best unit for such an endeavor."

"It goes against the order of things," the prince said. "If anything, I would think Druth Intelligence would be best equipped. Or perhaps the Tarians. Independent of all aspects of law enforcement, and beyond reproach."

"I appreciate the confidence, your Highness," Dayne said.

"I didn't mean you, necessarily," the prince said. "But surely Grandmaster Orren would have insight. One of the Adepts or Masters, yes."

"I appreciate the confidence in the Order," Dayne said, "but the Tarians couldn't do something like this. We are warriors, steeped in martial training. We know nothing of inspection or investigation."

"Which this would require, your Highness," Enbrain said.

"Which leads me back to Intelligence," the prince said.

Enbrain gave a glance to Satrine. "My unit is capable, and already versed in the particulars. We simply need Chief Quoyell to give his full cooperation."

"Feed my men to you, you mean," Quoyell said. He sneered at Satrine. "You want my duty rosters so whoever was working yesterday can be the laundry you hang. No, ma'am. You want to put my skull on the block, fine. But you can't compel me to give my men up."

"No, I can't," Satrine said. "But I believe he can."

"You're correct," Prince Escaraine said. "Were I to order him to, he would be compelled to give you that information. I am not, at the moment, inclined to do so."

"Might I ask why, your Highness?" Mister Montrose took the question before Satrine could, which was probably for the best.

"I'm still uncertain about what is best here," the prince said, scratching at his chin. "I must contemplate this further, and I appreciate all these points of view. For the moment, I will not gainsay your decision, Good Mister Montrose, and allow the commissioner and his Grand Inspection Unit to continue. But I will keep thinking on this, and take counsel with my cousin. I will leave you to your duties."

Everyone bowed to him—including Satrine—and he swept out of the room. Chief Quoyell made for the door.

"Chief," Satrine said. "I want those names, and I will want to interview them all."

"Maybe tomorrow," Quoyell said, "if the crown commands." He stalked off.

"Pleasant fellow," she muttered under her breath.

"He's rattled," Montrose said. "And you and yours would build as much of a wall around yourselves if the positions were reversed."

"Mine but not me," Satrine said. She knew well enough how the red-and-green wall worked, but she wasn't one to protect a corrupt stick if she had evidence. "But I appreciate that you are letting us do the job here, sir."

"It's largely a hot pot in your hands," Montrose said. "I'm not sure holding it will be desirable for very long. Though I'm surprised you didn't want the Tarians involved, Dayne."

"I think the Order needs to have a role, sir, but one

that is suited to us. I've sent word to the Grandmaster, whom I suspect I'll be hearing from—yes, here we are."

Jerinne ran in the room with a letter, and handed it to Dayne, giving Satrine a small nod as she approached. Dayne read through the letter and nodded, folding it up and putting it in his pocket.

"Good news?" Satrine asked.

"Somewhat," Dayne said. "The Grandmaster has agreed to assign members of the Tarian Order to guard the survivors tonight."

"That is well suited," Montrose said with a slight smile.

"You think—" Satrine still didn't want to give too much credence to Dayne's "Sholiar" theory, but she caught herself almost saying the name. "You think the killer will try to finish the survivors off?"

"It's worth the precaution," he said. "But he's asked me to protect Niall Enbrain personally."

"Niall's still at Riverheart Ward," Enbrain said.

"All the more reason for me to stand watch," Dayne said. "He's helpless right now. So with your leave, I'll be off."

"Of course," Satrine said.

"And you stay with her," Dayne told Jerinne. He was out the door before Satrine could tell him that was unnecessary.

"What's next for you?" Enbrain said, looking around a bit nervously.

"At this point, we have a lot of information, but very little analysis of it," Satrine said. "And it's late. I'll return to the stationhouse, consult with Welling, and return to this in the morning."

"Good, good," Enbrain said, though he had the bearing of a man who wanted to say more. "Then I'll let you get to it." He gestured for Satrine to leave. Perhaps the more he wanted to say was to the Parliamentarian. Satrine nodded and left, Jerinne still at her side.

"Are you going to follow me?" Satrine asked.

"Are we leaving now?" Jerinne returned. "If so, then yes."

Satrine sighed. If she was stuck with a shadow, there certainly were worse ones.

———◆—◆◆———

The Inquiry session had been a particularly brutal few hours, where Miss Morad delved in a number of Minox's past cases from the last three years, including some that he considered "unresolved."

She then held up the file for the Hieljam case, the one that had brought him to the Tsouljan compound. The one that had launched this Inquiry.

"This is where we'll stop, as we're nearly at six bells. I think everyone deserves to go home, and I believe our examination of this case in particular will require fresh minds. We will resume tomorrow at nine bells."

"Miss Morad," Minox said. "I do have open cases, an ongoing investigation."

"Perhaps you do," she said, "but this Inquiry must be resolved. Your captain will handle any adjustments that need to be made."

She packed up her satchel and went out.

Mister Olivant got to his feet, giving a slight nod to Minox. "Tomorrow, Mister Welling." Minox detected just a slight hint of sympathy from the man, which was definitely unexpected. Perhaps this process had cracked even his resolve to punish Minox.

"Well, all that went—I'm not sure," Cheever said.

"It went much like I feared it would," Minox said. "Thorough and callous. Though I did think there would be witness testimony."

"I think that Miss Morad still plans to do that. She's first establishing the particulars from the files, which she's clearly already given meticulous examination. I'm sorry I wasn't better prepared to offer defense, Inspector."

"Given that I wasn't expecting any at all, I am not

disappointed, Mister Cheever. Surprised to find you at my side, but not disappointed."

"Like I said, I'm interested in keeping justice from being miscarried. Be that in the courts or in here, to any citizen that needs my help. Such as it is."

"Tomorrow, then?"

Cheever offered his hand. "I will work on some motions and be better prepared, sir." He shook Minox's hand and went off.

Captain Cinellan was in the doorway before Minox could leave the room himself. "I apologize for this, Minox."

"It's necessary, sir," Minox said. "A crucible in which we can burn away the questions surrounding my fitness to serve."

"You seem confident," the captain said. He took the lead up the back stairs to the inspectors' floor. "That's good to see right now."

"I believe in a just system bringing the truth out. And I believe the truth is that I am a capable and fit man to serve as an inspector."

"More than capable," the captain said as they reached the inspectors' floor. "If I had my druthers, well—this is why it's strictly out of my hands."

"And yet you contacted Cheever, sir," Minox said.

"Me?" Cinellan asked, though the pitch change in his voice and twinge of his eye betrayed him.

"Someone let the Justice Advocate Office know about this, and I saw how distressed you were about the events of this morning."

"This morning was a terrible thing," Cinellan said. "I never should have allowed it." He led Minox into his office.

"One thing puzzles me about that, sir."

"One thing?" He went into his desk and produced a bottle of Fuergan whiskey and two glasses.

"How did the teashop agree to it?"

"Ah," Cinellan said with a chuckle. He poured two

glasses and passed one to Minox. "It's closing down, and the new owners were planning on tearing it down and rebuilding."

"Yes, of course," Minox said. He pulled out his pipe. "May I, sir?"

"Absolutely," Cinellan said.

Minox lit the pipe and picked up the whiskey as he smoked. Normally he did not care for the drink, but he recognized the gesture the captain was trying to make, and did his best to reciprocate. He certainly found it more appealing than beer or cider.

"That explains the largest flaw in the operation, why I was able to see through it so easily."

"Which was?"

"The location, off The Lower Bridge. The entire ploy needed me to believe that before checking in, Inspector Mirrell would cross to the north side and intervene on a wagon heist."

"I did point that out to Miss Morad."

"She remains a mystery here. What is her background?"

"Educated in law at Pirrell, years in the Archduchy Protector's offices, and then serving directly for the archduke."

"No cases of note?"

"Not in Maradaine," Cinellan said. "But she has led special investigations all over the archduchy: Kyst, Abernar, Maskill."

"Are you being vague, or is it her history?"

"Many of her investigations, once she was given her position directly serving the archduke, were kept under wraps. I don't have access to that information. And it's not like I can get quick word from Kyst."

"No, of course not," Minox said. He took another puff of his pipe. "I do appreciate your support here, Captain. What happens at the end of her Inquiry? She makes a decision, she presents her findings?"

"Formally, she'll present her report to us with her

recommendation. On paper, the archduke would review her work and make his own declaration, but that doesn't actually happen. Practically, her decision is all that matters."

"And avenues for appeal?"

"Best discussed with Mister Cheever."

Minox mulled over that and took another sip of his whiskey.

"Well, I hope this wasn't what your whole afternoon was like, or I'd be quite cross." Inspector Rainey was in the doorway. She held two newsprint-wrapped sandwiches from the cart outside, dropping them on the desk in front of her.

"Not at all," Minox said. "This is the first respite after a brutal afternoon."

"I know from brutal," she said, coming in and taking a seat. "Those are for you, obviously."

"Appreciated," Minox said, taking one. His stomach was more than growling at him. "I assume charged to my credit with Miss Wolman."

"She knew I wasn't buying them for myself." She turned to the captain. "Has he told you about the Parliament?"

"He hasn't," Cinellan said. "But I've heard a few snippets about it. Bad as they say it was?"

"Worse," Minox and Rainey said in unison.

Cinellan handed his whiskey to Rainey, who took it eagerly. "Go on."

Rainey told the story of the Parliament, the machine, and all the victims—which Minox only occasionally interrupted to add a salient detail when needed. Eventually she reached the part of her story where Minox was learning along with the captain, and he listened with intent.

"Well, that's horrifying," the captain said when she was done.

"Your account still leaves quite a few questions," Minox said. "Including how Sholiar managed to capture the twenty-two victims and get them and the crates of machinery to the Parliament."

"Sholiar?" the captain asked. "We have an identification for the Gearbox Killer?"

"Dayne Heldrin, the Tarian, has a past with the man," Minox said.

"We have a possibly theory," Rainey said sharply. "Based on what Mister Heldrin told us. But the name is all but meaningless."

"The skill and methodology matches Heldrin's account of events in Lacanja."

"Which we only have his word on," Rainey said. She took a deep sip of her whiskey. "I'm not saying it's not a good possible lead—it's more than anything else we have to go on—but we have no way of confirming what happened in Lacanja six months or more ago."

"I can make some inquiries," the captain said. "But that will take time."

"Tomorrow I'd like to bring in the marshals who were on duty, then talk to the other survivors. Corrie brought lists of everyone who was there, everyone who was supposed to be there, and so forth. If we could get the clerks to dig through the lists, find any discrepancies. And get a writ for the city to send us any and all building plans for the Parliament itself."

"I'd like to go over all that myself," Minox said.

"You have enough to handle tomorrow," Cinellan said.

"More Inquiry?" Rainey asked.

"Much," Minox said.

"Just in the morning? Or is he tied up all day?"

"I'm not sure," Cinellan said.

"Fine," Rainey said, in a tone that said it was anything but. "I've got the biggest case this office will likely handle for some time, and I could stand to have my partner on it."

"I'll get Miss Morad to do without him for the afternoon," the captain said.

A knock came at the door—Inspectors Mirrell and Kellman. "You want us to check in, Cap?" Mirrell asked.

"Where are you with the missing children?" Cinellan asked.

"Nowhere," Mirrell asked. "It's all cold trails, crazy stories."

"What kind of crazy stories?" Minox asked.

"Like a giant grabbing kids, pulling them into the sewers," Kellman said. "Seen anyone matching that description?"

Rainey chuckled. "We worked with a Tarian today who's a good head taller than you," she told Kellman.

"Cap," Mirrell said, taking another step in. "Tomorrow I need to . . ." He looked at Minox uncomfortably. "I need to testify. So we won't be digging any further with the kids."

"Kellman can dig," Cinellan said. "Darreck, take Iorrett and a couple of the squad and do some footwork tomorrow."

"If you say so, Cap," Kellman said. "Unless you want to trade, Tricky?"

"No, you can have Iorrett," she said. "And you do not want to trade cases with us."

"Yeah, but the blasted Parliament," he said. "The stories have been swirling, Trick. Sounds wild."

"Both of you work your own damn cases," Cinellan said. "Now all of you go home."

Minox left the office with Inspector Rainey. "You are going home, yes?" she asked.

"I am indeed," Minox said, heading over to their desks. He found a package of papers from Corrie—the sketches Jillian did. Perfect. "I require proper rest in my own space."

"Don't we all," she said. "I'll dig through papers in the morning, and we'll see where you're at when your done with the Inquiry." She paused for a moment. "Was it bad?"

"It was . . . invasive," Minox said. "To be expected."

"All right," she said. "The Tarians are sticking to this whole thing. The girl followed me here, and I'd bet a week's worth that she's waiting for me outside."

"No bet," Minox said. He was already convinced that Dayne and his younger charge would be diligent in their involvement, and it was better to let them help than shut them out. He gathered up the package and other documents. "My best to your husband and family, Inspector. Have a good night."

"You as well," she said. He nodded and went off to the stairs. Nyla and Corrie were already gone, home already. He was eager to do the same, even though he was certain that tonight he would find no rest.

Chapter 11

SATRINE WALKED OUT of the stationhouse to see Jerinne Fendall waiting outside, somehow managing to still look regal in her Tarian uniform despite the splashes of blood and char on it.

"Are you waiting for me?" Satrine asked.

"I thought I ought to," Jerinne said.

"I hardly need an escort," Satrine said. "I was alone on these streets when I was younger than you."

Jerinne chuckled dryly. "That explains a lot, ma'am. But begging your pardon, you took a nasty hit on the skull. And that killer is out there. Dayne and I both wanted to make sure that you got home without incident."

Satrine nodded. She appreciated it, even though these Tarians seemed to be a bit smothering once they decided someone needed their protection. "I'm fine."

"I'm sure, just—you were hurt protecting me. That doesn't sit right with me."

"Because you're supposed to be protecting people?" She started walking to the bridge. "You all aren't the only ones. What do you think the Constabulary is supposed do?"

"You're right."

"So did you go with Dayne to Riverheart to watch over Niall Enbrain?"

"I stopped by there briefly."

"How is Niall doing?"

"The doctors say he should survive, but he's been asleep all this time."

Satrine knew something about that. "And will he wake up? Still be aware?"

Jerinne was taken a bit aback. "I'm not sure what that means."

"My husband," Satrine said. "He had a horrible injury about six months ago. He survived, but . . . he hasn't been here since then." She tapped her forehead.

"I'm sorry."

"It's why I'm in uniform now."

"Huh," Jerinne said. "Sorry, ma'am. I took you for the type who had been doing this all her life."

"One way or another," Satrine said.

The walked quietly as they crossed the bridge to the north side. Finally, as they reached the northern shore, a thought burned in Satrine's head that she felt needed to be given voice. "What do you think of this Sholiar business?" Satrine asked. "I have to admit, I find the story rather . . . incredulous. But at the same time—"

"What happened at the Parliament defies credulity?"

"Rather."

Jerinne furrowed her brow. "Dayne doesn't talk much about Lacanja, what happened there. I know it devastated him, and—"

Satrine gave her a moment before prodding her. "And what?"

"He doesn't know I know this," Jerinne said. She looked like she was about to divulge something in confidence. "And I didn't really understand this until today. But Dayne . . . Dayne is apparently going to end his Candidacy without being promoted to a full Adept in the Tarian Order."

Even in Satrine's telepathically induced education, there wasn't much about the internal workings of the Tarians. She knew that they weren't truly members until they achieved the rank of Adept, but how that happened was a mystery to her. "Why is that?"

"Politics, from what I understand. The wrong people in the Parliament didn't like him. That's enough, apparently." She shook her head and chuckled ruefully. "Like we Initiates don't have enough to worry about."

They had reached 14 Beltner Street. "This is me," Satrine said, pointing to her door. "So you got me home safely."

"Should I—"

"Not necessary, Jerinne," Satrine said. "Go home. Or whatever you go to."

"The chapterhouse."

"Right. Go to your bed and sleep. Thank you."

Jerinne saluted and stepped back, but Satrine felt the girl kept watching her as she went inside.

"Hello, all," she called to the household. Warm and enticing smells greeted her as she came in.

Rian came over to the door, in the prim blouse and dress she wore when she worked at Henson's Majestic. She still looked as neat and pressed as she would have when she left in the morning. "Mother, what happened to you today?"

"Went to the Parliament, things blew up," Satrine said.

"You aren't making a joke, are you?"

"Not in the slightest. Is there dinner?"

Missus Abernand was at the table with Caribet, who wore a day dress Satrine noticed was starting to get a bit snug on her. Was she already starting to grow again? It was all far too fast. "Of course there's dinner," Missus Abernand said. "It's just amazing you're on time for it." They were putting out plates of beer-soaked sausages and onions, bread and butter.

"I'll clean up and be right out," Satrine said.

She went into her bedroom, where Logan was sitting up in the bed, muttering away as usual. When he first started being verbal again, it had been a lot of gibbering shouting. Now it was still meaningless, but at least it was relatively quiet.

"Evening," she said. She made an effort to talk to him; she had to believe there was some part of him still inside there, still capable of seeing and understanding her, even if that part couldn't reach out.

That part was in there, she knew it. And hopefully Major Grieson would make good on his end of things soon, and provide her with a telepath who could reach in and find that part of her husband. Find it, and bring him back to her.

"Today was a day, let me tell you," she said as she stripped out of her uniform. "The murders we've been following reached a whole new level. In the Parliament. An enormous murder machine on the Parliament floor. Many dead, several more injured and . . . it was too much."

She sighed, going over to the water bowl next to the bed. "We're still working out how he got all that machinery in there. I mean, he used the fact the whole place was nearly empty from the Saint Day—"

Logan suddenly perked up. "Say day! Say day sha mah! Say day sha mah!"

"Yes, that's right," she said. This had been the new change in his behavior in recent weeks—latching on to a couple of words she said and shouting a baby version of them back at her.

"Say day sha mah!" he shouted again, now very agitated. He kept saying it over and over again.

"All right," she said. She went to the cabinet and got out his medicine. "Medicine," though it was essentially *doph* and a few other unsavory things mixed together. But when he got like this, it was the best thing to calm him down. She poured out a portion in his cup, mixed with a bit of water. "Let's have it."

He fought her, as much as he could twist his head in his state. She eventually had to grab his chin and pry his mouth open, as he kept saying "Say day sha mah!" She poured the medicine down his throat and held his mouth shut to make sure he swallowed it. His arms flailed at her, pummeling her shoulders. It didn't hurt her—he didn't have much strength anymore—but she knew she would still get scratched and bruised from it. This was typical for these fits.

"I've got you, it's all right," she said.

His blows became slower and softer, and then stopped. She let go of his mouth—his eyes were only half-open now, dull and glassy. Just like he had been months ago. Medicine to put him back in that state, rather than this partial version of a man she had now.

"It's all right, my love," she said. "I'm going to find you, I swear."

She kissed his forehead and went back to washing off her face and arms. She wasn't sure if she had gotten all the blood and ash off, but it was enough to be presentable for dinner. Putting on the loose blouse she kept for wearing around the house, she went back out to the sitting room.

Missus Abernand was at the table with the girls, and a new visitor.

"Satrine," Commissioner Enbrain said, getting to his feet. "I'm sorry to intrude."

"No, of course," Satrine said. "You did—"

He pointed to the bottle of wine on the table. "I know how to be a proper guest."

"Well, join us," she said, sitting down for supper. "It's not every day I get to sit and eat with my daughters."

"I'm—I'm honored to be with you all." He sat back down. His face was ashen. Satrine knew exactly what he had gone through, and it wasn't likely to end anytime soon.

"I'm sure there's a lot to talk about," Satrine said, pouring him a glass of wine. "But for now, let's celebrate family."

"Yes," Enbrain said, holding up his glass. "To family."

———————◆———————

Minox took a tickwagon from the stationhouse up to Keller Cove and the Welling household. It wasn't his usual habit—he preferred to walk, or occasionally enjoyed the luxury of a cab. But today he was far too tired to walk, and after the intensity of the Inquiry, he felt he didn't deserve any kind of indulgence.

The sun had already gone down by the time he had reached the house, and the lamplighters had already done their work. Most of his street had gone into the quiet hush of evening. Most of the street, but the Welling house was lit and active. Much of his family—at least his generation—were out front on the stoop chattering about their day. His cousins Edard, Thomsen, and Davis—Uncle Timmothen's boys—and Colm—Aunt Beliah's youngest son—were engaged in hearing Oren—Minox's brother—tell some story of an outrageous case he had dealt with that day.

Corrie and Nyla were already there—somehow having beaten him home from Inemar Stationhouse—with Alma, Minox's youngest sister, still in her school uniform. Nyla's brother Ossen was up by the door, listening distantly to both conversations.

The absences were not notable. Ferah worked later shifts as a Yellowshield, and likely wouldn't be home for another few hours. Jace tended to stay late in Aventil; even though it wasn't his assigned shift, he demonstrated the same dedication to the Constabulary—and his lieutenant—that Minox did to his office as an inspector. And Evoy . . .

Evoy would never be out here.

"So this fellow is screaming to the saints and the sinners that his shipment needs to be let out of customs, and how dare we delay him any longer . . ."

"That was my whole day," Thomsen said. "It's been a dead calm out on the ocean, apparently, so ships that were scheduled to arrive for the past week all arrived today, and ships for today were still on the ocean, and then things are backed up from all the docks and customhouses having been closed for the Saint Day . . ."

Despite the jovial nature of this gathering, it was notable that they were all out here, and none of their parents were. It was distinctly unusual.

"Something's wrong," Minox said as he approached. "What's going on?"

Oren stopped his story, looking at Minox hesitantly. "Nothing is wrong, Minox. Do you want a beer?"

Minox hadn't drunk a beer on the front stoop with his family in—in so long he couldn't remember. And there was never a moment where Oren had offered him one.

Even if the deceit wasn't plain on Oren's face, that act of false fraternity was a sign that something was truly out of sorts.

"Is someone sick?" Minox asked. The last time he had seen anything like this—the memory came up so clear. The day they sent Grandpa Fenner to the asylum. They had all been sent out to the front stoop while the discussions were had inside.

But that was years ago. He, his cousins, and siblings had all been children then. Now only Alma, and possibly Ossen, could be considered that. Why would they all be sent outside so the parents could talk?

"Is it Evoy?" Minox asked.

"No, no," Oren said. "It's—"

"Saints rutting damn it," Corrie said. "No, Mine. It's her. She's in there."

"Her?" Despite Corrie's lack of clarity, Minox already had a strong idea what the answer would be.

"Rutting Miss Kendra Morad."

"I see," Minox said. Instinctively straightening his inspector's vest, he nodded to everyone and proceeded up the steps. He took off his belt with crossbow and handstick, hanging it in the entry foyer next to the belts and coats of the rest of his family.

Kendra Morad was in the chair in the sitting room, with Uncle Timmothen, Aunts Beliah and Emma all sitting around her. Uncle Cole—Emma's husband—paced a bit in the background, while Uncle Tal—crisp in his newly appointed Fire Brigade Chief uniform—stayed in the doorframe between the sitting room and the dining room.

Aunt Zura—Timmothen's wife—and Mother must be in the kitchen. They usually would be, in preparation for dinner, but if Mother wasn't here, then it must be to avoid Miss Morad.

"Miss Morad," Minox said as he came in. "This is highly inappropriate."

"I agree," Timmothen said. He looked like he was holding back his anger with every force of will he had.

"As I explained to your family, I am attempting to fulfill my mandate with minimal disruption."

"This is immensely disruptive," Timmothen said.

"What gives you the right?" Emma added. Her anger wasn't held back at all, but that was who Emma was. She never refrained from making it known that she was displeased.

"Missus Pyle," Miss Morad said with sharp authority. "Yelling at me won't change matters. Inspector Welling is under Inquiry. I will need to speak to many people who live in this household. I can order Writs of Summoning—Archducal Writs, mind you—and have you all escorted to Inemar Stationhouse individually with sheriffs as escort, or I can come here and manage it all at once with little muss."

"You have a very strange idea of little muss."

"I want to keep this as informal as it can be," Miss Morad said. She took a notebook and a charcoal stylus out of her bag and thumbed through the pages. "Now, I don't necessarily have to have interviews with individuals, but there are people of this household that I would require insight on that I do not see here. Jace Welling?"

"Jace doesn't always spend the night here," Timmothen said.

"I see, yes—he's with the Aventil house. I'll be visiting there in the morning anyway, so I can hold off. And Ferah and Evoy Serrick?"

"Ferah gets off her shift in an hour," Tal said sharply.

"And Evoy?"

"Ferah gets off her shift in an hour."

"Evoy won't speak to you," Emma said.

"I remind you I can compel—"

"Miss Morad," Minox said softly, holding down his own temper. "I will cooperate with you—as I have been—to the best of my ability. As will my family." He gave a glare to Emma. "But Evoy is not going to speak to you. He barely speaks to anyone in this household. Legal compulsion will not give you any additional insight from him. Please leave him be."

After a moment, she nodded.

Mother came into the room, standing behind Tal. "Supper is ready. If everyone could—"

"That can wait," Timmothen said.

"No, no," Miss Morad said. "Like I said, I want to minimize disruption. Proceed with your meal."

"Oh," Mother said. She gave a nervous glance to everyone, stopping on Minox. "Is she . . . joining us?"

Minox decided he needed to answer before Timmothen or Emma did. "That would be fine, especially if it helps expedite things."

Emma scowled as she stood. "I'll call the rest in." She walked past Minox, giving his arm an affectionate squeeze. "Whatever you need to fight this," she whispered as she went by.

"Thank you."

"Well then," Miss Morad said, getting to her feet. "If I may use your washroom."

"I'll show you," Beliah said, and led her out.

Timmothen came over to Minox. "You say the word, Minox, and I'll put in the papers to transfer you over to Keller Cove. You won't have any of this sewage there, I promise you."

"I appreciate that, Uncle," Minox said. "But this needs to be done, and resolved entirely by the book. I cannot have even the appearance of nepotistic interference hang over it."

"Even still, your captain—"

"Captain Cinellan is doing as much as he can for me while staying in the bounds of regulation. Which is the most I would expect from you in the same situation."

"As you wish," Timmothen said. "But we have your back in this, and everything else."

People took their places in the dining room as Mother and Zura laid out dinner—spiced pork with lentils and cracked wheat, lamb sausages, creamed onions, and heavy, hearty bread. The table was unusually quiet as people served themselves. At any normal dinner, there would be five different conversations; now, there were only muted requests to pass bowls.

"This meal is singular in its style," Miss Morad announced after she had eaten a few bites. She made a point of sitting opposite Minox, between Alma and Nyla—possibly the two members of the family least likely to attempt something violent if she did anything offensive—and watching him intently. "The seasoning and flavors aren't exactly what you'd find in the average South Maradaine household."

"Zura and I do all the cooking here," Mother said. "And neither of us are average."

"Yes, right," Miss Morad said, looking at them. "You both grew up in the Little East, no? In Caxa and Ashynnen? That's why this meal has Kellirac and Acserian influences, yes?"

The woman was grandstanding—letting Minox know she was completely versed in the details of every member of his family.

"Miss Morad," he said. "You said you had questions for my family, to save time. Now is the moment, if you please."

"Of course," she said, wiping her mouth with her napkin. "Now, a few months ago there was the inciting incident for this Inquiry. Inspector Welling was out of his proper senses, and as a result, a significant amount of city resources were devoted to searching for him."

"Including half this household," Timmothen said. "We turned out people, combed the streets."

"To protect him," Miss Morad said. "So that your family—or people under your command, Captain— would find him before Inspector Mirrell and his people did."

"We were all on the same rutting side," Corrie said.

"And yet, where did Inspector Mirrell find him? Here. Kept safe while the rest of you . . . put on a show?"

"It wasn't a show," Mother said. "Most of us were out of the house, either searching or with Beliah in Ironheart Ward."

"Yes, Missus Serrick," Miss Morad said, turning to Aunt Beliah. "You were injured by your nephew in the incident."

"No," Beliah said. "I was rescued by him."

"We all know that it's more complicated than that. Both you and Sergeant Corrianna Welling were present, and you both were hurt."

"We would have been a lot more rutting hurt by those Imach bastards, you know," Corrie said.

"Calm, Corrie," Minox said.

"No, it's sewage," Corrie said. "Everything she's doing is."

"Corrie, manners," Mother said.

"My rutting manners are fine," Corrie said, getting to her feet. "If they weren't, she'd be bleeding from her face." Corrie stalked off.

"I apologize, Miss Morad," Mother said. "Would you care for wine?"

"No, thank you," Miss Morad said icily. "So you would all attest that Minox, in his deranged state, found his way home on his own. None of you found him and brought him here? You would all testify that."

"They would, because it's the truth." Ferah was in

the entranceway to the dining room, in her Yellow-shield uniform, a smear of blood on her cheek. "Who is this, and what's going on?"

"Kendra Morad, special investigator for his excellency, the Archduke of Sauriya. And you must be Ferah Serrick."

"I am," Ferah said. "What is this?"

"She's here because of my Inquiry," Minox said. "Just tell her the truth."

"Oh, this," Ferah said. "I heard enough from the hall. You can leave the rest of them alone. Clearly you want to talk to me."

"Amongst others."

"Here's the story, ma'am," Ferah said, moving to stand behind Minox. "I got home from my shift, and most everyone else was out, either searching for Minox or staying with Beliah. Zura and Granny Jillian were here, as was Evoy out in the barn. Evoy fetched me because Minox was out there, in a feverish state."

"Sick? That's your contention?"

"Fevered. There's a difference, if you know medicine."

"And then you, what, cured him?"

"I broke his fever, and he recovered his senses," Ferah said. "Shortly afterward, Inspector Mirrell arrived, he and Minox spoke, and they left. If you need me to testify, swear on every saint on pain of fire, I'll be there."

"Zura, Evoy, and Jillian all saw this as well?"

"Evoy doesn't come inside," Beliah said.

"But Zura and Jillian?"

"Zura was in the basement, praying," Ferah said.

"Yes, I saw it." Grandmother Jillian came into the room on her cane. She didn't always come down for dinner, preferring to stay in her room on the top floor. Minox suspected she chose that space so she could make the excuse not to come down when she didn't want to. She was hardly as reliant on the cane as she pretended to be. "I saw Ferah save him, and I saw

Inspector Mirrell. And I see you, young lady"—she pointed her cane at Miss Morad—"coming here, being disruptive."

"I'm simply serving truth and justice."

"Justice!" Aunt Emma exploded. "That's a laugh."

"You doubt me?"

"I'm just shocked—shocked and appalled—that a woman like you has the ear of the archduke, and you waste your energy on harassing a gifted and effective member of the Constabulary instead of focusing on something that matters. Something that would better this city, this nation."

"I'm not sure of your meaning."

Nyla spoke up. "She means there's no pin on your lapel, Miss Morad." She pointed to the one on her own coat, that depicted a hand holding up two fingers.

"Oh," Miss Morad said, giving a withering look to Nyla, and then Emma. "You support the agitators."

"Suffragists," Emma said through gritted teeth, "are fighting for all women in this country." Minox now had a new assessment as to which family member would be violent toward Miss Morad.

Uncle Tal—Ferah's father—had gotten to his feet and stood behind Minox and Ferah, putting a supportive hand on Minox's shoulder. "Miss Morad, is there something more you need?"

"I've hardly begun—"

"Then perhaps you should consider Writs of Compulsion," Uncle Timmothen said.

"I see," she said, getting to her feet. "Thank you for dinner. Inspector, I will see you tomorrow."

"I'll show you the door," Timmothen said, and he led her out.

"You all right, Minox?" Ferah asked.

"As well as can be expected," he said.

"It'll take writs to get them to bring us in," Edard said.

"And they don't have the power to make us turn on you," Davis added.

Minox looked around the entire table, noting that almost all of them had the same expression of support and hope on their faces. All save Zura and Oren.

"Thank you, all," Minox said. "I appreciate the support."

"Good," Uncle Tal said, taking Miss Morad's plate away. "Let's get Ferah some dinner, shall we?"

"Not until she washes her face," Zura said. "She's a fright."

The rest of the family started eating and talking, back to a normal dinner on a normal night. Minox was about to start eating as well, when Mother took his hand—his normal one.

"No matter what," she said, squeezing his hand. "I'm always proud of everything you do. *Everything.*"

Minox smiled. That was enough for now.

        ◆━━◆━━◆

The ward floor in Riverheart was quiet. Dayne found it troubling. He felt, given the number of injured and dying being kept in the hospital ward, there should be more activity. But instead there was just the harsh, labored breathing of Niall Enbrain and the other patients.

Dayne stepped away from Niall's bed and walked up the hallway. There was a desk at the end of the hallway, where two nurses sat in a dim pool of lamplight, whispering as they wrote in notebooks.

They had come by to check on Niall earlier, and if either of them also had wanted Dayne to leave, they hadn't said anything. He knew his presence on the ward floor was probably inappropriate, but it didn't matter.

This man—Niall Enbrain—was nearly dead because Dayne had failed. Failed on so many levels. While Dayne slept just a few feet away, Sholiar had orchestrated this monstrous feat in one of the most sacred places in Druthal. And now there were at least eight dead and several deeply traumatized—more when he included the three men who had been in the boiler room—and Niall, now clinging to life.

All Dayne's fault.

"I knew I would find you here." The sultry voice of Lin Shartien, thick with her Linjari accent, startled him.

"What are you doing here?" He glanced around to see if the nurses had taken note, but clearly Lin had walked in with little trouble. Perhaps the nurses didn't care who came through at this hour. All the more reason for him to stay here. Sholiar had wanted Niall—not to mention others—dead, and Dayne's instincts told him that Sholiar wasn't done. He had a goal, a message, and that likely involved Niall Enbrain.

"Hemmit and Maresh are finishing up the printing of the morning issue—yes, your name is out of it." His expression must have spoken volumes. "They're writing about what happened, who the victims were, with some focus on Welling and Rainey taking the lead on investigation."

"I don't need more attention," Dayne said. "Especially with this."

She went over to a chair and sat down, placing a bag on the floor. "You're convinced this is about you."

"I don't think it's entirely about me," Dayne said. "But it can't be ignored as a factor."

"Because this Sholiar fellow wants to harass you, personally?"

"He did it before," Dayne said. "Is this why you came here?"

"That, and I figured you were hungry." She picked up the bag and handed it to him. He opened it to discover a newspaper-wrapped crackle fish and crisp. The sort of thing he used to eat in Lacanja out of necessity— not a favorite in Maradaine. He wasn't sure if Lin was teasing him somehow, or this was a genuine attempt to please him. He chose to accept it as a gesture from her saints rather than her sinners.

"It has been a bit," he said. "There's something else, though?"

"Welling," she said darkly. "He's a mage in the Constabulary."

"Right," Dayne said. "Thanks the saints. He was able to hold the machine still long enough to rescue the people we could."

"Hmm," she said. "You know it's not allowed, don't you?"

"Not allowed?" That didn't make any sense.

"By the Circles. None of them would allow a member to be a constable."

"That bothers you?" Dayne asked. He bit into the crackle fish—which was a bit greasy for his taste, but he wasn't going to gripe to Lin for bringing it to him. "I would hardly think you would care about that."

"Personally?" She shrugged. "The saints know that I wouldn't care about Circles if I didn't have to. If I could have dropped out of school with Hemmit and ignored the whole thing, I would have. But I didn't have the luxury."

Still eating, Dayne commented, "I didn't think your Circle exactly kept tabs on you or anything and prevented you from much of anything."

"Red Wolf Circle tends to give a fair amount of latitude, even cooperating with Intelligence," she said. "But not Constabulary. Never Constabulary."

Dayne didn't even want to pretend he understood that.

"So he doesn't have a Circle. So?"

"I'm a pretty middling mage," she said. "Beyond dazzles of light and sound—" She emphasized this by forming several colored spirals of spark and fire from her fingertips.

"Don't sell yourself short."

"I'm far more an artist who uses magic than a proper mage," she said. "But I did get pretty good at reading magic in school, feeling its taste. And I can tell you Inspector Welling tastes like nothing I've ever seen."

"That's a strange sentence," Dayne said, offering her some of the crisp in his bundle. She took it happily.

"Best I can describe. Look, he seems like a good sort, but he might be dangerous. In ways he doesn't even understand, because he never learned."

"You could teach him," Dayne said.

"Not my forte," she said. "I'm just saying, be aware, be careful. That's all."

"That's all I ever do," Dayne said.

She looked over at Niall. "You think Sholiar is going to come for him?"

"I have no idea what Sholiar is going to do," Dayne said. "I know one thing, though, and that's that Sholiar wanted this man dead, and he isn't. If Sholiar comes for him, I want to be ready, with shield and sword."

She got to her feet. "I'll not be a distraction, then," she said warmly. "Should we check on you in the morning?"

"I'll be here," Dayne said.

She winked at him and went down the hall.

Dayne would be here, until Sholiar made another move. It was coming, that much was certain. Dayne needed to be ready for it, whatever it might be.

Chapter 12

SATRINE WAS AMAZED that dinner remained pleasant. Commissioner Enbrain charmed the girls and Missus Abernand, and the conversation stayed on appropriate, engaging topics that had nothing to do with the horrors faced today. The girls laughed, and for a few moments, Satrine let herself enjoy it. A small slice of what normal was supposed to look like.

Caribet went to bed, Missus Abernand cleaned up the dishes and went up to her own apartment, and Rian went out to a friend's, supposedly to study. Satrine had suspicions about that, but decided it was well past time for her to trust Rian on her own out there. A little.

Satrine poured the last of the wine into two glasses. "So what haven't you told me, Wendt?"

He stood up. "You know I won my reelection by a hair, right?"

"I had read that," she said. The official tally had been that Enbrain had won by fewer than two hundred votes. Satrine feared that he hadn't won fairly. Major Grieson had grilled Satrine on her opinion of the commissioner, and she suspected that he and his people in Druth Intelligence had influenced the election in Enbrain's favor, based on her testimony to his character. "You think that's connected?"

"I think that I have enemies, in and out of the Constabulary. Commandant Undenway was pissed out of his eyes over losing to me. And he has a lot of north side captains loyal to him."

She needed to clarify her question. "Do you think that's connected to the atrocities that happened today? Why Niall was a victim?"

"I want to know what you think, Satrine," Enbrain said. "Saints, I can barely think straight right now, but I know one thing. Putting the Grand Inspection Unit in your stationhouse—south of the river, away from the halls of power, and with you and Welling in it—that was the smartest thing I've done all year."

"And to think you didn't want me as an inspector," Satrine said, drinking her wine.

"My mistake. Absolutely. Now that I've seen what you're capable of—especially you and Welling together—I admit that I was just wrong about that."

"I appreciate that," Satrine said. "Now if you could swing a raise?"

He nodded. "I know you're making a joke right now—"

"Not really," Satrine said. "We're barely keeping our chin above the river here."

"That isn't really something I handle, Satrine," he snapped. He paced for a moment, fuming, and then took a breath. "Sorry. I wish I could do more, but the commandants are all doing whatever they can to choke my authority, especially in terms of the budget. Undenway and his people do not like the GIU, and would love to see it fail. But I'm trying to empower Brace to do more. He—all of you—need to be something that can keep the rest of the force in check."

"All right," Satrine said. "How do you think that ties to the events in the Parliament?"

"I'm not sure, and maybe I'm just a crazy old man. I just . . . and I know this is egotistical, but it feels like this was an attack on me. The rest, I don't know, just so much theater."

Satrine sighed. The worst part about this was that he could be right. "This morning, before we even knew about the Parliament, Welling had a theory. Something of a reach, but not without grounding."

Enbrain took his seat. "What sort of theory?"

"The first seven victims were all seemingly random. No connection to each other, no obvious pattern. Different jobs, different ages, nothing in common."

"You're talking about the Gearbox Murders that led up to this. Clearly just the overture before his big performance."

"Welling thought that was also a message. The initials of the victims' names spelled out 'Enbrain failure.'"

Commissioner Enbrain just stared at her for a moment. "You can't be serious."

"I'm not saying it's necessarily significant, but . . . it is a fact. It might be a coincidence, or—"

"No, not possibly a coincidence," Enbrain said. He drank his entire glass of wine in one gulp. "Satrine, there is—" He hesitated, as if he didn't quite have the courage to say what he needed to. "There is a sickness within the Constabulary in this city."

"There's always been corruption, sir. It's just . . . that's the nature of the work."

"Not just corruption, though that's part of it. A symptom. But something greater, deeper, and I don't even know where it starts or ends."

"And this is connected . . . how?"

"Let me ask you this, Satrine. Since I became commissioner, crime in the city is down. There are fewer murders, fewer robberies. Most people consider Inemar safe to walk through, and the north side neighborhoods as well. The city is safer, and that's a fact."

"All right," she said, not sure where he was going with that.

"Despite that, people are dissatisfied with the Constabulary—"

"That will always happen, sir. No one likes us."

"But to look to Undenway and his cronies to fix it? Why them?"

"I can't answer that, sir," she said. "I don't know why—"

"I'll tell you who might be able to answer it," he said. He pointed to her bedroom. "Loren. He's one of the few people whom I trusted. I am certain he was not a part of this corruption. And that's what he was investigating the night he—he—"

"Are you serious, sir?" Why hadn't he told her about this? "What, exactly, was he looking into?"

"His investigation involved corruption in the Constabulary, tied to the City Protector's Office, the Council of Aldermen, the Archduchy Sheriffs, the King's Marshals . . . even further, maybe. But I don't have any details."

"Why?"

"We decided the best way to handle it was as a Brick File investigation."

Brick File. She had heard Loren use the term from time to time, and Welling had mentioned it a couple times as well—specifically with the Missing Children case. The idea was to keep all information on an investigation secret from one's fellows, especially one's superior—until you have the case ready for writs and arrests, when you can present the evidence in its entirety to the Protector. Mostly because if one was investigating one's fellows, it was best to keep it quiet.

"So how did that lead him to the docks?"

"I don't know. His case files vanished that same night."

Tears came fresh to Satrine's eyes. "Why . . . why didn't you tell me this before?"

"I'm not sure," he said. "I was angry. First at myself, and then at you when you pulled—when you got yourself into the Inemar house. And, frankly, I don't know who I can trust. Except, maybe, the two inspectors who live in this house."

This was too much for Satrine to hear. "I . . . I don't know what you expect me to do with this."

"Look, Satrine," he said. "I know that my Constabulary has an infection. And with this today . . . maybe that goes even further than I imagined."

"What do you mean?"

"I have enemies, working with Undenway. Maybe these enemies are also working with the Gearbox, or even the King's Marshals! Who knows where this goes?"

"You're sounding like Welling," she said.

"Maybe he's on to something."

"Sir," Satrine said. "This is . . . this is more than I can handle."

Enbrain looked like he wanted to say more, but nodded. "Of course. I'm—I shouldn't put so much on you. Not when you've already given so much." He got up and went to the door.

"We will get to the bottom of this, sir," she said. "Just . . . I need . . . I need time."

"I don't know how much we have, Satrine. But I'll give you as much as I can."

He went out. Satrine latched the door—Rian had her key—and went to her bed. She was far too tired to do anything else.

———◆◆———

After the anger from Miss Morad and her rutting sewage had drained off, Corrie came down and went out to the front stoop, and for the first time in months the night air was something resembling cool. Most of her cousins were sitting out here—save the youngest ones—surrounding a bucket with ice and bottles of Deeringhill beer at the base of the steps. Even Nyla was out here tonight, and she almost always turned in right after dinner if she didn't have a caller.

Ferah, still in the shirtsleeves of her Yellowshield uniform, pulled a beer out of the bucket and tossed it over to Corrie.

"Appreciated," Corrie said. "Blazes of a day, hmm?"

"For you, surely," Edard said. "We only got a taste of it."

"That's just a bit, Ed. Today, we saw some real chop. Like I've never seen. And then I saw the prince."

"What, like a Rose Street Prince?" Edard asked.

"No, the actual rutting Prince of Maradaine, Prince Escaraine. Right there, close to me as you are."

"Is he really that handsome?" Davis asked. She wasn't sure if he was teasing her or actually asking.

"Point is, I made a rutting fool of myself in front of him. And then there's that woman." Corrie looked back up to the house, the dinner table. Even though Miss Morad had left, Corrie could still feel her there. "Yeah, that woman—I . . . look. This morning I had to do something pretty rutting awful, thanks to her."

"You mean the 'exercise'?" Nyla asked.

"What's this?" Edard asked.

"They wanted to test Minox," Nyla said. "So they set up this whole fake hostage situation to see what he would do."

"And I had to rutting look him in the eye and pretend it was real," Corrie said. "Blazing awful."

Edard nodded, looking at the ground before he took another sip of beer. "You gotta do what you gotta sometimes."

"This whole thing of testing Minox is rutting sewage," Corrie said. "We all know he's the best damn inspector in the joint, and so what if he's a mage?"

Almost everyone cringed just a bit when she said that.

"That a problem, Thommie? Davis?" Corrie said, moving over to them. "He's a mage. We all know it, even if we never talk about it."

"Nah, course not," Davis said weakly. "Minox has a lid on it."

"Do we really know that?" Colm asked.

"What did you rutting ask?" Corrie shot back at him.

"Hey, it's a valid question," Colm said. She was half on top of him, but he was holding his ground. "It's gotta be asked. And I never shied away from talking about Evoy." He pointed over to the barn. "When he started to unravel, you all put your heads down and I was the only one who said it was a rutting problem. And now he's going mad in the barn."

"Nothing to be done about that," Edard said. "Like with Old Fenner."

"And maybe like with Minox," Colm said. "Don't tell me I'm wrong about that, Corr."

"How about I just knock your teeth?" Corrie said.

"He's not wrong," Ferah said. Corrie shot her a hot glare, but she stayed strong. "Hey, I fought for him in there, and I will anywhere, but let's talk some truth. You didn't see him that night. None of you did."

"It spooked you," Nyla said. "I remember that."

"Didn't just spook me. Spooked Evoy." She pointed to Edard, Thomsen, and Davis. "Made your mom lock herself in the basement."

"He was sick," Corrie said. "Poisoned."

"Magic poisoned. And his hand. I've seen all sorts of infections and maladies, Corrie, and I ain't ever seen anything like his hand."

"So you're all rutting traitors?" Corrie asked. "Ready to send him in the creek?"

"No one is saying that, Corrie," Nyla said. "You know damn well I'm going to fight for him."

"Unless Tricky is there."

"Don't bring her into this."

"Are you still griping on his partner?" Colm asked.

"She's a liar and a rutting fraud," Nyla said. Her voice was hot, and she almost never swore, at least not in front of Corrie.

"Who's a liar and fraud?" Jace, Corrie's youngest brother, came strolling up the walkway, late as always. Came with being part of that special Loyal squad under his lieutenant, trying in vain to clean up that neighborhood. One night in that place, and Corrie had nearly been killed. And Jace had probably been nearly killed more times than he could count.

"Tricky Rainey," Corrie said. "According to Nyla."

"And half the Constabulary," Edard said.

"Nah, she's aces," Jace said, as if that settled it. "Someone give me a beer?"

"Cadets don't get beers," Corrie said, as did most of her cousins in unison.

"Good thing I'm not a cadet, then," Jace said, opening his coat to show the brass plate on his chest. "You're looking at Patrolman Jace Welling."

A whoop of cheer came out of Corrie's throat, and everyone else joined in. She slammed her beer into her brother's hand. "Then drink that up, stick," she said.

"He's earned it," Nyla said.

Corrie didn't disagree, even if the rest of the family was trying to make her collar smoke. Minox needed them all to have him, shoulder to shoulder, and they were being a bunch of rutting bastards.

She shook the thought off. They were doing what they could, though it wasn't much. And Nyla holding her grudge with Tricky, that wasn't about Minox. Blazes, she even knew Nyla was trying to protect Minox from Tricky, in her own way. Even still, Minox needed more in his corner right now. That Kendra Morad was oily; Corrie could smell it. She was just going through the steps so she could find cause to pull Minox's vest off. Corrie wasn't going to have that, no way.

But she needed help.

Then she thought of exactly who should help her.

"All right, enough," she said, snatching the beer out of Jace's hand. "You got patrol tomorrow."

"Who doesn't?" Edard asked.

"Right, right," Corrie said. "I'm sacking out. See you all in the morning."

She went in, drinking the last drops of beer from Jace's bottle.

Nyla came in with her, following her up the stairs to their room.

"I wasn't kidding when I said I'd fight," Nyla said. "Who do you think told the captain to get Cheever in there?"

"Cheever?" Corrie shot back. She saw Nyla was hurt by that, and she softened her tone. "You're rutting right, it's something. I just wish this whole sewage wasn't happening."

"Well, it is," Nyla said. "So don't knock on my plan if you haven't got a better one."

Corrie nodded, getting ready for bed.

She had a plan now, though she wasn't sure it was a better one.

———◆—◆———

"Minox, could you come to the kitchen?"

Minox dutifully came at his mother's request, to find her and Aunt Zura cleaning the dishes and putting things away. Zura, as had been her method for the past few weeks, worked diligently without ever looking at Minox. She hadn't made eye contact or spoken directly to him since the night his hand changed.

"What can I do for you, Mother?" he asked. He was very much ready for his bed, which he hadn't come back to in three days. He knew she was annoyed about his long absence, but he hoped she understood why he did it.

She must understand. Father was the same way. Always one more ride, one more whistle call.

She picked up a tray with a covered plate and a cup of cider. "Evoy wouldn't answer the door for me or Beliah. He slammed it shut on Colm when he tried. The last time he ate was when Ferah brought him something two nights ago."

"So he answers to Ferah still?"

"Sometimes. He refused her yesterday."

"I will try. One moment."

He went to the foyer, noting the rest of the cousins drinking beers at the front stoop with Corrie. Sometimes he wondered if they were as burdened as he was by the dread sense of duty, the horrors of the city that needed to be stopped. Other times he knew they all felt it, just as he did. Beers on the stoop together was how they were able to get up each morning and go back out into the city. They had the same drive as he did, he knew. If anything, they were stronger than he was, because they had each other.

He knew he had them as well, but not in the same way. Other than Corrie and Nyla, that same trust wasn't there.

He knew that on some level, his fight was to keep himself from going into the barn just like Evoy, to the sanitarium just like Grandpa Fenner.

A fight he had to win.

Right now, that fight was with the Inquiry, with Miss Morad and Mister Olivant. Even though he welcomed it—it was fair and just for him to be questioned—he had to fight and he had to win.

And he had to resolve all the mysteries still hovering over the city.

Evoy could still help with that, even in his current state.

Minox picked up his satchel and slung it over his shoulder, and went back through the kitchen.

"What do you have there?" Mother asked.

"I've collected newssheets for him," Minox said. "Some north side ones he doesn't normally see."

"Hmm," Mother said.

"And I saw Jillian today . . ."

"Jill—how is—"

"She's well. And Corrie saw Sherien. They both seem productive and happy. In their own way. But I have some sketches from her that Evoy might like to see."

"You do?" Mother asked, her face brightening. "May I—"

He held up a hand. "I believe you would not like to see these, Mother."

Realization dawned on her face. "Are they . . ."

"Rather gruesome, yes," Minox said. He took a moment, and then said, "I could contact her, ask her if she might send you something. I think she would be amenable."

A hint of a tear formed at her eye. "I'd love to see her, you know. I would even . . . you know I'd love . . ."

"I know, Mother," he said. The rift between his uncle Terrent and the rest of the family kept the twins away, and Mother would far prefer to bury it all and have all three of them back in their lives. The real enmity was between Terrent and his sisters, Emma and Beliah, and that was not something that Minox or his mother could cure. Terrent's anger with his sisters was too deep, too raw, and it extended to everyone under this roof. As it had since Aunt Shenia died.

Mother took the tray and handed it to him. "Just see if he'll eat it."

"I will endeavor."

Minox went out to the barn with the tray. He stopped for a moment in the yard, glancing at his latest side project leaning against the barn. In Aventil, when he had to hurry to campus he had borrowed a pedalcart and dismantled its tow carriage. He had enjoyed the rush of racing through the street on it, even more than riding a horse. In the past few weeks he had taken a couple of old pedalcarts and rebuilt them as efficient two-wheeled pedalcycles. It had been a good thing to do to take his mind off the worry of the Inquiry. He was hoping he could convince Evoy to try riding it, but tonight was not the night. He had a feeling just a conversation would be hard enough when he knocked on the door.

"Piss off!"

"Evoy," Minox said. "I've got some new papers."

Minox heard some scrambling inside, and the latch bars on the doors came off. Minox thought they should make a point of keeping Evoy from actually locking himself in there, but no matter what they would do, Evoy would think of a new way to barricade himself in.

The only thing that would stop it would be the sanitarium. That was the sad truth.

Evoy opened the door, looking quite like a dead man who forgot to stop moving. His face was sallow and pale, the wild beard and hair the only thing keeping Minox from being able to see the bones under his skin.

"You're alone?" Evoy asked.

"Yes."

"And you're—well?"

"Tonight," Minox said.

"Good, good," he said. "Come in."

The scent upon entering was worse than ever. It was rank with illness. There were several plates piled in the corner, the food on them decayed to the point where they were indistinguishable from Evoy's waste, also in the same corner.

This couldn't last.

"Evoy, you have to take some care of yourself," Minox said sharply.

"Hush," Evoy said, taking the satchel from Minox's arm. "Too much to do. Too much to figure out. All the things are happening in this city, and I know—I've seen the pattern, but there's only . . . If I could get the letters, I'm sure there's letters." He opened up the satchel and pulled the papers out.

"Yes, but—"

"*The Veracity Press*!" he said with excitement. "I can tell you, I can tell you, these gents have a touch, they feel the pulse. The rest, they have hints and pieces. I think these fellows have seen it. They don't know what they've seen, but they have *seen* it."

"What, exactly?" Minox asked.

"What's happening." He pulled out the sketches. "Oh my saints and blessings. What is this?"

"That happened today."

"At the Parliament, yes? This is good, very good. Jillian?"

"You recognized?"

Evoy went over to the wall where he had affixed papers and drawings and his own scrawls. "She has a gift, there is no doubt. Never discount that girl." He started to put the sketches on the wall.

"Evoy, how—how can you even bear being in here?"

"I have to. Only wall big enough. Only place private enough."

"I mean the scent. The filth."

"I don't notice," Evoy said. He started studying the sketches of the torture engine from the Parliament. "This is quite the feat. Eighteen chairs, but more than eighteen victims. At least twenty-two, am I right? Including someone connected to Commissioner Enbrain?"

"How did you—"

"Obvious, really, from all the signs. And this is covered in signs, yes. Oh, our Gearbox Killer wants to tell his story, doesn't he?"

"Wants to?" Minox asked.

"Do you hear cheering?" Evoy wasn't paying attention to the wall anymore. "Ah, the rabble, yes."

"Our family," Minox said pointedly. If Evoy was dismissing everyone else as rabble, then there might be no bringing him back ever.

"Most likely Jace has passed his cadet examination and been promoted to patrolman. Good. Good. He's of use to us like that. He's got a sharp mind. Like you and me, yes? Don't you think?"

Minox worried about Jace sometimes. The boy was passionate and engaged in the work, fearless as he worked the streets of Aventil, loyal to the point of zeal to his Lieutenant Benvin. Minox was almost certain that Jace might get himself killed in service to the Constabulary, just as Father had. But he wasn't like Minox and Evoy, as far as Minox could tell. Jace would never lock himself away. He loved the service, he loved the streets far too much.

"I'll congratulate him shortly," Minox said. "What do you see about the killer?"

"Well, all this, it's just a ploy. Almost like a child, really."

"He wants the attention?"

"Yes, clearly. But the question is whose attention, exactly?"

"Commissioner Enbrain?"

"Too basic," Evoy said. "I mean, let's face facts, Enbrain is just a piece in a larger game. Barely won his election, and I suspect that was with some influence. Less than what should have been legal, yes. Not to mention the redistricting. Who is Panny Orshick to the folks on this side of the river? No one, but he's now the councilman for Seleth. And did the votes get taken? Can we trust the Scallic results? Who should be in the Parliament, let alone, can you trust Mister Hel—"

"Whose attention, exactly?" Minox asked, quickly interrupting Evoy before he went too far away from the point. He knew well enough that when Evoy went down a spiral, asking a question he had asked himself earlier was the key way to get him back on track.

"That is the question," Evoy said. "Maybe not attention, but audition . . ."

"Pardon?" Minox asked.

"Maybe nothing." Evoy sighed. He went over to the wall, carrying the papers. While he focused on that, Minox quietly pulled in magical energy and directed it to the rainwater barrel outside. With a gentle push, he drew the water out of the barrel—such as it was after this dry summer—and pulled it under the barn wall through the pile of refuse and sewage, washing it to the old horse sloughs and out the back. Minox was pleasantly surprised that he could feel where the water was outside through his hand, manipulating it without seeing it.

Whatever his hand had become, it was now part of his senses, and that seemed to be beyond the magical. He was still far from understanding it.

As far as he knew, no one understood it. Certainly no one he could ask.

Except there was now someone—Quentin Olivant, a mage of some note—who was downright demanding Minox's attention.

That could be something.

"Evoy," Minox said gently. Evoy barely paid him note.

"Evoy," Minox said again.

"Hmm, what? Still here?"

"I'm going now," Minox said. "I should sleep. Long day tomorrow."

"Hmm, yes," Evoy said. "There may be something here, I'll see what I can determine. Very clever, but very . . . needy. Yes. Yes. I will let you know if I have something."

"Good night," Minox said. "Eat that, would you?"

"Yes, of course," Evoy said, though it was clear he wasn't listening.

Minox left the barn and went back into the house. Indeed, there was now quite the celebration for Jace and his promotion. As much as Minox wanted to just slip upstairs, it was the least he could do to offer his brother well-earned congratulations.

Chapter 13

SATRINE AWOKE TO a sound she hadn't heard in her home for some time: girls laughing. Rian and Caribet rarely were anything but serious—or worse, squabbling—but today they were clearly engaged in something amusing. She only hoped whatever it was that lightened their mood would last.

"What's going on?" she asked as she came out to the sitting room. She was surprised to not only find breakfast on the table, but three young women sitting around it. That was one more than usual.

"Ma'am," Jerinne Fendall said, getting to her feet. Today she was in a full Tarian uniform, sword at her belt and proper shield.

"Wasn't expecting to see you again today," Satrine said. "Certainly not this early."

"My apologies—"

"Mother," Rian interrupted. "How do you know Jerinne?"

That raised Satrine's eyebrow. "How do *you* know her?"

"We met over the summer," Rian and Jerinne said in unison, followed by more laughter. Caribet rolled her eyes and went on eating her porridge. That, at least, explained what Satrine's question was going to be—namely, why Rian had let Jerinne into their house.

"At the store?" Satrine asked.

"Just so," Rian said.

Jerinne continued. "I was at Henson's Majestic on its opening day, as Lady Henson is—well she and Dayne are—" She made some awkward hand gestures, as if to indicate their entanglement with each other.

"I've got it," Satrine said.

"And I spotted Miss Rian working at the gloves, and I struck up a conversation with her."

"And oh my saints, Mother," Rian said, her face giddy. "She's a knight! Look at her! Isn't she amazing?"

"We don't use 'knight,'" Jerinne said. "And I've told you—"

"I know, just an Initiate." Rian shook her head. "Still so much more interesting than the girls in my school."

"I still don't understand why you're having breakfast here," Satrine said. She pointed accusing fingers at her daughters. "Shouldn't you be going to school shortly? And you, Miss Fendall, shouldn't you be doing, I don't know, Tarian Initiate things?"

"I should, yes," Jerinne said. "I told Madam Tyrell about you and Mister Welling and everything that happened, and she advised me that I should come to you and offer my protection to you until the situation is resolved."

Satrine scoffed, heading over to the teapot. "Why the blazes did she say that?"

"I believe her main reason was, 'someone needs to keep Dayne from annoying the blazes out of that woman.'"

Satrine laughed at that. "Even still, I'm a Constabulary inspector. I can't exactly have a Tarian Initiate hovering around." Under her breath she added, "The folks at the stationhouse give me enough grief as it is."

"Even still, given the nature of your current investigation—"

"What's the nature of it?" Rian asked.

"You don't need to know."

"Is it gruesome?" Caribet asked.

"I told you, you don't need to know."

"So it is gruesome."

"I've seen the newssheets," Rian said to her sister. "It's about—"

"Rian!" Satrine snapped. "We don't talk about that here."

"Fine," Rian said. Despite that, she whispered to Caribet. "Really gruesome."

"You have to navigate a different world than usual, ma'am," Jerinne said. "I can help with that."

"I can handle the navigation."

"Yes, but I'm familiar with the Parliament, the players . . ."

"Is this the usual sort of thing you get assigned?"

Jerinne shrugged. "It's hard to say what's usual. I mean, I'm an Initiate, I'm not actually supposed to be assigned to duties like this—"

"But yet you are?"

"It's complicated. Largely due to Dayne and Madam Tyrell and their—that doesn't matter."

"Right," Satrine said. She really didn't care about that. "But you Tarians are largely focused on things like protecting members of Parliament, or nobles—"

"Or election boxes!" Rian piped up.

"What?"

Rian was almost gleeful. "That—that was her and the huge guy."

"Dayne."

"Him. They were the ones who—"

"Fine," Satrine said. She really hadn't followed that story, or the assassinations of Parliamentarians. Anything north side or involving the national government. Her daily concerns were far more concrete, things like paying bills and keeping order on the streets. A girl like Jerinne probably had no idea what that meant. "Where'd you grow up, girl? Noble house?"

"In the servants' quarters."

That was the answer she suspected. This girl probably grew up being taught all the things that Satrine had to have crammed into her skull, and knew nothing of the sort of life Satrine had lived as a child. If she fancied herself a protector of people, she needed to—

Before she could finish that thought, there was a pounding knock on the door. A knock with an anxious urgency that Satrine immediately found familiar. She went to the door and found exactly the person she anticipated.

"Phillen," she said. "I haven't even dressed yet. I assume Inspector Welling has been at the station all night and has urgent things for me?"

Phillen Hace was standing dumbfounded with a letter in his hand. "No," he said after a bit. "Well, about Inspector Welling. He actually went home last night."

"But the letter is for me? Something urgent?"

"Yes, ma'am," Phillen said, holding it up.

"Well, don't just stand in the doorway, come in."

"Are you sure, ma'am? I wouldn't want—"

"Saints and sinners, Phillen, get in here." She pulled him in and shut the door.

"Who's this, Mama?" Rian asked, a bit of distrust in her voice.

"Phillen Hace, senior page in the Inemar Constabulary House, miss," he said with a nod of his head. "Rian and Caribet, I would gather. And—well, hello there. Don't know you."

"No," Jerinne said coolly.

"She's a Tarian Initiate," Satrine said as she went to the bedroom to change into her uniform. Somehow Loren was still asleep through all this. Not that he was connected to the world around him. But it was good that he would sleep, instead of infecting their morning with the yawps and yips he would make. "So she's none of your concern."

"Just you usually don't see anyone wandering around with a sword and shield—"

"Shield and sword," Jerinne told him like a correction.

"Pardon, miss?"

"I'm a Tarian, so it's shield and sword. It's part of the oath."

"You have an oath?" Rian sounded far more interested in the details of Jerinne's world than she had in anything else in some time.

"Of course we do. We're pledged—"

"Phillen," Satrine called out, not wanting the exact nature and history of the Tarian Order to be part of breakfast conversation, and certainly not to have those thoughts be bouncing around in Rian's head. "So what was this letter you felt should be run over to me in all haste?"

"Oh, it's—" She could hear him approach the door to the bedroom, but she knew propriety would keep him outside. "It came from the Aventil Constabulary House."

That raised a hair. Satrine pulled her slacks and blouse on and came out, vest in hand. "Lieutenant Benvin?"

"Who's Lieutenant Benvin?" Rian asked, with almost a hint of accusation.

"About the only officer in Aventil who gives a damn."

"Mother, language."

Satrine snatched the letter form Phillen. "Who brought this to you?"

"A cadet named Saitle."

That meant it was legitimate. She broke the seal and opened it up.

"What's the word?" Phillen asked.

Skimming over the letter, she said, "Looks like the lieutenant has built a solid case against one of the Aventil gangs. He could get the lot of them ironed up and sent to Quarrygate if—" There was the problem. She knew it wouldn't be that easy.

"If what?" Jerinne was asking.

"If he can get a writ to raid one of the safehouses where the evidence he needs is supposed to be. But he can't get one from his own office's protector, since his witness—" Saints, that was no good.

"What about his witness?" Phillen asked.

"She won't give her testimony on record until the gang leader is in irons." Made sense. Benvin couldn't get a writ from his stationhouse, but Hilsom could write one based on Promised Testimony, since the GIU had more investigative latitude. And she had made a promise to Lieutenant Benvin. "If we don't act soon . . ."

"It all collapses, yeah," Phillen said. His eyes hardened like steel. "What do you need, ma'am?"

She put on her inspector's vest. This was something good she could do this morning, instead of just staring at reports on the Parliament atrocity and worrying about Welling. "Let's be about it then, Phillen. Come along, Jerinne."

"Where are we—" Jerinne started.

"To Inemar, and then Aventil. Time for you to see the south side."

Giving final kisses to Rian and Caribet, she grabbed her weapons belt and headed out into the early morning with Phillen and Jerinne flanking her.

"There was something else, right, Phillen?" she asked as they were walking to the bridge.

"What do you mean?" he asked.

"I mean this wasn't the sort of thing that would compel you to run across the river to get it to me top speed. At least, you didn't know that."

"Well, I suspected—"

"Phil," she said sharply, "what's going on?"

"My mother," he said. "Her year at Quarry is about up."

"Your mother is in prison?" Jerinne asked with a sneer.

"Ease down, girl," Satrine said. "None of us pick our mothers."

"Yeah," Phillen said. "So she's getting out in a

couple days, and she named me as her pickup. And as much as I. . . ." He let it hang for a moment. "She's my mother."

"I hear you," Satrine said. They had now reached the bridge, crossing over the wide Maradaine below, filled with boats and barges. "But what do you need?" Phillen was a good kid who would make a good stick some day, and he had been there for her time and again, had her back above and beyond what should be asked of a page. This was the first time he had ever asked anything resembling a favor, and if it was something she could do, she'd damn well do it.

"I'm too young to be a pickup, but I can name a 'responsible escort' to be there with me—"

"Done," Satrine said. "You tell me where and when, and I'm there."

"Three days, around midday. It'll be at our station-house."

"All right," she said. "I've got you, Phil."

"Thank you, ma'am," he said. Glancing at the crowd building up at the end of the bridge, he said, "I'm gonna charge ahead, get that file to Protector Hilsom so he's already got it working when you get there. Good?"

"Good," Satrine said. Phillen dashed off away.

"Why is his mother in prison?" Jerinne asked.

"Because he turned her in," Satrine said. "Like I said, we don't pick our mothers. But we do pick who we stand by."

"Today I'm standing by you, Inspector."

Satrine mused for a moment. "We'll see how you feel about Aventil."

━━━◆ ◆ ◆━━━

Minox rarely came down to breakfast to find his sister and cousin waiting for him. Usually Nyla was up before dawn and out of the house before anyone else, and Corrie was dragging her heels any given morning, still getting her uniform on when he left for the station.

But this morning they were both ready—sitting with Mother in the kitchen—when he came down.

"This was not necessary," he told them as soon as he saw them. It was clear this was some form of solidarity, or an attempt to assist him where no help was needed or wanted.

"What wasn't?" Mother asked, handing him a cup of tea.

"This, these two," Minox said. "I do not need to be coddled."

"We're hardly coddling you," Nyla said. "I just decided to come in at the same time as you for once."

"And she woke me rutting up," Corrie said.

"I do not believe this obvious dissembling," Minox said. He drank the tea, which was too hot. Almost on instinct, he blew on it with a hint of chilling magic. Making things cold had gotten easier since the night his hand changed.

"I don't care what you believe," Nyla said.

"I don't either," Corrie said. "But I'll tell you blazing what. No one, certainly not that blasted Kendra Morad, is going to take you down without a fight from me."

"You will do no violence to Miss Morad," Minox said.

"That's not what I mean, and you know it."

"I'm not entirely clear on any of your intentions," Minox said.

Mother handed him his breakfast—three flatbread wraps of sausage and egg. "The girls are just there for you, Minox," she said. "Just appreciate it."

"We need to get moving, if you're coming with me," Minox said. "The tickwagon will be here shortly."

The ride to the stationhouse was subdued, as the other passengers were all buried in their newssheets, none of them making eye contact with Minox or the rest. The story was on the Parliament, and from what Minox could see without ripping a newssheet out of someone's hands, the article was filled with salacious details but low on facts.

"That is where my head needs to be at, Corrie," he whispered to her while pointing to the sheet. "Sholiar needs to be put away."

"Who is Sholiar?" Corrie asked.

"The Gearbox—" He stopped himself. "It's the possible alias of someone who might be the Gearbox Killer. Unfortunately the name is largely meaningless."

"Name's something to go on," she said.

They reached the stationhouse to find Joshea Brondar pacing in front of the building, looking like he was ready to start throwing punches.

"Morning, Joshea," Nyla said as she disembarked from the tickwagon. "Don't usually see you out here in the morning."

"Good morning, Nyla," he said, speaking very gently and deliberately. He was definitely making an effort to keep his temper, at least in front of Nyla. "There's been some news this morning."

"Go on in, Nyla," Minox said. "I'll catch up."

Nyla went inside, but Corrie planted her feet right next to them.

"Corrie, if you could—"

"No, I rutting can't," Corrie said. "We all can go inside if you want. But I have some blasted words for you, Josh, and you will rutting well hear me. And neither of you are going to keep any secrets from me. Not when all this rutting business is going down."

Joshea ground his teeth.

"Joshea," Minox said, "what's wrong?"

Joshea produced a piece of paper from his pocket. "This is wrong!" He passed it to Minox. It was a Writ of Compulsion for Minox's hearing.

"Who gave this—how did you—" Minox stammered.

"It was delivered to the butcher shop!" Joshea shouted. "Right there, in front of my father, two inspectors come in and shoved this paper at me. Saying I have to testify today, that I'm compelled by law to?"

"Yes, that's rutting what it is," Corrie said, taking

the sheet. "How many of these wound up at the house last night?"

"Probably very few," Minox said. "Despite her bluster, I do not think Miss Morad is interested in harassing our family."

"But mine?" Joshea asked.

"I'm so sorry," Minox said. "Does the writ give grounds?"

"Material witness in kcy moments of the incident of the fifteenth of Erescan. That's the day you—"

"I know," Minox said. "It's not untrue. You are a material witness."

"How am I supposed to explain that?" Joshea asked. His voice dropped to a hiss. "Does this Miss Morad know about me?"

"I don't think so," Minox said. But Miss Morad had been absurdly prescient and aware of fine details in Minox's life. If anyone could figure out Joshea's special relationship to Minox, it would be her.

"Rutting blazes," Corrie said. "Folks knew he was at the hospital." She grabbed both of them by the sleeve and pulled them into the alley. Out of the corner of his eye, Minox noted that Nyla had come back outside. Like she was standing lookout.

"That is likely what it is about," Minox said. "The fact that you helped at the hospital is well known."

"And the rest?"

"Do not lie on my account, no matter what," Minox said.

"Minox!" Corrie snapped. "You sure you want—"

"Let me be clear," he told them both. "I want to clear this Inquiry and return to duty with the full confidence of the Constabulary behind me. I want to do that without causing any difficulty to our family. Or yours, Joshea."

"If this goes public, if I get—" Minox had never seen such fear in Joshea's eyes. "My father cannot know what . . . that I can . . ."

"It never needs to come up," Minox said. "This is about me. Just say what happened to me. What I did."

"Minox," Joshea said quietly. "That could be damning."

"What did he do?" Corrie asked in a horrified whisper. "Look, you were rutting there, Josh. I don't remember much of anything of what happened in the hospital after he went—you unleashed that thunderstorm."

"Is that what it was?" Minox asked. He had been in such an altered state, he really had no sense of what he did. Or how.

"It's apt," Joshea said.

"All right, all blasted right," Corrie said. "We have to make sure our stories are straight about that day."

"There is no 'straight,' Corrie," Minox said. "I know this enrages you, but the only thing that matters is the truth. As much as I would despise it, if the truth means I am considered unfit, then that is what must be."

"No," Corrie said. "If it was me—rutting blazes, it was me in that hospital room with a knife at my throat— you wouldn't stop fighting."

"I never said not to fight," Minox said. He needed to make this clear. "But do so within the bounds of the truth."

"All right, then," Corrie said, turning to Joshea. "So rutting tell me first. What happened in that room? What happened after?"

"Right," Joshea said. "So Minox let loose that lightning, and the place filled with black clouds around him. The lightning mostly went for the Imachans, but it was everywhere. I . . . shielded myself."

"Magically?" Corrie almost spat the word out.

"Yeah. And I did my best to protect you and Beliah. But I—I really didn't know what I was doing properly. I tried to reach out to Minox, but he was gone. And then I saw it—that hole in the floor."

"I remember that," Corrie said.

"He somehow blasted it straight down to the sewer tunnels. I saw that he had dropped down with it, but he didn't just fall. It was like those black clouds held him up."

"So you jumped down after me?" Minox asked,

"Yeah," Joshea said. "Look, in that moment, everyone else was down. I knew—I saw—that the hostage situation was over. The rest of the constables could swarm in and grab them. I had to make a decision to save you. Even from yourself."

"So you jumped down?" Minox reiterated.

"Essentially," Joshea said. He was already massaging his testimony, as he likely used his own magic to slow his descent. But that was not a relevant detail.

"So you reached me, and—"

"And you were thrashing down the tunnel like the sinners were chasing you. We must have run, I don't know, three blocks before you collapsed and I caught you. And you mumbled to take you to the Tsouljans."

"Why the rutting Tsouljans?" Corrie asked.

"We had—" Minox corrected himself. "I had already engaged with the Tsouljan mystic in further educating myself in magic, in their methods. I must have assumed that whatever was happening to me, they could help."

"When you were a little clearer, you said as much," Joshea said. "So I got you there, using your coat and credentials to get past the patrolmen at the gate, and the Tsouljans tried to—do something to you."

"Something?" Corrie said. "Blazes, Josh, you got to be more specific."

"Something magic, I don't know. I don't even know if they were really trying to help you. But you freaked out at their treatment and ran out of the place. I tried to follow, but those red-haired guards of theirs kept me in the compound until . . . well, until you found me there, Corrie."

Nyla came over to the alley mouth. "Whatever you all are going on about, you better wrap it up. Rainey is coming up the avenue with a girl in a Tarian uniform, and that man Olivant is coming the other way."

Olivant. That could be a problem. "Joshea, did you take any *rijetzh* today?"

"Every day," Joshea said.

"There is a mage on the panel, and he might—be wary."

"Saints Veran and Soran," Joshea muttered. "I have some on me. I'll take a second dose, just to be certain."

"Stay here briefly, while we go inside," Minox said. "It's probably best if Olivant does not see us emerge together."

"Right," Joshea said.

Minox went back out into the street, Corrie and Nyla flanking him. Inspector Rainey came over to him, with Jerinne Fendall at her side.

"Morning, Welling. Wellings," she said. "Miss Pyle."

"Inspector," Nyla said, her voice with just a hint of bile.

"I assume you have further hearings now? Miss Morad didn't simply rule in your favor overnight?"

"No," Minox said.

"She rutting showed up at the house," Corrie said.

"That is troubling," Rainey said. "Should we go in? I need to engage Mister Hilsom for some writs."

That intrigued Minox, leading the way inside. "You have a revelation in the case?"

"In a case," Rainey said, holding up a letter. "Word from Lieutenant Benvin."

"Ah," Minox said. One of her unresolved cases. As much as he wanted her focused on the Gearbox and the Parliament, he couldn't begrudge her settling old business when new information came to light.

"He's got a rutting break?" Corrie asked. "That's trouble."

"Why?" Rainey asked. They reached the inspectors' floor, Nyla heading off to her duties immediately. She clearly did not want to be standing near Inspector Rainey any longer than strictly necessary.

Corrie tapped at her temple. "Seems a little odd, Benvin sends you blazing word he's got a thing, right when Jace makes patrolman? Probably that other kid too. What's his name?"

"Saitle," Minox said.

"I doubt he sat on this," Rainey said. "Even to get his squad up to full strength."

"Who's Jace?"

Minox realized that Jerinne Fendall was still with them, in her full regalia of Tarian uniform, with the blue-and-white buttoned coat with the shield emblem on the chest, as well as the shield on her back, sword at her hip. She looked like a drawing from a history book.

"He's our brother, 'bout your age," Corrie said. "He's newly minted patrol in Aventil."

"Miss Fendall wants to stick in my shadow," Rainey said, and it was hard to tell if she was amused or annoyed by this. Perhaps a bit of both, though Minox often found his partner's sense of humor inscrutable.

"And this morning you will be in mine, Inspector." Miss Morad came up with Mister Olivant and Mister Hilsom. "Where is your counsel?"

"I'm certain Mister Cheever will be here shortly," Minox said. "I've heard you've already been busy today." Inspectors Mirrell and Kellman came up the back stairs, pages in hand. That settled the one mystery. "She had you two delivering the writs?"

"We do what we have to," Mirrell said. "That's all this has been." He looked proud of himself, though Kellman seemed a bit ashamed.

"Shall we proceed?" Miss Morad asked. "I only have you for the morning, after all." She went to the back stairs, Mister Olivant right behind her.

"You, stay," Rainey said to Hilsom. "I need you right now."

"You shouldn't speak to me in such a tone, Inspector."

"Or you won't do your job?" she fired back. She clapped Minox on the shoulder—a rare physical display of solidarity from her. "Paperwork and arrests. Easy walk. I'll see you at midday."

Minox headed to the back stairs, and noticed for a moment his sister looked hesitant. He knew her well enough to know why.

"Corrie," he said, "surely Inspector Rainey will need a Special Response Squad in Aventil."

"I don't rutting need to—"

"Please," Minox said. "After all, someone ought to see Jace on his first day with brass on."

Corrie gave him a bright smile. "Don't let the bastards get you."

"Never."

He followed after Miss Morad, hoping he could muster as much confidence for today's Inquiry as he had just pretended to have.

Chapter 14

THE PATH TO Aventil Stationhouse took Satrine and her company along Lower Bridge, the street that defined the border between Aventil and the far calmer Colton neighborhood—a route that passed some of the corners where the Toothless Dogs and the Kemper Street Kickers were having their war.

Some of the buildings were just on fire. Not engulfed in flame, but slowly burning, wisps of smoke curling off their rooftops. Windows broken, doors ripped off their hinges. Shoeless kids running in the middle of the cobblestones—there were almost no carriages or horses or even mulecarts here. Shops looked deserted. A pair of old men sat on a stoop, one of them with an active head wound.

"Saints above," Jerinne said as they passed by. "What is happening here?"

"You don't cross the river much, do you, girl?" Corrie asked. She was in riot gear, with three of the squad trainees. The captain gave her only four patrolmen. He wasn't exactly cooperative, but his mind was on Minox. He didn't even give them horses, making them walk to Aventil. Satrine understood, since her mind was on Minox as well. But taking care of old business in Aventil was a good distraction.

Protector Hilsom hadn't been too cooperative

either, grousing about writing Writs of Entry and Search off Promised Testimony. He had admitted that Lieutenant Benvin had put together a good case, cut a deal with someone connected to the Kickers to testify against the gang, and knew that they had stolen goods in a series of apartments on Kemper Street. Most protectors couldn't write a writ off Promised Testimony, but Hilsom, as the protector for the GIU, had more latitude in his authority, though he'd have to explain himself to the court.

But all the Aventil sticks had to do now was kick down doors and make arrests, since Satrine was bringing the writ.

"It's a territory war between two of the Aventil gangs," Satrine said. "The Toothless Dogs on the west, and the Kickers on the east. After we help Benvin's squad with arrests, the Kickers will be done. Which means this bit of war will be over."

"How can they have a war over a few run-down blocks of street?"

"That's what there is in Aventil," Satrine said. "Nothing but pubs and pride."

"There's, what, six gangs in this rutting neighborhood?" Corrie asked.

"Seven," said Bankly, one of her patrolmen.

"Were seven, then six, now seven again," said Ebber, another patrolman.

"You keep track of that?" Corrie asked.

"Ebber lives here," Jints—the third patrolman—said.

"That going to be a problem, Ebber?" Satrine asked. If he lived here, then he might be tied indirectly to one of the gangs.

"We're hitting the Kickers, supposedly?" he asked. "Then, no. I got—" He thought for a moment, then shrugged. "I got some kin in the Orphans. Nothing too close, but kin nonetheless."

"Just follow orders."

Jerinne shook her head, confused. "These Aventil gangs, are they really that organized? Formal?"

"It's a strange neighborhood," Satrine said. "Other neighborhoods, east and north of here, their underworld is usually all controlled by one or two bosses. Or you go out farther west, in Seleth or Carroll Creek, there's just a mess of crews, hardly any organization at all. Aventil hits an odd balance—organization with no single overboss."

"And you all—I mean the Constabulary—you don't just arrest them all?"

"It's not that easy," Satrine said. They had reached the stationhouse. Aventil Stationhouse was a run-down corner whitestone, nothing like the old fortress that the Inemar house had been constructed from. Aventil was a younger neighborhood than Inemar, but all the neighborhoods were younger than Inemar. There were probably parts of Inemar that were old when Oscana started the Rebellion against the Kieran Empire twelve centuries ago.

Satrine didn't remember all the details of the Aventil gang territories—not that it mattered, since the streets they controlled changed every day—but the stationhouse was near where the Toothless Dogs and Hallaran's Boys clashed. Neither gang tried anything right next to the stationhouse, so it was more of a no man's land. Or Constabulary land, at the very least.

"Come on," she told Jerinne. "Lieutenant Benvin is probably waiting."

Satrine waved her way past the front desk clerk, going up to Benvin's squad room. It would probably irritate half the sticks in this house, but given how lazy or useless any of the folks outside of Benvin's squad were, Satrine couldn't care less.

Lieutenant Benvin was in his squad room, going over a report with his people: Sergeant Tripper, Wheth, Pollit, Saitle, and the newly badged Jace Welling.

"Left, she's here," Jace said.

"Lieutenant," Satrine said. "I've brought you papers and muscle."

"And I need both," Lieutenant Benvin said, turning toward her. "Right now we—saints, is she a Tarian?"

"Yes," Satrine said.

"Initiate," Jerinne said. "Inspector Rainey said I should see this part of the city."

Jace and Saitle almost fell over each other approaching Jerinne.

"Hi, Jace. Jace Welling."

"Saitle. Hesh Saitle."

"Fire it down, boys," Corrie said. "She could probably knock both of you on your ass without even trying."

Lieutenant Benvin came over and shook Satrine's hand. "I appreciate this, Inspector. Especially after—"

"No need," Satrine said. "We're all on the same side."

"Yeah, supposedly," Benvin said. "Here's the deal. We have the Kemper Street Kickers ready to wrap up. Names of the bosses, places they use as flops and holeups, and Miss Linnia over there ready to give us the full testimony we need to tie a bow on it all."

Satrine noticed Miss Linnia—she looked like any street rat girl would look after twenty years hustling for a gang. Drawn and worn out. Linnia was probably ten years younger than Satrine, but looked older.

"So what's the problem?"

"Problem is, someone in this house must be taking grift from the Kickers, because they got word and took steps. Now we've got nothing."

"Nothing?" Satrine said. "I've got writs a plenty. Let's clap some iron and bring it in."

"Nuh-uh," Linnia said.

"Why nuh-uh?"

"Because they got my boy, stick," Linnia said. "They'll carve a new smile on his neck if I give testimony now."

Now it clicked. She wouldn't talk unless the boy was safe, and the writs were based on her Promised Testimony. Just by implying she might not testify, their enforceability would fall apart, and the whole case would crumble.

"So you're saying we have a rescue mission," Jerinne said.

All eyes went to her.

"I mean, that's what we do, right? Get the boy, then when he's safe, she can testify and it's fine, right?"

Linnia looked about at the constables surrounding her, and then her eyes locked onto Satrine. "He's gotta be safe, hear? Then I'll do whatever. But you gotta get him, and Musky isn't going to let him go. He'll probably kill him if there's even trouble."

"Musky, that's one of the bosses on our writs, right?" Pollit asked. He went over to the slateboards. "We've got him making a den in this tenement on Firebolt and Hedge."

"Up on the fourth floor," Linnia said.

"Well then," Satrine said. "It's real simple. I'm an inspector in the GIU with a writ. I'll go in there, get that boy out. And then we lock the rest down."

"Just walk in there?" Linnia asked. "You think it's going to be that easy?"

"Oh, no," Satrine said. "But it's what I'm going to do."

———•———

"There are several things that should be covered by this Inquiry," Miss Morad said from her place at the table. Minox noted an even greater formality to today's setting, as if yesterday was just a preliminary session to whet Miss Morad's appetite for the proper feast. Now there was no gallery hiding behind the glass. At the table with her were Captain Cinellan, Protector Hilsom, and Quentin Olivant. Two clerks—one from the stationhouse and one from the Protector's

Office—took notes on the proceedings. Inspector Mirrell was sitting off to one side, likely to be called to give testimony when Miss Morad was ready for him.

Inspector Kellman was in the hallway. He had been given the task of keeping the other potential witnesses waiting for when they were to be called. Minox wondered why that hadn't been assigned to a patrolman or sergeant. He would have thought that Iorrett would have been eager for such a duty. Minox mostly wondered what was being done about Mirrell and Kellman's cases while this Inquiry was going on. He couldn't believe that this would take priority over investigating the missing children.

Mister Cheever came in, this time with his valise and papers in good order. Possibly because Nyla was right with him, carrying a handful of notebooks and writing supplies.

"I see you've begun," Cheever said as he took his seat next to Minox.

"Had you been more punctual, you would have been here for the start," Miss Morad said.

"I do apologize," he said. "I was arranging for a clerk of my own to transcribe these proceedings."

"Miss Pyle, is that what you're doing?" Captain Cinellan asked.

"It's what Mister Cheever needs," Nyla said. "The Justice Advocate Office couldn't spare anyone for him."

"Then who's on the desk on the inspectors' floor?"

"It's covered," she said. "If you feel you need to dock me the day's wages, Captain, I understand."

Captain Cinellan sputtered. "That isn't—Miss Pyle, you under—I didn't—"

"Can we continue, Captain?" Miss Morad asked.

"Please," Cinellan said.

"Inspector Henfir Mirrell, please rise."

Mirrell stood, smoothing his inspector's vest as he rose.

"Are you ready to give testimony to the events that caused you to insist on initiating this Inquiry?"

"I am, ma'am," Mirrell said. On her nod, he started. "On the morning of the fifteenth of Erescan, I was called to Ironheart Ward in response to a hostage incident involving people who had been brought in from the riot in the Little East the night before. Specifically Assan Jabiudal and his associates. They had taken control of one of the ward rooms, holding thirteen patients and members of the ward staff."

"Taken control how?"

"I do not have firsthand knowledge of the details, but I understand they had knives and surgical instruments as improvised weapons. There were four people holding the room, so they specifically held the nurses at knifepoint to keep the others at bay."

"And that's important, why?"

"Because some of the patients were also constables, including then patrolwoman Corrie Welling."

"The sister of Inspector Welling?"

"Yes, that's right."

"A question," Mister Cheever said. "You said you did not have firsthand knowledge."

"I have the reports of the other officers who were on site before my arrival. The reports are largely in agreement about the events."

"Are you disputing his testimony of these events, Mister Cheever?" Miss Morad asked.

"Establishing the particulars, Miss Morad. And performing my function. I will challenge his testimony as I see fit. Proceed."

Mirrell looked annoyed. "When I arrived, Inspector Welling had already taken authority over the event. He was in the midst of capitulating to one of the demands when the incident in question occurred."

"Objection," Cheever said. "'Capitulating' is a loaded word choice."

"It's the word I choose," Mirrell said.

"Describe the incident," Miss Morad said. "In your own words."

Minox recognized that unnecessary addition was solely meant to irritate Mister Cheever. From the look on Miss Morad's face, she was quite amused by that.

"When I arrived, Jin—Inspector Welling was in the room with the hostages, the hostage takers, and Mister Brondar."

"Who is Mister Brondar?"

"He's a civilian," Mirrell said. "I'm not sure why he was there."

"So you admit to not being versed in the particulars of the situation?" Mister Cheever asked.

"I'm saying I don't understand why Welling chose to involve him," Mirrell said.

"Ah!" Cheever said, taking one of the files out of his portfolio. "That's very interesting. You admit that your other testimony is based on the reports of the officers on scene, and not your own firsthand knowledge. By saying you don't know, you invalidate that claim!"

"How so?" This came from Hilsom.

"Because I have here the reports from patrolmen Caggs, Unster, and Mascien. They make clear in their reports that Mister Brondar—a retired soldier—volunteered to assist so none of the hospital staff would have to be put in harm's way."

"What's your damn point?" Mirrell asked.

"My point," Mister Cheever said, "is that Inspector Mirrell's testimony is based entirely on secondhand appraisal of reports that he hasn't even properly absorbed, or is intentionally misrepresenting. We would never accept such testimony in the court of law, and we should maintain the same standard here."

Hilsom nodded. "I'm inclined to agree, Miss Morad."

"Constrain your testimony to the things you saw, Inspector," Miss Morad said.

"Well, I saw a thunderstorm explode in the room," Mirrell said. "Welling was the apparent source of it.

He filled the room with dark clouds, lightning. They're the only words I have to describe it."

"And you're certain this came from Inspector Welling?" This was Mister Olivant.

"Look, I'm just a stick who's worked hard and made inspector," Mirrell said. "I don't know about magic or how it works, save that I know Welling here has it. I know he blasted that room with lightning, knocking out just about everyone in it, and then burned a hole in the floor and ran off through it."

"Which ended the incident," Cheever said. "The hostages were all safe, the malefactors arrested, yes? Thanks to Inspector Welling."

Mirrell shook his head. "As far as I saw, he caused a mess of destruction and ran away from it, not bothering to check if the situation was resolved. Which is, frankly, just as much menace as Jabiudal and his people were."

"What did you do, then?" Miss Morad asked.

"I called an All-Eyes to find Inspector Welling and we swept through the neighborhood to find him."

"And where did you find him?" Miss Morad continued.

"At his home."

"And his demeanor there?"

"Calm, attentive. He insisted we meet with Inspector Rainey to solve the murder of the Fuergan dignitary."

"And did he?" Cheever asked.

"Mister Cheever!" Miss Morad said. "I have given you a fair amount of latitude, but this is my hearing, and it goes by the rules I set, which are not the same as a court of law."

Cheever pulled a small book out of his case. "You do not set the rules of this hearing; there is a set procedure which echoes that of a trial. And in such a case it is my sworn duty to root out any corruption and dishonesty that would send the citizen I represent to an unfair ruling. Answer the question, Inspector!"

Mirrell hesitated. "Between him and Inspector Rainey, they got a confession and made an arrest."

"Let me get something clear," Cheever said. "You didn't see Inspector Welling do anything, but you believe his magical ability ended the conflict with Jabiudal, and then he needed to recover, and you found him home and in his full senses. As a result, you turned out a massive manhunt, drawing resources and manpower away from a massive crisis in the Little East."

"Mister Cheever, I would remind you—" Miss Morad started.

"No, Miss Morad, no," Cheever said, getting to his feet. "The entire basis of this Inquiry is the complaint filed by Inspector Mirrell, who, in my opinion, was acting in a manner unfit for an inspector. If an inspector brought an investigation to arrest and trial based on such spurious evidence, the case would be thrown out of court, and the inspector would be brought up on charges! It is only due to Inspector Welling's intense levels of polite calm that an Inquiry wasn't called on Mirrell. I think he deserves it."

"This Inquiry—"

"You are missing a critical point here, Mister Cheever," Olivant said, interrupting Miss Morad. "It's fundamentally about his fitness to serve because he's an untrained, unverified, Uncircled mage."

"And that is not in dispute," Miss Morad said coldly. "I'd like to excuse Inspector Mirrell and call the next witness, Mister Joshea Brondar."

Mirrell opened the door and called out Joshea's name, and immediately Minox felt a bristle of magical energy from the hallway. Almost like a sharp spike that ran up his arm from his left hand.

Olivant perked up. He felt something as well. If Joshea came in, Olivant would sense him, and he'd be exposed. It would ruin him.

"Wait," Minox said. "If this is entirely about my magery, then further testimony is pointless. I confess that I am an Uncircled mage. Does that make me unfit to be a inspector? I say it doesn't,"

"That's hardly for you to say, Inspector," Miss Morad said. "We must—"

"I will tell you in detail what happened to me that night," Minox said.

"Inspector, you don't have to—" Cheever said.

"It is all right, Mister Cheever. Your aid has been most welcome. But there is no need for further witness statement. I will give you the best account I can of what happened, and accept your judgment, on one condition."

"Which is?"

Minox took off his glove and held up his hand, black and glassy and shining with magical energy. "If Mister Olivant can explain what my hand is, and how it became this way."

———— ◆■◆ ————

Satrine's shirt was coated with sweat, in part from the sheer heat of the day combined with her heavy riot coat, and in part from the nerves of what she was doing. It was a terrible, horrible plan, but it was the only one she had.

That wasn't entirely true. She could have just left Aventil, decided this wasn't her problem. But she couldn't live with that. She had earned a small sliver of trust from Lieutenant Benvin, who just wanted to make Aventil a better, safer neighborhood. He was exactly the sort of constable the city needed: decent, uncorrupted, and willing to fight the good fight.

If he was doing that, the least she could do was match it, prove to him, to herself, and everyone else in Maradaine that there were sticks ready to do the right thing. What it meant to serve the city, serve the people.

This is what Loren must have felt, even as he lost the fight that took him from her.

Whatever happened, she was going to keep fighting.

In her walk to the Kemper Street Kicker den, she noticed plenty of Kickers taking note of her, trailing her along as she went up to the tenement. None of them made a move, but they all kept her under close watch. They weren't nervous. Why should they be? As far as they knew, she was alone—single Constabulary inspector, walking through Kicker territory without anyone backing her up. Why should that worry them?

The tenement was crumbling, covered with Kicker inkjobs, and half the windows were broken. In a couple of those windows, up on the fourth floor, she spotted archers taking aim. Bows had become popular again in this neighborhood, it seemed. A lasting influence of the Thorn, possibly.

Posturing on their part. Even if they thought she was alone, there was no way they would kill an inspector in broad daylight. They would have to know a stick full of arrows in the middle of the street would bring the full weight of the Aventil Constabulary on their skulls. The Aventil house might be lazy and half corrupt, but plenty of them liked an excuse for a brawl.

Also, Satrine wasn't alone. Jace and Saitle were in position near the entrance, dressed as cart boys hawking salteds with mustard. Saints, Jace had spent a fair amount of time coming up with his character—he couldn't just pretend to be a food hawker, he had to have a story about a family business and a sick mother. Saitle tried to do the same, but his creativity didn't match his energy. It was fun to see them just love their work, enjoying being constable patrolmen in disguise as something else.

Benvin, Wheth, Tripper, and Pollit couldn't play the same game—all of them were too known on the streets to play any sort of disguise. They were paired off and walking the neighborhood a couple blocks away. Far enough that the spotters in the windows wouldn't notice them, or realize which building they were targeting. Close enough to hear whistles and come running.

Corrie and her boys were on horses, slowly working

their way up Lower Bridge, ready to thunder in when the whistles came.

But Satrine was alone when she went into the building. She had her whistle palmed in her left hand, but if things turned bad, she'd barely get a chance to blow it. Hopefully her backup would get there in time to help her, should she need it.

All that backup was official and in Constabulary uniform—save Jace and Saitle. But there was also Jerinne. Satrine wanted her to hang back with Corrie, or at least with Benvin. Jerinne wanted to go in with Satrine, but Satrine wasn't about to allow that. Last thing she needed was a girl with shield and sword coming in with her. This had to look official but friendly, and Jerinne would be neither. So she went and had a cider at the dive across the street from the tenement—surely a Kicker hangout—looking as subtle as a runaway cart.

The tenement had a wide lobby, where the tile floor had cracked and broken to reveal wide patches of dirt. In some places, sickly weeds were even growing. At least a dozen boys and girls—Kickers all by the kerchief tied around their ankles—hung about on the steps and rotting benches.

"What's what?" one of them asked, hopping to his feet as Satrine entered. His kerchief was blue, as opposed to everyone else's gray, so he was a captain. "What are you walking in our place of sanctum, stick?"

"Place of sanctum?" Satrine knocked back. "You've got an awfully high opinion of this sewage hole."

"Maybe so, but it's our sewage hole. You're not welcome here."

"Doesn't matter if I'm welcome here. Got to talk to a man named Musky."

"Oh, you got to," he said. "Well, that's different."

"Saints Ilmer and Soran," one of the other Kickers said. "She ain't just a stick, she's a specs!"

"Ain't no lady specs," one of the girls said. She had a nasty scar on the side of her face, nearly taking her eye out.

"Are so," Satrine said. "Right in front of you."

"No chance," the girl said. "Ain't allowed, I'm sure."

The captain shoved his way over to Satrine. "What ain't allowed is her coming in here looking to make a ruckus on us."

"Make a ruckus?" Satrine asked. "I've got some questions for someone named Musky. That one of you?"

"What do you want to talk to Musky for?" the captain asked.

"That you?" she asked. "If not, it's not your business."

"People who want to talk to Musky is my business, stick."

"Look," Satrine said, pulling out one of the writs. "I've got a Writ of Seizure here that says I can come in here with a whole passel of patrolmen, haul every last one of you away in irons, and put everything that isn't nailed down in lockaway. But that's gonna be a mess. I ask Musky some questions, and maybe this can all just slip away nice and easy."

The writ said nothing of the sort—it wasn't a Writ of Seizure, and a Writ of Seizure didn't even mean what she said—but she was banking on these kids not being able to read more than a handful of words. All they had to do was get out of her way and let her go up the stairs. She already knew from Linnia that Musky hung out in a flop on the fourth floor, and he was likely keeping her son there with him. Yetter, that was the boy's name.

"Nice and easy, we can make things, skirt," the captain said. He moved a bit closer to her, putting his hand on the handle of her handstick. "You wanna go up, you leave your weapons behind."

"No," Satrine said. "That's not how it's going to work."

"Oh?" He moved in a bit closer, his lips curling in a grotesque way as he came deeper into her space. He stroked her handstick. "And how is it gonna work?"

"You take a step away, and I go up those stairs," she

said. "And you go to bed tonight grateful that your arm isn't broken."

His hand went up to her face. "Now that isn't easy—"

Satrine grabbed his forefingers and twisted. He screamed and dropped to his knees.

"See?" she said. "Just fingers."

"You crazy slan! Why did you—"

She turned to the rest of the group in the lobby, putting as much fire in her eyes as she could. Saints knew this was just a bluff. "Anyone else need something broken? Or am I going to go up there now?"

The captain skittered away, cradling his hand to his chest. "Saints, lady, you didn't have to—"

"I don't need any trouble," she said. She pointed to the girl with the facial scar, who had been impressed with her being an inspector. "You, come on. Bring me up to Musky."

"I ain't supposed to—"

"Well, today you are. Come on." Satrine made for the stairs, and Face Scar came with her and led the way up the three flights to the flop. She gave a few hisses and whistles to other folks as they went up. Warnings: there's a stick in the building. Satrine could hear a bit of scurrying behind the doors as they went up.

The girl knocked on the flop door on the top floor.

"What's what?" someone shouted.

"There's a stick inspector lady here to talk to Musky."

The door opened, and an unkempt man peered at Face Scar.

"Inspector lady? The blazes?" He then noticed Satrine. "Saints, she is the blazes!"

"And she needs to talk to Musky," Satrine said. "Step aside."

"Or what?"

"Do we really have to press that?" Satrine asked. "I've got writs, I've got questions. This can be smooth as butter if you let it be."

"Let the stick in," someone called from inside. "I want to know what she wants."

Unkempt stepped back, letting her into the flop. Face Scar followed behind, looking more like she was getting away with something, coming into the boss's flop when she normally wasn't allowed.

The place was a dingy, moldy-smelling hole. Four more Kickers sat at a table covered with beer bottles and greasy plates. Short-haired woman with a pair of knives on her hips. Dusky-looking fellow with a pair of hatchets. Short guy with a tetchball bat. Ugly bruiser with thick arms and an eyepatch.

And Musky—obviously Musky—lying on a bed in the middle of the room in his skivs.

Behind the table—over by the stove—was a young boy. Dirty face, nibbling on a hunk of dried meat as he sat on the floor.

"This is an inspector?" Musky asked. "They certainly are making a better breed of them nowadays."

"That's lovely," Satrine said, letting the contempt flow out of her voice. "Mister Musky, I presume."

"You've got writs, you've got questions?" he asked, sitting up in the bed. "You ain't one of the specs from Aventil."

"No, I'm with the Grand Inspection Unit," she said. She paced a bit, to put herself close to the window, so she wouldn't have the table between her and the boy. "We're stationed out of Inemar, investigating large-scale crime throughout the city."

"Fancy," he said. "And that brought you to me?"

"Well, it brings me everywhere," she said. "Yesterday I was at the Parliament."

"Meet anyone special?" he sneered at her.

"Prince Escaraine," she said.

"Really?" Eyepatch said.

"Shut it," Musky shot at him. "What do you want, skirt? What're your blasted questions?"

"I just have one question," Satrine said. "Hey, Yetter?"

The boy looked up.

"Wanna go home?"

The four at the table got on their feet. Before they were all the way up, Satrine had the whistle to her lips, and her handstick out with her other hand. She swung out, crashing through the window, as she sent out the call as loud and as sharp as she could.

Now she just had to live long enough for help to arrive.

Chapter 15

SATRINE HAD SEVEN people between her and the door, and she had to get Yetter out that door with her. Four bruisers: Eyepatch, Hatchets, Short Hair, and Tetchball Bat. All of them brawlers, surely. Both Disheveled and Musky looked past their prime, but they couldn't be discounted. Face Scar was farthest away, right in the doorway. She didn't look like much, but Satrine knew not to minimize her threat. Any one of these people could put an end to her.

Eyepatch looked the roughest—and the closest. Satrine spit her whistle out at him, right at his good eye. That startled him enough for her to bring her handstick into his chest, and then flip it over across his head, while driving her knee into his tenders. As he dropped, she kicked at the table, knocking Hatchets and Short Hair back.

No one between her and Yetter, she charged toward him, drawing her crossbow with her left hand. She fired—a wild shot. She had been hoping to hit Musky, but instead got Disheveled in the leg. He screamed out and went down. When she reached Musky, Tetchball Bat was on her. He swung like he hoped to score a Triple Jack with her head. She darted backward, feeling the wide edge of the bat fly just past her nose. The hard swing threw him off balance, and she lurched forward, cracking her crossbow across his head. It shattered into a mass of splinters, and he stumbled dazed in front of her.

Grabbing Yetter's arm with her left hand, she shoved her way past Tetchball and tackled Face Scar through the door. This got her in the hallway, dragging the kid along with her.

Face Scar screamed out, clawing at Satrine's head, pummeling her on the shoulders and back. Not effective, but not pleasant either. Satrine pulled herself out of Face Scar's paltry grip, and cracked her handstick across her jaw. Then she knocked her again, dropping the girl.

Now to the stairs. Satrine was already dizzy and winded, and her right leg was reminding her that she had been shot twice in the thigh this year. She was many years from the street brawler she had once been.

Or that girl who trained on a slow boat to Waisholm in between her psychic instruction sessions.

"Get up. Do it again." Grieson watched from his deck chair as his four goons stepped away from the sparring circle.

Trini wiped the blood off her lip as she got on her feet. "Why can't he shove this sewage in my brain like the princess stuff?" Her head was a swirly mess already—not just a bunch of useless book learning, but garbage about dinner forks and dresses and the sorts of things swells worried about. She was having dreams of going to the fancy school she had never been in and having friends she'd never met. Getting clobbered by Grieson's goons over and over again didn't help. They were all taller, stronger, and trained. Trini had bested plenty of street rats who had been the first two, but not the third. And certainly not four of them.

"Doesn't work that way. This has got to be in your body, in your muscles. He can't do that for you."

"I can brawl fine," she said, getting in the stupid stance he made her hold.

"Brawling is all right if it's just you and someone

else. You got to hold up against three, four, five others—"

"You get killed."

"You control the situation or you get killed."

"There's no way to fight that many people and not get beat."

"True," Grieson said. "The secret is to keep going despite getting beat. Again."

She took a moment to catch her breath, and pushed through the pain to pull little Yetter with her to the stairs.

A doorway in front of her burst open, and Short Hair came out, knives drawn. Satrine glanced behind her, and Hatchets had come out of the apartment she had just come from. Obviously the rooms up here were connected. And it wouldn't be too long before the rest of them recovered enough to get out here.

"Back to the wall, kid," she said, drawing out her handstick.

Short Hair and Hatchets both leaped at her at the same time. Short Hair pounced like a cat, knives first, while Hatchets swung in tight circles—not enough space in this hallway to really go wide. Satrine stepped to the side—to keep Yetter between her and the wall—knocking one of Short Hair's blades with the handstick before pivoting and sweeping the stick at Hatchets' tight swings.

She caught the handstick against the hatchet handles, below the blades, and pushed hard to throw him off balance into the wall. Short Hair came up with another swipe, which Satrine pulled back from. She could feel the blade pass by as it barely missed the tip of her nose. She kicked at Short Hair's knee, while bringing the handstick into the girl's sternum.

Both Short Hair and Hatchets reeled for a moment, and Satrine pushed Yetter toward the stairs. "Run!" He went like a crossbow bolt down the hallway, and Satrine tried to shove past Short Hair to do the same.

Instead something yanked at her leg and Satrine fell to the floor.

She flipped herself over to land on her back, just in time to get her handstick up to block the two knives coming at her chest. She tried to pull up her leg, jam a knee into Short Hair's side, but Face Scar was on the ground with her, holding on to her boot.

Satrine kicked, knocking Face Scar in the nose while holding back Short Hair's desperate press to bury her knives into Satrine's heart. Satrine kicked again, and this time her leg was free—as her foot had come completely out of her boot. She kicked Face Scar again, pushing the girl into Hatchets, who fell on top of Short Hair's legs.

That distracted Short Hair enough for Satrine to jerk the knives to the side. Short Hair tried to push harder, but just jammed her knives into the floor. Satrine gave her two quick jabs to the face and scrambled out from under the girl.

She was on her feet at the same time as Hatchets, and he just looked annoyed. Satrine was already bruised and winded, a gash on her arm that she only now noticed, one leg aching and the other one with a bare foot.

He came at her with arms like windmills, hatchets spinning, screaming like he was on fire. It would be bad business for Satrine, but he brought the hatchets down in a predictable rhythm that was easy to block. He was swinging too wide, so Face Scar and Short Hair were stuck behind him. Satrine knocked his hatchet blows away as she stumbled back. Quickly he caught on to what she was doing, and tried to switch up his method. He did a fancy spin that looked impressive, but left his back unguarded. She slammed her handstick into his spine, grabbed his shoulder and hurled him into the wall. Both his hatchets got stuck in the wall.

She wasted no more time getting to the stairs, even though she she could only hobble on her uneven feet.

"Someone get that lousy stick!" she heard screamed from behind. As she tried to catch up to Yetter, she could hear plenty of bruisers giving chase, and even more brawling below her.

<hr />

Olivant stood dumbstruck for a long while, staring at Minox's hand. The rest of the room was silent, save for Nyla's quiet sobs. Minox understood that. She had known that something had happened to his hand, but she had no idea the extent of it. His reveal was surely something of a shock.

Eventually Kendra Morad broke the silence. "Mister Olivant, I'm waiting for you."

"I just—" was all the man could say, though he started to move from behind the table, slowly drifting toward Minox as if pulled by a river current. Minox stayed with his hand outstretched, hoping that it would spur the man to a definitive response.

"If there isn't an answer, or an action, then I am closing the file on this entire charade," Captain Cinellan said. "And you will have to file petitions with the commissioner and the entire Table of Commandants, Miss Morad. I will not care—"

"Everyone should leave this room," Olivant said quietly.

"Don't you dare tell me my job or my authority, Captain," Miss Morad said.

"Minox?" Nyla said, her voice quavering, ignoring the rising argument between the captain and Miss Morad. "How is that—is it even flesh?"

"I don't know," Minox told her.

"Is it even human?"

"I really think everyone—" Olivant said again.

"No one is going to—" Protector Hilsom was putting himself between Cinellan and Morad.

"Saints almighty!" Olivant shouted. "Please! Everyone leave except myself and Inspector Welling."

"I don't think I can agree to that," Mister Cheever said.

"Please," Olivant said, his voice quieter, though he clearly was anything but calm. "This is—I need to—I need some quiet and sense before I can address this."

Miss Morad stepped over. "Mister Olivant, I will confess that I don't even remotely understand what I'm seeing here or what it means. But it's clearly a dangerous secret that Inspector Welling kept to himself."

"Not true," Cinellan said. "Welling showed it to me when this happened. And Inspector Rainey is fully aware."

"But you don't understand what . . . this is, any more than I do. Or Inspector Welling!"

"I need a moment with the inspector," Olivant said. "I really must . . ."

"It's fine," Minox said. "Everyone else can go."

"I would prefer not to leave you," Cheever said. "I'm not afraid of . . . whatever it is Mister Olivant is afraid of."

Nyla moved over to Minox, grabbing his shoulder and squeezing. "I'll stay as well, if you need."

"It's not necessary. I would like the best answer from Mister Olivant he can give. If that means leaving me alone with him, that's fine. Same to you, Mister Cheever."

"Let's leave them," Cinellan said, ushering Hilsom and the clerks out. "But we'll be watching from the next room."

"Fine," Olivant said. They all left—Nyla giving one last affectionate touch to Minox's arm—and Olivant stared hard at the hand. Miss Morad lingered for a moment, watching Olivant, her face unreadable. Even after they were alone in the room, Olivant didn't speak for some time.

"So what do you think, Mister Olivant?"

"I'm out of my element, here," he said. "Did Professor Alimen see this?"

"He did not explicitly," Minox said. "And I assume he did not mention it to you."

"He told me . . ." Olivant trailed off. "That there were chaotic and impossible swirls of magic around you. Like you were out of control. He assumed that was because of your untrained status, but clearly . . . more is at play here."

"What is it?"

"This happened to you recently?" Olivant asked. "You had a normal, human hand months ago?"

"Do you know what it is?"

"Please, Mister Welling, be calm." Olivant peered hard at his hand. "Tell me how this happened."

"Do you remember the murders of the Firewings and the fellow from Light and Stone a few months back? You represented Jaelia Tomar."

"Yes. And you lost control of your magic during the interview."

"I did nothing of the sort."

"You don't even know what you—" Olivant looked down at Minox's hand again and stepped back. "It doesn't matter. Continue."

"The murderer also targeted me. He captured me and started his killing ritual before he was thwarted."

"I recall reading about that."

Minox wasn't entirely sure if he should reveal these details, but if he was going to learn anything, he needed to be as open as possible. "Part of his ritual involved using mysterious spikes of an unidentified metal, which sapped magical energy."

"Like dalmatium?" Minox must have made a confused face, because Olivant added, "It's the metal in mage shackles."

"No, very different from mage shackles," Minox said. "I compared them, and we also brought a spike to a Major Dresser, who was unable to identify it."

Olivant made a face that made it hard to tell if he was familiar with Dresser, or what his opinion of him was. "And where are these spikes now?"

"I don't know," Minox said. The full truth was that they were somehow stolen from evidence, along with any documentation about them.

"And you were exposed to it?"

"It was driven into this arm, right at the wrist."

"Dear saints," Olivant said.

"It did not heal properly, causing discomfort and occasional disruption to my magical ability, but not until I became sick did it change into this."

"And the sickness?"

"Was the result of exposure to a Tsouljan pollen that becomes a poison when magically activated."

"This is absurdly complicated, to the point of sounding fanciful."

"I am telling you the truth, sir!" Minox's anger hit him sudden and strong, flexing his hand instinctively.

"Calm down!" Olivant shouted. He had turned suddenly pale, and then gingerly stepped closer. "You probably don't even see the way the *numina* swirls around and within this thing."

"Numina?" Minox had heard that word in passing before.

"Magical energy," Olivant said. "Really, you are . . . it's actually somewhat remarkable. Perhaps your magical senses aren't very keen, and perhaps you just don't have the training. But to me it's rather clear. And the *numina* around it gets stronger when you are agitated."

"Magic is how I move my hand," Minox said, flexing the fingers.

"Saint Benton, that's troubling," Olivant said. "You have been keeping it still during this proceeding, haven't you?"

"I've now practiced enough that it's largely natural and instinctive."

"Son," Olivant said quietly. "I'm trying to respect that you largely did not have the opportunity to get the education you desperately need about this, but . . ." He muttered to himself, pacing away. "That is our mandate to Lord Preston, isn't it? To teach? Saints and sinners, Quentin, you are not built for this."

"Mister Olivant?"

"How's your appetite, since this happened?"

"Ravenous most of the time," Minox said. "But that's no change."

Olivant shook his head and sat down. "Let me try to explain the gravity of what I see, looking at your hand. The forces you have contained in there are . . . beyond my capacity to describe. The amount of *numinic* flow you generated flexing your fingers could flatten this building. I should . . ."

"I don't think I have a greater amount of magical power, if that's what you're saying."

"You don't think—" Olivant stammered. "You don't even comprehend the sort of—I'm out of my depth. This is not—"

"Mister Olivant, please," Minox said. "I need guidance."

"I'm not qualified for this," Olivant said. "I'm not a magical theorist, Inspector. I barely made passing marks in those classes, and that was thirty years ago. I'm a paltry mage who also studied law so I could be useful to my fellows."

"Then find me someone who can help! Bring in experts from the university!"

"Help? I will definitely be reaching out to the academic community, but I imagine that anyone I speak to would certainly say the same thing that I am thinking. You should be locked up with as many mage shackles as we can find, and even then I fear it wouldn't be enough. It's not just that you're untrained and unskilled in your magic, sir." Olivant pointed at the hand, as if he was afraid to come in contact with it. "What you've become, whatever that is. . . . I fear it could command enough magical power to destroy this entire city."

"Surely—"

"You ask if I think you're fit to serve as a constable?

That's irrelevant minutia to me. I think you're a menace beyond the scope of my comprehension. I will likely spend the rest of my nights lying awake terrified, praying you don't lose control of the unholy power you use to wiggle your fingers."

The whistle call shot through the air, and Corrie charged her horse like the sinners were chasing her. After all this sewage with Minox and the Gearbox Killer, she was more than ready to crack some skulls, especially ganger wastes in Aventil. Jace had told her enough stories about the Kickers and their main rivals, the Toothless Dogs, to make her hate every last one of these bastards. The fact they were holding some kid hostage made them even worse.

As she pounded toward the tenement, she realized everyone at the stationhouse had Tricky all wrong. Especially Nyla. She couldn't think of anyone else who would walk into a gang flop and then blow her whistle for backup. That took steel, for damn sure.

Almost no one else. Minox would. And Pop would have. Pop would always stay out there beyond his shift, no matter how much Mom would cry and fuss over it. And it wasn't for extra crowns. He'd always say, "There's always one more ride you can take before you go home."

Then he had taken one more ride, and it was his last.

Corrie charged into the intersection outside of the tenement, and it already was a war zone. Arrows were raining down from the upper windows, and Jace and Saitle were pinned under their salt bread cart. Benvin and the rest of his people were under fire half a block away. Which meant Tricky was alone in there.

Arrows struck her horse, and Corrie almost went flying as it collapsed from under her. She managed to roll with the fall, banging her arm up as she went down. More arrows came at her—saints and bastards, they were armed like a fortress up there—and she was in the open. People were screaming and scurrying in all directions, and the panic in the street was holding up the rest of her squad.

She drew out her crossbow, looking up to those top floor windows. Arrows were raining down on her, but she might still get one shot off before they took her down.

Sorry, Mama.

Then a shadow passed over her, and those arrows became a series of metallic drumbeats.

Nothing had hit her.

Instead she was pulled to her feet. That Tarian girl was in front her, shield high. "Can you run?"

Corrie didn't even realize what had happened. "Blazes, yes," she said.

"Then stay with me." Jerinne drew out her sword and tore forward to the tenement, keeping her shield overhead. The storm of arrows didn't touch her, didn't slow her down as they pummeled her shield. Corrie stayed right with her—under that shield was the only safe spot on the street. They got to the front of the tenement, and Corrie and Jerinne pressed flat against the brick wall.

"At least nine shooters, third and fourth floors," Jerinne said.

"And Tricky's on her own in there."

"Probably on the fourth floor. The lieutenant and his folks aren't going to make it in until we stop that barrage of arrows," Jerinne said. She noted Jace and Saitle, behind their cart fifty feet away. "They might make a dash if I cover them."

"That's still only four of us," Corrie said.

"They won't stand a chance," Jerinne sent back with a wink. Before Corrie could say anything else, the girl whistled to Jace and Saitle, dashing out to them. More arrows came at her, which she blocked. While Jerinne brought the boys over, Corrie stepped out a bit and took a shot at one of the archers. She heard someone cry out as she pressed back up against the wall, now with Jace next to her.

"Blazes of a first day, eh, sis?"

Rutting idiot was grinning.

"When we get in, we've got to go for the stairs," Corrie said, reloading her crossbow. "That lobby is probably full of Kickers, and whoever can get through, pound your boots up to the top."

Jerinne raised her sword. "I'll make a path for you." She charged the door.

"Saint Ilmer, what a woman," Jace said, going after her.

Corrie followed right behind. No way was she going to let her little brother show her up.

Jerinne was tearing a swath through the dozen or so Kickers in the lobby—a brutal dance with her sword, and those gang rats had no clue what their steps were. They came at her with knives and tetchbats and other improvised weapons, and none of them could touch her, while she clobbered them with the flat of her blade. Jacc was in a tussle with one Kicker—holding his own, but not making any headway.

Two Kickers were standing firm at the bottom of the stairs, sporting cudgels and knucklestuffers. Both bruisers who towered over Corrie by a good head and a half.

"Rutting saints," Corrie muttered, taking a shot at the one on the left. The bolt stuck in his thick muscled arm, and he did little more than grunt in annoyance.

Jerinne burst out of her scrum and slammed into one of them with her shield, knocking him into his buddy. She looked to Corrie.

"Go!"

Corrie sprinted up the stairs. "Tricky!" she shouted as she reached the second floor. She cocked a new bolt into the crossbow and took aim down the hallway. Clear. She went halfway up the stairs to the next floor when she nearly collided into the kid.

"Oh saints and sinners!" the kid shouted.

"Hey, hey," Corrie said, looking him over. He seemed dirty and too skinny, but all right. "Is there a stick up there with Waishen hair?"

"She said to run!" the kid said. "But—" This was the kid they came to rescue. Corrie should bring him down the stairs, get him out. That was the job.

But that meant Tricky was up there alone.

"Go," Corrie said. "Find a constable. Or the girl with a shield."

The kid ran, and Corrie went up to the third floor. Blood was smeared on the floor here, leading to the hallway. Corrie went in, crossbow raised. A few feet in front of her, a fat man in his skivs was limping ahead, hatchet in his hand. Just beyond him, Tricky was grappling with some short-haired skirt. It wasn't much of a grapple—Tricky had the girl in a headlock and was clobbering her. But that had her full attention; she didn't see the fat man with the hatchet coming.

Tricky dropped the slan to the ground, and the fat man was moving in.

"Stand and be held!" Corrie shouted. "You are bound by law!"

He turned, like he was about to come at her, but he saw the crossbow aimed for his heart. "You come in to my house, rotten sticks, and think you can—"

"She said stand and be held," Tricky said. Looking at Corrie she added, "Took you long enough."

"Streets are a mess," Corrie said, tossing her irons over to Tricky. "This guy the boss?"

"Musky," she said. "Drop the hatchet, because she doesn't miss."

He let it fall to the floor. Tricky limped over—one of her feet was with just the stocking—and ironed him up.

Corrie leaned in closer while taking the boss by the irons. "We've got archers on this floor, peppering the rutting streets. Keeping the rest of our boys from getting in here. We need to take them out and get back to the lobby."

"Hey, archers!" Tricky shouted. "We got your boss in irons, so lay them down and come out quiet. We've got plenty of search and arrest writs, so don't give us an excuse."

A couple doors opened, and some Kickers stuck their heads out.

"Hands on heads," Corrie said, aiming her crossbow at them. "And march to the stairs nice and blazing civil."

They did as they were told, and Corrie only hoped the situation in the lobby was under control. If it was still a fight, bringing these guys down only made it harder. She let them lead, walking behind them with her crossbow trained on their backs. Tricky took Musky behind her.

"Where's your boot?"

"Up there somewhere. Hopefully still."

The lobby was a scene, but not the one Corrie was expecting. A dozen-odd Kickers were all on the ground, moaning and wheezing. One of those big bruisers was being held down by Jerinne twisting his arm and pinning her knee on his back. The kid was here, clutching onto Saitle's leg.

Jace paced around the fallen Kickers. Despite blood gushing from his nose, he still had that stupid grin. "You are all bound by law!" he announced. "You will be ironed and brought to the stationhouse where charges of crimes will be laid upon you, and you will stand trial for those crimes. These charges may include, and not be limited to, assaulting an officer of the law, resisting a lawful writ, and being a menace to the public trust. Does anyone have any questions?"

Only groans came in response.

Benvin came in with his squad, and the rest of the boys from the GIU. "What's the score?"

"A safe boy, a boss named Musky, and a whole lot of Kickers to send to Quarrygate," Tricky said. "There's a handful more upstairs to be mopped up, but I think your squad can handle that."

Benvin gave a nod, and Wheth and Pollit went up the stairs.

"Bring me my boot if you find it!" Tricky yelled up after them.

"Not rutting fair," one of the Kickers said from his place on the ground. Looked like at least one arm was broken. "Bringing a Tarian knight in to do your job."

"Didn't realize I had to be fair, Reginick," Benvin said. "Saitle, call for some wagons and Yellowshields. Your arm is bleeding, Inspector."

"Just a nick," Tricky said, coming the rest of the way down the stairs. "You all right, Jerinne?"

Jerinne popped up to her feet as Bankly and Ebber ironed up her bruiser. "Quite spirited folks in Aventil. Thank you for letting me assist you all."

Benvin gave her a grudging nod. "We appreciate all the help we can get down here."

Yellowshields came in, and a couple went right to Jace, who protested a bit too much given what a mess his face was. Benvin's people ironed and carted off Kickers, and they started searching through the tenement. Tricky waited patiently while a Yellowshield wrapped up her arm. "Just the bandage," Tricky said. "I can have the Inemar Stationhouse ward surgeon stitch it up. So how does this do by you, Benvin?"

"Assuming the arrests hold, this will gouge the Kickers. Now we need to keep the other gangs from taking these corners over, or a new one from springing up out of the ashes. But this is a big win."

"Call if you need help with another," Tricky said, shaking his hand.

"Will do." He leaned in with a nod of his head. "If you brought that shield girl with you again, I wouldn't hate it, either."

Pollit came back down with a shredded boot. "One of them took out his anger on this."

Tricky sighed and went over to the Kicker called

Reginick, placing her stocking foot next to his boot. She then pulled it off him and put it on, over his annoyed protests.

Jace came over and embraced Corrie. "Stay safe," he said. "And find out where I can write to Jerinne."

"She's too much for you to rutting handle," Corrie said, smacking him on the head playfully. "Now go do your blasted job, Patrolman."

"See you at home, Sergeant," he shot back. "Specs." He saluted to Tricky and went off with Benvin and the rest of his squad.

"What do you think of that kid brother of mine?" Corrie asked Tricky as they left the tenement, Jerinne and the GIU boys behind them

"I think he's a Welling," Tricky said. "Let's get back to our house. Still plenty of our own mess to clean up today."

Chapter 16

MINOX HAD RETURNED to his desk, still trying to process what Mister Olivant had said. Miss Morad had, true to her word, ended the hearing for the day, and she claimed she intended to present her report tomorrow morning at the latest, if not sooner. "There's more than enough information at this time." That at least meant she wouldn't be harassing his family or Joshea any more. She went off with her notes to a back office with Mister Olivant.

All the notes and files from the Parliament had been piled up on his desk, as well a delivery from the East Maradaine Stationhouse. He opened that up right away, finding exactly what he had hoped to find.

Charcoal drawings, scores of them. Jillian probably had not slept, drawing through the night. He had suspected she would, that she would be inspired by what she had seen, gripped by it, and produce more from memory. And her memory was remarkable, as was her capacity to render what she had seen as image. In many ways, Jillian was cut from the same mold as Minox and Evoy. Jillian used her art to expel the sinners from her skull. That rendered images that were almost as detailed as being there.

It gave him many faces: victims, marshals, other people on the scene. Minox hadn't been in a position to pay close attention as people were rescued, being too occupied with holding the machine in place while Dayne and the trapmaster freed the victims. Amongst the packet of work, Jillian had painstakingly crafted images of all the victims, the living and the dead.

That would be a great help, because he wanted to confirm that the victims were who they were supposed to be. Going through the initial reports, he had already found something interesting that stood out in the twenty-two victims. Possibly nothing, but worth looking into. He had already sent a page to get a roster of the Parliamentary functionaries.

"Hey, Jinx." Inspector Kellman had come over to the desk. "Look, I know this ain't the best time, but—"

"Is this about a case?"

"The missing kids," Kellman said. "You had said something about matching witness statements, but I'm not finding anything in the files."

Minox sighed. Perhaps he had been unclear, but more likely Kellman was not paying close attention. He wondered, if he were to lose his place as an inspector, how many cases would get shoddy care. Cases that he might have solved. "The reports of the giant who grabbed kids from the alleys."

"That?" Kellman said. "Saints, I thought that was, just, you know, *doph*- or *effitte*-dosed punks seeing things."

"It could be, but it's a consistent point that was given separately by several different people," Minox said. He hadn't bothered to transcribe the more fanciful details that he had been told, like the shiny, scaly skin, black eyes, or oversized teeth. Fanciful, but recurring and consistent. "Not to mention many of these reports were from children, so even someone your size might be called a giant."

Kellman shrugged. "Yeah, all right. Is that across the city?"

"The matching reports were mostly involved in the ones in Dentonhill, Inemar, and Keller Cove—

especially Dentonhill. But there were a few on the north side of the city as well."

"Hmm," Kellman said, nodding like that meant something specific to him.

"Do you have a theory? Or a suspect?"

Kellman shook out of his small reverie. "No, nothing like that. It just . . . it feels like it's too damn big, you know. I can't get my head around it all."

This man had been assigned Minox's case, the case that Minox had put together and proved to Captain Cinellan was larger than anyone else suspected. This man couldn't get his head around it. Him and Mirrell, a man who usually decided the solution to his cases when he first received them, and fit his investigation to that. A case like this, where there was no obvious suspect, meant Mirrell would have to do actual work to solve it. Minox imagined that meant Mirrell had already signed it off in his mind as unsolvable, ready to send the case files to the archives as soon as it was politically feasible to do so.

Kellman might not have the intellectual capacity to solve this case, but he was showing that he cared about it, which was leaps and bounds beyond Mirrell.

"Were this my case," Minox said carefully, "I would get a map of the city, and track the locations of each known abduction with dates. Find the center, find when things expanded from the center, and what circumstances changed. Use that information to lead you to the next piece of evidence."

Kellman seemed to take that in. "Yeah, that sounds like something that could be useful." He nodded and went off.

Minox had, of course, already done the work, but if he had flat out told Kellman what that yielded, the man would likely ignore it. Instead, it was best to let Kellman do it himself, and then come back to Minox when he couldn't figure out what it meant. Likely two days for that. There was time. If Minox's own analysis was correct, the next wave of abductions would be in two weeks.

Inspector Rainey came over to their desks, her arm bandaged and several scrapes on her face, including a decent-size bruise on her cheek. Also her boots no longer matched—one of them had a colored kerchief wrapped around it. Despite that, her mood seemed almost jubilant.

"How was your morning?" he asked.

"Rough," she said. "But I rescued a boy and helped take down a gang, so it was worth it."

"And you lost a boot?"

She sat down and put the foot with the foreign boot on her desk. "But I got a trophy. From a Kemper Street Kicker captain."

"I wouldn't go around wearing that for normal duty."

"No. It fits, but not well. I've asked Nyla to bring me a new pair. And she barely gave me any grief for it."

"Her mind is probably elsewhere. My morning was . . . harrowing."

Rainey sat up properly. "That bad?"

He quickly briefed her on Olivant's dire statements regarding his hand. When he finished, her expression was filled with sympathy, and even a hint of fear. He could hardly blame her for either, but he felt he needed to soften things with her. "It may be that Mister Olivant was merely being hyperbolic. He seems to be prone toward the dramatic."

"That he does," she said. Likely sensing that he was not in the mood to discuss it any further, she said, "Have you had any chance to go over these files and notes?"

"I have, to a limited degree. I have a list of the victims. I have Mister Leppin's reports on the ones who died, and he has confirmed all of them."

"Good," Rainey said. "We should first go back to the Parliament, walk through the floor and all the entrances. There's no way that much equipment was brought without leaving traces. Then question the marshals."

"Specifically the ones who were on duty the day before yesterday."

"Chief Quoyell was reluctant to give us those names. I doubt he's changed his mind."

"After that, we should visit all the survivors—those who are in a condition to talk to us—and get another statement from each of them," Minox said. "But about that. I've been going over the list of victims, and I've found something odd."

"Odd in what way?"

"The names of the victims are wrong."

———◆·◆———

"I'm going to ask you to define 'wrong,'" Satrine said.

"Perhaps it is a strong term. I'm not saying that the victims aren't the victims. But there is an odd quirk as to who the victims are that has a discrepancy. A minor detail which may be nothing, but I think it is notable."

Satrine had long since learned to trust when Welling thought something minor was notable. "A pattern that's broken?" she asked.

"Exactly. All the victims are support staff to Parliament members, except the one who was killed as the 'example'—he was the husband of one of the women. He didn't work for the Parliament in any capacity."

"You think that's why he was the example? He was abducted with her, but not specifically part of the plan?"

"Likely," Welling said, "but not my main point. You see, the other victims are specific functionaries to specific members. All of them are staff chief, head clerk, or office secretary."

"All right," Satrine said. "Except someone isn't?"

"Not exactly. You see, I've learned that there is a formal order to the members of Parliament, based entirely on tenure in the body, rather than party, chair number, or archduchy represented."

"Right," Satrine said. As soon as he said it, that bit of civics unlocked in her brain. "So how do these two things connect? What's the discrepancy?"

"It's subtle, so much so I'm almost inclined to ignore it. Almost." Welling handed her the list. "If you list the victims in the formal order to their respective member of Parliament, it goes in rotation: staff chief, head clerk, office secretary, in that pattern. Except for three, and those three are specifically the ones from the boiler room."

That got Satrine's attention. "That can't be coincidence. You're wondering about who are the three who should have been there instead."

"Exactly," Minox said. "Why were they passed over? It's possible that, for whatever reason, it wasn't feasible for our 'Sholiar' to get to them."

Satrine bristled at that. "I'm not comfortable with taking this Sholiar thing at face value."

"You don't trust Mister Heldrin?"

"It's less about trust, and more about examining all the possible evidence," she said. "I mean, it seems Dayne has done the thing you always hate Mirrell doing."

"Deciding the truth before considering all the evidence." Welling furrowed his brow. "And I will confess I was eager to absorb a possible solution in lieu of any other leads."

"I can understand that urge, trust me," Satrine said. "But still, literally the only evidence we have for Sholiar—even that there is such a person—is the say-so of Dayne Heldrin. We can't build a case on that."

"True. And it's also true that this operation requires a massive amount of support and infrastructure. The kidnapping, the delivery of materials."

"This isn't a man, it's an organization."

"Dare I even say, a conspiracy."

Satrine laughed a little. "I don't like going there, but in this case, it seems apt." There was no way this could have been pulled off without a lot of people working together, and several inside the Parliament system. "We can call it the Sholiar Conspiracy if you like."

He frowned. "Are you making one of your dark jokes, Inspector?"

"Yes," she said. "I'm sorry. Just, instead of chasing after shadows or Dayne's own personal nemesis, we need to look at the elements that are concrete. And your three missing functionaries sounds like a good place to start. If there is a conspiracy, I'd wager those three would have answers."

Welling nodded. "Once the page returns with the roster I requested, we'll be able to identify them."

Almost as if on cue, Phillen came charging up the front stairs and burst past Nyla's desk as if he were on fire. He got to their desks completely out of breath, dropping a file in front of them. He then fell to his knees, gasping and wheezing.

"Mister Hace," Welling said harshly, "I appreciate your enthusiasm, and while I did ask for this file as quickly as possible, I did not mean to the detriment of your own well-being. There was no need to run with such abandon."

"I came—" Phillen gasped out, still unable to catch his breath. "I came—"

"Easy, Phil," Satrine said. "No need to hurt yourself."

He gasped and gulped air again, grabbing hold of Welling's chair to steady himself. "I came from the Parliament," he got out.

"Yes, of course, and you didn't need—"

"The King's Marshals," Phillen said. "They're coming. I heard them. They're coming to reclaim the case. And all the evidence."

Welling grabbed the file Phillen had just brought and sped through it like it was about to burn up in his hands. Then he closed the folder, grabbed a pile of charcoal sketches and shoved them into an envelope. He stood up and tucked the envelope into his trousers. "We probably don't have much—"

"Attention, attention!" At the entrance to the inspectors' floor, Chief Quoyell stood with a dozen King's Marshals. "Everyone stand up and step away from your desks. I am here with writs from a Grand High Judge and a royal seal." He pointed across the floor, staring hard at Satrine and Welling. "I am here to claim royal jurisdiction over one of your cases and take all pertinent files, reports, and evidence. Interference will result in arrest and charges of High Crimes against the Crown."

Satrine stood up and stepped away. She wasn't sure what would happen next, but she was certain of one thing: any chance that this case would end in justice for the victims had just turned to smoke.

— • —

Minox kept his hands up as he moved away from the desk. Chief Quoyell signaled his men to spread out into the room. Captain Cinellan stormed out of his office.

"The saints and blazes is going on here?"

Quoyell deposited his papers in Cinellan's hands. "What's happening is this Parliament case—and by extension the entire Gearbox Killer case—is now under Royal Jurisdiction. King's Marshals are going to be handling it. I would appreciate that you give us everything you have and don't give us any difficulty."

Cinellan frowned as he thumbed through the pages. It was clear from his face that everything looked legitimate, and he was powerless to put any stop to it. "I'll have you know that Commissioner Enbrain is directly involved in this case and has declared it high priority."

"You can imagine how little I care about that," Quoyell said. He turned to his men. "Every file, report, and piece of physical evidence. I presume someone can lead my people to your examinarium and evidence lockroom?"

Cinellan point to Hace. "You, show them the way."

Hace saluted and waved for a handful of marshals to follow him down the back stairwell. Three marshals descended on Minox's desk.

"Captain," Minox said, noticing Joshea was talking to Corrie and Nyla by Nyla's desk. "We should probably escort all the civilians off the floor during this— situation."

"Not a terrible idea," Cinellan said.

"I'll handle it," Minox said. "It's not like I have anything else to work on right now."

He went over to Joshea, taking him by the arm and directing him toward the main stairs. "I need a favor," he said in a low voice.

"Now?" Joshea asked as they left the floor. "I think that—"

"Please, this is critical. You're a civilian so the marshals won't—"

"Fine," Joshea said, though he looked put out. "I've had to deal with a lot of sewage here today."

"I understand, and I will make it up to you," Minox said. It wouldn't be fruitful to mention that he had sacrificed himself to Miss Morad and Mister Olivant to protect Joshea's secret. This was not the moment. "Take these sketches across the river to Riverheart Ward; look for a man named Dayne Heldrin." He pulled out the envelope and slid it under Joshea's vest.

"How will I recognize him?"

"He's a seven-foot-tall man in a Tarian uniform."

"So he stands out," Joshea said.

"Yes, rather." For once, Minox got the joke Joshea was telling, even if this was not the moment. "You should hurry."

"But what do I—"

"Go over those sketches with him, tell him I sent you. I will join you both as soon as I can."

"The last time we were both in a hospital ward—"

"We will endeavor not to repeat that."

Joshea gave him a big grin, and with a slap on the shoulder, went down the stairs.

Minox returned to the inspectors' floor, where the marshals were nearly tearing apart his desk.

"What is this?" Minox said, feeling heat and magic flow to his hand as he came up to Chief Quoyell. "What do you think you're doing to my work?"

"We're taking everything connected to the case," Quoyell said. "It's not my fault that your files and reports are so disorganized."

"Is this about the Gearbox?" one of the other marshals asked, pointing to the slateboard.

"Not exclusively," Minox said. "While I'm certain you have the authority to claim evidence, reports, and files, I'm also certain that you are not empowered to claim anything that isn't an official part of the investigation."

"I have a royal edict—"

Minox didn't let him start on that. "Even the king himself couldn't empower you to claim my personal notebook or my slateboard musings without specific writs to that end."

"We could charge you with Crimes against the Throne and claim them as evidence for that."

"Do not be petty, Chief," Minox said. "You have what you need."

Leppin came up the back stairs, still in his blood-spattered examinarium apron and gloves. "I want to file a protest against these marshals! Damaging evidence! Tampering!"

"Who is this fool?" Quoyell asked.

"Fool?" Leppin nearly spat in his face, his north-western Druth accent thickening with anger. "This fool is Maricus Leppin, Master of Sciences. This fool has no less than three Letters of Mastery from RCM and The Acorian Conservatory, and I know about more things than you've even thought of. And I know that even with a damn Royal Edict and writs of any sort, the proper handling and transfer of evidence requires more than a handful of meatheaded cretins shoving things in crates with a sinner's care!"

"Leppin," Captain Cinellan said calmly. "We're obliged to cooperate."

"The way they're—the integrity of evidence is at stake, sir. I thought that mattered when solving a crime is paramount."

"That's not your problem, little man," Quoyell said. "Where are we, gents?"

The marshal who seemed to be in charge of Minox's desk gave a halfhearted shrug. "I think we've got it all. I can't read half this handwriting."

"Err on the side of caution," Quoyell said. "If you're not sure, take it."

"I have material on several cases—" Minox started.

"Try my patience, constable," Quoyell said, cutting him off. "Maybe a night in the marshal's holding pens would cool you off."

"You wouldn't—" Leppin said.

"The both of you. All of you." Quoyell locked eyes on Inspector Rainey, who had been cool and impassive all this time. No, not that. She had been watching and studying Quoyell. "You have anything to interject?"

"Not right now, Quoyell." She made a strange point of over-pronouncing the syllables in his name, as if his name itself was an insult she was emphasizing.

He scoffed, and then his expression changed. "What are you burning in here?"

Minox realized that the glove he wore over his altered hand was lightly smoking. He didn't realize how much heat and anger he had shunted into that hand. He quickly drew energy back, taking control over himself.

Maybe Olivant was right about him.

"All right," Quoyell said, noting that his people seemed to be finished. "This office will, as of this moment, cease any further pursuit of the Gearbox Killer case and the Parliament Atrocity. Any further revelations made by this office should be reported immediately to the King's Marshals. Good day."

The marshals all marched out.

Captain Cinellan waited for them to be gone, and then closed the main doors to the inspectors' floor. "Enough gawking, people. Back to work. I'm sure you all have something to do." He went back into his office.

Minox sat down at his nearly empty desk, only a handful of notes and paper scraps remaining. Rainey sat down, and Leppin came over, his face filled with anger. Then he leaned down. "I have copies of all my own reports, sketches, and findings. Those were hidden and safe."

"Were you expecting this?" Minox asked.

"If not this, something like this," Leppin said. "Ever since the spikes vanished, I'm taking no chances with anything. My own files, my own evidence."

"That will be helpful," Minox said. "Though this might just be an academic exercise from now on."

"We're not giving up on this, I assume?" Rainey said. "Even if this goes to the 'unresolved,' I can't imagine you'd just let it go."

"Hardly," Minox said. "While I may not have the files, I still have my memory. And no Royal Edict can stop us from interviewing people who were *not* listed as victims of the Gearbox or the Parliament Atrocity."

"So who are the functionaries we're going to visit?" Rainey asked.

"Three men by the name of Tenning, Hunsen, and Cole."

Chapter 17

THEY WERE ACTING in deliberate defiance of the King's Marshals and Royal Writs. Despite that, Satrine hadn't felt more excited in months. The fight with the Kickers had gotten her blood up, and she was hungry for more. It was clear Welling was in the same frame of mind. He looked like he was ready to take on every bit of corruption in law enforcement in Druthal. Probably the axe over his head had lit the fire in his belly.

Not that Welling was ever lacking in that. He always had drive, but now he seemed to have passion as well.

"All three addresses are on the north side," he said as they left the stationhouse. "Are you going to be all right with that?"

He pointed to the Kicker boot she was still wearing. Nyla had said that it would take a few days before they could get her a new pair of boots. Satrine imagined Nyla wasn't exactly pushing the paperwork through with any great expedience.

"It's fine," she said, though it wasn't true. The boot fit, essentially, but there was something about it that was bothering her. Too stiff along her ankle. She'd make do until she could get new ones.

Jerinne was waiting outside, looking concerned. "I saw the marshals come and go. Everything all right?"

"The case isn't ours anymore, officially," Satrine said.

"And unofficially?" Jerinne asked.

"Unofficially, you should probably check in with your superiors," Welling said. "Given the change of case, they may not wish for you to be shadowing us any further."

Jerinne's face fell a little. "Are you sure, Missus Rainey?"

"Unfortunately, yes," Satrine said. Then something occurred to her, "but stop by my house if you can later this evening. I'm sure Rian would appreciate it."

"Yes, ma'am," Jerinne said, her face brightening immensely. "It was a bracing morning, to be sure."

"You were amazing," Satrine said. "Thank you."

Jerinne saluted and went off.

"All right," Minox said once she left. "I need to stop at Missus Wolman's."

He went up to the food cart camped on the other side of the square from the stationhouse, always Welling's favorite. Though it was probably his favorite just due to its proximity to the stationhouse.

"How many today, Inspector?" Missus Wolman asked, working her flatbread dough and throwing her mysterious meat substance on her grill.

"Three," he said.

A perverse urge struck Satrine, probably because she hadn't eaten anything since this morning. "Make it four."

"Really?" Missus Wolman asked. "You ain't afraid it's cat kidneys or something?"

"Is it?"

"I ain't telling you."

"Just give me one," Satrine said, pulling out a tick. She noticed even Welling looked surprised. "I'm starving. I literally forget to eat when I'm not out there with you."

"You're usually quite critical of the fast wraps."

"Well, if half a dozen Kickers can't kill me, then what can this do?"

Missus Wolman flipped the flatbreads over, and then portioned the meat in each one, and with practiced dexterity, rolled them up and then wrapped them in yesterday's newsprints. "You two are in the prints a lot more of late," she said as she finished the last one.

"That won't last," Satrine said.

"The bastards are boxing you out?"

"Where did you get that idea?" Welling asked.

"Boy, I sit outside that stationhouse all blasted day," she said. "I saw a swarm of marshals drop on your head. And it was your head, eh?"

"It was," Welling said. "But that's over, and we have further work to do."

"Get all the bad ones off the street," she said, passing over the wraps.

Welling tucked into the first one as they started walking toward the bridge. Satrine unwrapped hers a bit more gingerly. Despite the number of times Welling would eat as they walked the streets, she had never quite mastered his grace in juggling food while navigating the crowd.

Also, the spicy, fatty scent was already giving her regrets.

Still, she was hungry, so she cautiously took a bite.

It wasn't as horrible as she feared, but it certainly wasn't good.

"I can't believe you eat, like, ten of these a day."

"They are convenient in location and price," Welling said, already working on his second. "Especially since Missus Wolman only charges constables half price."

"At least someone appreciates us."

They crossed the bridge, went through Satrine's High River neighborhood to North High River. Satrine always felt this neighborhood was warm and inviting, in part because the shops here all spilled out into the street, and just strolling through the walkway brought about kind and well-meaning solicitation. As opposed to Inemar or Aventil, where the invitation to purchase something almost felt like an assault.

Also, when people saw her and Welling, in their Constabulary uniforms, they would nod and say "good day" instead of shoving their hands in their pockets and keeping their eyes to the ground.

"Tenning first?" she asked.

"He's the farthest out," Welling said. "I thought it made sense to go to him and then work our way back."

"What do we know about these three?"

"Other than they should have been in the Atrocity—is that the formal name for this event?"

"That's what the marshals called it."

"Apt, but terrible. Anyway, our information is limited. I only had time to read the files to find names and addresses."

They came to the address—a tony and posh-looking building with intricate brickwork and several trees and flowers bordering its front walkway, much like every other building in this part of the city.

"Second-floor apartment," Welling said, leading them in.

The obvious thing when they got inside was that something untoward had happened in this building. There was a hole smashed in the wall—recent, to Satrine's eye—and the handrail of the stairwell had been knocked loose. With just a nod of mutual understanding, she and Welling pulled their crossbows out and went slowly up the stairs. The door to the second-floor apartment was broken—like it had been kicked in.

"Mister Tenning?" Welling called out. "Are you there?"

No response.

"City Constabulary. Is everything well? I will presume a lack of response means you are in need of aid."

In this, he was going by the regulations. Which was probably wise, given that they were well off the path at this point.

After a reasonable pause, Welling pushed the door open, and he and Satrine went in, quickly sweeping through the apartment.

Satrine almost slipped on the blood on the floor.

"Sweet saints!" she cried.

There was a dead man on the floor, at least two stab wounds in his neck and chest. And the room was a mess—when this man was killed, there had been a fight.

Welling crouched down next to the man, touching his face briefly.

"He's dead. But for barely an hour, I'd guess," he said. "The question is, is this Tenning, or did this man come for Tenning and he killed him and ran?"

Satrine looked closer. "I'm not sure, but I can tell you—this was one of the three men in the boiler room."

"Really?" Welling, for once, showed some surprise. "But that would mean . . . you're certain?"

"Rather," Satrine said. He was the one who had all but lost his mind in there. "But we had different names for them, right?"

"We did," Welling said, frowning. "And I didn't memorize all the details, but the names of the men in the boiler room—we were told—were Ollick, Brens, and Gennan. So is this man one of them, or is he Tenning? And in either case, what does this mean?"

"I know one thing this means," Satrine said, pulling out her whistle. "We've got to call this in."

◆━◆━◆

The dead body of Mister Tenning was definitely a curiosity. Everything about the situation raised questions. First of all, the body was definitely Tenning, unless the neighbor who identified him was part of a larger conspiracy. Minox did not suspect that was the case—there was too much shock and honesty in the neighbor's reaction when he saw the body.

Which meant that Tenning had been one of the three in the boiler room that Rainey had rescued. And if that were the case, why was his name removed from the roster of the survivors, and replaced with another? Was it as simple as Tenning, Hunsen, and Cole giving false names, and if so, why? Why had Tenning been killed now? And by whom, in a simple, rough, and violent way?

One thing was certain, it was not the work of the Gearbox Killer—or, at least, not his signature work.

That was probably fortunate, as it did not raise any need for explanation to the North High River constables about the murder or what they were doing there. Minox and Rainey had simply introduced themselves as inspectors with the GIU and that they had come to ask some routine questions when they found Mister Tenning dead. The North High River inspectors were quite pleasant and cooperative, willing to share any revelations their investigation brought with the GIU. One of them, when his partner was otherwise occupied, slipped his calling card to Minox, hoping to be transferred to the GIU if an opening arose.

"You all are doing great stuff," he said. "I'd love to be a part of it."

Minox agreed to pass the card to Captain Cinellan. He could even do so in good conscience—these inspectors both seemed engaged, inquisitive, and competent. They were everything that inspectors ought to be. Minox thanked them for their help and gladly passed the case on to them.

"And now to Cole?" Rainey asked as they left. It was already midafternoon, a bit too much time wasted at Tenning's place.

"With some urgency. It's just a few blocks this way," Minox said. "Hopefully it won't be the same scenario. The North High River Stationhouse would probably have some concerns." Them finding two dead Parliamentary functionaries in North Maradaine would likely get the marshals' attention, if the first one alone didn't.

Cole's apartment was not the same scenario, but it did have similarities. There was no body, or signs of a struggle. It was a similar mess, but a mess that put Minox in mind of someone quickly gathering a few necessary belongings and running off. Including a lockbox that had been taken out of a hidden spot under a desk and left open and empty on the bed.

"So, was Mister Cole robbed or did he run?" Rainey asked.

"My guess is run," Minox said. "But why and to where?"

"Why is likely because he doesn't want to get killed like Tenning."

"Presuming he's aware. Presuming he isn't the one who killed Tenning."

"So here's the big question in front of us," Rainey said. "These three, Tenning, Cole, and Hunsen, were missing from the list we had for a reason. Tenning we know was one of the three in the boiler room. I don't know about Cole and Hunsen . . ."

"We have my cousin's sketches, including her sketches of the victims and other parts of the scene."

"I thought those were claimed as evidence."

"She did another set from memory—it's something she does—and I gave them to Joshea to bring to Dayne. Since those were her personal sketches, sent to me personally, they were not official evidence."

"Did she even see the three in the boiler room?"

"I'm not certain. At least some of her drawings were of the aftermath—Yellowshields treating victims and such. She may have something useful there."

"Hmm." Rainey sat down on Cole's table, flexing her foot. The replacement boot from the Aventil gang member was clearly annoying her. "I'm assuming you trust Joshea here."

"Implicitly."

"I'll accept that. I still barely know the man. And you think Dayne can be trusted? I like Jerinne, I'll admit, but I still have my doubts on him."

"I believe that Dayne is fundamentally honest with us. That the Gearboxes match the events in Lacanja, that Dayne really did see and confront this Sholiar character who was, nominally, the perpetrator of those crimes, and the Gearboxes and the Parliament Atrocity were, if nothing else, engineered with similar craftwork. Does that mean Sholiar is really in Maradaine and responsible?"

"Or real?"

"I think the answer to both might be irrelevant. But my instinct is that Dayne Heldrin is someone who is invested in justice being done here, and has little faith in the marshals to do so."

Rainey nodded. "And given that this investigation might get us in trouble, all the way up to the royal level, keeping him involved might give us cover."

"How so?"

"Prince Escaraine was of the opinion that if anyone had the authority to investigate the marshals independently, it would be the Tarians."

"The prince just told you this?"

"I have my charms, Welling."

Minox let that go. "Even still—" He paused for a moment. "Dayne's situation in Lacanja. That put him out with the Benedict family, yes?"

"Right."

"Mister Cole is the staff chief for Wesley Benedict."

"You think that's connected?"

"I think it's interesting that someone who probably has specific knowledge of the events in Lacanja was involved in this situation, and their name is missing from the victim list—"

"Replaced with a different name."

"Yes. And that man has now vanished."

"Cole," Rainey said absently, like it was a clue in and of itself. "You think he could be the key to this?"

"I think he could be crucial to find."

"I don't think we'll find anything else here, unless he left a letter detailing the entire conspiracy."

Minox pointed to a rubbish bin filled with fresh-looking ashes. "Anything like that he seems to have burned."

"Then we should move on to Hunsen in all haste."

Satrine had been keeping one question in all afternoon, and as they walked to Hunsen's place, she knew she had to ask it.

"So what's the worst outcome, realistically?"

"You are going to have to be more specific than that," Welling responded.

"To your Inquiry. Let's say they find you unfit, which I honestly can't imagine."

"Can't you?"

"No, I can't. Yes, I know what Olivant said to you, but I don't believe that for one jot."

"Why not?"

"Because I know mages, especially ones like Olivant."

"Your experience extends beyond Major Dresser?"

"It does. And in my experience, they're absurdly paranoid about authority outside their own. Now, I also know the history—"

"Public executions with no trial, spurious arrests. I'm aware."

"The point is, yes—you scare them. Olivant. Dresser. Professor Alimen on campus . . ."

"He was explosive."

"You scare them because they think your loyalty ought to be to them, when it's to this," she said, pointing to her vest.

"Is it?" he asked.

"You're one of the few people whom I have no doubts about on that. And I don't mean the Constabulary itself, the green wall. I mean justice and order."

He furrowed his brow. "I need to confess something to you, Inspector Rainey."

She had been waiting for this for a couple weeks now, ever since they had the situation in Aventil. "That you know who the Thorn is, that it's not the man who went to jail for it, but you don't want to arrest the actual Thorn?"

"You've known?"

"I deduced."

"I should have assumed."

She paused for a moment, looking up at the building that was Hunsen's apartment. "Commissioner Enbrain visited me last night. He's certain that the Constabulary is filled to the top with corruption. Including Vice Commandant Undenway."

"His victory in the election over Undenway was by a disturbing small margin," Welling said. "And I suspect that was affected by vote tampering."

"Really?"

"There were an unusual number of disturbances on election night in western and southern neighborhoods, which lowered voter turnout. Unremarkable on its own, but they would have had an effect on the city district races, like the alderman seats where the Chair District was drawn unevenly."

"You've studied this?" she asked.

"My cousin Evoy did. Though the mapping of it was not something I quite understood."

"Hmm," she said, not sure what to make of it. Perhaps she was right about Grieson tampering with the election in Enbrain's favor.

She was going to have to get a straight answer from him about that, if it were possible.

"But my point is this," he said. "I do believe that Commissioner Enbrain is correct, and I am concerned deeply about the Constabulary in this city. You deduced my confession about the Thorn, but not why I don't wish to see him arrested."

"Because you think he's a good man?"

"Because I think he's a man who can do good that we can't." He sighed. "I almost—" His voice choked up, which was more then unusual. Overcome with emotion was not something she had ever seen on Minox Welling.

"What is it?"

"The Constabulary is my life, and I embrace that calling," he said. "But I almost wish that . . . that this Inquiry does drum me out of it. So I wouldn't be surrounded by so many people unworthy of the colors."

He cleared his throat, looking sheepishly at the ground. "Present company excluded, of course. Forgive my lack of decorum, Inspector."

"Always," she said. "This is it."

They made their way up the stairs to the third-floor apartment belonging to Hunsen. Immediately they saw things were amiss—the door hung open, the framing and hinges cracked. Satrine brought up her crossbow, as did Welling. In harmony, they went into the apartment, sweeping through the kitchen and sitting room, and then to the bed.

"Body," Welling said as he came in.

Satrine knelt next to the figure, lying on his back. He was dressed like he was about to leave, even run off—boots and a coat, despite the heat. A sizable bruise covered his face, but not so much that Satrine couldn't tell he wasn't one of the three from boiler room. She told Welling as much.

"He may have been one of the main victims, I didn't see them all," he said.

She touched the face and neck of the man. Still warm. "This didn't happen long ago," she said. "Maybe his attacker is still—"

She was interrupted by a shuddering cough from the body, and then he wheezed.

Still breathing.

"Yellowshield," she told Welling. "We need to get him to a hospital ward."

Chapter 18

D AYNE WASN'T SURE what to make of this Brondar fellow. When he first arrived with the envelope of sketches, saying he had come from Inspector Minox Welling, Dayne thought he was just a courier of some sort. But then he stuck around, asking questions. Then it became clear the man was an associate of Minox's, but an informal one. Not part of the Constabulary.

Brondar pulled up a chair and started chatting, first asking about the Tarian Order and the training involved. Then he started talking about the Army. That lit the man up, as he told one animated story after another about his service.

Dayne had to admit, it was engaging, and the man definitely had some fascinating experiences in Eastern Druthal and on the Kellirac border.

But there was something else there. The charismatic storyteller was a performance, Dayne could see. Brondar was holding something back, something he was ashamed of. Perhaps something happened during his service, perhaps he had seen or done terrible horrors. This was a man who clearly bore the weight of sins on his back, as much as he pretended not to.

More than he wanted to admit, Dayne understood what that was like.

Nonetheless, it was a welcome distraction while watching over Niall in the hospital ward. The nurses insisted that Dayne keep a certain distance from Niall's bed, so they could work without him underfoot. Niall still hadn't woken up, but he had stirred and shown signs that the doctor called "encouraging."

"What I don't understand," Brondar said after the nurses had done another round of checking on Niall and heading off, "is why the government never did anything to integrate the Tarians and the Spathians and such into the military."

"Well, that's not entirely true," Dayne said. "I mean, not for the Tarians and the Spathians, but many of the other Elite Orders were folded into the military. The Braighians became the pikemen in the Army, the Marenians essentially became the Navy. . . ."

"Right, but . . . like your training, the Spathians. The Army could benefit from that."

"Wouldn't we lose what makes the Tarians unique, though?" Dayne asked. "We are supposed to represent an ideal."

Brondar shrugged. "Well, sure. But if there was better integration, if someone doesn't make the standards of the Tarians or the Spathians, then they'd still be a well-trained soldier."

Dayne wasn't quite sure how to respond to that, given that he was doomed to finish the third year of his Candidacy without being fully inducted to the Tarians. That might not sting as much if he knew that he would automatically be placed somewhere else in service of the country. In theory, his liaison role between the Parliament and the Order could continue even once he cashiered out of the Tarians next year. But he had a hard time believing that was anything other than an appeasement from the Grandmaster.

"Besides," Brondar continued, jumping on Dayne's silence, "then you'd have a better sense of where the Orders fit in the hierarchy and the chains of command.

I heard some from Minox what a mess this whole matter was in terms of jurisdiction."

"Which appears to have changed, you say."

"I don't know much about that, other than Minox wanted me to skirt away when the marshals arrived."

"So why were you there if you aren't part of the Constabulary?"

"Sort of what I was talking about," Brondar said. "The constables want to put together a squad with something closer to Army training, use what we do on the streets here."

"They could use it." Jerinne approached. She looked like she had been in something of a scrape, a bandage across her scalp.

"What are you doing here?" Dayne asked.

"Knew you'd be here," she said. "The marshals cracked down on the constabulary investigation, and Missus Rainey chased me away."

"She'll do that," Brondar said. He offered his hand to her. "Joshea Brondar."

"Jerinne Fendall," she said coolly. "I helped her with some gang trouble on the south side, other constables in Aventil. Frankly, I don't know what they would have done without me."

"This is what I mean," Brondar said. "Shouldn't all of us be on one side in all this, working together and maximizing the good we can do? Instead we have marshals and constables and Elite Orders and Mage Circles all doing their own thing."

Curious he mentioned Mage Circles in that.

Dayne turned back to Jerinne. "So you came here? Did you hear anything else? Should I be somewhere else?"

"Weren't you assigned to protect him?"

"Right, but if this all is back in the hands of the marshals, shouldn't I be liaising or such with them?"

She shrugged. "I gathered they would prefer if you stayed away."

"Right. Maybe to exile me here."

"Does this guy need protecting?" Brondar asked. "I mean, has anything happened?"

"How long have you been here, Dayne?" she asked.

"Since five bells last night."

"Oh, saints, Dayne," she said. "I'm sure the Grandmaster didn't expect you to forgo sleep or—"

"I dozed on the chair."

She shook her head. "I'll go to the chapterhouse and get this cleared up. You shouldn't—"

Before she finished her sentence, a pair of ward doctors and a nurse came crashing down the hallway with a gurney, a man laid out on it. The man was thrashing and coughing. Inspectors Welling and Rainey were chasing right behind them.

"Did you see what happened?" a doctor shouted. "Where was he injured? How?"

"We're not sure," Welling said. "But he might be the best witness we have."

"What happened?" Dayne asked, stepping forward. "What's going on?"

"Please give us space," the other doctor said. "We're going to need to work. Get this coat off him!"

"We'll explain shortly," Welling said. "Just let us—"

Dayne nodded, watching as the gurney rolled past him.

He saw the face of the man the doctors were working on. A face he'd never forget.

"Sholiar!" he shouted.

In that moment, the nurse who was trying to remove his coat screamed as a metallic device snapped shut on her hand. Blood spurted from it, spraying on the doctor's face.

Sholiar sat up, suddenly unburdened by cough and seizure. A crazed, maniacal grin crossed over his face as he took in the room. The nurse still screamed, and the two doctors were in a state of shock. The rest of the room froze.

"Dayne, old top," Sholiar said. "Capital to see you here. I guess the jig is up!"

Dayne lunged at him—as did Welling and Rainey—but before he could close the distance, Sholiar pulled something from under his coat and slapped it on the wrist of one of the doctors, and in a maneuver so graceful it was almost poetry, he whipped a cord around the neck of the other doctor. As soon as he let go, a hideous grinding sound came from the device on the first doctor's wrist, and the second doctor was pulled over the gurney into the first. Both of them screamed in horror and pain, and Sholiar slipped off the gurney and started off down the corridor.

"Get him!" Dayne shouted at no one in particular, though both Jerinne and Brondar were in position to block Sholiar's escape. Dayne, instead, went to the two doctors. One was being choked, and the other was having his wrist torn up. Dayne grabbed the device and the cord, trying to keep at least the cord from tightening any further around the one doctor's neck. The device kept grinding and winding, though.

Welling came over and touched the device with his gloved hand, and it shattered into a dozen pieces, freeing both doctors. The first one's arm was still a mess of blood and mangled flesh, and the second gasped for air. Rainey had her hands full with the nurse, still screaming in agony and panic.

Dayne looked up, and Sholiar was darting around the corner. Jerinne and Brondar were both on the floor, covered in some rancid smelling syrup. Jerinne was emptying the contents of her stomach on the floor, and Brondar looked like it was taking all his effort to not do the same.

"I'm in pursuit!" Welling shouted to Rainey, and went off after Sholiar. Dayne gave one last look at the two doctors to confirm they were in no further immediate danger, and charged behind Welling.

"Stand and be held!" Welling roared as he rounded the corner. "You will be ironed and brought to justice."

Dayne caught up in time to see Sholiar pivot just as Welling reached him. With that same precision, he wrapped another infernal clockwork on Welling's gloved hand, and spun a wire around the inspector's neck.

"Hold there, Dayne, old top," he said, pointing a threatening finger at Dayne while keeping the other hand on the device on Welling's wrist. "I'm about to flip this key, and then in a matter of seconds, the good inspector's head will come clean off. You come any closer, and that's what will happen. And that will be yet another life lost because of your foolery."

"Sholiar—" Dayne growled, but he didn't take another step. He wasn't ready for this—his shield and sword were still sitting by Niall's bed.

"Now, the good inspector and I will keep walking—and he isn't going to try anything if he wants to keep his head. And once I'm at the door I will slip off into the night, and you will just have to live with that."

"I'm not going to—"

"I want to hear 'I agree to your terms,' and nothing more."

"I do not," Welling said, and his gloved hand burst into a blue flame. The clockwork device and the wire turned into ash, and Sholiar cried out, waving his own hand like it was on fire.

Welling spun around and was on him, kicking Sholiar's leg out from under him. Before Sholiar could recover, Minox had his irons out and was putting them on Sholiar's wrists. "You will stand trial for crimes. If you need them named, they will include and not be limited to assault on officers of law and assault of members of the citizenry. Do you understand what I have told you?"

"Oh, I do," Sholiar said, leering up at Welling despite having his face in the floor. "You're more than I bargained for, Inspector Welling. I won't forget that, and there will be a reckoning."

Welling got up and hauled Sholiar to his feet. "The

only reckoning there will be is the justice you will face."

Sholiar grinned at Dayne and gave him the tiniest of winks. "We'll see about that. Eh, old top?"

———◆—◆■—

Satrine had managed to stem the bleeding, at least on the nurse's hand, all the while shouting for more nurses or doctors to come. But the device on the nurse's hand—some sort of small spring-loaded jaw trap—was something Satrine wasn't able to get off.

"Jerinne! Joshea!" she called at the two on the floor. "Get someone! Hurry!"

Jerinne got to her feet, though she looked a bit shaky. "I'll—just a—" she said as she stumbled. A truly horrid putrescence came wafting off the girl.

"Stay down," Satrine told her. "Doctors! Help!" She couldn't take her hands off the nurse's wound, and both the doctors in front of her were useless. One of them was still coughing, even though Minox had burned up the thing on his neck. The other was desperately trying to wrap up his own wrist.

A couple other doctors came running over. "Sweet saints, what—" one of them exclaimed.

"Just help them!" Satrine said, passing the nurse to one of them. She drew out her crossbow and went down the hall. "Joshea, if you could—"

"I've never . . . it was . . ." was all Joshea said, not getting up off the floor. Satrine didn't have time to worry about him right now.

But then Minox came back around the corner with Dayne, and the man Dayne had called Sholiar in irons. Minox looked exhausted, his eyes sunken. Like he was putting all his effort into just staying standing.

"You got him," she said. "Sholiar, I presume?"

"I never said that," the man said. "That was this tall one."

"He is Sholiar," Dayne said. "I would swear to it in any court."

"I challenge you to find a single official document with that name on it. Certainly not one you can connect to me." He leaned forward to Rainey. "Please, Inspector, my name is Tandus Hunsen. I am the staff chief for a member of Parliament. This is some dreadful error."

"Really?" she asked.

"Reach into my pocket and take my papers," he said.

Satrine almost laughed at that. "You really think that I would fall for that? That I didn't see what you've got in your coat?"

He broke out into a low cackle. "Well, you never know what surprises might be there, that's true."

"Enough of this foolery," Dayne said.

The man suddenly took on a thick Waish accent, leering at Satrine. "Ye even hold a wisefast wit, *quia*, sure as yer finger."

That was very strange, and not just for the fact that he addressed her by the rank she held when she was undercover in Waisholm.

"I don't recommend we attempt to remove his coat," Welling said.

"No, certainly," he said. "You do it wrong, it might be bad for both of us."

"He's slippery," Dayne said. "I wouldn't trust he wasn't hiding something unless he was naked."

"Saints, at least ask my father's permission, squire."

"And not even then."

"Really," the man—Sholiar or Hunsen or whoever—said. "This is a misunderstanding, borne from this Tarian stalking me for a year. He blames me for his own failures, the death of his mentor."

"You attacked those three people," Welling said. "And tried to hold me hostage. We are taking you in to the stationhouse."

"Of course, but I demand counsel," he said. "I want the Justice Advocate and my own lawyers as soon as we arrive."

"That's your right," Satrine said. "But I don't think it will help you."

"Well, I'll explain everything when I have counsel and witness. You're working with this brute, so I don't trust you to treat me fairly."

"Then let's go," Satrine said. She turned to the doctors treating the three injured people. "Please come to us at the GIU in Inemar if you need to press further charges or questions." She laid her calling card down where they could get it when they weren't as busy. "I apologize for the disruption."

Jerinne had finally righted herself, though she still looked very out of sorts. She had helped Joshea up, and he was walking with her. While Dayne led Sholiar or whoever he was out the door, Satrine hung back with Welling for a moment.

"You all right?" she asked, taking some dried lamb from her pouch. Welling took it eagerly.

"Too much, too fast. I got—cocksure, I think, listening to Mister Olivant. I assumed I had immense power at my fingertips, literally, and— I was very careless in using too much. Turning metal into dust is more involved than I had assumed."

"We'll stop—"

"No," he said. "Let's get this man, this Sholiar, under proper custody. Joshea, are you well?"

"I've never seen anything like him," Joshea said, still staring at the prisoner as Dayne hauled him away. "He moved like a . . . like he was touched with grace."

"Hardly the word I'd use," Jerinne grumbled.

"Well, yes, horrible," Joshea said quickly. "But a horror that inspires nothing short of awe."

Satrine didn't have time to worry about Joshea's bizarre response to being assaulted. Welling needed to be brought back to the station quickly, and they had an arrest. A solid one. And if Dayne was correct, an arrest that would also solve the Gearbox deaths.

In the pit of her stomach, though, she had her doubts about Dayne.

Chapter 19

MINOX COULDN'T LET anyone see how he felt—weak as a newborn, ready to fall down at any moment. The magic he had invoked in the hospital, turning Sholiar's machines to ash, had put too much strain on his body. Whatever Mister Olivant thought about his supposed power, it was a gross exaggeration.

And he had let Olivant's words make him overconfident. Even foolhardy.

Inspector Rainey clearly realized his condition, despite his attempt to dissemble. Dayne and his young associate probably did not, as they were not as familiar with him as Inspector Rainey. And Joshea—Joshea normally would notice, but he seemed slightly out of sorts. The encounter with Sholiar had spooked him, somehow.

As they delivered Sholiar to the Inemar Stationhouse, Minox ate all the dried beef he kept in his coat pocket for emergencies. This clearly was one, and while he no longer felt as hungry, he still had a bone-deep exhaustion that made every step a trial.

But that would not deter him. He had Sholiar, clearly the Gearbox Killer and the architect of the Parliament Atrocity. He had him in irons, and would take him to be questioned, and book an arrest that would set a trial in motion.

His duty, fully executed, and it would keep at least one thing from going to the unresolved.

Right now, that would give him a bit of peace.

As they entered the stationhouse, the desk clerk at the front just raised his eyebrow. "You leading a parade, specs?"

"We're bringing in an arrest," Minox said, pushing Sholiar forward. "And they all will make witness statements."

"What's he guilty of?" the clerk asked, his tone even more disrespectful than the usual trouble the floor staff would give him and Rainey.

"Besides attacking us and people in the hospital?" Rainey shot back. "Well, he's probably guilty of the Gearbox Murders."

"I really expected the press to do better with that," Sholiar said. "It's a terrible name."

"What?" the clerk asked. He turned to a nearby page. "Get the captain!" The page scurried off.

"Process him and set him for questioning," Minox said. "But be aware, he's got tricks in that coat of his."

"Why else would I be wearing it in this heat, hmm?"

"Hush," Rainey said.

"We can't take him in without a weapons search," the clerk said.

"And I don't recommend you forgo that procedure," Minox said. "In fact, be beyond thorough in your examination."

"Gentlemen, I think I should be courted a little first," Sholiar interjected.

"Can we muzzle him?" Dayne asked.

"What's with the rutting knights, specs?" the clerk asked.

"Two members of the Tarian Order, who were helpful and instrumental in his capture."

"Minox?" Captain Cinellan had come downstairs. "What's all this?"

"We've apprehended this person, who we believe is responsible for the Gearbox Murders."

"Based on?" Cinellan asked.

"He was identified by Mister Heldrin here—"

"And I will gladly make a statement," Dayne added.

"And he had devices on his person that match the gearbox machines in style and form."

"That's good," Sholiar said. "Oh, that is a good one. I thought he had nothing but Dayne, but that is good."

"I can't—" the captain started.

"Regardless of the charge holding, Captain," Rainey interjected. "He attacked us, three staff members at Riverheart Hospital Ward, Miss Fendall, and Mister Brondar. Those assaults are not to be ignored."

"But he's a suspect for the Gearbox?"

"Yes, of course," Minox said.

Captain Cinellan sighed. "Then I have to send word to the King's Marshals. It's their case now." He whistled for a page to come over as he grabbed a notepad.

"Sir, we should—"

"I have to, Minox," he said. "You can hold him in questioning and do what you can before the marshals get here, but it's on them. If they don't like him as a Gearbox suspect, then you can charge him for the other assaults."

Miss Morad and Mister Olivant came purposefully down from the stairway to the inspectors' floor. "Is he back?" Miss Morad asked. "We need to—"

"I am in the middle of things, Miss Morad," Minox snapped. "Whatever you have will have to wait while I attend to my duties." He grabbed Sholiar's irons and pulled him toward the back stairwell. "I'm going to question him until the marshals arrive. Please send someone to transcribe."

Rainey was at his arm as they went down. "I don't know how wise that was," she said.

"I'm not interested in wisdom," he said. "I'm interested in resolution."

Minox noted that Dayne had followed them down to the questioning rooms. Inspector Rainey took point on trying to dissuade the Tarian. "You can't come in here, Heldrin," she said. "We've got to follow some procedure here."

"You didn't search or disarm him," Dayne said.

Minox nodded, as Rainey took Sholiar in. "It's a risk I'm willing to take right now. And he's not booked as an arrest right now. The marshals can handle disarming him and his coat of gearwork monstrosity."

"Even still—"

"We have little time to waste before the marshals sweep him away. Trust me, I will not drop my guard around him. And you can observe from there." Minox pointed to the observation room. "You can jump in if action is necessary."

"All right," Dayne said, clapping Minox on the shoulder with his giant hand. "Caution."

Minox went in, to see that Rainey had secured Sholiar to the chair, and was sitting on the other side of the table.

"I notice that you have not brought in either private counsel or Justice Advocate for me," he said. "I imagine that's a violation."

"Do you want either of those brought to you?" Minox asked.

"Not particularly. After all, what do you actually have on me, Inspectors?" Sholiar asked. "I mean, truly, what?"

"You attacked a nurse and two doctors."

"Did I?" Sholiar asked. "Or did they put hands on me, and accidentally injure themselves on my equipment?"

"You were identified by Mister Heldrin," Rainey said.

"Oh, yes, his word," Sholiar said. "The word of a semi-disgraced Tarian who, from what I understand, crippled a young boy and then fled Lacanja. So he's made me the monster of his nightmares. I'm just the victim of his delusions."

"You tried to hold me hostage," Minox said.

"Did I?" Sholiar asked again. He shrugged. "Perhaps it seemed that way, but I did have a large, delusional man who insists that I'm some sort of monster bearing down on me. My actions were merely in self-defense."

"And the Parliament?" Rainey asked. She had a look on her face that said she wasn't remotely interested in his games of denial. "How did you do that?"

"How did I?" Sholiar asked. "I can't answer that. Now, were you to ask how *might* I pull off such a feat, even then I'd be at a loss."

Rainey presented one of the devices from the hospital, which she had taken out of her pocket. "This is pretty intricate work. We saw similar things at the Parliament. It wouldn't take much for a person to decide the connection between the two was reasonable enough to presume you were the architect of all these machines."

Sholiar's eyes narrowed, a smile creeping over his face. "Oh, she's clever. But no. I mean, I'm sure a corrupt and compromised justice system could convict me, and that will be mine to bear. Especially once the marshals come for me. I'm not even sure what you're here to ask me, Inspectors."

"So you deny that that's your work?" Rainey asked. "Someone else was able to build that monstrosity of torture?"

There was a glint in his eye. "You're trying to hit my pride, Inspector. I respect that. What if I told you, *quia mosha*, that what you found in the Parliament was my design, my equipment, but I was not involved with its implementation?"

"I'd say that was lacking credibility," Minox said.

"Come now," he said. "That isn't really my style. Were I even this monster you think me to be."

"You aren't?"

"Some might say artist."

Rainey made a disgusted noise.

"And like any artist, I'm often in need of a patron. You have to audition to show them you can compose a symphony of death, a lasting work of profane and disturbing beauty."

"Who did you 'audition' for?" Rainey was taking point in these questions, which Minox was grateful for. He wanted to just observe the man, see through this performance. But he was also exhausted, which Rainey surely noticed. She was keeping Sholiar's attention on her so he wouldn't see how weak Minox actually was.

"It hardly matters, especially speaking in the abstract. Which I certainly am. The point is, some people want a masterpiece, and some people think the master's tools are all they need. And so you get no profound poem on the fragility of life. Instead it's a belch of random slaughter. Imagine, *quia mosha*, that you're busy playing the first notes of the overture, and some cretins plagiarize your libretto."

"You're really saying—"

"I'm saying that were I the man your Tarian friend thinks I am, then that facade of an atrocity at the Parliament would be beneath me. I almost had to just lie down at your feet and get caught to get some justice."

"Justice?" Minox found himself shouting the word.

"We all have our methods of justice, Inspector Welling. Each is very personal. And my work is deeply personal to me. That's why I put those three in the boiler room. Rushed on my part. So I had hoped to make an example of Mister Hunsen, but he. . . ."

"So you're no longer claiming to be Hunsen?" It was only through pure willpower that Minox did not throttle this man. To be so . . . glib about the torture and death he had caused, it was infuriating. Minox could feel that anger bubbling up in his gut and slowly feeding into his hand. He needed to get control over it.

Sholiar laughed drolly. "Damnation, I had forgotten that bit. Too much on my mind, that's for certain. I had such games planned for the two of you, and instead . . .

it's all just crassness now. That's what rushing gets you: sloppiness instead of art."

Someone pounded on the door. "King's Marshals are here!"

"Oh, our time is at an end," Sholiar said. "The marshals will, if they have any sense, throw me in a hole and then throw away the hole."

"Seems about right," Rainey said. If she was feeling the same rage Minox was, she was keeping it hidden. Though four months had taught Minox that she was adept at masking her feelings.

"But given what you've discovered, what you know, what's the one question you should be asking yourself. Come on, Inspectors? Do I have to spell it out for you?"

"Did you kill Tenning?" Rainey asked. "Or Cole or Hunsen?"

"You know I didn't, there was no showmanship there," he said. The door started to open. "Out of time."

"Who did kill him, then?" she asked, moving closer. "And where are the other two?"

Chief Quoyell came in with Cinellan. "All right," Quoyell said. "This is done."

Sholiar winked at Minox and Rainey. "I guess this is the end. But that was the right question."

———◆·◆———

"Come on out," Quoyell said, glaring at Satrine. "We'll be taking him." He looked like he wanted to drag her and Welling out of the questioning room by their hair.

"Then take him," Welling said.

"Get out of here," Quoyell said, grabbing Welling's arm, pulling him out to the hallway.

"Are you taking him into your custody?" Satrine asked, glancing at the curtain to the observation room. Dayne was in there, even if she couldn't see him right now. She didn't want to leave Sholiar—damn it, she had accepted that was who the fellow was, hadn't she?—without eyes on him. Dayne would have to do.

"We'll question him," Quoyell said. "And then we'll decide if he's of interest to *our* case." He spit that word at her with much venom. Satrine kept herself half in the doorway, where she could still pay attention to Sholiar and see Quoyell and Welling. Four marshals were in the hallway, waiting with their hands resting on sword pommels.

"Rainey, let's just let this go," Cinellan said.

"No, I'm not," Quoyell said. "The fact that I had to come down here, twice, because of your overzealous people—"

"My people did their jobs," Cinellan shot back hotly. "You will respect me and my house, and my people—"

"What I'm going to do is get a Royal decree to crawl up inside the Constabulary, especially this Grand Inspection Unit, and tear it apart."

"Just try it, *Chief*." Cinellan made the man's rank sound like a slap.

"Your man Enbrain can't protect you!"

"Enbrain," Sholiar said lightly. "There was something for him, too. But that's past. You all ruined it."

"Shut it," Quoyell said. He turned to his men. "Take him out of here." The four marshals came into the room, brushing Satrine aside.

"Coming here wasn't my plan in the first place," Sholiar said. "But sometimes a man has to improvise."

He whipped his arms around and the irons came flying off, smacking one marshal in the face. Then he hurled three darts at the other marshals. All three fell to the floor in a fit, foaming at the mouth.

"And, yes, *quia mosha*, you should have checked the coat."

———◆———

Dayne knew he shouldn't have let that rat Sholiar out of arm's reach. Four men down in a breath. And with the marshals on the floor, Welling and Rainey wouldn't be able to get at him easily. But it also meant that

Sholiar would likely try to jump through the curtain into the observation room to make his escape. Which left it up to Dayne to stop him.

"Stay back, miss," he told the clerk who had come to transcribe the questioning. She had already jumped out of her chair and scurried to the back corner.

"Don't think I don't hear you, old top," Sholiar said from the other side. He tore the curtain open. "You think this can help you atone?"

"You're not going anywhere," Dayne said. Rainey and Welling were trying to get over the fallen marshals, Welling's hand now lit up in blue flame.

"Maybe, maybe not," Sholiar said, stepping farther into the questioning room, putting the table between him and the window to the observation room. "Doesn't change the fact that somewhere in Lacanja there's a crippled boy, all thanks to you."

"That was your doing!" Dayne tried to get into the room, but the window from the observation room was small, and Dayne could barely squeeze through it. He had only managed to get his head and one arm through so far. At least Sholiar couldn't get past him.

"I didn't smash him with a barrel lid, old top." Sholiar kicked the table, knocking it into Rainey, pinning her to the wall. "You weren't the one I had wanted to play with, dear," he said to her.

"Were you trying to get my attention?" Welling asked, getting in front of him. "The Enbrain message?"

"You noticed that?" Sholiar asked, ducking a swing from Welling's handstick. "Oh, Inspector, I could kiss you." He popped up, grabbed Welling's head, and did just that.

Welling startled, and the flame around his hand lit up into white-hot. Sholiar grabbed the inspector and spun him toward Dayne. Welling's hand smashed into Dayne's face, and suddenly Dayne was engulfed in light and pain.

After a momentary eternity, Dayne pulled himself out of the window, breaking contact with Welling. He felt like every part of his body was on fire, and even trying to use his eyes was painful. But he had to see, he had to move. Sholiar was already gone.

Dayne pushed himself out of the room, despite the pain, forcing himself to stay on his feet. In the hallway, Sholiar had grabbed the clerk and was holding a cord around her throat.

"Now," Sholiar said loudly. "I'm going to walk out of here, because you all want this girl to not bleed all over the floor. Am I clear?"

Rainey and Welling were in the hallway, both looking slightly dazed.

"Nyla," Welling whispered. Then his voice rose to a roar. "You will release her!"

"Nothing doing, dear Inspector," Sholiar said, dragging the woman down the hall. "No one is going to try to stop me. All I have to do is jerk my wrists and she dies."

"Minox, please," the woman said.

Rainey had her crossbow up, but she wasn't aiming at him yet.

Sholiar was at the stairs.

"Stay with them," the Constabulary captain said. He had a bleeding gash on his face. Sholiar must have struck him on his way out the door.

"Everyone keep away from me!" Sholiar shouted as he went up. Dayne charged after him, despite every nerve in his body crying out. Welling looked like he was feeling the same way, nearly collapsing as he tried to pursue Sholiar. Rainey grabbed him before he fell, and hauled him with her up the stairs to the main stationhouse work floor.

Sholiar was crossing the room, still holding the clerk by the throat.

"No one, and I mean no one, even come close to us," he said.

Dayne drew out his sword. "You will let her go, Sholiar."

"Try it, old top," Sholiar said. "You probably will

kill me, I've no doubt, but she'll die, too. You want that on you?"

Welling raised his hand, but instead of it being engulfed in flame, it just sparked and crackled, like the last embers of a dying campfire.

"I really expected better," Sholiar said. "But now I can at least get things back on track. And you'll help, won't you, dear?" he asked the clerk.

"Please," she whispered. "Anyone, help."

"No one can," he whispered back. He had crossed over to the entry desk. Ten more feet, and he'd be outside.

Then suddenly the device around her neck flew out of his hands, and Sholiar went flying in the air, crashing into a wall.

The clerk collapsed, and someone ran in to catch her before she hit the ground.

"Got you," Joshea Brondar said.

Sholiar was on his feet in a heartbeat. "Well, that's interesting."

Dayne tried to make his legs charge forward, but they felt like wood, rooted to the floor. Rainey raised up her crossbow and took a shot, but Sholiar slipped to the side. Her bolt embedded itself into the wall.

"That's enough of that," Sholiar said, and barreled through the one patrolman who stood between him and freedom. Rainey ran after him out the door, while Welling stumbled toward the clerk and Brondar.

"Are you—did you—" Welling said, gasping for breath. Dayne could barely keep his own feet and let himself collapse to his knees. His sword fell from his hands, clattering to the floor.

"It's fine," Brondar said. "I'm fine. She's safe, that's what matters."

Chief Quoyell and the Constabulary captain came up the stairs. "Where is he?" Quoyell asked. "Did he escape?"

Dayne tried to answer him, but he couldn't even get

words into his mouth. Minox Welling had also dropped to the ground.

"Yellowshields, doctors, hurry!" Dayne heard some-one yell, before his vision blurred, and then everything went quiet.

Chapter 20

SATRINE HAD LOST Sholiar. She ran down the alley she assumed he had gone down—based on the scatter of the crowd in the square—but there was no sign of him there. There was no point in just running blindly, wasting more time. She returned to the stationhouse.

"Is everyone all right?" she asked as she came in, even though it was clear the answer was no. Nyla was on a bench normally reserved for new arrests, looking Poasian pale as Brondar and Corrie hovered over her. Joshea Brondar's attention wasn't completely on her, though, as he glanced furtively around the room.

It was his magic that had separated Sholiar and Nyla, not Minox's. It didn't occur to Satrine until now, seeing the guilty look on his face. Probably no one else in the stationhouse would make the connection, save Minox and Corrie. No one else needed to know, as far as Satrine was concerned.

Welling and Dayne were both on the ground, as a couple of Yellowshields attended to them. Mister Olivant stood over them both, scowling, while Jerinne paced aimlessly.

Captain Cinellan was having his face bandaged, while Chief Quoyell was dropping a Riot Call on his head.

"What sort of outfit are you running where a prisoner is not properly searched and disarmed before putting him in holding?" Quoyell shouted. The other marshals were being carried out on stretchers by Yellowshields.

"He wasn't in holding—"

"My men are down, your house is a shambles. If you thought I wouldn't bring down the weight of the crown on you before—"

"Get out of my house," Cinellan said quietly. "And if you come back you better bring a box of writs and a Grand High Judge with you."

"Don't think I won't," Quoyell said. He pointed a thick finger at Satrine. "Stick to your side of the river." With that, he left.

Satrine went over to the captain. "Thank you, sir."

He shook his head. "Someone will have to be hit with the hammer for this, you know." He looked over to Welling, still lying insensate on the floor next to Dayne, who was in the same condition.

"What happened to them?" Satrine asked.

"Foolishness," Olivant said. He held his hands over the two of them, a faint violet nimbus surrounding him. "I have no idea how, but the inspector managed to bind himself to this Tarian fellow with some sort of *numinic* tether. Sucked half the life out of them both."

"Can you—" Satrine started.

"Maybe," Olivant said. "But try to remember I'm a lawyer who happens to do some magic."

Satrine took this as a cue. "I can go get someone. At the university? Or I know a few—"

"I've already started, and I've stemmed the bleeding, so to speak. They won't get worse. But if I hadn't been here, they'd have both died here on the floor."

"We appreciate it," Captain Cinellan said.

"I really don't care what you appreciate. I should just let him die from his own incompetence. But Welling dragged this other fellow into it, and he doesn't deserve that."

He yanked both his hands apart, and the violet nimbus shattered like glass. In that moment, both Welling and Dayne opened their eyes and gasped for breath.

"Easy, easy," Jerinne said, crouching next to Dayne. "You're going to be all right."

"He's probably starving. The both of them," Olivant said. He shook his head and stepped away from them, giving an odd glance over to Brondar at the bench with Nyla and Corrie. All three of them had gotten to their feet to look at Minox.

"Kid," Satrine said to one of the pages who was standing in the middle of the work floor, gawking. "Run out to the wrap stand and get as many fast wraps as Missus Wolman can make. Tell her it's for Inspector Welling, and it's an emergency." The page ran out.

"What happened?" Welling asked. "I never—I don't—"

"You had no control, Inspector," Olivant snarled. "Like I've been saying."

"No need for that," Satrine said. "They both nearly died."

"And thankfully someone who knew what he was doing was on hand," Olivant said. "I've been saying this, and it is the formal opinion of Lord Preston's Circle." He pointed over to Miss Morad, who had been quietly sitting at a desk writing in her journal. "Regardless of her decision, rest assured that *we* will be taking action, and filing an injunction with the Trust of Circles—"

"This is not the time," Cinellan snapped. "You do what you want, but you do it elsewhere."

Olivant raised an eyebrow, and gave one last disdain-filled glance at Welling, and then another to the bench. "Constabulary. Always building a wall around themselves." He flung his capelet over his shoulder and stalked off.

"Rainey—" Welling said, reaching up past the Yellowshield. "I can't—"

"Just stay put," Satrine said.

The page ran in with a handful of fast wraps. "She's cooking more. Is this enough?"

"It's a start," Satrine said, taking one and kneeling next to Welling. Jerinne grabbed a couple and got close to Dayne. Welling wasn't able to hold it, barely able to get his head up. She had to feed him directly, which he accepted voraciously, though she could see shame in his eyes.

At least there was something in his eyes. Otherwise this would be far too close to how it was when she fed her husband.

"All right, all right," he said when he finished a fourth. "I think . . . I think I can get on my feet."

"As can I," Dayne said weakly. "I've never . . . I've never felt anything . . ." His Yellowshield was now checking his face and eyes.

"You're both lucky to be alive," Jerinne said.

"My fault," Welling said.

"Sholiar," Dayne said hotly. "Blame no one but him."

"Where—" Welling started to ask.

"In the wind," Satrine said. "I'm sorry, he got outside, and I . . . I just lost him."

"Not your fault," Welling said. "He . . . I don't know . . . used me against Dayne, or . . ."

"It doesn't matter," Dayne said, getting on his feet. "We must find him and—"

He stumbled to his knees.

"I'm taking you back home," Jerinne said, helping him up.

"I'm going to rutting do the same for you," Corrie said, coming up to Welling. "You and Nyla should both get home and rest."

Cinellan coughed.

"With your permission, Captain," Corrie added.

"No," Miss Morad said from her place at the desk.

"I'm sorry?" Captain Cinellan asked.

"Mister Welling cannot leave until I've presented my decision, which I'm now prepared to render." She stood up and crossed over to them. "The rest is of no moment to me, but I will follow some procedure here. This has all already been far too irregular."

"It's fine," Welling said.

"But—" Corrie started.

"Take Nyla home."

"Like rutting blazes I'm leaving you to get home alone," Corrie said.

"Language," Miss Morad said in gentle song.

"I can . . . I can wait," Nyla said weakly. Satrine didn't believe she meant it, and clearly no one else did either.

"Nothing doing, Miss Pyle," the captain said. "You should go home and rest. Blazes, most of us should."

"I can take her," Brondar said.

"Are you certain?" Welling asked.

"Absolutely," Brondar replied. Minox stumbled closer to them for private counsel, and Satrine kept her distance.

Jerinne came up, half holding Dayne's massive form up with her shoulder. "I'll bring him back to his apartment, and then come back—"

"I cannot condone that," the captain said. "I appreciate the . . . involvement of the Tarian Order today, but as we are no longer dealing with the Parliament case or the Gearbox Murders, it's not appropriate."

"But Sholiar—" Dayne said weakly.

"Is out of my hands," Cinellan said. "Frankly, from what I saw, maybe you and yours should be the ones to handle it."

Jerinne nodded, and gave Satrine as much of an embrace as she could manage while holding Dayne up. "If you need—"

"Come to the house when you can," Satrine whispered. "I have . . ." She faltered. The idea was still only half in her head, nothing she wanted to formalize as a real idea. "I have something to talk to you about."

Jerinne nodded, and took Dayne off. Nyla and

Brondar also left, after some embraces and handshakes with Welling.

Corrie led Welling over, and Satrine got on the other side to support him. "Shall we do this then?"

"Come along, then," Miss Morad said to Welling, beckoning him to the stairs upstairs. "Inspector Rainey, there's no need for you to bother."

"Like blazes," Satrine said, taking a small amount of joy from the wince in Miss Morad's face at that. "He's my partner. Right next to him is where I'm going to be."

Minox wanted to get up the stairs to the inspectors' floor unassisted, but despite his best efforts, he was unable to. Corrie and Inspector Rainey did their best to aid him only when he absolutely needed it, which amounted to almost every step.

He almost thought that Miss Morad was doing it this way to watch him suffer. If that was the case, then he was giving her a very good show.

On the floor, Inspectors Mirrell and Kellman were pacing about, going over a large map of the city. It looked like Kellman, at least, was taking Minox's advice seriously, and Mirrell seemed to be engaging in the idea. For some reason, Iorrett and the rest of the Special Response Squad were milling about as well, like they were waiting for something. All of them, including Mirrell and Kellman, looked expectant.

It was obvious that Miss Morad was going to deliver very bad news. She had gathered the squad, as well as Mirrell and Kellman, to be on hand in case Minox had reacted badly.

Then he spotted them: mage shackles hanging on Iorrett's belt, as well as Mirrell's. Were those a precaution, or part of the plan? Was Miss Morad's decision to incarcerate him?

In his current state, he couldn't do anything about that.

"No matter what happens," Minox said to Corrie, but loud enough for Inspector Rainey to hear as well, "do not do anything foolish."

"It was a friendlier rutting reception at the gang house this morning," Corrie said.

"That's the truth," Rainey muttered. "Saints, this could get ugly."

"Please, for me, do not make it uglier."

Minox couldn't get a good enough read on any of them to be sure of their intentions. Iorrett looked anxious, even nervous. Mirrell's face had a hint of guilt. Nothing that confirmed his worst fears, nothing that couldn't be applied to them anticipating having to subdue an angry, untrained mage. It might be that they didn't even know. From his analysis of Miss Morad, that was likely. She was a woman who kept her own counsel, and it was probably better for her plans if the others here didn't know what they were going to have to do.

Of course, all this manpower was sitting around upstairs, when they could have been used to keep Sholiar from getting out the door. The only reason Sholiar hadn't been able to escape with Nyla as his prisoner was because of Joshea. Thank the saints he had been present and had taken action, even at the risk of exposing himself. Mister Olivant had surely noticed something was amiss, so now he might be suspecting Joshea of also being an Uncircled mage.

Mister Olivant was going to be another problem, certainly. But a problem for another day.

Of course, it was very clear that Mister Olivant was correct. This hand of his was beyond his understanding or control. He doubted Sholiar truly knew what he was doing when he distracted Minox and threw him into Dayne, but the results were real and markedly dangerous, nonetheless.

He was going to have to do something to maintain control over himself, his life. Even if that meant wearing a mage shackle around this cursed altered hand for the rest of his days.

"Let's proceed," she said, pointing to Cinellan's office.

"Here is fine," Minox said, almost falling into one of the desk chairs. "There's nothing you're going to say that won't be the subject of gossip anyway, so let's be open about it."

She gave a slight respectful nod. He had to remind himself that she was not some villain, eager to deprive him of his calling and livelihood. She was a servant of the people, here to do a job to the best of her ability, with dogged determination. In any other context, he probably would have admired her.

He had to force that thought through his head, but he also knew, in his core, that "the best of her ability" was likely affected, if not corrupted, by treating him like some sort of laboratory specimen, the freak who is an Uncircled mage, who thought he deserved to be an inspector.

He tamped down that anger. Even in his weakened state, it was flooding his body, including the hand, with magical energy.

"Inspector Welling," she said, opening up her folder. "By my authority granted by His Grace, the Archduke of Sauriya, in accordance with the Constabulary Charter of the City of Maradaine, I have reviewed your case work and capability in regard to your untrained magical ability. I have found your work and dedication to the craft of investigation and diligence in your duty to be beyond reproach."

"Thank you," Minox said.

"This is what I've rutting been saying," Corrie said.

"Sergeant," Captain Cinellan hissed.

"That said," Miss Morad continued, "your magical ability is chaotic and untested. While I am not versed in the terminology to judge your raw power and capability, it disturbs me. More than once in my presence, you've demonstrated that you can do great and terrible things."

"That's bunk," Corrie said.

"Corrie!" the captain snapped. "I don't want to pull you out of here."

"The events of this evening only solidify my point," Miss Morad said, closing the folder. "Your loss of control, that . . . thing that is your hand." She stepped closer and tapped his glove. "No one even knows what this is. Especially you."

"That's hardly his fault," Rainey said, stepping protectively in front of him.

"Please," Minox said. "Let her finish."

Rainey nodded, but didn't yield her position.

"I cannot, in good conscience, remove an officer from the Constabulary who has such an impeccable record and clarity of purpose. But I cannot also allow such a potential menace to be on the streets, interacting with the public in the name of the city. If it was merely a matter of you being an Uncircled mage, I could ignore it, but we both know that this goes far beyond that."

Silence hung over the room for a moment, until Captain Cinellan broke it. "So what does that mean?"

"My decision is that Inspector Welling is removed from active casework, and restricted to desk and file duty—at three-quarter pay for his inspector rank—for a period no less than one hundred days, at which time his capability will be reassessed."

"Where are you getting this from?" Rainey asked.

"It's the same protocol for debilitating injury, Missus Rainey," Miss Morad said. "I'm sure you're familiar with it."

"He ain't debilitated," Kellman said.

"We don't really know that," Mirrell said, lighting his pipe. "And that's the point."

Minox nodded. He hadn't been thinking about his hand along these lines, pretending that everything was as normal as it could be. As normal as he could be. But the truth was he had been grievously injured, magically, and that injury was never treated.

"So what's the point of a hundred days?" he asked. "Nothing will change before then."

"Maybe not," Miss Morad said. "But I'm going to urge the archduke's office to compel various Circles—Lord Preston's, Red Wolf, whoever will cooperate—to work with you and study what your hand has become. Ignoring and condemning you is . . . reprehensible. And dangerous. And I won't have it."

"That doesn't sound very enforceable," Minox said.

"There are limits of our authority, especially over the Mage Circles."

"Fine," Cinellan said. "Welling, as of now you are off active case work, including any investigation of crime scenes, interview of civilian witnesses, and questioning suspects."

"Where does that leave me?" Rainey asked.

Cinellan held up his hands. "Let me work out the specifics, we'll discuss it shortly." He waved at Kellman, Mirrell, and the squad. "And you all, stand down. You're disturbing me."

He turned to Minox, but couldn't quite look him in the eye. He stood this way for a moment, waiting for the words to come, until he eventually shook his head and went into his office.

"This is blazing sewage, you know this, yes?" Corrie said.

"I know," Minox said.

"I'll be back in one hundred days," Miss Morad said, handing Minox a card. "Of course, you have nine days to exercise your right to petition an appeal."

"You bet he will," Corrie snapped, almost spitting in Miss Morad's face.

Miss Morad did not seem fazed. "And you can contact me through the archduke's office if you have any questions or if you . . . need any assistance."

Corrie snatched the card, and for a moment looked

like she was going to strike Miss Morad. "We've had enough from you."

"Try to see the fuller picture, Sergeant," Miss Morad said. "Good night to you all."

Minox got to his feet—a struggle, but he had recovered enough to manage. Slowly he stumbled to his desk, and took off his inspector's vest, leaving it on his chair. No need to keep it on. For the foreseeable future, and possibly forever, he would not be an active inspector anymore.

———◆—◆—◆———

Five blocks from the stationhouse, and Nyla's heart hadn't slowed down. Joshea wanted to take her home in a cab, but the last thing she wanted to do right now was sit. She needed to move, she needed to feel her feet working, make every step and every breath mean something.

She could still feel the wire around her throat.

She didn't want to talk as they walked, and Joshea picked up on that without question. Normally he was so gregarious, telling all his stories, but he maintained the silence now. When they had gone two blocks, she quietly gripped his hand. He simply took hers, comfortingly, and did nothing else but walk with her.

That was all she needed right now. Right now, she just needed her heart to stop racing, threatening to burst out of her chest.

Fortunately, for whatever reason, the streets were quiet as well. It was like the whole city had held its breath so she could have a moment of peace.

Then five blocks away from the stationhouse, someone stepped in front of them.

"You! You're the source of magic, I knew it!"

Mister Olivant's many-ringed hand was pointing accusingly at Joshea.

"I don't know what you're talking about, old man," Joshea said.

"The blazes you don't," Olivant said.

"Please," Nyla said. "We've been through—you were there . . ."

"Yes, I was there, and I saw what he did."

"He caught me," Nyla said. "He was there for me, while you stood there. If it hadn't been for him and Minox, I would have been—"

"Minox?" Olivant said. "You think it was his magic? No, no. This one. You, Mister Brondar." His eyes flashed with understanding. "You Uncircleds are working together. That's why he stopped you from testifying. Didn't want me to see you, but I did."

Nyla's head was swirling. This man was talking madness, and she couldn't handle any more right now. "Stop it, just stop it."

"She said to stop," Joshea said, brushing Olivant aside. "Leave us be."

"No," Olivant said. "You are going to be known for what you are, sir. We will stalk you down and drag you out into the light so *everyone will know*!"

Joshea spun on his heel and grabbed Olivant by his coat, pulling him into an alley. From the depths of his throat he roared, like nothing Nyla had ever heard before. "You will do nothing of the sort. You will leave me and her alone or by every saint I will put an end to you!"

Nyla swore when he said that, the air dropped to a bitter winter's chill.

"Josh, stop," she said. "Let's just get out of here."

"There he is," Olivant said. "There's the man I was looking to—"

His last word was cut off by a blade coming through his throat. Blood spurted from his mouth as he dropped to the ground, hitting Joshea in the face.

Nyla screamed, unable to hold anything back.

"I didn't—I don't—" Joshea started, but then he fell to the ground, twitching and foaming. And standing over the two bodies was him. That same greasy, horrifying man.

Fear froze Nyla's feet.

"And there's the man I was looking to find as well," he said, looking at Joshea's collapsed form. He then glanced up at Nyla, an evil grin playing over his face. "You slipped away once, miss. But I'm going to need you to deliver a message."

Chapter 21

MINOX GATHERED UP his personal journals from his desk, and did his best to straighten it out from the mess it had become when the marshals ransacked it this afternoon.

"Don't pretend like it wasn't already a blazing mess," Corrie said, hovering over him. "And roll these bastards. Let them deal with it."

"Much of these notes are important to me and my own personal endeavors," Minox said. "And while I trust Inspector Rainey to treat them with care and concern, someone else might get assigned to this desk in the meantime, and I cannot assume they would be as considerate."

"No one else is sitting here," Rainey said. "I won't—"

"We cannot assume that. You will get assigned a partner, your career needs to continue."

"And the unresolved?" Rainey asked.

Minox allowed himself a small chuckle. "I am being taken off active cases. Nothing can prevent me from continuing to do the work that was already off the books to begin with."

"And I'll be there for that," she said. "Though now you have less excuse to send me pages in the middle of the night."

"Yes, I think that will be on hiatus," he said.

"All right, everyone, listen up!" Cinellan called out, coming back out of his office. He looked in more disarray than when he went in—his shirt was unclasped at the collar, and his coat looked like it had been removed and poorly put back on. Minox surmised that the captain had had a drink from the bottle of Fuergan whiskey he kept in his bottom drawer. Possibly more than one. He had a handful of letters in his hand, which he was waving about slightly haphazardly.

"What's up, Cap?" Kellman asked.

"There are a few things that we weren't going to move forward for a few more weeks—new directives, and so forth. But since we're already having changes imposed on us, we're going to do this now. All complaints can be filed to the back of the stables."

"This will be some blazes," Corrie whispered.

"In the coming weeks, we're going to be getting a few more inspectors, from houses around the city, to increase the scope of the GIU. So I want to make it clear that this is our house. We are holding the banner in Inemar, hear?"

"As I said," Minox said quietly, "someone new at this desk."

"Wait," Satrine said.

"So effective tomorrow, Inspector Mirrell is promoted to First Class, and will be Chief of Inspection." A few of the squad gave a smattering of applause, but mostly people looked perplexed. Especially Mirrell.

"Really, Cap?" Mirrell asked. "I mean, I ain't gonna turn it down—"

"You've got the years for seniority, Henfir, and the record for closing cases."

His record for closing cases was dubious as far as Minox was concerned, but in terms of pure numbers, he couldn't disagree.

Cinellan continued. "Kellman, Welling, and Rainey will all get bumped to Second Class . . ."

"Captain," Minox said, "given my situation, is that remotely appropriate?"

"Well, your three-quarters salary will be based on that, for one. And when you're back on full duty, I want to make it clear what I think of you and your work. And I want the new third classes to know the four of you are who they should look to. Even during the time you're desk bound."

"If you say so."

"And Kellman and Rainey, you'll be partners from tomorrow on. At least until Minox is fully sorted."

"What?" Rainey all but shouted.

"It's what's best," Cinellan said. "Look. . . ." He took a moment, looking at the floor. "Between this business with the marshals, and with Minox, I want to nail down everything with this house and this unit, so no one can sweep in and rut it all up. I need all you . . . the folks I trust, the house I built . . . I need you to be the Grand. Understand?"

"We got it, Cap," Mirrell said. "That all?"

"Not quite," Cinellan said. "This is the part you all are going to hate. As part of the GIU expansion, we're expected to have inspectors on duty at all shifts, as well as the Special Response. That means everyone— and I mean everyone—will pull night shifts in rotation until we've got that full staff."

"Starting?" Kellman asked.

"Tonight," Cinellan said. "So you, Iorrett, Riggock, and Murd will stay tonight."

"Aw, Cap," Riggock said.

"I'm too old for night shifts," Murd added.

"You're bunking out here, so get used to it." He gave a pointed look at Rainey. Minox understood what it meant, what this new policy would mean for her schedule and family. She just nodded, though.

"That's all. Now get out of here if you ain't supposed to stay." With that, Cinellan went to the stairs and left.

"Rutting blazes," Corrie muttered.

"Rainey?" Minox asked. "You all right?"

She put on a smile that Minox read as pure artifice. "Another seven crowns six a week. That can make the difference to pay Missus Abernand to stay the night."

Mirrell and Kellman both approached, looking a bit sheepish.

"Hey, Ji—Minox," Mirrell said. "I want you to know, I never expected that . . . I was just thinking . . ."

"There is no need," Minox said. "You did what you considered your duty given the situation, and I do not hold it against you."

"You might rutting not," Corrie said, nearly growling at Mirrell. "Bastard gets promoted to chief for rolling you?"

"It is not that simple, Corrie, and you know that," Minox said.

"And let's make this all work as best we can," Mirrell said. He pointed over to the map that he and Kellman had been looking at. "I mean, Kellman tried your idea and all we learned is neither of us are good with maps."

Minox could have told them that part already. "So your plan is to have me do the piecework here while you all work the streets?" It was likely he could become the Evoy of the stationhouse, holed up in some archival room. What worried Minox was how oddly appealing that sounded.

"I won't pretend that I don't think most of your ideas aren't sewage, Minox," Mirrell said. "But when you hit the center mark, saints, do you ever."

"That's a pretty strange compliment," Rainey said.

"Right," Mirrell said. "Anyhow, I think our priority needs to be Darreck and Tricky working this kids case. Maybe that starts with the HTC Imports dockside warehouse, or not, I don't know . . ."

"Nah, that's nothing," Kellman said quickly.

"What's HTC?" Rainey asked.

"Some import and export company," Mirrell said.

"They got a warehouse on the north side, on the West Hetrick Docks in Trelan. That was where things centered on the map after Kellman did what you suggested."

"West Hetrick?" Rainey repeated, looking stunned.

"It probably shouldn't be dismissed out of hand," Minox said. His results from the analysis had showed him the same area, but he hadn't researched the specific businesses there. "If it's a lead, you should pursue it."

"I'm just saying, I probably just rutted up reading the map and doing what you suggested," Kellman said. "But, yeah, Tricky, we'll . . . we'll get on that in the morning. Though I might not be worth a blazes staying here all night. You all right, Trick?"

Rainey shook out of the reverie she was in. "Yes, of course. Just a lot to take in today."

"Put Iorrett and his boys on watch duty, and bunk out in the back room," Mirrell said to Kellman. "Tell them to wake you only if there's an issue you need to handle. Saints, we're all going to have to do this for the next month. I should get home to the wife while I still can. You both as well." He pointed to Minox and Rainey. "Do like the captain said. In the morning, we'll get things in order here." He slapped Kellman on the shoulder. "Night, Darreck."

Minox watched Inspector Mirrell walk off, fascinated by his behavior. The man had done his best to undermine him ever since Minox had earned his vest, and now that he had succeeded, it seemed his guilt was driving him toward camaraderie. And that convivial behavior also spilled over to Rainey. If that made Minox's exile to the archives somewhat tolerable, he'd take it.

"Right," Rainey said. "I'll see you tomorrow. Get him home safe, hmm?" This was directed to Corrie.

"I'm going to pour several beers down his throat, so help me," she said.

Minox was about to object, but for once, Corrie's

idea sounded like it had merit. He nodded to Rainey. "Have a good night. My best to you and your family."

***

Satrine left the stationhouse, her head swirling. Too much had happened today, and she needed clarity. West Hetrick Docks on the north side. Where Loren was found. Just hearing the name spooked her. Saints, she could hardly believe that the fight in the Kemper Street Kicker tenement was this morning. Of course, the boot digging slightly into the side of her foot was a stern reminder of that.

She was going to need new boots. The salary bump to Inspector Second Class would help with that. But even that was strange. Captain Cinellan was stewing on something beyond what she obviously knew about, and between the marshals and Miss Kendra Morad, he snapped and took action. She wasn't sure what else was troubling the captain, exactly, but she needed to get her head around it before too long. She could see it in Welling's eyes, he was probably thinking the same thing.

"Bastards," she said out loud to no one in particular. She wasn't even sure who she meant. But she knew it wasn't right, what happened to Welling today. She'd cope with being partnered with Kellman for now—he was decent enough, for being such a clod—but she wanted to have Welling at her side again as soon as she could.

And then those words of Pra Yikenj hit her again. *You're working with a traitor.*

She shook it away. Yikenj didn't know what she was talking about, just trying to rattle Satrine.

Then Enbrain's fears from last night came at her. There were traitors in the Constabulary, he was certain, or at least corruption, beyond the petty grift of places like Aventil Stationhouse. Was that her problem? Had that taken Loren from her? She had no idea.

Taken from her, at the West Hetrick Docks.

She stopped walking and looked up. Saint Limarre's Church. Instinct had brought her here, knowing she needed wisdom. Or at least a friend.

She went into the church, dropping a pence at the feet of the statue of Saint Limarre. Evening services were just ending, with the preacher giving a final prayer to the small crowd, with Sister Alana and one of the other cloistresses of the Blue attending him at the altar.

As the parishioners shuffled out, other cloistresses helped guide them out and tidied up the pews. The young blonde girl—Sister Myriem?—walked past Satrine and stopped, turning.

"Hello, Inspector," she said, her voice almost a song. "You missed the service."

"The duties of work," Satrine said.

"Is that why your boots don't match?" Sister Myriem asked, keeping her eyes locked on Satrine's.

Satrine stepped back a bit. "I was hoping for a word with Sister Alana."

Myriem glanced to the altar, where Alana was engaged with the reverend on some issue. "She seems engaged, but I'll get her for you." She moved closer to Satrine. "I feel I owe you, Inspector. I ruined your tea and pastries yesterday morning."

"It's not a problem," Satrine said.

"Even still," Sister Myriem said, reaching under her robe and producing a paper bag. "I have a pastry here, and I'd like to give it to you."

"That . . . that isn't necessary," Satrine said, but Sister Myriem pushed it into her hands.

"I went across town to get that, Inspector," she said with quiet intensity. "And I really think you should take it."

Satrine put the bag in her coat pocket rather than argue. Myriem smiled brightly, and went over to the altar and Sister Alana. Alana noticed Satrine from across the church, and with a quick word to the reverend, came over.

"She spooked you, didn't she?" Alana asked. She glanced over to the altar, where Sister Myriem was arguing with the reverend over something. "Well, what would we be if we didn't take in broken girls? Where would I be?"

"Maybe I missed my calling," Satrine said.

"Oh, no," Alana said. "I think . . . I don't think the saints needed you here in the blue. You're doing your own good work."

"Am I?" Satrine asked. "Sometimes I wonder."

Alana touched her face. "You've been in a scrap today. I bet that did some good."

"In theory we busted up an Aventil gang. But another will take that territory, or one will splinter."

Alana gave her a hard look, one that said so much with no words—mainly that she wasn't going to take any sewage from Satrine.

"Welling is busted to his desk, the King's Marshals are on top of us, we completely rolled up the Gearbox investigation—sorry—"

"It's fine."

"And I'm going to have to partner with Kellman."

"I thought you said Kellman was all right."

"Well, he's better than Mirrell—who is now going to be chief of inspection for the GIU."

"Is that bad?"

"Probably, but . . ." She couldn't put the feelings to words.

Alana led her over to the pews and sat her down. "So what do you need, Satrine?"

"A week on the Yinaran coast?" Satrine said. She sighed. "Something my mother used to say, I don't know why. I don't think she'd ever been to Yinara. I'm not sure if she had ever left Maradaine, until . . . well . . ." She didn't feel like saying it.

"Until she left you." Alana shrugged. "I believe it's best to just say what things are."

"You know, for all I know, she went two blocks

away." Satrine sighed. "I mean, I don't even know why. I presume there was a new man who didn't want to deal with a street kid daughter, and she . . . I don't even want to talk about it. I'd rather actually talk about a week on the Yinaran coast, you know. Supposedly Kellman and I are going to check out a dockside warehouse tomorrow. Maybe I can jump on a boat and . . ."

She stopped. What was the name of that importing company? She had been so focused on the West Hetrick part, she hadn't even thought about the company.

"You wouldn't do that to your daughters—"

"Shush, Lannie," Satrine said. "HTC Imports?"

"What's that?" Alana asked.

"I'm not even sure," Satrine said, as ideas crashed together in her head.

"Don't try to change the subject," Alana said. "Your daughters and your husband—"

She remembered Loren, last night, so agitated when she mentioned the Saint Day. Yelling "Say day sha mah" over and over. And he had been attacked—found—on the docks on a Saint Day. West Hetrick Docks, in Trelan. The same set of docks as for HTC Imports.

"It was a Saint Day," she said. "And most official stuff shuts down. But he was still investigating something. . . ."

"Who? Minox?"

"No, my husband," Satrine said. "Was he investigating a shipment on the holiday?"

"You're not making sense."

This must be what it feels like to be Welling. "That's what Loren was trying to tell me. He was saying 'Saint Day shipment'! And HTC must—"

HTC. Suddenly it was clear.

Satrine got to her feet. It was a crazy idea, probably nothing, but maybe it was everything. Almost everything. "Maybe just a coincidence, but I need to find Minox and . . . I don't even know." She kissed Alana on the cheek. "Thank you!"

She ran out of the church, barely hearing Alana's bewildered, "You're welcome," before reaching the door.

She would tell Welling. If anyone would believe—would understand—this crazy idea, it would be him.

Chapter 22

CORRIE WHISTLED DOWN a cab and pulled Minox into it. He wasn't arguing, or talking at all. The ride up home, he quietly pulled out his pipe, packed the bowl with his Fuergan tobacco, and smoked it in silence. As they reached the house, he was already on a second bowl.

"Come on, you rutting fool," she said as she brought him up to the house. No one was at the front stoop tonight, but it was already dinnertime. Corrie didn't know how she had lost track of time like that. She had barely eaten all rutting day.

"Maybe I should just go upstairs," Minox said, puffing on his pipe. "Finish this outside and just go up."

"Nothing blazing doing," she said, grabbing his chin. "Look at me, hmm? You're gonna get through this, hear? And you're going to do it because every rutting one of us in this house is going to have your back, starting with me."

"Every one? Even Oren?"

"To blazes with Oren if he gives you guff. He knows I'll knock him on his ass, and I will."

"I know you will, Corr," he said. He took another puff and looked up at the sky. "I know . . . I know I have a hard time saying, you know, things that matter."

"Like blazes you do," she said. Minox was the most honest person she knew.

"No, I mean . . . I mean . . ." He looked like he was struggling with the words.

"You don't have to rutting say it, you fool."

"I do," he said. "I sometimes have doubts. In myself, in the Constabulary on the whole, but . . ."

"Hey, hey," Corrie said. "I get it, I do. Especially with Iorrett and the other pisswhistlers in the squad with me."

"But never you," he blurted out. "You've always been a beacon for me, Corr, and I'm so proud to call you my sister."

Corrie felt tears threaten to burst forth, but she forced them down. "Oh, saints, big brother. You can't do that to me, you know?" She wiped away any rebellious tears that might have escaped. She resisted the urge to embrace him. Even now, he wouldn't like that, she knew. "And Pop would be proud of you, you know?"

"I hope so," he said. He looked like he was about to say something else, but then snuffed out his pipe instead. "We should get inside."

Just about everyone was at the table, including Jace, who was almost never home by dinnertime.

"There she is!" Jace shouted. "You all should have seen it. Arrows pouring down from above, and she comes riding in like it's nothing—"

"Hush up," Corrie said. "Ain't nobody needs to hear about that sewage."

Jace paid her no mind. "Her horse gets shot out under her, and she just rolls off, and then this Tarian girl. And I mean, this girl—Ma, Aunties, forgive me, but—this girl was like a saint come back down."

"I needn't hear you blaspheme," Zura said.

"Hey, enough," Corrie said. "Look, I'm sure you heard some of this from Ny—" She looked about the table. No Nyla. "Nyla ain't here yet?"

"She's not with you two?" Uncle Cole asked.

"She left before us," Minox said. "With Joshea. She was . . . there was an incident at the stationhouse, and she was—"

"Was she hurt?" Aunt Emma asked, getting to her feet.

"Shook, but she's fine," Corrie said quickly. "Like we said, Joshea walked her home. Maybe they stopped for a tea or something."

"She's with Josh?" Aunt Emma asked, cooling down. She even smiled a hint. "Well, then I'm sure that's fine."

"So what happened?" Davis asked.

"A prisoner escaped," Minox said quietly. "My fault. And he tried to hold Nyla hostage. She got free, but . . . he slipped away."

The table went silent, everyone glancing uncomfortably at each other.

"Well," Oren said eventually. "I'm sure it wasn't really your fault." He said it in such a way, it didn't really sound like he believed it.

"It was," Minox said. "But that hardly matters. I've been reassigned to desk duty, pending further study and investigation of my capabilities."

"Your capabilities?" Uncle Timmothen asked. "I've seen your file, you've got a blazes of a record. How much more capable could you be?"

"That's not what I mean," Minox said quietly. "I mean my other abilities."

"He means magic," Corrie said sharply. "They're afraid of his magic, just like half of you rutting are."

"Corrianna!" Mama snapped.

"Tell me I'm wrong."

"Corrie, it's fine," Minox said, sitting at an empty chair. "I am quite famished."

"I've got you," Mama said, getting a plate for him.

"Same for me," Corrie said, going over to the icebox. She grabbed a couple bottles of Deeringhill and brought them over to Minox.

"I don't know if I should—" Minox started.

"Sewage," Corrie said. "Drink up."

He took the Deeringhill and sipped gently. Corrie popped open her own and sat next to him. As Mama brought over plates of sausages and bread for them, there was a knock at the door. Jace hopped up and ran to it.

"So, what are you going to do?" Edard asked.

"Work in the archives for a hundred days, while they figure this out," Minox said, holding up his gloved hand. "Because I, apparently, defy explanation or understanding." He took another long drink from his beer.

"A hundred days?" Uncle Timmothen asked. "That's just—I'm going to file a protest. I'm going to—"

"Please don't," Minox said, eating his bread. "All it will do—"

"Minox?" Jace said from the archway between the dining room and the sitting room. "Someone's here for you."

Tricky Rainey came into view, looking like she had run here from the stationhouse. "I'm terribly sorry to disrupt your dinner," she said. "But I needed to speak to Minox."

"Who's this?" Mama asked. Everyone—save Jace— looked at her like she was a viper. Maybe it was a good thing Nyla wasn't back yet.

"Sorry," Tricky said. "Satrine Rainey. Inspector. I'm Minox's partner."

"You heard the captain, Inspector Rainey," Minox said. "I'm not your partner anymore."

"Maybe not," she said. "But I think—"

"Miss," Uncle Timmothen said sharply. "Maybe your stationhouse enjoys your presence, but in this house, we don't cater to cheats."

"Hey, hey!" Jace shot back. "You shouldn't—"

"You shouldn't give me lip, boy!"

"This lady did things you wouldn't—"

"I know what she did!"

Suddenly everyone was shouting and yelling, pointing at Tricky and saying things that even Corrie wouldn't say at the dinner table.

Enough of this sewage.

Corrie pulled her whistle out of her pocket and blasted it until everyone shut the blazes up.

"Listen up, you all," she said, putting her whistle on the table. "Tricky has enough going on that she wouldn't come all the way out here unless it was really blazing important. And if it is, I want to rutting hear it."

Minox looked up, the spark in his eyes glowing just a bit. "As would I. So what is it, Inspector?"

She smiled. "I think I've resolved something."

With just that, the spark in Minox's eyes lit.

— ◆ ◆ —

Satrine felt the combined heat of over a dozen pairs of Welling eyes boring into her. She knew that she had walked into a house that was far more aligned with Nyla than Minox, but she wasn't quite ready for the raw loathing coming off some of them.

Some, but not all of them. Corrie was giving her a slight smirk of approval, like she expected Satrine to give fire and blazes to anyone who crossed her. And Jace looked like he was going to brawl any and all of his cousins who gave Satrine any lip.

"Minox, why don't you and Missus Rainey go into the sitting room," one of the older women said. Probably Minox's mother, since she had some clearly Racquin features, the same sort of nose that Minox and Corrie both sported. "I'll bring out some tea."

"That isn't necessary," Satrine said.

"Of course it is," she said. "You're our guest." She then pointed an accusing finger at some of the other older folks. "You all were more civil to that woman last night who was trying to end his career. Whatever else you think of this one, she's had his back and saved his life. Shame."

The one in the captain's uniform looked cowed at

that, and on his nod, the rest all stopped their angry glares. Minox got to his feet, and led her to the couch of the sitting room.

"So what is it?" he asked her as he sat down.

"Something a bit too odd to be a coincidence," she said. "My husband, when he was attacked, was found on the West Hetrick Docks, the same set where HTC Imports is."

"Right, the business that you and Kellman are going to investigate," he said. "So you think your husband's attack was connected to the missing children?"

"Maybe," Satrine said. "But something else jumped out at me. HTC Imports. Who owns it?"

"I have no idea," Welling said. "I would hazard a guess that it's three businessmen in partnership, and the letters represent their three family names. That's not uncommon."

"Right," she said. "Three family names like Hunsen, Tenning, and Cole?"

That startled him.

"That is . . . I hesitate to use a word like 'coincidence,' and while that's certainly intriguing, but I'm not entirely sure how it connects."

"The atrocity in the Parliament," Satrine said, letting the ideas flow in her head. She wasn't even sure where she was going with it, but the connections were coming together. "What was it, ultimately? We thought it might have been some sort of message to Enbrain, including Niall in it. But that was just a piece of it, and maybe an intentional mislead. I think the whole thing was just a giant distraction."

"A dozen dead and a massive breach of the security of the Parliament, a distraction?"

"And just about every constable, Yellowshield, marshal, and journalist focused on the Parliament. An enterprising thief could have emptied out a goldsmith house and carted its wares out without notice."

"You think it was a goldsmith house robbery?"

"I don't know what it was, but my point is that if you

needed law enforcement distracted, you could hardly come up with a better way."

The older woman came out with a tray of tea and small cakes. "Thank you, Mother," Welling said, confirming Satrine's theory.

"It's good to finally meet you," she said to Satrine. "He admires you so much."

"Thank you, Mother," he said, even more pointedly.

"It's very kind," Satrine said. "You have a lovely home, Missus Welling."

"Amalia," she said. After Welling glared at her for a moment, she said, "I'll leave you." She went back to the dining room.

"Presuming you're right, then what do you think it all is? What's the distraction from?"

"What, I don't know," Satrine said. "Let me break down what I think happened. We know that it has to have been organized with a plan, someone from the inside. If we take what Sholiar said at face value—"

"A dubious proposition."

"He spoke with passion that felt—"

"Veracious?" Welling said.

"Exactly. Someone else executed his plan, and that annoyed him. If I'm right, that was spearheaded by Hunsen, Tenning, and Cole, who pretended to be victims and then were 'allowed' to go free once the eighteen chairs were filled."

"Sholiar said he put them in the boiler room."

"Exactly. He caught them and put them there; that wasn't part of their original plan."

"And they give false names to the Constabulary, slip their Tarian protection, and go about their business, the supposed business they organized the distraction for in the first place?"

"I think," she said with an unconfident air. No, she was confident in what she was saying, she believed it was right. She was also aware how odd an idea it was. "I think there's more to it all, but we don't have the information to see it."

"That's very true."

She swallowed hard, nervous. "My gut tells me it's the docks. And . . . this might be even crazier."

"I've entertained lunacy, and it's been correct on occasion," he said. "Go ahead."

"Loren has been trying to tell me something."

"Your husband speaks?"

"He makes noises. But it's been the same noises lately. And I think he's been saying 'Saint Day shipments.' I think . . . I think someone, maybe with or through HTC, is doing clandestine shipments, smuggling things in or out of Maradaine, usually using the quiet of a Saint Day as cover."

He looked to the side for a moment. "Then perhaps . . . Thom!"

One of his relatives—a burly, handsome young man—came into the room. He wore a River Patrol uniform. Thomsen, a cousin, middle child of the nurse aunt, if Satrine remembered the various extended Welling clan correctly. "What's on?"

"You said there were dead calms out on the ocean. Ships were late?"

"Oh, yeah. Winds picked up, though. All sorts of ships that were supposed to come in all last week arrived yesterday."

Welling snapped his fingers in excitement. "And thus whatever was supposed to happen on the Saint Day—"

"Couldn't happen until yesterday," Satrine said.

He jumped to his feet. "I think no time should be wasted. It's late, but you can get a Writ of Search from Mister Hilsom, just send a page—"

"Me?" Satrine said. "We should go . . ."

His face fell a little. "I'm off active cases, Inspector," he said. "Fortunately, your partner, Inspector Kellman, is dozing at the stationhouse now. You'll just have to—"

He was interrupted by a pounding on the door. Thomsen ran over to answer it.

"It seems everyone is knocking on your door tonight," Satrine said. "I don't care about any of that. Or Kellman. I want you at my back, no matter what."

He smiled, ever so slightly—such a rare sight from him. "That matters, Inspector. But—"

"Sweet saints, no!" Thomsen screamed from the door. "What the rutting blazes?"

Welling ran over to the door, and Satrine instinctively followed, hand going to her crossbow.

Nyla was standing at the door, tears streaming down her ashen face.

Her neck, arms and body were encased in a mechanism of ticking gears and springs.

"Please help me," she whispered. "Dear saints, please help me."

<hr />

"What happened?" Minox said, pushing past Thomsen. This was Sholiar's work, surely. "How did—"

"Minox, you have to step back," Nyla said, almost panicked. As he reached out to her, a bell started to ring, and the gears turned faster. "Step back!"

Inspector Rainey grabbed him and pulled him back. The ringing bell stopped. "Let's do nothing rash," she said.

Thomsen reached out and took Nyla's hand. No bell, no speeding up of the gears. "I got you, Ny," he said.

Everyone else came into the foyer, and screams and panic filled the room. Uncle Cole pushed to the front.

"What the saints and sinners?" he said. "Nyla, who did this to you?"

"I have . . ." she said, trying to force words through her sobs. "I have a message to deliver. To Minox. But you can't come closer to me, Mine. You can't."

"What is this, Minox?" Uncle Cole demanded. "What happened to my daughter?"

"A madman named Sholiar," Minox said. He charged his hand up with magical energy. The bell started again.

"Bring it down," Rainey hissed at him. He released it, and the bell stopped. "I don't know how, but there's some sort of magical sensor on this machine."

"He was ready for me," Minox said.

"Who? What is all this?" Cole was in his face.

"Sir," Rainey said, interceding between Minox and Cole. "That doesn't help."

"This is our family," Cole shouted. "You shouldn't—"

"Stop shouting!" Nyla yelled out. "You have to listen to me."

Corrie had pushed forward, taking Nyla's other hand. "Let her rutting speak," she said. "What's the message?" Aunt Emma had come through as well, taking Thomsen's place.

"Minox," Nyla said, looking at him. "I have to say this exactly right. He made me memorize it, word for word."

"Who?" Cole asked again.

"Joshea Brondar and Jerinne Fendall are currently guests at the Kittrick Hotel, at the corner of Holmes and Mudgett. They will not survive the night unless Minox Welling and Dayne Heldrin, and only them, come to the hotel to rescue their companions by nine bells."

Minox went over to his coat to fetch his notebook. "Where is that, Holmes and Mudgett?"

"This is madness, what?" Timmothen said. "Let's bring everyone we know in. All-Eyes, All-Hands."

Nyla continued, raising her voice. "If any other member of the Constabulary or the Tarian Order, or any other law enforcement entity comes to the Kittrick, Joshea Brondar and Jerinne Fendall will die, as will . . ." she choked on the words for a minute, "as will Nyla Pyle."

"Saints, this is stupid," Edard said, coming over to Nyla with a hammer. "Let's get this sewage off her."

Corrie leaped up and tackled him to the floor.

"Are you a rutting idiot?" she shouted. "You know what this is? You roll this up, she dies!"

Rainey stepped forward. "What else, Nyla?" she asked. "He made you memorize that, what else?"

Nyla nodded, as best she could. "If any member of this household other than Minox Welling leaves this house, Nyla Pyle will die."

"That's rubbish," said Timmothen, heading to the door. "I'm calling in all my squads. I'm going to—"

As soon as he opened the front door, the bell on Nyla's collar started to ring, and gears moved faster again.

"Close the door, Tim!" Cole shouted. Timmothen did, and the ringing stopped.

"How—how is that possible?" Davis asked. He put on his spectacles and peered at the absurd machinery Nyla was wearing.

"There's gotta be a way to get this off, Davey," Edard said. "You can figure it out."

Davis looked up at his brother, and shook his head. "I wouldn't even know where to begin. And I doubt any of you do."

"Minox, magic it off," Oren said. This brought the room silent, save for the ticking gears on Nyla, and a shocked gasp from Aunt Zura.

"I can't," Minox said, even though he was feeling his power bleed and burn through his hand. He was losing control again, out of his anger and helplessness. "The madman thought of that. He thought of everything."

"We have to do something!" Aunt Emma said.

"Nyla," Rainey said calmly again, locking her eyes onto her. "You're sure those are the exact words? Exactly the conditions?"

"Yes, I'm certain," Nyla said.

Minox stalked over to the table and absently picked up one of Mother's cakes, eating it in one bite. It did nothing to satiate him, to stem the burning hunger from the bleeding magic. He ate another, still felt empty. Rainey came over to him, taking a paper bag out of her pocket. She took a pastry out of the bag and handed it to him. He chuckled as he took it—she had reached the point where being ready to support him like this was automatic. He was going to deeply miss her partnership in the days to come. He ate the pastry gladly—it was actually excellent—but noticed that she was focused on the bakery bag.

Everyone was arguing, crying, demanding that someone do something.

"He had a wife and a bakery," Rainey whispered.

"What are you saying?" he asked.

Rainey grabbed his arm. "Minox," Rainey said. "There's a loophole, and I know what to do."

Chapter 23

"**A** LOOPHOLE?" UNCLE Cole asked. "What the rutting blazes is she talking about?"

Minox ran over Nyla's speech in his mind. "No member of the household but me can leave," he said. "I can get someone, perhaps, who could—"

"No, no, you won't have time," she said. On everyone's immediate reaction, she shouted down the room. "Minox has to play the game, save Joshea and Jerinne—"

"Who the rutting blazes is Jerinne?" Oren asked.

"She's the Tarian girl!" Jace said.

"But I could—" Minox started.

"Holmes and Mudgett are on the north side of the city," Rainey said. "In Fenton. You'll barely have time to get Dayne and get there by nine bells."

"You have to," Nyla whimpered. "Please."

"So what's this rutting loophole?" Corrie asked.

"No member of the household can leave," she said, going to the door. "That means I can."

She opened the door. The bells didn't start this time.

Minox came over to her. "But what can you do? I have to go, and go alone—"

She held up the bag the pastry came in, lowering her voice a bit. "This might be crazy, or a sign from the saints, but . . . I think I know where to find that trap-master who helped at the Parliament."

He saw it in her eyes. Whatever it was, whatever leap of intuition she had made, it made perfect sense to her. He told her the only thing she needed to hear.

"I trust you."

Corrie came over, her place by Nyla taken over by Mother. "What's the rutting plan?"

"Plan is, we go," Minox said. "I'll play Sholiar's twisted game."

"And I'm going for someone who can get Nyla out of that," Rainey said. "I will be back as soon as I can."

Corrie nodded. "Then I got one rutting job. Keep them all from doing something stupid."

"I don't envy you," Rainey said, and she went out the door.

"Stay safe," Corrie told Minox.

"Always," he said, and followed Rainey. "Wait!" he called after her. "Where are you going?"

"Junk Avenue, over in Seleth," she said. "You have to hurry."

"We both do," he said.

"I don't suppose you have a pair of horses in that barn," she said.

"No," he said. "Not horses. But about as fast."

———◆═◆———

Satrine needed a bit of practice to get the hang of Welling's crazy two-wheeled cartless pedalcart, but once she got herself into a rhythm, she was flying down the streets of Keller Cove, across the creek bridge and into North Seleth. It wasn't until she turned onto Junk Avenue that she realized she had no idea how she was supposed to stop the thing. She elected to jump off it—aggravating her bad leg and irritating her oddly booted foot—and let the pedalcart just sail riderless into the alley wall.

It made a frightful noise when it crashed, but didn't appear to be obviously damaged.

"Shut it!" someone yelled from across the street.

North Seleth was a neighborhood filled with run-down buildings, shops with broken windows and doors that looked like they were about to fall off their frames. But the Junk Avenue Bakery was a solid brick building, everything neat and tidy. It also had a sign reading "CLOSED" and looked dark inside. But there were lamps burning in the upstairs window.

Satrine pounded on the door. "Constabulary! Open up!"

She heard some scrambling upstairs, and a window opened up. A woman stuck her head out.

"We're closed! Come back in the morning!"

"Constabulary," Satrine yelled up. "Grand Inspection Unit."

"What the blazes does that mean?"

"It means—are you the proprietor of this bakery?"

"I am," the woman said. "What of it?"

"And are you married?"

"I am, though I don't see what business it is of yours." A cry pierced the air. "You've woken the baby."

"I apologize," Satrine said. This whole thing might just be a complete waste of time, a lark she went on because of a pastry wrapper. "But I need to speak—"

A man stuck his head out. "You need to stop shouting in the street."

Even in the dim of the evening, she recognized the face and voice.

"Come down and I'll stop, sir," she said.

"You'll—" He peered at her for a moment. "Saints above, how did—stupid question. What are you—I don't even want to know." He went back inside.

"I need your help!" Satrine called out.

Through the bakery window, Satrine saw the woman from upstairs storm over with a wailing toddler in one hand and a lit lamp in the other. She threw open the latch and the door flew open. She immediately laid into Satrine.

"Do you have a writ of some sort? A summons or a

search? Or are you just here to harass perfectly decent folk on the west side? Are you even from here?"

"No, ma'am," Satrine said. "I'm from the Grand Inspection Unit, and we have a—"

"You have what? We already know you don't have a writ, so you can't question us or arrest us. So what is your problem?"

"I need your husband's—" Satrine tried to say over the child's screams.

"Pick your next word very carefully, miss."

"Help."

A suspicious eyebrow went up. "Help with what?"

The trapmaster came into the light. "It's all right, Raych," he said. "This is the officer from the thing at the Parliament. What are you doing here, miss?"

"There's another machine," Satrine said. "And a young woman is trapped in it. I don't know—"

He held up a hand. "Where?"

"A house in Keller Cove."

He sighed. "All right, let me get my tools." He slipped off again.

The baker looked sheepishly at the ground. "He didn't really tell me what happened at the Parliament. Pretended he couldn't."

"I understand," Satrine said. "But . . . he saved a lot a lives. Even if . . . I presume he doesn't want the credit."

"No," he said, coming back with a satchel strapped over his back. "Let's keep my name out of the prints, shall we?"

"I don't even know your name," she said.

"Let's keep it that way, hmm?" He shook his head. "My brother would not believe I'm helping the Constabulary."

"You're helping the woman who's trapped," she said, going over to the pedalcart. She picked it off the ground. It was well built; save a few scrapes, it seemed in perfect shape.

"What is that?" he asked, looking at it carefully.

"A stripped down pedalcart my partner made," she said.

That seemed to get his attention. "That is fascinating. Rather."

She took her seat. "Get on and grab hold. We're going to go pretty fast."

He did as he was told, sitting behind her and grabbing her waist.

"Get back here safely," the wife said, looking at him. "None of that—just don't—"

"Love you, too," he said. Satrine started pedaling, and after a slow start, hit a good speed back to Keller Cove.

"How *did* you possibly find me?" he asked over the rushing wind.

"A cloistress gave me a wrapper from the bakery," Satrine said.

"Well, that makes perfect sense," he said. "Carry on."

❖

The Parliament halls were quiet, at least from Dayne's apartment. Such a stark difference from yesterday. In the next few days, it would be filled with commotion again. Soon the standing members would return from their archduchies, the new members would settle in, and the latest convocation of the Parliament would meet.

In a hall violated by death and blood for the second time.

Dayne wondered if that was going to be his legacy. No matter how much he tried to be a vessel of peace, to be the shield between the people and harm . . .

No matter what, there were still deaths.

Today he had failed again, with Sholiar right there. He had failed and the killer had escaped. His fault, yet again.

Jerinne had gotten him back to the apartment in his weakened state, made him rest. He must have fallen asleep for a short time, and when he woke, Jerinne was gone. The sun had gone down—it was probably half past eight bells at this point—so she probably had to return to the Tarian Chapterhouse for the night.

Dayne should sleep, should let himself recover fully from the physical and magical ordeal he had been through.

But there was no chance he was going to sleep. Sholiar was here, in Maradaine. At liberty to kill countless more.

Dayne wouldn't allow it. Not one more death, not if he could help it.

He washed his face and took out a fresh uniform. His dress uniform, bright blue with the kite shield emblem in gleaming silver on his chest. He wasn't just going to stop Sholiar, he would show him who was stopping him. A Tarian. A trained warrior of the Order.

He strapped the shield onto his arm, once again saying the oath, if only for his own ears.

> *"With shield on arm and sword in hand*
> *I will not yield, but hold and stand.*
> *As I draw breath, I'll allow no harm,*
> *And hold back death with shield on arm."*

He glanced over to the looking glass hanging on the water closet basin. "Now get out there, Tarian," he said to himself.

As he opened the door, Inspector Welling was standing there, about to knock.

"Inspector," he said, trying to keep his surprise from showing. "What are you doing here?"

"I need your help," Welling said. "You're . . . very ready, I see."

"Sholiar is out there," Dayne said. "I'm not going to fail again."

"That's why I need your help," Welling said. "He's apparently taken two new victims—my friend Joshea, and your protégée."

"Jerinne?" Dayne asked. "How? Are you certain?"

"Honestly, no," Welling said. "Sholiar captured my cousin and left her on my front stoop with a message for me. For us."

"Another one of his games," Dayne said with a sneer. "What's the message?"

"You and I go to the Kittrick Hotel in Fenton by nine bells. Or else they die."

Dayne understood this game. "And there would be consequences if any other Constabulary or Tarians show up?"

"So I'm led to believe."

"Then let's waste no more time," Dayne said. "I'll not fail you, Inspector. Not again."

"Nor I you," Welling said. "We'll save our friends, and bring him to justice."

Dayne smiled and bolted down the hallway, calling out, "Come on. We'll hold back death together."

Jace was standing just in the entryway of the Welling home—just within the bounds of not breaking the rules—when Satrine rode up with the trapmaster on the back of the pedalcart.

"That was fast," Jace called out as she ran up the walkway to the front stoop. "Which is good. Corrie's been having a blazes of a time keeping everyone at bay."

"Language, son," the trapmaster said with a smirk.

"Who's this fellow?" Jace asked, following them both as they came into the foyer.

"He's the guy who disarmed the contraptions at the Parliament," Satrine said. "And that's all you need to know."

"It's already a bit too much," the trapmaster said.

They came into the sitting room, where Nyla now stood in the center, the furniture cleared away from her. Only Corrie, Nyla's parents, and the Yellowshield cousin were still in there with her; the rest had decamped to the dining room.

"All right," the trapmaster said. He took a deep sigh and looked around the room. "I don't suppose any of you care to clear out of here."

"I'm not leaving my daughter," her father said.

"I understand, Mister—" The trapmaster looked at his badge. He almost choked for a second, and covered it. He glanced back at Satrine. "Get them all out of here. I don't care what you have to do. I'm going to get set up."

He pulled a small table and chair over and opened up his toolkit.

Satrine tried to appeal to them. "Mister and Missus Pyle—"

"Sergeant Pyle!" Nyla's father shouted.

The trapmaster slammed his hand on the table. "Out!"

"This is delicate work," Satrine said. "The fewer distractions he has, the better."

"Cole, dear," Nyla's mother said. "Maybe we should—"

"Mama!" Nyla called.

"Tricky," Corrie said. "You're sure you got this?"

"I'm sure this is her best chance," Satrine said. "That's as sure as I can give you."

"Emma, Cole," Corrie said. "Let's clear the blazes out."

"I can't—" Emma cried.

"Go!" Nyla shouted. "Please, I love you, please."

The Yellowshield touched Satrine on the shoulder. "I'll be just in the next room if you—if anything . . ." Her eyes were full of tears.

They all went into the dining room, where the rest of the Wellings were congregated. The trapmaster crossed the room to shut the door on them. "Sure, I'll go help," he muttered. "In a huge Constabulary family house."

"Get it together," Satrine whispered to him, grabbing his shoulder. "That girl is terrified and you're her only chance."

"I know," he shot back. Glaring hard at her, he added, "I'm about to save the daughter of the man who killed my father, so you'll grant me a moment to collect myself."

Satrine stepped away from him, not sure what she could say to that. She went over to stand at Nyla's side.

"Why are you still here?" Nyla asked her, her voice trembling.

Satrine grabbed her hand. "Because if this goes poorly, your family already hates me."

Nyla squeezed her hand back so hard, it felt like it was going to break. "Please, please, I can't—"

"I know," Satrine said. "Just look at me."

"All right," the trapmaster said, sitting down in front of Nyla. "Let's see what we've got here."

Nyla looked up at the ceiling, breathing slowly and deliberately. "I'm not going to die here," she said slowly. "There's no way I'm going to die holding your hand."

"That's the spirit," Satrine said. "Trust me, hate is a fantastic survival tool."

"Trust you, sure," Nyla said. "A cheat and a fraud."

"This is fascinating," the trapmaster said. "I mean the work, not your squabbles."

"Can you disarm it?"

"I'm going to give you a very qualified 'maybe.'" He got up and walked around her. "Latch, hasp, gear, gear, and . . . yes."

"Yes?"

"I found what I'm looking for, that yes," he said. He counted the ticks of the gears for a moment. "Yeah, time to move fast."

"Fast?"

"Rather," he said, grabbing a tool. "I'm not certain, but I think this thing will decapitate her in two minutes."

"What?" Nyla screamed.

"Or sooner," he said. He gingerly patted her by her shoulders. "Yeah, I was afraid of that. Springs are poised to release, and the turning of this mechanism is holding them back."

"Which means?" Satrine asked.

"It means I can't just take out the screws or jam the gears. The mechanics running is what is keeping her alive. If I stop the gears, clonk."

"Clonk?"

"Forgive my ineloquent language," he said. "Now, if our man who made this is true to form, there're a few fail-safes in here. He's a redundant cuss."

"Mister," Nyla said. "Please, I don't want to die." She clutched at Satrine's hand again.

"Right," he said. "Damn and blazes. Tell me quick, I saw a whole lot of people in that next room. All family, Miss Pyle?" He was taking out a number of tiny clamps and cutters and was placing them in various spots on the device on her body.

"Yes," she said.

"So, who're the two who've got the best hands? I'm talking about precision."

"Davis and Ferah!" she said quickly.

"I like the certainty," he said. "Davis! Ferah! Get in here!"

The door flew open and they ran in. "What, what?"

"All right, here's the thing," he said as he walked around to her back. He further fiddled with the device while giving instructions. "You want her to live, four things have to happen simultaneously. Ferah, you're the Yellowshield, hmm? Stand at her right side, get your hands on that clipper. Davis, grab the handles of those clamps at her waist. Don't waste time, just kneel down."

They did as they were told.

"All right, Inspector, you get the worst job," he said. "And we've got seconds. Grab this right here."

Satrine moved around to Nyla's back, where he had cut away at some fabric to reveal a pull zip holding the device shut.

"The cuss used a strappercoat as the base of this,

which helps us out," the trapmaster said. "Now, I'm going to count to three, and *on three*: Ferah, you snip; Davis, you clamp; and Inspector, you unzip that thing like it's on fire. Which it just might be. You got me?"

"Got," Satrine said.

"All right, Miss Pyle," he said, cupping her face. "I'm going to pull on this evil thing, and you got to jump back out of it as fast as you possibly can."

"Fast as I rutting can," she said, sweat pouring off her forehead.

"That's the spirit," he said, placing his hands on the front of the device. "Prayers if you've got them. And one, two . . . three!"

Satrine pulled down the zip as hard as she could, and in the same moment Ferah and Davis acted, while the trapmaster twisted two parts and yanked. Nyla screamed and jumped back, falling onto Satrine.

The trapmaster hurled the thing across the room, where it suddenly became alive with snapping and slicing, shredding itself in the process.

Nyla cried out, grabbing Satrine in a frantic embrace. "I'm alive, I'm alive, he did it, I'm alive."

"Saints and sinners," the trapmaster said, sucking on his finger. "Got a piece of me. Not a good couple days for my fingers."

Nyla scrambled to her feet and threw her arms around him. "You did it you did it every saint be praised." She kissed him repeatedly on the cheek.

"All right, all right," he said, extricating himself from her. "I am a married man."

The rest of the family rushed in, grabbing Nyla and hollering in joy.

"Do you want me to look at your hand?" Ferah asked the trapmaster.

"It's a scratch," he said quickly. He stepped away to the foyer. "Not a worry."

Nyla's father strode right at him. "Sir," he said, grabbing the trapmaster in a mad embrace. "You've done a great service."

Satrine extricated the man. "All right, don't smother him."

"I did . . . what any decent man would do," the trapmaster said. "Much to my surprise."

"Even still." Nyla's father dug his calling card out of his pocket. "You ever need anything, I am in your debt."

The trapmaster took the card and nodded. "I suppose you are," he said.

"I'll see you out," Satrine said. She grabbed him by the arm and led him out the door.

"I think I can find my own way back home," he said sharply once they were outside, pulling himself free of her grip.

"Thank you," she said.

"Yeah, well . . . she didn't deserve to die because her father . . . yeah. I appreciate your discretion, though," He shook his head, looking at the calling card. "I suppose you should get back to your people."

"My people?" she asked.

He pointed to Nyla's father in the window as he flipped the card over his fingers with the practiced ease of a born thief. "You're both Waish, aren't you?"

"Where do you—"

He showed the card to her. "Cole Pyle. That's a Waish name if I ever heard one. Thought I suppose it'd be spelled something frightful—"

The gears in Satrine's own thoughts suddenly snapped together. The trapmaster had unlocked the thing that had been bothering her for two days.

"Corrie!" she cried out. Turning to the trapmaster once more, she said, "Thank you, absolutely. Saints' blessings on you and yours." She ran back into the Welling house, calling for Corrie again.

Now it made sense.

"Corrie," she said, coming into the room where the Welling family was celebrating. "Do you have your writ pad here?"

"Of course," Corrie said, handing it over. "What the blazes for?"

"Because we need a Writ of Search," Satrine said, filling out a request. "Now. I need a page."

"What do you need?" Jace asked, stepping up.

"You ain't a blazing page!" Corrie said.

"You need someone to run," Jace said, looking at Satrine. "I can do that."

Satrine tore off the request and put it in his hands. "Head to the Inemar office, give this to Inspector Kellman. Have him put in the writ, and once he has it, meet me at HTC Imports on the north side."

"Meet us," Corrie said, grabbing her belt and coat off the hooks by the door.

"You're coming?" Satrine asked. "Shouldn't you—?" She nodded to the rest of the family.

"It's fine," Corrie said. "Minox is out in the night, going after the bastard who did this to Nyla. That's where I want to be as well."

"Let's go, then," she said. "One more favor, Jace?"

"Name it, Tricky," he said with a wink.

"Head to 14 Beltner after that, in High River. Let my family know it's going to be a very late night."

Chapter 24

MINOX HAD NEVER been in this part of the city before. Most of the Fenton neighborhood was reminiscent of the stretch of "loyal houses" in Keller Cove that the Welling family lived in. Older houses, built larger and farther apart. No brick whitestones cramped together here, let alone crumbling tenements.

But while the houses had a certain elegance, even in the dark of night it was clear that many of them were in disrepair. Fallen eaves, collapsed porches, and half-dead trees that tangled through broken windows. Houses like this were noticeable in the southern part of the neighborhood, but once he and Dayne were in the northern part, they had become the norm. As far as Minox could tell, these blocks were nearly unpopulated.

"Here's the absurd thing," Dayne said, noting Minox's confusion. "This neighborhood is expensive to live in. Or at least, it recently became that. It was a neighborhood for artists, writers, performers, and it was very popular for a few years near the end of the war. So rents went up, and soon the artists all left, and the allure faded. The money stopped flowing here. So you had people with houses they couldn't afford to sell or repair."

"And the shops that serve the neighborhood closed

up," Minox said, noting a block of stores and restaurants that were all dark. Not even the lamplighters were bothering here. "So even more people leave the neighborhood, because they have to travel ten blocks just to buy food."

"I don't understand why the city doesn't make an effort—" Dayne stopped. "Well, no, I understand, especially with this latest election."

"I suppose," Minox said. "I'm not familiar with the city aldermen who represent this side of the city. Or my new one."

"I didn't think there was much change in the Council of Aldermen."

"No, but our house was in the thirteenth district, and now it's in the ninth. I'll confess, examining the details of local government has not been my priority."

"Get on that," Dayne said, striding toward the large brick building that sat at the corner of Holmes and Mudgett. Like most of the other places around, the windows were boarded up, but two oil lamps hung over the main door.

"It's definitely not my priority in this moment," Minox said.

The faded sign over the door read "The Kittrick Hotel," with fresh paint scrawling "Under new management" in red and black over it.

"This is his style, certainly," Dayne said. "I haven't heard any church bells—"

"If there are any we could hear in this area."

"But I don't think it's nine bells yet." He opened the door. "So we've jumped his first hurdle. There will be more, Inspector."

"Noted," Minox said, going in.

The lobby of the hotel had likely been warm and inviting at one point, but now most of the furniture had been stripped away, the carpet chewed by rats, and the lamp sconces hung loosely on the walls. But someone had recently swept and dusted, as there was none of the expected detritus on the floor.

"Oh, excellent. Customers."

An older man stood behind the counter, wearing a suit that looked like it was last in style when the hotel had closed. Given its holes and loose threads, it likely had been sitting in a closet somewhere in this hotel all this time. The man smiled at them, but at the same time, he was trembling with nerves.

"I'm glad to see you both made it on time," he said. He chuckled nervously. "Yes, very glad indeed."

"Who are you?" Minox said, coming up to the counter. "Where is Sholiar?"

The man nodded. "Yes, your rooms are ready. I'm sure you'll be anxious to go up and get settled in."

"We aren't going to do anything of the sort," Minox said. "You're going to tell us what's going on. Where is Sholiar? Where are Joshea Brondar and Jerinne Fendall?"

The man's brow was drenched in sweat, and it visibly dripped down onto the ledger in front of him as he pushed it to Minox. "If the two of you could just sign in."

"Where are they?"

"I'm not at liberty to discuss other guests of the hotel, sir," he said. "Surely you understand."

"Do I have to arrest you?" Minox asked. "Is that what I have to—"

"Minox," Dayne said gently. "His leg."

Minox looked over the counter and saw. The man's leg was shackled to the floor. Not merely shackled: it seemed to be clamped on with some sort of bear trap device that threatened to chop his leg off if it released.

"He's as much a victim as us," Dayne said. "Do you need help, sir?"

"I—" The man's voice broke, and for a moment he sobbed pathetically. Then he composed himself best he could. "I need to check you both in, explain the rules of the hotel."

"Of course," Dayne said. "Go ahead."

"Sign here," he said. "Those last two spaces on the ledger."

Dayne started to write, and then dropped the pen.

"What is it?" Minox asked.

Dayne pointed to the names on the ledger, thirteen of them. The first seven were the same as the original Gearbox victims, all of them marked as "checked out." The next six were all names Minox recognized: Jerinne and Joshea, as well as Hemmit Eyairin, Lin Shartien, Maresh Niol, and most surprisingly, Ezaniel Rencir.

"Rencir?" Minox said out loud.

"Who is that?" Dayne asked.

"He writes for the *South Maradaine Gazette*."

"A friend?"

"An acquaintance," Minox said.

"Another tool to turn your hinges," Dayne said. "Just like my friends on *The Veracity Press*. Are they here as well, sir?"

The man nodded. "If they aren't marked as checked out, then they should still be on the premises. But the . . . the checkouts haven't been updated tonight yet. As far as I know."

"Let's get on with it," Minox said. He was in no mood for any of this. He had arrived, that was enough of playing Sholiar's game. He was of half a mind to magically tear the building apart, brick by brick, until everyone was found. On the desperate look of the man, he picked up the pen and wrote his name under Joshea's. Dayne took the pen and wrote his own.

"Here are your room keys," the man said, handing them over. "Up the stairs, right at the top. It's crucial that you each go into your own rooms, and at the same time."

"We won't switch," Dayne said quickly. Clearly in one of his previous experiences with Sholiar, Dayne had attempted to subvert the rules of the game.

"One more thing, Mister Welling." The man reached under the counter and came up with a gauntlet, like the kind worn by knights centuries ago, but with a lockbolt of iron shackles at the wrist. "I'm afraid you must put this on."

"You want me to wear that?"

"Those are the rules, Mister Welling. It was—it was made very clear to me that you had to put that on."

"Of course it was," Minox said. There was no value in arguing these things. He pulled the gauntlet on his left hand, covering the glove that kept the blackened thing hidden from sight, and then on the old man's encouraging nod, he shut the lockbolt. Now without the key, he couldn't remove it. And he immediately felt the effects, which were exactly what he expected. The gauntlet must have been made of the same material as mage shackles, but even more effective. His hand went dead inside, his connection to it numb. The rest of his magic was just as muted.

"Is that all?" Dayne asked.

"Weapons," the man said. "But I was told you can keep the shield, sir."

"Well, that's something," Dayne said as Minox placed his crossbow and handstick on the counter.

"That all?" Minox said.

"All," the man said, gesturing to the stairs. "Please enjoy the hospitality of the Kittrick."

———◆–◆–◆———

"You need to make one thing clear to me, Trick," Corrie said as they crossed the great bridge to the rutting north side of the city. It was a quiet night, almost eerily so, which surprised the blazes out of Corrie. But maybe the past few days had been so crazy the whole city needed to take a moment to breathe. The two of them weren't quite running, but they were walking as fast they could without breaking into a sprint. Corrie wished they had horses under them.

"I'll try," Tricky said.

"Which of the bastards are we going after right now?"

"What do you mean?"

"I mean, what case is this? It's not the rutting Parliament case, right?"

"Not directly," Tricky said. "It's sort of the missing kids, but sort of the Parliament. And maybe that all ties to this Sholiar character."

"Saints and sinners," Corrie said. "You've been around Minox too much."

"Maybe so," she said with a wicked grin. "But I found that trapmaster who saved Nyla because of a bakery package."

Corrie didn't even know what to make of that. "This is why I'm not going to be made inspector."

"You never know. It's in your blood."

"It's in Minox's blood. I'm just an angry cuss who doesn't quit."

"That's Minox as well."

"That was our pop," Corrie said. She thought about what Minox had told her, that he had taken the transfer to far westtown to keep Minox from there. The job that killed him. "Saints hold him close."

Tricky stopped walking, getting her bearings, and looked back at Corrie. "You all right?"

"Nothing," Corrie said, wiping away the hints of moisture that were threatening to become tears. "You think Minox is all right?"

"I hope so," Tricky said. "He won't underestimate Sholiar. Though Sholiar kidnapped the only other person whom Minox would tear the city apart to rescue."

"Right," Corrie said. She was glad Minox had found Joshea, that he had someone to talk about magic stuff with. He had no one in the family, really, save Evoy. She knew she hadn't made herself available to him about that. That was a mistake that led to this stupid rutting Inquiry. Now he was going to be stuck at a desk when he should be working the streets with her. "So where the rutting blazes are we going?"

"There," Tricky said, pointing out one of the buildings on the dock side of the street. Run-down-looking place, but there were a few lamps burning in the windows. But that was all Corrie could see through the windows, the flicker of the lamp flame. They had covered every window with butcher paper or something to keep prying eyes out.

"Well, that place looks suspect, all right."

"It does indeed," Tricky said. She moved down the street, her attention away from that building. She looked out in the distance, holding up her hand like she was lining up a shot.

"What?"

"You can see the Parliament from here, and *that* building, between here and there, is one of the station-houses for the King's Marshals."

"That supposed to be significant?"

"Maybe," she said cryptically. "I'm going to check something else. Stay here, keep an eye on that, and wait for the writ."

"Presuming Kellman comes the blazes through with it."

"He damn well better," Tricky said. "Eyes sharp, ears up."

"You too," Corrie said. Tricky went off around the corner.

Corrie looked back to the HTC Imports building. Through the shadows on the butcher paper, she could see that someone definitely was in there.

Maybe they'd do something that would give her cause. Then she wouldn't even need a writ.

She pulled out her crossbow and waited. Just in case.

◆——◆◆——◆

"Why do we split up?" Minox asked as they reached the two rooms at the top of the stairs.

"Because that's the game we're supposed to play," Dayne said. "If we have any chance of catching Sholiar . . ."

"I doubt we even have that," Minox said. He mostly hoped to bring Joshea out safely, as well as the others.

He also hoped that Inspector Rainey had been successful in her plan to free Nyla from her trap. Or, failing that, that the deal Sholiar laid out had proven true: by coming here and following the terms, her safety was ensured.

"Either way, let's do this," Dayne said. He put his key in his door and tried to turn it.

It didn't budge.

"What's wrong?" Minox asked.

"It doesn't move," Dayne said, the muscles in his massive arms straining. He stopped trying. "The key would snap before it turned."

"It's the game," Minox said, putting his own key in. "To keep us honest, it's probably rigged that we have to turn both our keys at the same time."

Dayne muttered some invective under his breath. "Let's to it then. On my count?"

"Go ahead."

Dayne counted, and they turned their keys together. This time, they both turned smoothly and easily.

Trapdoors opened up beneath them.

Minox barely had time to register this as he fell down a metal chute, sliding through it and bursting through a metal grate that shut behind him when he landed.

As soon as he was on the ground, the clicking sound of gears and chains surrounded him. Something had just started moving, activated by his entrance.

"Dayne!" he called out. "Are you here?"

"Yes!" Dayne's voice echoed from every direction, no way to determine where it was coming from.

Minox took a moment to get his bearings. A dim hallway, lit by oil lamp globes on the low ceiling. Along the hallway walls, chains were cranking along, pulled by unseen gears. In the distance down the hall, more sounds echoed and reverberated. The was a regular constant clang, heavy and hard.

Then a scream.

Minox ran down the hall.

He emerged in a large chamber—impossible to tell what it might have been in the original architecture of the hotel—but now it housed another of Sholiar's atrocity machines. It resembled a large printing press, slamming down with great force every few seconds. Three people—Rencir and Niol and Miss Shartien—were shackled around their necks, the chains pulling them into the press. They struggled to stay clear, but the slow, relentless pull of the chain brought them closer and closer.

Iron bars separated them from Mister Eyairin, who was locked in a cage. Dayne came running over from the other side of the iron bars, able to reach Eyairin's cage but not the man himself.

"Help! Welling, help!" Rencir shouted. The press slammed down again, and began its slow crank back to being open. Minox's first instinct was to reach out magically and snap their shackles, but his power spurted and fizzled. The gauntlet blocked him.

Dayne was frantically trying to open Eyairin's cage, but he wasn't succeeding. "Get them out of there!"

Minox looked around for anything he could use as a tool to break their shackles, but there was nothing remotely usable. He spotted three control levers, accessible only from Eyairin's cage.

The press slammed down again.

"What are those levers?" he asked Eyairin.

"I don't know," Eyairin said. He grabbed one and pulled it down.

Rencir's chain slackened, and he was able to pull himself a few feet away from the smashing maw of the press. Eyairin screamed out in pain and let go. The lever snapped up and Rencir was drawn in again.

"What happened?" Dayne asked.

"Hot!" Eyairin cried out. "Scalding!"

Niol and Shartien were dangerously close to the press as it slammed down again.

"Do it again!" Shartien called out.

Eyairin tried to pull his sleeves over his hands as he

pulled down the next lever. This released Niol's chain enough to get him away from immediate peril of the press. He got farther than Rencir before Eyairin screamed again.

"It's too much!" he said.

"Please!" Shartien said. The chain had now pulled her over the lip of the press, which was almost to the top of its cycle before it slammed down. Minox grabbed hold of her waist and pulled as Eyrain pulled down the third lever, yanking her out of harm's way as the press slammed down. Eyairin screamed again.

Dayne tried to bend the bars of Eyairin's cage, but he couldn't get any purchase.

Eyairin's hands were smoking, tears streaming down his face. "I can't do any more, I'm sorry."

"You bought us time," Minox said.

"What are you doing, Welling?" Rencir shouted. "Get us free!"

"I'm thinking," Minox said. They only had moments before Rencir and Niol were in deadly peril again, and Shartien moments after that.

He looked at the machine. Followed the gears, the chains, the pattern. He couldn't see the mechanism that pulled their chains because it was behind the press, as were whatever Eyairin's levers controlled. It had to all connect somewhere back there—probably with a steam pipe that heated the levers.

Minox just needed to get back there. Rencir and Niol were already being pulled back into the press. "Dayne! This is Sholiar's game, so what are the rules?"

"There're no rules," Dayne said. "It's just cruelty!" The press was about to slam down again, and despite his struggles, Niol was about to be smashed by it.

But there were rules. Minox had to put on the gauntlet, block his magic. Dayne was allowed to keep his shield. This had to be for a reason.

"Dayne! Shield!"

Dayne seemed to understand exactly what Minox meant, and tossed him the shield through the iron bars. Minox caught it and wedged it in the lip of the press as it came down. It jammed the press before it could crush Niol, but the chains pulling all three inside didn't relent.

Dayne tried to reach through the bars of Eyairin's cage, get at the levers himself, but they were too far away.

The shield started to buckle.

Minox darted into the press, crawling through it to the machinery on the other side. It was challenging, with one hand numb and unresponsive, but he pulled himself through.

"Pull the levers again, Hemmit!" Niol shouted.

"I can't!"

"Minox, get out of there!" Dayne yelled.

From inside, he could see the gearwork. It didn't make much sense to him, but he could see what he presumed were the release controls of the chains. That lever was glowing red hot.

"The shield is breaking!"

Minox swung his left arm so his numb fingers in the gauntlet wrapped around the hot lever. The metal sizzled and stuck, which was good enough. Minox pulled as hard as he could.

The chains released completely, and the machinery stopped. Eyairin's cage popped open. Two of the iron bars separating Minox's side from Dayne's fell down, leaving enough space for someone to pass through.

"Well done, well done." Sholiar's familiar voice reverberated around them. "I'm quite impressed by your teamwork, gentlemen, including your sacrifice, Inspector."

"Where the blazes are you?" Dayne shouted.

"Mind your temper, Tarian," Sholiar said. The voice seemed to come from every direction at once. More of Sholiar's clever madness, or did he actually have magic on his side? He definitely understood magic, enough to make the gauntlet and the trigger of Nyla's trap.

Minox managed to pull his gauntleted hand free of

the lever. The metal had been scorched, but its ability to dampen his magic hadn't diminished.

But if his hand had been normal flesh, it probably would have been irrevocably destroyed by doing that.

Sholiar said his sacrifice. Maybe Sholiar didn't know about Minox's hand, what it was. That he didn't feel any pain through it. No reason to let Sholiar know different. He could play that high card later. As he extracted himself from the press, a key fell down from a hole in the ceiling. Rencir picked it up and unlatched his collar, and then gave it to Miss Shartien.

"What the blazes is this, Welling?" Rencir asked. The poor man looked an absolute fright, his skin pale and clammy. He looked like it was taking every bit of willpower he had to not vomit.

"This is Sholiar, the Gearbox Killer," Minox said.

"Saints, for real?" Rencir said. "I thought . . . but why . . ."

"I had to give these boys a test," Sholiar said. "See how much resolve they had when the victims are people they have mild affection for."

"So now what?" Dayne shouted.

"Now, you all have a choice," Sholiar said. Two doors—which Minox hadn't even noticed before— opened on their own. One of them revealed a back alley outside, the other a staircase. "You are all free to leave, if you wish. Or delve further into the adventure."

"Jerinne and Joshea," Dayne said.

Minox nodded. "We don't all have to make the same choice, do we, Sholiar?"

"Oh, it would be delicious to torture you with that, wouldn't it? Make you choose between taking the beefy mustache there to a doctor or saving the others. But I'm not in the mood for that. Each of you can make your own choice, without hurting the others."

Rencir bolted outside.

"Go," Dayne told Miss Shartien. "Get Hemmit to a doctor."

As she and Niol helped Eyairin to the door, Sholiar's

voice came through again. "That said, should any Constabulary or marshal or even a fire brigadier come too close to the hotel, well . . . I can't be responsible for what might happen."

"Are you going to be all right?" Shartien asked Dayne.

"We will," he said. "Go."

They went out the door, and then it slammed shut. A moment later, the shield in the printing press snapped and it slammed down as well.

"Oh, I wish I could take credit for that," Sholiar said. "You best hurry, gentlemen. Gears are turning, springs are winding. Miss Fendall and Mister Brondar do not have all night."

Chapter 25

SATRINE STALKED AROUND to the other side of the HTC dockhouse. She wasn't sure what she was going to find, if anything, but even though she was deep within her own whims of presumption, she couldn't shake the feeling of absolute certainty. It felt right.

She only wished her foot felt right as well. The damned boot kept digging into the arch of her foot, and it annoyed the blazes out of her. After tonight Nyla damned well better rush a requisition for her to get a new pair. Nyla would probably never stop hating her, but she should at least start giving Satrine some grudging respect.

She couldn't get to the HTC dock from here, not without blatantly trespassing, and that would spoil whatever case could be made. She had to keep that in mind. She was already flirting with all sorts of trouble. If she was right, this would come right up to the edge of the jurisdictional fight they had already lost to the marshals. Of course, if she was right, then that part wouldn't matter. But that wasn't something she could prove at all. Not yet. She could see to the river, though, and that at least confirmed the gut feeling she had had about coming here right now.

There was a ship at the HTC dock, heavy in the

water. Loaded with cargo. A few men worked rolling crates, with an expectant energy to their actions. None of the ships' lamps were lit, though. Nothing she saw was illegal, but there was every sense that the ship was being prepped for launch very soon.

And no one runs a ship at night with no lamps unless they were doing something very shady.

She strained to hear their voices, hoping to catch something that would justify going in right now. She knew it would be ridiculous to charge in, just her and a crossbow. She should wait for the writ. Wait for Kellman and the squad.

Kellman. She was going to have to be stuck partnering with him while Welling rotted in the archives. That was a waste. Kellman wasn't horrible, but he had definitely picked up Mirrell's worst habits. She might be able to train him, though. He at least listened to her.

He wasn't a bad sort, she kept telling herself. He had stuck up for her when she was found out. He had gotten hurt helping her fight Pra Yikenj, and he got up with a smile and went back to work the next day.

Kellman would work out. She'd make it.

And Welling . . .

She just hoped Welling survived the night. She feared that Joshea Brondar and Jerinne Fendall were already dead, and Welling and Dayne were just going to walk into their own deaths. She didn't know what to make of Sholiar, but he was clearly a deranged genius, and nothing about the man could be safe or trusted.

No. Minox was brilliant as well. He'd see it all clearly, he'd figure it out. If anyone was going to outthink Sholiar, it would be Minox Welling.

Presuming he was thinking straight.

Satrine was so deep in her own reverie she didn't notice the horse cart pulling up to the dockhouse. Someone had come outside to greet it. Even from this distance and the dim moonlight, Satrine could recognize that one. He had screamed at her enough in the boiler room. She wasn't sure if it was Cole or Hunsen, but that didn't matter. His presence was enough to confirm at least that part of her theory. She moved as close as she dared to not be spotted.

"What are you doing here?" he asked the cart driver. "You weren't supposed to be here until midnight."

"Time's gone short," the driver said. "I need the ones for Senek, and that boat needs to get gone." That voice was familiar, but Satrine wasn't certain if she was right, or just wanted to be.

"Saints and sinners," the man at the door said. He opened up the dockhouse doors. "Get in here."

As the horse cart pulled in, Satrine slipped over to the main door. Now, as far as she was concerned, she had cause. But she still had to find out more, find out for sure. She checked her crossbow—loaded and ready.

As they closed the dockhouse door behind the cart, she went through the main door and trained her crossbow at the two men.

"What a surprise seeing the two of you together," she said as they turned around. "Hands high, nothing fast."

"Who the blazes are you?" the man from the boiler room asked.

"Inspector Satrine Rainey of the Grand Inspection Unit," she said. "I saved your life yesterday, remember? And you would be either Hunsen or Cole. But I'm guessing Cole, yes?"

"Shut it," he said.

She looked at the driver. "He's Cole, isn't he? Your, what, nephew or distant cousin? And that's why you're connected to this, aren't you, Chief Quoyell?"

Corrie hadn't seen Tricky for too many clicks, and still no sign of Kellman, Iorrett, or anyone else from the stationhouse. It was a whole mess of trouble, that was for damn sure.

She was tempted to declare cause—a missing

inspector certainly qualified—blow a Runner Call on her whistle and charge in. At least, if she was wrong, she'd be the one to take the heat from the City Protector. Mister Hilsom hated her anyway, and the feeling was mutual.

But if she blew her whistle, then she might screw things up for Tricky. Screw up the writ that was probably on the way. Jace went to get it, and he would pester the sinners out of Kellman until it was on the way. And if it wasn't, she knew damn well Jace would run here himself to tell them.

That kid, he was something else. Proud as blazes of him.

Which made her wonder how their brother Oren had turned out to be such a knob. Probably the influence of Timm's boys.

"Hey, hey, skirt."

She looked up to see two footpatrol steves wandering up to her.

"That's Sergeant Skirt to you tossers," she said. "What's your stumble?"

"What are you, south side?" one of them asked.

"Yeah, Inemar," she said. "You from Trelan Stationhouse?"

"That's right," the other asked. "You really a sergeant?"

"Yeah," she said, pointing to the chevron on her sleeve.

"She's young for sergeant."

"I ain't seen any sergeant this young. How old are you, skirt?"

"Nineteen, you got a problem with that?" she asked. "I did my—never mind, boys. Look, I've got a specs who went investigating something and she's overdue."

"*She's* overdue?" the first asked. "They do things different in Inemar. Skirt inspectors, skirt sergeants."

Rutting blazes, these two.

"Right," she told them. "Look, I've got cause to run at that dockhouse, and I'm going to whistle the Runner

Call, and you two'll need to have my rutting back, hear?"

"That dockhouse?" one asked. "That one right there?"

"Yeah, that rutting one, tosser."

"Hey," the second one said. "That spec you're missing, is she a Waishen-haired slan?"

"Yeah, she—"

Corrie knew she had rutted up as soon as she said this. His handstick was already coming down on her arm, knocking her crossbow out of her hand.

"You blazing little pisswhistle," she said, introducing her fist to his teeth.

"Oh, she's got fire," he said, spitting out blood. "I bet she's good for all kinds of spar."

"You want some spar?" she asked. She pulled out her handstick and jammed it at his gut. "I'll give you some rutting spar!" She moved in close, driving her knee into his tenders. He screamed and grabbed her hair. His teeth full of blood, he hooted and slammed her nose with his head. That filled her eyes with rutting stars, and she fell to one knee.

"She's gonna make a good one, she is," he said.

"Saints, stop playing," his partner said, and a handstick cracked across her skull.

She saw nothing but stars as she was dragged away.

"You aren't supposed to be here!" Quoyell shouted at her. "You don't have the right or jurisdiction—"

"Jurisdiction?" Satrine shot back. "So you admit that this is tied to the events at the Parliament."

"I'm not saying anything," he said. "You are engaged in clear Constabulary misconduct by invading privacy without cause."

"Oh, I have cause. I even have a writ of search on the way. What I didn't quite have was the connection, but this confirms the little buzz I had in the back of my head." She turned back to Cole, pushing her point again. "So what is he? Uncle? Cousin?"

That threw him. "How did—what—I mean . . . what a ridiculous idea."

"It's not. It was bothering me for the past two days. I should have seen it sooner, but . . . it's been rather busy."

"Oh, really?" Quoyell said. "Please, explain your great elucidation, Inspector."

"Your name is Waish," she said. "I spent a few years in Waisholm, and so I recognized that. But what I had forgotten about is how Waish spelling is a bit odd compared to ours. Same letters, different rules. So what would get pronounced 'Quoi-yell' here, when you *say* it like the Waish would, is just 'Cole.'"

"Truly," Chief Quoyell said flatly, "I'm dizzied by your deduction."

"I don't care," Satrine said, letting her anger build. "I don't know what you're doing here, but it's going to be stopped. You—I know my husband was onto you—"

"Your who?"

"Inspector Loren Rainey!" she shouted. "He was found beaten and half-drowned right out there!"

"First I've heard of him," Quoyell said. "You mistake me for someone who cares."

"You should care!" She almost shot him with the crossbow right then. "You . . . you're a goddamned King's Marshal! You're supposed to uphold the law and serve the king!"

"No, I'm supposed to serve the throne and Druthal," he said. "It's a subtle difference."

"I don't care how you justify it! You're responsible for a dozen deaths, and for what?"

"What is your point?" Cole asked. He almost looked bored.

"The point is the two of you colluded to stage that atrocity on the Parliament floor—a horror show like the city has never seen before, and why? To divert all the city's attention over there to buy yourself a few extra days, because that boat couldn't arrive until now."

"That's patently absurd," Quoyell said, though his tone indicated she was hitting at the center. "You will never understand the reasons."

"And then you scrubbed the names of Cole, Tenning, and Hunsen from the victim lists because you didn't want anyone to know they were involved. And I'm guessing that Tenning got cold feet, or was otherwise problematic, so you killed him today."

"If he'd just stayed calm," Cole muttered.

"Shut it," Quoyell said.

"So the only question I have right now is, where is Mister Hunsen?"

"Oh, him?" Quoyell asked. "He's behind you."

A hand grabbed the top of Satrine's head, and slammed her into the floor.

Chapter 26

"ARE YOU HOLDING up?" Dayne asked Inspector Welling as they reached the top of the stairs.

"I'm fine," Welling said. "I'd rather we were done with this, with Sholiar in irons."

"That's not going to happen, boys." Sholiar's voice echoed above them. "Though I respect the determination."

"You're unwell," Welling said.

"Yes, you would know about that, wouldn't you?" the disembodied voice said. Dayne was amazed at Sholiar's technical ability—as always, the greatest shame was that genius of this level was tied to such a diseased mind. The good a man with Sholiar's capacity could do if he were so inclined.

Sholiar went on. "I mean, with your grandfather, your cousin Evoy. And you and Jillian aren't far behind, are you?"

Welling didn't respond, but his face said volumes.

"Now what, Sholiar?" Dayne shouted. The stairs had led to a small chamber with no obvious exits, beyond going back where they came. Dayne could hear the grinding of gears all around, though. "Is this your clever trap for us?"

"Dayne, old top, there's no trap for you. You already live in your own trap. Let me show you."

The wall opened up to reveal a large chamber, nearly the length of the whole building. Several of Sholiar's machines were winding and cranking all around, but the center of Dayne's attention was at the far end of the room. Jerinne was there, shackled at the ankles and waist. Dayne quickly saw the purpose of the machines: they were repeatedly firing crossbow bolts, steel balls, hammers, and other blunt instruments at Jerinne.

She had her shield, and despite being immobilized, she was doing her best to block the attacks. Attacks barraged her from every direction, and her body was covered in welts. Sweat and blood pasted her hair to her face. She looked exhausted. She couldn't possibly keep up.

"Look at her, old top," Sholiar said. "I expected her to pass out after twenty minutes, but she's been at this for nearly an hour."

Dayne charged forward on instinct, and before he knew it, he had pulled a tripwire. Three new machines sprang to life. Jerinne struggled to compensate, moving her shield as fast as she could, but took a steel ball in the leg. She cried out, but stayed standing.

"Dayne, look out!" Welling yelled. Another machine flung a bladed disc across the room, which nearly hit him in the arm. Welling grabbed him and pulled him back up.

"Be smart about it," Welling said. "Watch the machines, learn the pattern. They've only got so much wind in them."

"She doesn't have that kind of time," Dayne said.

"Just get the keys and unlock her, old top," Sholiar said. Dayne saw it now: three keys hung on hooks from the ceiling. Right in the center of the room. Right in the crossfire.

"You don't have a shield," Welling said, clearly seeing what Dayne was about to do.

"I'm a Tarian," Dayne said. "I am the shield."

He charged forward, bounding up on one of the machines and grabbing the first key. A hammer whizzed past him, inches from his ear. As he went for the second key, Welling darted into the room, sliding low and grabbing one of the steel balls that had already been fired. Winding his arm like pitching at tetchball, he hurled it at one of the machines, knocking it out of alignment. It fired its crossbow bolts far to Jerinne's left.

Dayne had the second key, and was about to grab the third when another bladed disc flew at him. He twisted to dodge it, but it sliced his arm as it went by.

"Dayne!" Jerinne yelled. "Don't—"

She missed her block, focusing on him. A hammer hit her in the chest, and she collapsed as much as her shackles would let her.

Dayne threw a key to Welling, who had managed to get closer to her, despite the waves of bolts and balls. Jerinne recovered, back on point with her shield, but she looked like she could barely get her breath as she struggled to defend herself.

Welling crawled toward her with his key, while Dayne grabbed the third key and charged over to her. Welling was able to get the key into one of her leg shackles, but was struck with a ball in his side before he could turn it. Another bladed disc flew, and Welling scurried out of the way to save himself.

It didn't matter. Dayne was at her, putting himself between her and the salvo. Everything bombarded him, striking his back and legs. He bore it, he had to, as he unlocked the shackle around her waist. Free of that, she reached around him with the shield, protecting him as he bent down and unlocked her legs.

He heard great crashes behind him. He risked a brief glance to see Welling disabling more of the machines with well-thrown steel balls.

One more ball came, knocking Dayne in the head.

Despite his senses spinning, despite the pain, Dayne got Jerinne free, and pulled her off to the side. Though he started to stumble, and she ended up pulling him as much as he did her. They both collapsed on the floor near Welling.

"You shouldn't have done that," she said.

"You'd have done the same."

"How are you?" Welling asked. For the moment, the space they huddled in was safe, and Welling seemed to have an eye out, watching for that to change. "Both of you?"

"Nothing a week in the hospital ward won't heal," Jerinne said.

"I . . . I will—" Dayne tried to say he'd recover, but the words weren't finding their way to his mouth.

"You're addled," Welling said.

"That's his prison, you see," Sholiar's voice came. "All I had to do was give him a nice dangerous charge to save someone, and he would move the world to let himself take their pain."

"Can you walk?" Welling asked, though his question seemed directed at Jerinne.

"I think so."

"Stairs that way, down and out. Get him and yourself to a Yellowshield or a doctor as soon as you can."

Dayne grabbed Welling's arm, and tried to tell him that he wouldn't leave, he wouldn't abandon Joshea Brondar, that Welling needed his help. But all that came out was, "You . . . Joshea . . ."

Welling picked up a hammer off the floor. "Get out of here. I'll get Joshea and be right behind you."

Dayne wanted to argue more, but Jerinne was pulling him up, dragging him toward the exit. He couldn't leave Welling, but he couldn't let her go alone, either. Welling gave him a nod—he understood. Neither Dayne or Jerinne were in any shape to be of any use to him. As Dayne reached the door, he heard Minox Welling call out to the room.

"All right, Sholiar, let's play the last game."

Satrine found herself somewhere dark and cramped, her hands tied behind her back. Mouth gagged. And her head was killing her. She must have blacked out when she was knocked to the floor. She needed to stop getting hit in the head.

So this was trouble.

"What are you going to do with her?" she heard someone ask. "Throw her in the river?"

"See, that's just wasteful." That was Quoyell. "There's no need to throw away something we can get value out of."

Satrine stayed still for the moment. Let them think she was still out. Wait until it was an opportune moment to try to free herself.

"So put her on the boat?"

"No, no. On the cart. Senek can have her."

"I thought he just wanted the children."

Children. They were involved in that. She was right.

"He's apparently branching out now. I was told he needed 'mothers.' More of his . . . experiments." Quoyell gave an audible shudder. "I think we're better off not knowing."

"So the other one?"

"Boat. Young and strong, that one. And a pain in the ass."

"Older than most of the ones we're sending."

"But young enough to sell." Satrine was suddenly heaved up—whatever she was inside was lifted and moved. She was being placed on the horse cart. "Either way, get that boat launched. In a few minutes we're going to want to be gone."

"There're still a few crates to load."

"Forget them. Just get the ship launched."

"And the papers?"

"Burn them."

"And what about me?" Third voice. Probably Hunsen.

"I don't care. Lie low here, hop on that boat and see the world. Doesn't matter."

"I didn't sign up for either of those."

"There's a lot we didn't sign for, son," Quoyell said.

It sounded like he was getting into the driver's seat of the cart. "But this is what we get."

"After what we did? What we went through? You do get that the two of us almost died in that boiler room? We weren't even supposed to be a part of—"

"But you didn't die," Quoyell said. "Stop dwelling, unless you want to join Tenning."

"He was just scared—"

"We don't have time to argue this. You've got money on the boat. Sail out or take your share and hide here. It's not my problem. I have the Brotherhood to answer to." The reins snapped and the cart started to move.

Satrine took advantage of the noise to see how much she could move. She was definitely in a trunk of some sort. Not much space to move. Her hands were pretty well tied, almost no way to get any leverage. Her legs were bent back behind her, so she could touch her feet. Not that it did her much good.

She could feel that her belt and coat had been taken. So, no crossbow, no handstick, no irons. Not that they would help her in this predicament.

But she did still have her boots, including the one that kept digging into her foot.

She was rolling in the street now. If she didn't have a plan to get out soon . . . she didn't want to think where that would lead.

Certainly nowhere good for her. Or for Loren and the girls.

She had to think, for their sake. She tried twisting her hands about, but definitely got nowhere in terms of getting herself loose. She managed to thrash about a little—hopefully not enough to get Quoyell's notice— and pushed the lid of the trunk a little. So it wasn't latched. If she could get loose, she could get out.

What had she even said last to her girls this morning? She couldn't remember. She had left in a hurry with Phillen and Jerinne.

Saints, if nothing else, let Jerinne be all right. She

was already fond of Rian. She might just do what Satrine wanted to ask of her out of her own volition.

But if Satrine did get out of this, she was going to ask Jerinne. She needed a plan, in case of the next emergency.

"All right, Tricky, how would you get out of this?" she asked herself. Of course, she didn't get out of it when this exact thing happened to her at fourteen. And that led her to Waisholm and everything that followed.

"Fine," she muttered. "What would have made a difference then? What do you have now that you didn't?" She had training, experience, knowledge. But she'd trade all of those right now for a knife hidden in her sleeve.

"Wait a minute," she said, even though there was no one to talk to but herself. Why *was* the boot digging into her foot?

She stretched backward just enough that she could manage a few fingers inside her boot, feeling around. There was something there. A lump pushing inside the boot.

Oh, thank every saint for gang boys and their crazy schemes. The boot had a goddamn secret pocket.

And that pocket had a knife.

As Minox wound his way up the spiral staircase to the next floor, Sholiar seemed to have gone quiet. No more comments or needling. Perhaps that had been for Dayne's benefit. Perhaps he didn't find Minox quite as much fun.

Minox had an urge to call out to Sholiar. So many questions. How did he know about Fenner and Evoy? How did he know about Jillian?

Then the answer was obvious. He had had Nyla captive for hours. Surely she divulged much personal information about Minox, if that's what Sholiar sought.

The real question was, why did he take Joshea? He saw Joshea at the hospital, and at the stationhouse. But why would he know to take him as a means to bait Minox?

As Minox approached the door, the answer came to him: the same reason he had taken Rencir. Sholiar had been planning some sort of "game" for Minox for a while, because Minox was the one talked about in the newsprints, especially in Rencir's articles.

Though that raised the obvious question, why had Sholiar ignored Rainey? She had been mentioned less in Rencir's articles, out of the man's own prejudices. Perhaps Sholiar had assumed that Minox was the inspector to pay attention to.

And perhaps that presumption had allowed Rainey to save Nyla. Hopefully. He had to take that on faith.

The door was shut, and did not open when Minox tried it.

"Sholiar!" he called out. "What's next?"

There was no response.

"Sholiar!"

The echoy voice reverberated through the room. "What is it, Inspector? I'm busy." Now, Minox could focus on the source of the voice. Earhorns and pipes lined the ceiling. So where was Sholiar? Was he behind the door?

"Where is Joshea Brondar?"

"He's not your concern, Inspector. Go home, Inspector. I'm sure you have a long day in the archives tomorrow."

"Where is he?"

Silence.

Minox decided not to waste any more time. The door in front of him was the only way. He examined it quickly. Heavy wood. New hinges. Possibly reinforced with metal. Not like anything else in this building, and certainly not something he could easily bash down.

Not easily.

But unless it was bolted and bolstered on the bottom, a well-placed kick should crack the door lock and give him access.

He stepped back, and then charged forward, delivering a strong kick. The door cracked a bit, but didn't give completely. He stepped back and gave it another kick. Then a third.

On the fourth, it opened.

The scene was now familiar. The gearbox machines, the victim strapped down.

Joshea was on the ground, stripped to his skivs and leather straps holding him at the wrists and ankles. Four gearbox machines surrounded him, each with a cleaver poised to drop on Joshea's limbs.

Not poised. Held back. Joshea's hands were surrounded in a sickly orange nimbus, thin and barely visible. As were the cleaver heads. They were dropping on him, and only his magic kept them from coming down on him.

But there was also Sholiar's voice, now a silken whisper.

"Because your duty was to serve, soldier. Yet you failed. What of the Sauriyan Eleventh? What of Casper, and Menkin, and Onterin?"

"Shut it," Joshea said through gritted teeth.

"And what would your father say—"

"Stop it!" Minox shouted. He stepped toward Joshea. He would get him out of those straps easily.

"Don't move, Minox!" Joshea shouted. Minox stopped, and then he saw it.

The entire area was surrounded by spiderwire, crisscrossing in every direction. Minox saw no way to get to Joshea without disturbing it.

"Tear this apart!" Joshea called. "I can't hold it back much longer!"

Minox tried to summon his magic, but everything in him was numb. The gauntlet blocked him; he couldn't even get a grasp on the power. "I can't!"

"So sad and helpless," Sholiar said. "That great inquisitive mind can't help you here. No puzzle to solve, no mystery to unlock. Just a man facing his inevitable demise, and you as witness."

"What's this game, Sholiar?"

"You keep saying game, Inspector, when this is deadly serious." Sholiar's voice echoed. "But you know about deadly, right, soldier? You've seen it."

"You let him go! That was the agreement!"

"The only agreement was that if you didn't come here by nine bells, he would die. I never said he wouldn't if you did come."

"Minox," Joshea whispered, tilting his head up. "Don't risk yourself for me. Just get him."

"So noble, soldier. Where was that when your duty was at stake?"

"Shut it!" Joshea shouted. "I did . . . I did. . . ."

"I know what you did," Sholiar said. "You thought you could hide it, control it? Even with your . . . kindred spirit here, you know you're out of control. You're nothing but a dirty, stinking mage. Isn't that what your father would say?"

"Stop it!" Tears were on Joshea's face. The magical energy holding the cleavers at bay was faltering.

Minox couldn't get close. Not without hitting the spiderwire, and there was no telling what that would do.

"Sholiar!" Minox called out. "Your quarrel is with me!"

"No, Inspector. Yours is with me."

"I promise you—" Minox started.

"Here is my promise, Inspector. I'm going to walk out the front door, and you're going to helplessly watch your Uncircled compatriot die. And I will vanish into the night. My next murder in this city might be tomorrow, or next month, or in a hundred years. It doesn't matter, because you've helped make me more legend than man. The Brotherhood asked me to orchestrate a symphony of fear, and you've so helpfully played your instrument. Killing Brondar here, that's the grace note."

"Who are they?" Minox called out. "Who are you talking about?"

There was no answer. No sound but the grinding of gears and Joshea's strained breathing.

"Sholiar!"

"Go, Minox," Joshea said. "You can't save me. But you can get him."

"I'm not going to leave you." Minox tried to unlatch the gauntlet, claw it off.

"You have to."

"No," Minox said. He dropped to his knees and smashed his hand against the floor. "No one is going to tell me what I have to do." He hit the floor again. "No one is going to be master over me." Down on the floor again.

Olivant had said this hand was beyond his imagining. It held power that terrified him. But that power belonged to Minox; he would own it and tame it. No Circles, no special inquests, and certainly no saints-be-damned gauntlet would stop him.

And he would not lose the one person who understood.

He hit the floor one more time, and the gauntlet cracked slightly, and through that crack a spark flashed in the center of his hand. Minox held on to that spark, and pushed it until he could breathe it into a flame. The gauntlet wanted to quash it, dry up every drop of power he had within him. It was almost like trying to fight a living thing, an angry beast trying to eat his hand.

But now that he had that flame, he wasn't going to let it go. Olivant said he held enough power to destroy the city, and by every saint, he would wield that now, no matter the cost.

"Minox, go—" Joshea whispered.

He couldn't move. He couldn't breathe. All he could do was hold on to the flame inside him. He pushed it against the gauntlet, while bringing up his arm one more time, bringing it down to the floor.

The gauntlet shattered, the floor cracked open, and a rush of magic flooded through him.

And Minox was the fire, the flood, the storm.

Everything poured out of him, enveloping around

Joshea as the machines snapped the cleavers down on him.

Minox's energy hit the machines and turned them to dust.

Minox pulled Joshea to him, the magic burning the spiderwire and gearboxes to ash. Joshea went limp, and Minox held his inert body close as he surrounded himself in a sphere of green fire.

"I can't—I can't—" Joshea muttered.

Minox expanded the sphere. "And you don't have to. No one will face this house of death again."

He pushed out farther, burning through the floor, and he and Joshea dropped down to the ground floor, landing as gently as stepping off a curb. His energy followed in his wake, turning every stone, every pipe, every blade and gear and chain into so much ash and dust.

Minox noticed the front desk was now unmanned. Whether the clerk had been let go, or was always Sholiar in disguise, he neither knew nor cared. It didn't matter.

Carrying Joshea over his shoulder, Minox walked out into the street, as the Kittrick Hotel fell apart behind him.

Chapter 27

SATRINE SLOWLY SLID the knife out of the boot with just two fingers. The cart rolled to a stop while she did that, but then started moving again, turning right. Away from the water. She didn't know the Trelan streets well enough to know how far they had gone, where she was now. But the distance between her and the dockhouse was growing.

She managed to flip the knife around and work it into the knot of the rope. She sawed away at it, hampered by her lack of leverage. She sensed they were now on a major road, based on the echo of the wheels, the sound of other carts around them. Even at this hour, there would be some people in the streets. If she got out, there would be witnesses. That was all she needed.

Was Quoyell in his uniform? Would people see a constable trying to subdue a marshal, or an ordinary citizen?

Would that matter?

She cut through some of the fibers of the rope. Not enough to get loose, but enough to give her a bit of play with her wrists. Enough to move the knife into a better position.

Minutes were passing. The cart was getting farther away. Was she still in Trelan, or some residential neighborhood? Where was she being taken? They mentioned someone named Senek and experiments. Somewhere on the Royal College campus? No, that was in the other direction.

What the blazes was Quoyell into?

Another couple blocks. Another few fibers. She had no sense of where they were, or how long she had before they were out of the public eye. She had to get free, and quickly.

She cut through another bit of rope, and she now had enough play to twist her hand out of the knot. Her wrists were ravaged, raw and torn, but she had one hand out, and then the other.

The cart hit a hole in the road, bouncing Satrine up into the lid of the trunk. It popped open. She sat up as quick as she could, looking around and getting her bearings. Darkened road, houses and shops, a few streetlamps lit. She was in one of five trunks on the cart.

Quoyell turned from the driver's seat, noticing she was out. He dropped the reins and lunged at her.

Rather than let him grab her on his terms, she jumped backward off the cart. He overreached to get hold of her, and she latched on to his wrist as she fell. That pulled him off the seat, and they both tumbled onto the cobblestones as the cart trundled on.

She landed on her back, sharp pain shooting through her. Despite that, she got on her feet. Quoyell was up as well, his great fist coming down on her head.

"I will not let you—" he started.

She didn't let him finish, taking a jab at his nose, knocking him back, and then burying the knife in his shoulder. He screamed and dropped to his knees. A couple of people on the street ran over, either to help or to gawk.

"Constabulary!" she said, kicking him down so she could force him on his face. "Get to a whistlebox and call me a wagon!"

"But I—"

"Stop her!" Quoyell shouted. "I am a King's Marshal and I order you to stop her!"

Satrine planted her knee in his back, keeping him

on the ground. The two people stood dumbly for a moment. Fortunately, Satrine was still wearing her inspector's vest, while Quoyell was out of uniform.

"Call a wagon," she said calmly. "And let them sort it out."

One of them—the man of the couple—ran over to the corner and called the wagon. The woman still stood, staring transfixed at Satrine.

Quoyell stopped struggling. "You're a fool, Rainey. You can't charge me. You don't have authority or jurisdiction."

"You tied me up and put me in a trunk," Satrine said. "That's abduction, and of an officer of the law. That's definitely in my jurisdiction."

"Based on your word?" he sneered. "Against a marshal's?"

"And mine," the woman said quietly. She looked up at Satrine. "I'll bear witness to whatever you need. Saw you come out of that trunk." She handed a calling card over. Missus Irilia Hammond.

Two horsepatrol rode over. "What's what?" one of them asked.

"Pass me your irons," Satrine said. "I'm Inspector Rainey of the Grand Inspection Unit, and I've got a lawful arrest here."

"She does not!" Quoyell shouted. "I am a King's Marshal!"

"I read about her," the other horsepatrol said. He tossed his irons over to Satrine. "She's a right lunatic, but she's the real thing."

Satrine accepted that, shackling Quoyell up and hauling him to his feet. "Thank you, gentlemen."

"What you need, Inspector?" one of the horsepatrol asked.

"Get control over his cart," she said, though the horse had stopped walking with any urgency. "There are four other trunks, and I bet they aren't empty."

The horsepatrolman trotted off and led the cart back over to them.

"This is illegal seizure!" Quoyell shouted. "You have no right or cause—"

"I was abducted and put in that open trunk," Satrine said. "Cause enough to search the others."

The patrolman had hopped onto the cart and opened one up. "Oh, sweet saints," he said. He looked over to Quoyell. "What sort of sick business were you doing?" He hurried to open the other trunks.

Passing Quoyell over to the other horsepatrolman, Satrine went over to the cart. Each of the trunks had three small children piled into them, shackled together. None of them were moving. Satrine reached in, touching their faces and chests. All warm. All breathing. Thank every saint.

"What is this, specs?" the horsepatrolman asked.

"Saints only know," Satrine said. She turned to Quoyell. "I will see you thrown into a very dark hole for this."

Quoyell didn't speak. And his expression told her he wasn't planning on it. It didn't matter.

"Call me a wagon to get to the docks, and then get this one to the Inemar Stationhouse for processing. And let's bring these victims to Riverheart, or whatever hospital is closest."

A wagon came in a few minutes—far more efficient here on the north side than in Inemar—while a cadre of Yellowshields came for the children. After they were secure, the horsepatrol escorted Satrine and her lockwagon back to the HTC docks. When she arrived, Kellman was there with a squad and Leppin's people, as well as Mister Hilsom, who was looking both angry and exhausted.

"Rainey," Kellman said as they approached. "Where the blazes were you? We got here, no sign, but we served the writ and started our search."

"I was abducted," she said. "But I brought back a prize."

Hilsom looked in the back of the wagon. "That's Chief Quoyell of the King's Marshals."

"I'm aware. He abducted me."

"But why—"

"Because he was behind this. Along with whatever Hunsen and Cole were doing here in the HTC. You have the ship?"

"Ship?" Kellman asked.

"They were loading a ship," she said. "You're telling me it's gone?"

Leppin came over, carrying a waste bin that had wisps of smoke coming out of it. "Didn't see a ship at all."

"Call out the River Patrol," she said. "There's probably a ship heading downstream to the ocean, with no lamps. Maybe Corrie saw it, saw when it launched. It must just be downriver, we should—"

"Corrie?" Kellman asked. Was he going to repeat everything back to her as a dumbfounded question?

"Corrie Welling," Satrine said. "She was here with me. She was keeping watch just a ways away while I— She isn't here?"

Kellman looked pale and spooked. "No, Tricky. Haven't seen a hair of her."

Blast and blazes. "Go find her." She looked at the rest of the squad. "Spread out, look for Sergeant Welling!"

Kellman nodded and called out orders to the squad, his voice cracking with desperate urgency.

Satrine looked to Leppin. "Did we find anything in the search, at least?"

He nodded. "A few crates, with children, shackled and drugged."

"The missing ones?"

"I don't have any way to identify them right now," he said. "We're calling Yellowshields in. Hopefully they'll recover."

Satrine shuddered. "They said they had already loaded some on the ship. And others were on the wagon that Quoyell took me away on. What the blazes were they doing with these kids?"

"Unless the kids can tell us, we probably won't find out." Leppin held up the bin. "A handful of ledger books, badly burned."

Satrine shook her head. "So we have nothing? This was useless?"

He shrugged. "I'll see what I can do. I have a few tricks for these books that might tell us something."

Hilsom came back over. "You're going to press and testify for abduction?"

"Absolutely," she said. "Between that and the children, we must have him for a dozen charges."

"Maybe. We can at least get him for you, with strong testimony."

"He had children in the cart with him as well," Satrine pointed out.

Hilsom nodded. "That'll help." He glanced over to the lockwagon, where Quoyell sat stoically. The marshal didn't look the slightest bit nervous or worried. "I'm just saying, my instinct is that it won't be an easy case."

"Is it ever?" Satrine asked.

"No, but he's sure to—"

Before Hilsom finished that thought, a blinding violet light engulfed the lockwagon. Satrine shielded her eyes and grabbed Hilsom as the light burst out throughout the street corner in a deafening blast. They both were knocked to the ground, covered in ash and splinters.

"What—what was that?" Hilsom shouted. Satrine imagined his ears were ringing as badly as hers.

"Magic," she said loudly. The world was dull and muted, her eyes filled with the echo of light. But her vision had recovered enough to see the lockwagon had been reduced to nearly nothing, and its passenger a pile of charred bones.

"Saints, is that—" Hilsom said as they approached.

"Chief Quoyell," Satrine said, looking around. "Did anyone see where that came from? We have a mage assassin here!"

Patrolmen scrambled, but Satrine wasn't sure if they were running to search for the killer, or to hide.

Not that it mattered. Chief Quoyell was gone, and with him, their best chance for answers.

Kellman came back over carrying something. "Found this in the alley refuse." It was a crossbow. Constabulary issue.

"Nothing else there?" Satrine asked.

He shook his head mournfully. "I . . . I don't know what to say . . ."

Then Satrine remembered what she had heard in the trunk. The other one, going to the ship. Young, strong, pain in the ass.

Corrie.

"They got her, too," Satrine said, tears blurring her vision as she watched the dark river. "They got her on that goddamned boat."

———◆———

There had been no sign of Sholiar in the remains of the hotel. No sign of anyone. Minox had to hope that the hotel register was an honest document, that no victims were left behind.

The only other witness of the whole thing had been Rencir. He obviously hadn't run far, once he was clear of the place, instead standing on the curb across the deserted street.

"What happened in there, Minox?"

Minox had barely taken four steps away, now propping up Joshea as he weakly limped with him. "Are you asking me as a source?"

Rencir took a moment, and then said. "Not if you don't want to be. And . . . I shouldn't write a story that I was a part of."

"There shouldn't be a story," Joshea whispered.

Rencir nodded. "If you feel that way, Minox, I'll honor that."

Minox considered this, and he didn't have an answer.

There was too much to digest. "For now, leave it be," he said. "Are you all right?"

"Well, this has been the worst night of my life," he said. "But I'm glad to be standing here, breathing."

"Did you see anyone else leave?"

"The ones I was with—the *Veracity* folk? They left right behind me. I stayed and saw the big guy and some girl, and then the whole place collapsed and you two are here."

No Sholiar. He probably had his own way out.

"We should get you to a hospital ward," Minox told Joshea. "Probably you as well, Rencir."

"I'm not injured," Rencir said.

"No hospital ward," Joshea said. "I can't—"

"The stationhouse doctor, at least," Minox said. "Just to be checked out before you go home." Joshea acquiesced to that. The three of them stumbled out of the desolate neighborhood until they reached a main avenue, and finally hailed a cab that took them back to Inemar.

Minox let himself collapse in the cab's seat, the full weight of everything he did finally hitting his body. Joshea lay there, half asleep, while Rencir sat in awkward silence. Minox wasn't certain if it was because he was refraining from asking questions, or if he was still in shock from his own experience.

When they crossed the bridge, Rencir got up to hop out. "I'll check in with you in a few days," he said. "I won't print anything unless you agree."

"Thank you," Minox said, and Rencir went off into the night.

"Are you hungry?" he asked Joshea.

"Ravenous," Joshea said. "That's what I need more than to see a doctor."

At this hour, the options were limited. Missus Wolman and her reliable cart were surely home for the night. He remembered one of Corrie's suggestions. "There's a pub about half a block from the stationhouse that serves stews and sausages deep into the night. I understand it's a favorite of the night patrol."

"You realize he's just in his skivs," the cab driver—a man who looked like he could be Acserian or Imach, though his accent was pure far-north Maradaine—told them, turning his attention from the road. "And you barely look better. Whatever business you all had tonight, and it looks rough, you can't go in some pub like that."

"Also, money," Joshea said.

"You two better have money," the driver said.

Minox wasn't sure if he did.

"Then go to the Constabulary stationhouse, sir," Minox said. "I have some bills in my desk."

"You expect me to wait here for you?" the driver asked.

"Yes," Minox said. "I'm an officer of the Constabulary, sir."

"Fine. But the naked man stays."

"Bring me a coat or something," Joshea said.

Minox stumbled out of the cab—he felt as weak as a kitten, and made his way to the stairs to the inspectors' floor. There was an unusual amount of commotion and activity on the main work floor for the late hour. He was so distracted by that and his exhaustion, he was taken by surprise when someone grabbed his coat and pulled him into a closet by the staircase.

He reacted defensively, or at least tried to, but he didn't have the strength to even push back. But in a moment he saw it was Inspector Rainey.

"Minox," she whispered low. "Why are you here?"

"I came back after—why are you? Is Nyla—"

"Nyla's fine, I got her free. But—a lot has happened, too much to explain right now."

"I could say the same. In the morning—"

"Yes, but . . . do you trust me?"

"Of course," he said.

She glanced around cautiously, despite the fact they

were in a closet and no one else was around. "Then continue to trust me, no matter what I say."

"Of course."

She nodded. "Joshea, Jerinne? They all right? Dayne?"

"Everyone is . . . alive and not significantly injured," he said.

"And you didn't bring in Sholiar in irons."

"He's escaped again, yes. And . . . many things happened. I'm not sure how I can make a proper report of it."

"Then don't," she said. He must have shown his surprise. "Just . . . you weren't there in any official capacity, and don't write anything." She sighed. "I will explain, it's . . . I made a significant . . . revelation, if not arrest and . . . that's not important. Just . . . I'm sorry, Minox. I'm so sorry."

"What?"

"Your sister came with me, and . . . she's gone."

Minox's breath stopped. "Corrie's dead?"

She seemed to be holding back tears. "I don't even know for certain. We only found her crossbow."

"Only—" He couldn't even conceive.

"Just hold yourself together," she said. "I know, I know it's a lot, if anyone—"

"No, I—" He paused. "We all know each ride out could be our last."

He said the words, but he didn't feel them. His heart was screaming, but he couldn't let that show.

"There's so much more that happened, Minox," she said. "But this is the most important part: I'm pretty sure we were betrayed. Someone warned them we were coming."

"Who?"

She shook her head. "No way of knowing. Kellman or the boys on Iorrett's squad had easy opportunity, but frankly it could be anyone working late in this house or in the Protector's Office."

Minox took this in. He remembered Leppin telling him about evidence going missing, including all records that the evidence even existed.

"And you suspect that this betrayal involves a grander scope."

"Almost definitely. This was the children, Minox."

"You found the missing children?"

"We rescued fifteen," she said. "But . . . who knows how many there were total."

He took this in, but he was having a hard time concentrating. Between his fatigue and the news about Corrie . . . he could barely think straight. "I need to handle other things right now . . ."

"Of course. Go upstairs, do whatever you came here to do."

"Get some money and clothes for Joshea."

She furrowed her brow. "I'll be upstairs in a moment. I have an idea, and just— no matter what I do . . ."

"I trust you." He meant it.

She prodded him out of the closet, and he went up the stairs. As he went to his desk, Kellman and a few of the squad were all standing around, their faces downcast.

"Jinx, hey," Kellman said. "What are you—did you come in because—"

"I just need some things from my desk," he said.

"No, sit down," Kellman said. "Saints, you look like blazes."

"With good reason."

"Yeah, sure, but—saints, someone has to tell you. I'm sure the cap would want to do it in some official way, but . . . Tricky and your sister went to stake something out, and we got the writ request and went out to join them. By the time we got there, they had both been nabbed—"

Both? Minox took that in.

"Tricky had managed to get away, and bring back the crook. That rutting chief from the King's Marshals."

"Quoyell? He abducted them?"

"Yeah, but . . . I'm sorry, Jinx. There ain't no sign of Corrie. And the guy—he was killed before we brought him in. So we don't have much to work with."

Minox nodded, standing up. "I apologize, Inspector. I . . . I am not in an emotional state to handle this right now."

"Yeah, yeah," Kellman said. He held up some notes. "I've had runners come from Trelan, High River, they've got their people doing a full search. River Patrol is trawling and hunting as well. We're on this."

"Thank you. I should—"

"You should go home, tell your family what's up, and tell them to trust it's being handled. All right? We're not going to let one of our own vanish into the night."

Minox looked up at Kellman. His face showed no pretense. He wanted to find Corrie almost as much as Minox did.

"You hear me?" Kellman asked.

Minox nodded. "I appreciate your attention."

"Of course. I was about to send a runner to your house, but, with you here . . . I just . . . I couldn't not tell you."

"I appreciate that."

"Oh, he appreciates it." Rainey had come up the stairs. Her voice was dripping with scorn. "We go out there, working the case, and where were you?"

"Hey, ease off, Tricky," Kellman said.

"I'm not gonna ease off. You were off running around on some wild chase, with your new Tarian friend, weren't you?"

Minox understood what she was playing, and went along. "We were following a lead—"

"Oh, a lead? And did you bring anyone in here in irons?"

"No—"

"No." She slapped her hand on the desk, and in that same moment, she winked, so that only he could see.

She shook her head in a show for Kellman and the others. "And so the one who pays the price is your sister."

"Hey, hey," Kellman said. "That's far in the yellow, Tricky."

"Yeah, yeah," she said darkly. "Maybe I'm just tired."

"Yeah," Kellman said. "Both of you head home. We'll . . . we'll see about the rest tomorrow."

"Fine," she said, clapping Kellman on the shoulders. "I'm just glad I'm going out with you tomorrow, instead of the Jinx." With that, she left.

Minox had to admit that stung, even when he knew it was performance and artifice. He understood her game: pretend to be upset with him, craft the appearance of a rift, so the two of them could look at different angles for the corrupt infiltrator in their ranks. He understood and respected the tactic.

But it still hurt.

Kellman stood dumbfounded.

Minox grabbed the things he needed from his desk: money, a few pieces of dried fruit he kept there for emergencies, and the heavy coat he had left by his desk all summer. Without giving further commentary to Kellman or Iorrett's squad, he left.

"Everything all right?" Joshea asked as he came back outside. "Saw Rainey stomp off."

"Definitely not," Minox said, handing money to the driver and the coat to Joshea. "I'd rather not speak of it right now."

Joshea nodded. "I understand." He put on the coat, almost shivering as he did. "A night like this, it's a sinner's night."

"A sinner's night indeed," Minox said quietly as the cab started up again. "Perhaps that's why Sholiar bested us."

Quietly, in a whisper so low Minox almost thought he imagined it, Joshea said, "He's a genius."

Chapter 28

SATRINE WALKED HOME in her bare feet, carrying her boots and stockings. It somehow felt horrible and liberating at once. Even with the secret knife out of her appropriated boot, it still hurt like blazes to wear. And she and her feet had been through enough tonight.

As she crossed the bridge into High River, she was surprised to see one person sitting at the street side tables of the High River Wine Club. She was certain the place was closed at this hour.

"Well done, Satrine," the person said, holding up a wineglass.

"What the saints are you doing, Major?" she asked Major Grieson, taking the glass from him. She wasn't sure if he was offering it or saluting her, but either way, she was drinking the wine.

"I had been avoiding being seen with you, but since you dropped my name to Colonel Altarn, there's hardly a point now."

"Colonel Altarn, right," she said. "I presume she's a new authority in the Service."

"She's behind that Altarn Initiative you heard about." He shook his head. "I don't know what it's all about, but it's funneling money to special projects, departments of the university. And it's cordoning off sections of the Service from each other."

"And why are you telling me?"

"Because you're not a part of it, Satrine. So you're one of the few resources I still have."

"I'm a resource now?" Satrine asked. "What about what you are supposed to do for me?"

"I'm working on it," he said.

"Working on it?" She almost threw the wineglass at his stupid pointy chin. "Get a telepath to fix my husband, and then we'll talk." She walked away.

"I don't have anyone," he called after her.

"What?" she said, turning back.

"I don't have a telepath," he said. "At least, not one that I'd dare to trust on delicate work. Not one you would want."

She remembered the thing Oster had told her years ago when he was working on her mind. "Telepathy is a hammer. Very easy to smash something with. It takes work to become a sculptor."

"How could you—"

He shook his head. "Because I'm being boxed out. Carefully. Slowly. But it's happening, and I'm running out of options I can trust."

"Because of Altarn."

He pulled a paper out of his pocket. "You arrested Chief Quoyell tonight? And then he was killed?"

"That's right," she said, taking the paper. It was a memo deploying a special asset, with Quoyell's name written on the bottom. "She did this? She's in with whatever he was doing?"

"I think more correct is he was part of what she's into. And I don't know who's loyal to me. Or the crown."

"So you come crawling to me."

"I'm warning you, Satrine," he said. "You think I didn't notice that HTC is where your husband got knocked down? That whatever she's into connects to that, the marshals, the Parliament, the Constabulary?"

"Right," she said. "Commissioner Enbrain was saying the same things. This whole business with the Parliament, with Sholiar, I think it was moving a lot of gears. And one of them was embarrassing Enbrain."

"Sholiar?" he asked.

"The Gearbox Killer, supposedly," she said.

He rubbed at his chin. "I've seen that name before. I can't recall where."

"Maybe you need your own telepath."

He chuckled. "Maybe."

Maybe he knew something about the other elements of the evening. "Quoyell tried to take me and some of the children to someone named Senek. Does that mean anything to you?"

He nodded. "I don't know anything else, but I've seen the name Ithaniel Senek on some documents. Money vouchers, that sort of thing." He glanced around the street, even though no one else was in sight. "Look, I can't—I don't know what else is safe to tell you right now. But if you hear about anything happening to me—"

"How the blazes would I hear that?" she asked.

"If you do," he stressed. "That tinkerer I brought you yesterday, you can find him at—"

"The Junk Avenue Bakery, I know."

He gave her an approving smile.

"Right. Go to him and ask for his brother."

"His brother."

"He's like you. Retired."

"Fine," she said, handing him the empty wineglass. "It's late and I'm going home to my family."

"Enjoy that and them," he said. "I'm glad you got to have a few years of normal."

Satrine left him, walking briskly the rest of the way to 14 Beltner, letting herself into the apartment. Low lamps and low voices greeted her as she came in, leaving her boots, belt, and coat at the doorway.

"Who's still up?" she called out as she came into the

sitting room. Rian was at the table with Jerinne, both drinking tea.

"Mother!" Rian said as she came in. "You look a fright!"

"I've been a fright," she said. Though she noticed Jerinne looked the same way, with a sizable bruise on her face. "You've had a night as well."

"Nothing that won't heal," Jerinne said.

"Shouldn't you be somewhere at this hour?" Satrine asked.

"I should ask you where you've been, Mother," Rian said. "That overeager patrolboy you sent said you'd be late, but not this late."

Satrine just gave her daughter a look, and poor Rian withered with embarrassment. Jerinne picked up on this and spoke up.

"I already was kidnapped and put in a death trap," Jerinne said. "So I'm not worried about demerits from Madame Tyrell."

"Hush," Rian said. "Do you hear her? She acts like it's nothing—"

"But you're fine?" Satrine asked Jerinne.

"Yeah," Jerinne said solemnly. "Dayne took a heck of a battering for my sake, really dazzled his wits. But I got him to the chapterhouse, and our doctor said he's going to be all right."

"It's so exciting," Rian said.

Satrine pointed to the bedroom door. "Bed. Now." She must have said it firmly enough that Rian went without argument, just polite goodnights. Satrine sat down at the table, taking Rian's tea for herself.

"Why did you come so late, after the night you had?"

"There was a serial killer on the loose, grabbing friends and family of people who worked the case. I did think your family was at risk."

"Fortunately, it seems Sholiar didn't think much about me," Satrine said. "Rian seemed happy to see you."

"Yeah, well . . ." Jerinne trailed off, and then blushed. "She's sweet."

"Very." Satrine took a deep breath. "I want to ask you a favor."

"Name it."

"Actually, I think 'favor' isn't weighty enough for what I'm going to ask. I . . . want to impose a burden on you, and that's not fair. But I feel I need to ask someone else, and you're the best candidate."

Jerinne raised an eyebrow to that. "I'm an Initiate for another year, presuming I become a Candidate."

"Is your future in the Tarians that uncertain?"

"I don't take anything for granted."

Satrine understood that. Would that she had that kind of wisdom when she was Jerinne's age. "No matter what happens to you in the Tarians, I want you to stay friends with Rian. As close as you can be."

"Is that all? Gladly."

"And if anything happens to me—"

"Don't—"

"I'm serious. If anything happens to me, you stay with her, as her protector, no matter what."

"I— why would she need that kind of protection?"

"I've had a very colorful past, Jerinne," Satrine said.

"I've gathered a bit of that."

"You have no idea, girl," Satrine said. "Swear on your saint that you will keep this secret."

That gave the girl pause, and then she said, "In the name of Saint Justin, I will hold your secret or risk damnation."

That was good enough. "I was a spy in Druth Intelligence. For four years I navigated court intrigue in Waisholm, and was instrumental in placing King Kelldyshm II on the throne."

Jerinne let out a low whistle. "And now you're just a constable inspector?"

"I work to take care of my daughters. Including Rian, potential heir to the Waish throne."

"You—" Jerinne stared dumbfounded for a moment, and then shook it off. "You're serious."

"Utterly."

She seemed to drink this in, and got to her feet. She extended her hand to Satrine. "Then I pledge my shield and sword to her."

Satrine took her hand, and then pulled her in for an embrace. "Thank you."

"Always," Jerinne said. She said her good-byes and went into the night.

Satrine went into the bedroom, where Loren lay in the bed. He was quiet, but seemed to be awake. At least as awake as he ever was.

"Quite a day, love," she said. "Broke up an Aventil gang, took down a corrupt King's Marshal. Maybe one step closer to avenging what happened to you."

She kissed his forehead.

"Say Day?" he said quietly.

"Yes, I figured that out. HTC Imports, Saint Day shipments. I don't know all the details, but that, at least, is shut down."

He closed his eyes. Satrine wanted to imagine that he understood, that it gave him some peace.

He deserved that.

Especially since she would get none in the coming days.

—◆—

Minox ate at the pub with Joshea, mostly out of pure necessity. He couldn't go home until he had the strength to handle what he would need to do there.

He and Joshea didn't speak, beyond the pleasantries of ordering their food, which they ate in joyless silence. After finishing off several plates of sausages, Joshea stood up. "I should go home. I don't . . . I don't know how to explain what happened to my father."

"The truth?"

"My truths are too complicated for him," Joshea said. "He believes in meat, he believes in service, and he believes in God. Anything that goes outside his world of those three things, he lashes out at."

"Leave out the magic and the Constabulary. And me."

"And what I'm left with is I was abducted by a madman." Joshea shook his head. "My father would be crushed that I let myself be taken. That I failed that much."

"You didn't fail."

"I failed myself and my training. And I failed Nyla. I don't—" He took a moment in silence, taking a single step away from the table. "I don't know what to think about this night. I just know it's one of the worst ones in my life."

"Mine as well."

Joshea turned toward Minox, and extended his hand. Minox took it, and then Joshea pulled him up in an embrace. Minox didn't know how to react to that, but let Joshea express himself.

"Thank you for coming for me, brother," he whispered. "Thank you for thinking I deserved to be rescued. I'm not sure anyone else would."

Minox didn't have a response to that, and Joshea did not seem to expect one. He pulled away, giving one last grim smile, and left the pub.

Minox sat and ate another plate of sausages, nursing the beer he had ordered to have with it. He had never been a fan of beer, but Corrie always had been, and he felt he owed her some small honor. Right now, it was the only thing he could do for her.

He put down the pint of beer, and noticed that the glove he wore over his left hand was in tatters. That wasn't surprising, given what he had gone through tonight. It was a miracle that his clothing was largely intact. He'd need a new uniform for work tomorrow.

Work in the archives.

Work without Corrie.

He would have to swallow that. He had to go home and let them know what happened.

He flexed the hand. What was fascinating was how impervious to harm and pain it seemed to be. There was no sign that smashing it against the ground or singeing it had caused any damage. He ran one finger over it. He had the vaguest sensation of it being touched, but only like the memory of the touch.

"Oav! Vo vhuith kridge! Ranktae tsu asuvinu! So ekexo tsu asuvinu!"

A very old man, half stumbling and half carried, was being taken to the door by a younger woman. He was struggling, pointing at Minox. *"Sno, shay-sha,"* she said back to him, pulling him along. "I'm very sorry," she added to Minox.

Minox recognized the language—Sechiall, the old Kellirac tongue. Both the old man and the girl were Racquin, which was clear by their dusky complexion and woven vests. Minox had only picked up a few words from his mother, but he could make out that the man was talking about his hand. "What did your grandfather say?" He wanted to let the girl know he understood a little, including that she called him *"shay-sha."*

"I'm very sorry, about him," she said. "He drinks too much."

"Sno! Vour tsu asuvinui kixo! Asuvinu!"

"Quiet," she told him. "Please, sir—Inspector. He's just a drunk old man"

"Asuvinu! Szonsov, vinije! Asuvinu!" The old man pulled frantically at her.

"I'm not angry—" Minox started. *"So o ortije."* He knew he was mangling the language. At best, he said, "Anger not is me becoming."

"Asuvinu!" He pulled away and ran, and the girl, giving an apologetic look, chased after him.

Minox settled his tab and walked through the warm night to the house in Keller Cove. There were still lamps on inside the house, at least in the sitting room, and one hung by the door. He resisted the urge to blow it out when he came in. Perhaps Corrie was still out there, fighting her way home. The lamp would be there for her when she returned.

Ferah and Edard were in the sitting room, nursing beers and talking in low voices.

"Minox," Ferah said as he came in. "Everything all right?"

"Definitely not," he said. "I assume my mother is asleep?"

"She was in the kitchen, and I didn't hear her go up," Edard said. He leaned to look through the dining room. "I think there's a lamp burning in there."

"I will check on her," Minox said. "Is everyone else in?"

"My pop and Tal are out on night duty. And Corrie, well, I thought she was with you."

"She's not," Minox said. He felt his voice tremble. "I've been told she cannot be accounted for."

Ferah was on her feet. "Then let's be about it."

"No, Ferah," Minox said, though it made his heart shudder. "We've been asked to . . . trust that everyone is doing their job."

"Pfah," Edard said. "Where's the search going?"

"North side," Minox said. He needed to say the hard things that he knew were true, as much as he hated it. "Trelan Docks and surrounding. And none of us know that area. We'd just be in the way."

"Saints," Edard said. He shook his head. "Corrie's a fighter. She'll be fine."

"Yeah," Ferah said. Neither of them looked like they were convinced.

"I'm going to look in on Mother," Minox said. "We'll tell everyone in the morning."

He went to the kitchen, where his mother was sitting at the table, slumped down asleep. Two candles were burning low, as was an oil lamp. She had her journal out, inks and pen. Minox gently shut the journal and sat down next to her, touching her on the arm.

She looked up.

"Minox," she said dreamily. "Did you just return?"

"I did," he said.

"Did you . . . were you successful?"

"The people we went to rescue were rescued," he said.

"That's what matters," she said. "What's the time? Are you hungry?"

"I'm fine," he said.

"You certain?"

"I just need to rest."

"If you say so." She smiled and touched his face.

He needed to tell her, but he hated to break this moment. Even still, she must have seen it on his face. "What's wrong?"

"Many things," he said. He selfishly chose the one that concerned him personally first. "Do you know what an *asuvinu* is?"

She looked surprised by that. "Haven't hear that one in a while."

"What is it?"

"It's an old Kellirac legend. You know, stories to frighten children. It means . . . 'shadow of the Storm.' Wild magic of the Storm changed people into—" She paused, glancing at Minox's hand. "Foolish stories is all." Her face showed that she wasn't going to tell him anything else right now. "Did Corrie get back yet?"

He took her hand and squeezed it. "No, Mother. Not yet. Let me get us some tea."

Chapter 29

INSPECTOR DARRECK KELLMAN had spent the hours before dawn back on the north side of the river. He had gone back over to the dockhouse, talked with Leppin and his crew, who had spent the whole night searching the place completely. He had checked in with Trelan Stationhouse, talked up patrolmen on the streets, screamed at River Patrol, and stalked the docks himself.

No sign.

Only one choice left.

He went to the house—ironically in the Welling neighborhood—before the early haze of dawn had washed the darkness away fully. He didn't care about the hour, he didn't care that he'd be making a ruckus. It had been enough.

The houses here were wide and sprawling, fences and walls between each property. The kind of houses that showed off the money of the people inside. He charged up the porch and pounded on the intricately carved wooden door.

A servant of some sort opened up. "Is there a problem, Officer?" she asked.

"Get your master," he snapped, pushing his way inside. "Don't dally."

She scurried up the stairs, and a moment later Kellman heard a minor commotion. The woman returned, followed by an older man wrapping himself in a robe as he descended. This jowly, balding man who was the source of Kellman's woes.

"What in salvation are you doing, Inspector?" Commandant Undenway said as he came down. "This is unseemly."

"Unseemly?" Kellman snapped back. "I've been up all night, on the Trelan Docks. By HTC."

"Saints above, don't tell me that was boggled. I thought it was taken care of."

"Taken care of?" Kellman shouted.

"Lower your blasted voice, man," Undenway said. "I have a wife, children."

"Do you want to talk about children right now?" Kellman was not going to let that go. "Do you want me to tell them—"

"Leave my family be."

"You know who else has family, Commandant? Sergeant Corrie Welling."

"Who is that?"

"Who is she?" Kellman wanted to slap him. "She's part of my house who has gone missing. Quoyell and his people thought it a good idea to abduct two officers from my house—Welling and Inspector Rainey."

"Saints, Rainey. Would that I never hear that name again." Undenway shook his head ruefully. "But still, handled, thanks to you."

"No, not handled, because when we got to HTC, Rainey got free and dragged Quoyell in irons. And then a mage assassinated him. Do you think that will protect you, sir? You think I will?"

"I definitely think you will, Inspector." Despite being a few inches shorter, Undenway still managed to stare Kellman down. He pushed Kellman in his chest with two fingers, directing him to the embroidered chair behind him. "Let's be clear. You will make sure that HTC is a dead end."

"That's not going to be easy with fifteen children at Riverheart!"

"Find a way," Undenway said. "Make sure it goes away. That no one pays mind to what the children say. That any evidence found—"

"Leppin is on to us with the evidence."

"Then take care of it. Or him." He went over to a desk in the corner of the room. "Is money an issue, Inspector? Is a hundred more crowns enough to get you to *do your job*? You already failed enough that we have this mess. Your mess to clean up, Darreck."

"It's not about the crowns!"

"It is, though," Undenway said, coming over with goldsmith notes. "There's three hundred. I know your mother needs her medicine, Darreck. I know your brother and his wife are behind on their rent." He shoved the notes into Kellman's hands. "Get it done. You've got enough people there to keep your house looking clean, man." He shoved Kellman to the door. "And never come to my home again."

"Damn it, sir," Kellman said, even though he was leaving. "Where is Corrie Welling?"

"I don't know," Undenway said. "Though I can imagine. And if you open up your thick skull, I think you know exactly where as well."

He shut the door.

Kellman's stomach curdled. He had already been imagining all night exactly where he feared Corrie had gone.

Corrie's head had been in a fog for hours, perhaps days. She hadn't been sure. She wasn't sure of anything. Her insides were unsettled, her head was pounding, and her wrists—

Her wrists were shackled.

She instinctively yanked as hard as she could, and the shackles didn't yield more than a couple inches. Bolted to the wall. Nowhere to go.

The rutting place was dark and stank like the sewer of the dead.

"Hey!" she shouted, though her throat felt like it had been stomped onto the cobblestones. "What rutting gives?"

Her stomach couldn't figure out which way was down. She wanted to puke her guts out, but she felt like there was nothing there to vomit.

The place also stank of vomit. Fresh.

"Hey!" she shouted again. "What rutting sewage is this?"

Something moved near her.

"Stop shouting," someone murmured. "It won't help."

"What do you rutting mean?" she asked. She pulled at her chains again. Not a rutting bit of extra give, even as her wrists started to bleed. "When I get out of this—"

"Shut it!" A voice in the dark.

She forced herself to her feet, even though the shackles made her stoop down. "I'll shut you and then—"

"Calm down, girl!" Another voice in the dark. She could make out shapes and figures. Movement all around. Maybe thirty people around her. Maybe more.

"If you think you can—"

"Sweet saints, she's a stick!" someone else said. Someone young.

All these voices were young.

"Yes, I'm a rutting stick," she said, pulling on the chain. Bolted to wood. Wood would give, break away. She might not break the chain, but she could get free. And then she would rutting show them. "And I'm going to start cracking skulls and clapping iron if I don't—"

She was interrupted by the whole room lurching, throwing her against the wooden wall. Somewhere outside, wind howled and water splashed.

She was on a boat.

"So help me—" she whispered.

Light crashed through the ceiling, blinding her for a moment. A silhouette dropped down from the source of light. "What's the goddamn ruckus?" Older man. Heavyset.

"The stick is making the noise!"

Corrie's eyes adjusted, and she could see where she was, what she was surrounded by. The hold of a ship, and dozens of folk shackled to the wall. Some of them were kids, some just a few years older. She might be the oldest one there. All the rest of them were in rags and scrap. Street rats, the lot of them.

"You're the ruckus?" the old man asked. He came closer—too close, his wretched teeth black and breath hot on her face. Too close, but still too far for her to slam her head into his nose.

"What the rutting blazes is this?" she asked. "When I get out of here—"

"Out of here?" he asked. "Oh, girl, you ain't getting out of here until we make land. At least a month to whip around."

"I've got family in the sticks, in the River Patrol . . . they're going to turn the city over to find me and when they do—"

"Shame we're not in the rutting city, then," he said. "Being a stick—or family to sticks—don't matter on the open sea."

She lunged at him, but she couldn't get any closer.

He laughed and walked over to one of the other girls. "You've got something, girl. You'll be good coin, all right."

"What?"

"But you're gonna behave," he said. "Or there'll be trouble."

"You think you're going to beat me?" she shot back. "You rutting think I can't take what you got? Unlock these and I'll blazing well show you!"

He picked up a cudgel that was lying in the center of the room—far from anyone else's reach. He strolled over to one of the other girls. A wisp of a thing who couldn't be older than fourteen. He brought up the cudgel and wailed the girl in her chest.

"That was the warning," he said. He pointed the cudgel at Corrie. "You make a stink, someone else pays. Get?"

"Got," Corrie said. She couldn't rutting well let him make these kids suffer—suffer any blasted more—on her account. She'd have think her way through this. Use her eyes, use her rutting head. Plan the long game. What Minox would do.

Minox. Saints, he would tear the city apart looking for her.

They all would, but he would never rutting quit. He'd go so far, he'd end up like Evoy in the barn. Or worse.

So she had to rescue her own self, for his sake.

The old man climbed up to the hatch. "Good. You all behave, now. It's a long way to Imachan."

Imachan.

Good coin.

This was a rutting slave ship.

"You're a constable, right?" Little girl next to her. Younger than Alma. "Are you going to help us?"

"I am, kid," she said.

"My name's Eana," the girl said

"Corrie," she said. "Corrie Welling. Don't worry, Eana. I'll get us out of here."

Somehow.

———— ◆◆ ————

Minox had never gone into Saint Limarre's church, except in his capacity as an inspector. The only times he ever went to church as a patron were when he went to Saint Veran's with his mother, on the outskirts of the city. Those were rare occasions, on specific Saint Days, or on Racquin holy days.

The past few days had made that a daily pilgrimage. Mother went every day, and Minox accompanied her most of the time. Jace and Alma usually did as well, as did most of the cousins. Oren even went once, but usually he was "very busy."

The past few days had been quiet for Minox at work, as he had been down in the archives. He barely saw anyone, except the occasional check-in from Leppin, and Captain Cinellan's morning chat to assure Minox that he hadn't been forgotten.

Nyla had not gone into work for those days.

Rainey had worked cases with Kellman, of which he heard very little. She did not speak to him in the stationhouse. But she did send a note to him to meet her here, in Saint Limarre's, early in the morning.

When he arrived, the only other person in the chapel was Dayne Heldrin, trying to look inconspicuous. But at almost two meters tall, nothing he did kept him from standing out.

"What are you doing here?" Minox asked.

"I was about to ask you that," Dayne said. He held up a letter. "Did you send this?"

"No. In fact I was expecting Inspector Rainey."

"Here." She came out from the back of the church, with the cloistress who had been her old friend. "You know Sister Alana."

"I recall," he said.

"Why are you here, Dayne?" she asked.

"I received a letter, telling me to be here today, at this time. You didn't send it?"

"No," Rainey said. "You actually got it in the city post?"

He nodded, handing it over to her.

"That would take two days, and—" She shook it off. "I suppose I should accept the blessing."

"Yes, you should," Sister Alana said, taking the letter. Her face was deeply troubled.

"Yes," Rainey said. "I'm actually glad to have you here."

"Whatever you two need, I'm here for you," Dayne said.

"I apologize for my behavior the past few days," Rainey said to Minox. "I needed—"

"You wanted to establish the appearance of a rift between us, so the rest of the stationhouse would not suspect us of collusion," Minox said. "I figured that out from the beginning."

"I knew you would," she said. "You still deserve the apology."

"It's accepted," he said. "You've determined there is significant corruption in our stationhouse."

"In all our stationhouses," Satrine said. "And at every level. The King's Marshals . . ."

Dayne nodded. "The King's Marshals have something rotten within them."

"You don't think it was just Quoyell."

"In the months since I've returned to Maradaine, I've seen several incidents with the marshals that give me grave concern."

"Isn't that why you're in your 'liaison' position?" Minox asked. "As some form of oversight?"

"No. It's a feckless post," Dayne said. "I need to do more."

"I've felt the same way in the archives," Minox said.

"Well, I need you," Rainey said. "Right now, Minox, you and I are working a Brick File case. Secret to everyone else."

"Investigating the corruption in the Constabulary?"

"The sickness in the entire city," she said. "I think it touches everywhere."

Minox nodded. That was what Evoy had been saying, and while he felt the same thing, he wondered if he had just been slipping into the same hole as Evoy. But Rainey had clarity of thought, and focus. She saw it, and she wanted to root it out.

"So you want my help as well?" Dayne asked.

"If it's available."

"And the sister?" Dayne asked.

"She's our insurance," Satrine said. "Everything we

find, every bit, we also give to her. Saints forbid anything happens to us—"

"I go to the press with everything I have, invoking the Rite of Final Intent," Sister Alana said.

Dayne sat down. "I've had a sense that there is something deeper at play, and . . . it's little more than a sense in my gut—"

"I trust your gut," Minox said. "You were the one who knew about Sholiar." A flash of memory from that night came to him. He had been so engaged with Joshea, focused on how to save him, that it didn't register in his mind at the time. "Sholiar said 'the Brotherhood' asked him to create a symphony of fear."

"Quoyell mentioned that too," Rainey said. "And Nerrish Plum said it too, didn't he?"

"Who are they?" Dayne asked.

"I've seen some reference to a 'Brotherhood of the Nine,'" Minox said. "Little more than a name, but it's had my attention."

"Is that the center of this corruption?" Rainey asked.

"It's a theory," Minox said.

"Then are we resolved?" Sister Alana asked.

"I am," Dayne said.

Minox nodded. He still had his mind, and for the time being, all of his wits. He had been exiled to the archives, but he would use that, find the secrets lost in the files. There *was* a larger conspiracy and corruption infecting this city. Perhaps with Dayne's knowledge, Rainey's cunning, and his resolve, they could dig it out and bring it to the light.

Maybe even find out what happened to his sister, and get some small portion of justice for her.

"Good," Rainey said. "For now, we work through Alana. Minimize direct contact. She's our Brick File."

"And may the saints protect me," she said.

"I shouldn't dally," Dayne said. "I'm supposed to be helping new members of the Parliament acclimate to the city. So if you'll excuse me."

"Similarly," Rainey said as Dayne left. "Today's the day I agreed to help Phillen with his mother's release."

"Be well," Sister Alana said.

"And you." She went to the door, passing Minox. She stopped and touched his shoulder. "We're going to get all these bastards. For Corrie."

"And your husband," he said. "And every other victim of this sickness."

She patted his shoulder one more time and left.

Sister Alana still looked troubled, examining Dayne's letter.

"A problem, Sister?"

She looked up at him, and put on a smile that he read as insincere. "I was just thinking about one of the young girls in the cloister here. She's—she's subject to violent spells. And I was thinking I should pray for her. I'll pray for you as well."

She left, and Minox wondered about the strange combination of honesty and deceit in what she had just told him. But her offer of her prayers for him was legitimate.

That gave him some small amount of solace. The days ahead were filled with uncertainty, especially about himself. Any aid he could receive, he would gladly take. But he feared the blackness that had consumed his hand was only the beginning, and he would succumb to it completely sooner or later.

The best he could hope for, in the long run, was to take this city's banes with him as he went down.

Epilogue

"SIT DOWN, PHILLEN. You're going to wear through your boots."

Satrine needed the boy to calm down; he was a mess. Not that sitting would make it any better. He'd spent the first few minutes since they had been called down for the Quarrygate carriage arrival sitting on the bench, but the whole time he sat, his leg was trembling. Foot hitting the ground like a jackrabbit. After a few minutes of fidgeting, he got up and started pacing.

"She'll probably stab me," Phillen said. "I bet you, she'll have a knife."

"She won't have a knife," Satrine said.

"She'll have made one," Phillen said. Then he shook his head. "No, no. Far too industrious. She'd do something lazy."

"She's not going to hurt you."

"Maybe not here, not in front of you," Phillen said. "Not with witnesses."

"Probably not."

"But I'm going to have to take her home. She'll smother me when I sleep, you know."

"Your mother is not going to murder you," Satrine said. She gave him a slight smile. "I'll make sure of it."

"Thank you," he said. "I mean, really, thank you for being here. It really—I don't have anyone else to . . ."

"Phillen," she said softly. "You need anything, I've got you. You've had my back when no one else except Well—" She choked on that for a moment. She had to maintain the illusion of her squabble with Minox, even in front of Phillen. "You had my back," she said again. "You have a place to stay, place to bring her, right?"

"Yeah," he said. "Ain't much, but rent is paid for now."

"All right," Satrine said. "If you don't want to be alone with her for a bit, I'll—"

"I couldn't ask you that," he said. "You've got people to get to."

"At this point, you're definitely one of my people," she said. For a moment, he smiled hesitantly.

Then the sergeant interrupted. "Number 89211, Berana Hace. Released to the custody of Phillen Hace and Inspector Satrine Rainey."

"Berana?" Satrine asked, taken aback. "Your mother's name is Berana—"

"Well, isn't this wonderful?" The voice, a razor-scrape gravel of scorn, hit Satrine in the pit of her stomach.

Phillen's eyes were already full of tears and fright, looking to the sergeant and the doorway. Satrine followed his gaze and saw her.

The hair was grayer, the body stockier, the face lined and weathered, but Satrine knew exactly who she was looking at. Her voice left her; there was nothing she could say. Despite her desire to scream and howl, nothing came from her throat.

"Both my useless children are here," Mother said. "And saints help me, both of them are blasted, rotten sticks."

Appendix

The Druth Parliament

The government of Druthal is a Parliamentary Monarchy. Druthal is reigned over by the king, who is determined by the rules of succession from the royal line, and whose coronation is approved by the Parliament and the Church of Druthal. The king is both the head of state and the head of church. The current king, Maradaine XVIII, was crowned in 1213. He is the thirteenth king in the current royal line: The Line of Maradaine, the longest in Druth history, which began with Maradaine VII in 938.

Despite his position as head of state and church, the Druth King is actually quite limited in power. His authority is limited to acting as executive over the High Council, whose role is to implement policy as decided by the Parliament. He can issue edicts to the Parliament and the High Court, but neither body is obliged to obey him. The Druth Throne is far more of a symbol of power, and the true authority of the king is dependent on the love of the people.

The Parliament was originally conceived during the Reunification of 1009, and first convened in 1015. It is composed of one hundred Druth citizens, ten from each archduchy. The ten archduchies are Maradaine, Patyma, Sauriya, Acora, Oblune, Monim, Yinara, Kesta, Linjar, and Scaloi. Members of the Parliament ("Chair") are elected within their archduchy, and they must be citizens and residents of that archduchy. They also must neither possess nor have reasonable claim to any noble title. Every Chair serves a five-year term.

There is a Parliamentary election every year, in which each archduchy votes on two of their ten parliamentary chairs, in rotation. Over the course of five years, all ten chairs from each archduchy have stood for election. Elections are open to many candidates—often over twenty on the official ballot—and the two candidates with the most votes claim the chairs. If circumstances have opened an additional chair (the death or resignation of a chair who would not be up for election, for example), the third-ranking candidate claims that chair.

Within the Parliament, there are essentially six Party Affiliations:

- The Traditionalists (Dishers), whose primary platform is supporting the rights and authority of the noble class, which includes giving nobility greater freedoms for implementing taxes and policies within their own regions.
- The Loyalists (Crownies) support the leadership and authority of the throne, and work on policies that further the King's agenda.
- The Free Commerce Party (Minties) supports trade and business, including policies of minimizing taxes and tariffs to facilitate the growth of the merchant class.
- The Ecclesials (Books) support the church, and are often former members of the clergy. Their platform is one of enabling moral guidance and personal responsibility.
- The Functionalists (Frikes) have a platform of effective governance, focusing on policies that work and accomplish real goals over furthering specific partisan agendas.
- The Populists (Salties) represent the common man, beyond the interests of the nobility, throne, church, or merchant class. This is the smallest party in the Parliament.

The current parliament is controlled by a Ruling Coalition of the Loyalists, Functionalists, and Free

Commercialists. The Traditionalists and Ecclesials are united in a Coalition of Opposition. The Populists do not form a Coalition with either group, but frequently vote with the Ruling Coalition. But with recent assassinations of members of Parliament, and the elections of 1215 bringing in new members, the balance of the Parliament is poised to shift.